HEAVEN CRIES

A Novel

HEAVEN CRIES

by

Stephan A. Silva

www.penmorepress.com

HEAVEN CRIES by Stephan A. Silva

ISBN-13: 978-1-942756-58-3(Paperback)
ISBN :-978-1-942756-59-0 (e-book)

BISAC Subject Headings:
FIC014000 FICTION / Historical
FIC032000 FICTION / War & Military
FIC 037000 FICTION / Political

Editing: Chris Wozney
Cover Illustration by Christine Horner

Address all correspondence to:

Penmore Press LLC
920 N Javelina Pl
Tucson AZ 85748

Dedication

This book is dedicated to all the civilians who suffer in war, even when history is blind to their tears.

There is nothing noble in being superior to your fellow man; true nobility is being superior to your former self.
— Ernest Hemingway

Disclaimer

This is a work of fiction. A Novel. Names, locations, political and historical events and incidents are purely the product of the author's imagination and used in a fictitious manner. All characters and events in this book, even those that allude to real people, living or dead --and any references to historical or political events are purely coincidental.

Editor's Note

Poetic license allows a writer to bend, even break the rules of grammar in the service of rhyme, meter, or for the sake of a good line. Prose writers are usually held to more rigid standards; nevertheless, we invoke poetic license for this story. Sometimes in songs the tense will shift from past to present to involve the listener in the moment with all the immediacy that the singer feels. Even some recent novels have openly embraced this technique. Therefore, when the narrative of this story shifts from the conventional past tense to present tense, please recognize it as an intentional invitation to become part of the story. Certain experiences are so vivid, so extraordinary, they transcend time—the person tastes eternity in that moment. The present tense comes closest to expressing that sense of timelessness.

Review

Stephan Silva has written an important first novel that depicts the dilemma that the Italian people faced in World War II. The armed forces originally were fighting on behalf of an independent Italy for colonial expansion in Africa. Their integrity was compromised by Mussolini's alliance with Adolph Hitler and Nazi Germany, with terrible consequences. Before long, Italy was embroiled in a war on its own soil. Allied forces were conducting an aerial bombardment, even as German SS Troops terrorized Italian citizens. Worst of all, political factions arose to fill the void of a government collapse. The most brutal of these were the communist partisans who gave and received no quarter from the Nazis. These irregular forces had an eye on post war Europe and wished Italy to be placed behind the Iron Curtain as a Russian satellite nation.

Based on the actual World War II experience of the author's Great uncle, a pilot in the Regia Aeronautica, **Heaven Cries** conveys the disillusionment, anguish, and indomitable spirit of people betrayed first by their elected leader, then by their ally. It shows with chilling realism how the desire for freedom can become a commitment to overthrown an oppressive regime. Most significantly, it reminds us of the true spring waters of freedom: hope, kindness, courage, and love.

In the dark light of recent events, this history is particularly relevant. **Heaven Cries** is not simply a taste of our past: it is also our future.

Nicholas Gage

Author of the bestseller *Eleni*

CHAPTER 1
San Giorgio Mountain

Mountain people think they can escape the turmoil of the lower altitudes. It is their proximity to the heavens that engenders this false hope. In the lives of men, some troubles are so great, they rise like thermal currents. No amount of denial can cool them.

Autumn arrives early in bucolic northern Italy. The morning's first rays of sunlight bring no warmth, yet the afternoon heat will make you look for the shade of a fig tree. The weather may be mercurial, but life in the mountains changes little from generation to generation. San Giorgio, like most of the Apennine mountain chain, is isolated from the cities in the valley. For a country boy, life can be adventuresome, and lonely. It consists of hunting rabbits as they scurry in and out of briar thickets, eating wild raspberries right off the bush, or just inhaling the aroma of Mama's freshly baked bread. There is also the matter of avoiding chores, such as carting wood down to the city of Piacenza, or digging up truffles with the help of the neighbor's dog, a well-mannered, black Labrador retriever, whose personality changed when a truffle found its way into her mouth. Then the event became a wrestling match with the jaws of a growling cur. Artemio, named after his grandfather, also a good rabbit hunter, was a carefree boy, but he often imagined what life off the mountain would be like. There was a gnawing inside him whispering that he was meant for greater things. "Stop staring at the clouds, boy, and get to work!" was a common admonishment from Rafaello, his father.

Artemio liked looking up into the sky to watch the biplanes as they dropped in altitude, to land at Malpensa airport near Milan. Oh, to be a pilot and fly through those clouds! It would be exciting to see new lands and meet different people.

Poverty was rampant in post World War One Italy. There were few jobs, and the employed were paid subsistence wages. In the mountains, you could scavenge for food, but the rabbit and fowl meat had to be sold, the money used to pay government taxes and fees, or bribes to magistrates. The mountain people would eat wild greens like arugula, or tomatoes, like the ones mother planted in the garden. Life for city dwellers was harder. Multitudes of people were leaving Italy in search of a better life. Steamships departed every day, bound for New York and other cities in the new world. They were overbooked with the destitute looking for work.

The Battaglia family struggled to make a living in these hard times. Only the most enduring of souls could eke out a living. The restaurants in Piacenza would buy kindling wood, game meat and truffles from them for a pittance, barely enough to replace their threadbare clothes and hole-riddled shoes.

Some mornings, a pea soup fog blanketed the city with only the *campanile* bell tower rising above it. The view from the mountain was breathtaking: a layer of fluffy white cotton, a funeral shroud, laying over the valley floor with a marble sewing needle piercing through it. Artemio knew it was sights like this that made his father proud to be a Piacentino; he, however, felt separate, with no special connection to this place.

On such days, the moisture in the air was heavy and clung to the ground, especially the uneven stone roadway, a rain cloud that had landed on earth, still yielding it tears. Artemio could see his stooped father making slower and slower starts on these cold, wet mornings. The rough life on the mountain had aged Rafaello beyond his years. He had married late in life—an arranged marriage. His parents had been confronted by old Signora Fastidioso, the town *paraninfo* or matchmaker, a woman who knew every one's business in and around Piacenza. Another family had an older, unmarried daughter, and people were talking: "Why are these two singles not finding anyone?" or "They are right under each other's noses, but cannot see." The Signora thought Concetta would make a good spouse for Rafaello; both were approaching thirty years old and had no prospects. There was a meeting of both sets of parents and Signora Fastidioso. All agreed: the two young people would be made to sit next to each other at the coming chestnut festival.

A short courtship followed, and marriage. Rafaello and Concetta were happy, but the union bore no fruit. After many years of trying, they believed God's plan for them was to be childless. Then one day Concetta cornered Rafaello in the house; she had a wide grin on her thin face. He was concerned at how silly she was acting, until she told him that she was with child. The news changed the grizzled old man. He went to church every Sunday and lit a candle, thanking God for this, the greatest of all blessings.

The elderly couple doted on Artemio, their only child. He was intelligent, too smart for working in the mountains as a laborer. Concetta would read to him every night. During the day he disassembled anything mechanical: locks, tools, Grandpa's old time piece, just to see how they worked. The boy had legerity, especially with gears and moving parts.

He would ask his father questions of why the world was the way it was, and Rafaello had unlimited patience with his inquisitive son. The question he asked most often was, "Why did your brother leave for America?" Each time he tried to explain, Rafaello realized there were layers of complexity to the answer, far more than the young boy could grasp. However, Artemio did sense the pain in his father's voice as he listened to the answer yet again. Artemio knew Bruno's actions tore at the family's heart.

Rafaello missed his older brother. Bruno had been a lanky youth who would always win the local bicycle races, which made him a hero with the Piacenza girls. In the fifteen years since he had left for America, he had done well for himself. He had risen from a spaghetti cook in a storefront window to owning his own restaurant off Broadway in the theater district of Manhattan. Artemio had heard the family stories, that Bruno was a maverick. How angry he would get when the topic of politics came up! He would shake his fist in the air and say things no one else dared: Italian society was top heavy with landowners and the idle rich; they made social mobility impossible. These powerful people controlled the banks and kept the economy stagnant. The politicians and police all took bribes; they were in the pockets of the rich. Bruno believed the only thing that could save Italy was an iron-fisted dictator, a Napoleonic figure, who would destroy the status quo and unleash the raw energy of the

Italian people. In the end he had realized there was no way for his country to shake itself free of the rigid class structure which the church and monarchy imposed. Bruno bought a one-way ticket on a tramp steamer leaving out of Genoa.

This day, walking down the wet, slippery grass of San Giorgio Mountain, Rafaello recounted the tale of that cold winter's night with greater detail. "Your Grandmother burst into tears when Bruno delivered the news. Her heart ached as if it were the death of her firstborn son. She cried for weeks, and when the crying stopped she was never the same. She had lost a son. Your Grandfather never said a word, just stared into space. I begged my brother to stay, but he would have none of it. There was no convincing him. He may have been born in Italy, but in his heart he was a true American." When he finished the story, the old man turned as if to adjust his scarf against the cold morning breeze and dried his tears so that the boy would not see them.

A little later, Rafaello noticed that up ahead his son and the donkey were on the roadway. He yelled, "Artemio, I told you to keep her on the grass!"

"I am trying, Papa, but Contessa has a mind of her own today." Actually, Contessa was always stubborn. Artemio would make excuses for her. "She is still young," he would say. Contessa was two years old, full load-bearing age. Her duties were to transport supplies up and down San Giorgio Mountain. The young lad considered her his pet and took care of her. Even though he loved her, today he was getting annoyed; she was not being obedient. "C'mon, girl, behave and stop getting me in trouble," he admonished her.

The boy tried pulling the donkey off the poorly maintained, ancient Roman road. The better sections were uneven, flat granite stones quarried from the mountain by long-forgotten masons. Most stretches of the crumbing roadway were just dirt. In its heyday, two thousand years ago, Rome had kept the road in perfect working order. Back then it would have been used to expedite men, armor, weapons, horses, and wagons into Gaul—present day France. The Roman Legions had to be mobile, to suppress internal uprisings and insurrection, as well as to fight barbarian hordes on the walls of the Empire. These ramparts were needed to maintain a certain purity within and to keep the dregs out.

The more force the boy used to pull on Contessa's rope bridle, the more she resisted. The moisture on the stones made them slick. The donkey's hooves started to slip, the bales shifted, her legs moved faster as she tried to regain her balance. The young animal lost her footing and her front shoulder hit the stone roadway hard. There was a great thump, then a second sound more ominous then the first: the air rushing out of her lungs. Both men were paralyzed with fear for the injured donkey. Contessa let out a howl, not the usual bray one gets from an angry donkey, but a wail of pain. She thrashed about, all four legs moving wildly, unable to right herself. They both ran to her, but did not know what to do. It was as if they were watching a movie and had no control of the story. Rafaello removed the kindling wood from her back, while Artemio held her head in his lap. He closed her eyes with his hands, stroked her long snout, and spoke gently to soothe the donkey. "It's okay, girl, you're going to be all right." The boy's touch had a calming effect on Contessa; his voice gave comfort and soothed the pain. The thrashing subsided.

A rumbling could be heard in the distance, like far away thunder; but instead of subsiding, the mechanical clattering grew louder, eventually drowning out all natural ambient sound. Around the curve of the road, obscured by a thick outcrop of trees, suddenly appeared two Moto Guzzi motorcycles, followed by a long black sedan. The two motorcyclists approached the boy and his injured Contessa. Their front tires stopped within inches of the injured animal's tense legs. The donkey, laying on her side, breathing in short, quick breaths, was still unable to stand. Her dark eyes tracked the movements of the strangers with suspicion.

The riders were Piacenza policemen and they were escorting a VIP limousine. The car's driver was exposed to the elements, while the occupants were protected from the wet weather. The chauffeur, in his goggles and long white raincoat, stopped the vehicle several yards back, in what looked like a security procedure. The two policemen dismounted and walked up to Artemio and the injured animal. They were well dressed in their ornamental uniforms. Feathered hats and gold epaulets convey a sense of authority, as much as the guns and the badges. The boy saw these men in their blue uniforms and black leather riding boots, and he felt confident that they could help. The father was older and more experienced. He approached the two officers with his hat in his hands, to explain the events. The taller policeman, resting his right hand on his gun holster, put his left hand on Rafaello's chest to make him keep his distance.

Before Rafaello could speak, the shorter officer, sporting a fashionable handle bar mustache, said with a note of sarcasm, "What do we have here? Two idiots with an injured animal!"

Both father and son tried to explain.

The taller officer had chiseled facial features; when he spoke his voice was deep and commanding, "You do not know how to properly handle a beast of burden. Your foolishness has created an impediment in the road." Artemio was starting to lose confidence that these men could be of help. They were acting surly, as if the wounded animal were a nuisance.

The policeman made his decree. "This animal has gone lame; there is nothing that can be done for it."

Rafaello struggled against the officer's hand and said, "Please sir, I am a poor man here with my son; this animal is all we have. Please let us take her home, I can nurse her back to health."

The senior officer barked, "By the order of the King, we must keep this road open!"

"No, No!" yelled Rafaello, as he grabbed the policeman's arm to prevent him from drawing his handgun. This only angered him, and he pushed the frail old man to the ground. Methodically he drew the police issue semiautomatic handgun from its holster, as he had done hundreds of times in training. Artemio, sitting on the road with Contessa's head in his lap, looked into the man's face. He saw a look of determination, a desire to perform a despicable act. This man could dispatch life and say he was "just following orders." Artemio looked deeper: the face shifted and changed. The good-looking face became ugly. Sharp, rugged features morphed and became weak. His jawbone was moveable, like jelly; all humanity drained from him. When Artemio realized the unthinkable was about to happen, time moved slowly. His heartbeat banged loudly in his eardrums and his muscles froze. Rafaello got up from the ground and scurried over to his son. He put his hands under the boy's armpits and dragged him away from Contessa, leaving tracks of his heels in the dirt. There was an explosion from the Beretta. A single copper-jacketed bullet traveled through the donkey's skull, killing Contessa instantly. A few postmortem jerks of the legs were all that remained of her life. The cries of the donkey were silenced. The only sound now was of the Bugatti limousine idling in the background. All four men stared at the donkey's lifeless body.

Artemio and his father were in shock. Rafaello cried to himself, but his son bawled. The policemen bent down coldly and pulled the carcass to the side of road, then kicked it off the embankment and down the mountain. It rolled and slid, coming to a stop in a dense growth of bushes. The policemen mounted their motorcycles and kick-started the "V" twin engines. With a slow release of the clutch, first gear engaged, both Moto Guzzi rolled past the father and son peasants.

The long black sedan followed the policemen, passing the two disconsolate figures on the side of the road. Artemio was able to see inside the limousine's windows as it passed them. Two women and a man were talking and laughing, oblivious to all outside events. The man was an obese, balding figure facing forward, drinking from a champagne glass. Artemio recognized the man as Silvio Marchese, the mayor of Piacenza. The woman to his left wore a bright red dress with matching hat and gloves. The hat had a black mesh webbing that extended down, stopping at the end of her nose. This allowed her long cigarette holder access to her mouth. The second woman facing the mayor had no clothes on. The mayor was not interested in poor people; he pandered to the rich land owners. Today he only had time for the prostitutes in the car. The limousine passed, leaving a blue-gray exhaust fume.

Without speaking, Rafaello tied the wood that Contessa had carried onto his son's back. Both walked silently down the mountain. The midday sun had burnt off all the fog, and they were getting tired and sweaty as they traversed the steep slopes. Exhausted, the old man said to his son, "Let's rest here. Put down your burden."

Artemio felt a rage inside him, an emotion he had never felt before, and it consumed him. He did not know how to control himself; he wanted to punch his father. Why could he not protect Contessa? It was his job to protect the whole family! Rafaello, after taking the wood of his son's back, offered him water. He refused it.

There was more silence. Artemio was seething. The father knew something must be said. "Do not let this trouble you, son. We will get another donkey."

Artemio flew into a tirade. "Like always, you will do nothing! You cannot do anything! You are powerless!"

"It is all right. We will get through this," the old man said stoically.

"No. Not this time. I am sick of this country and the rich people who abuse us." He looked to where Contessa's carcass might have come to rest, but saw only the grasses, trees, and wild flowers of the mountain. He turned back with acrimony and said, "In the morning I am leaving for America. I will live with *Zio* Bruno." He knew this pronouncement would hurt his father more than a fist.

Rafaello would not lose his son as he had lost his brother. He put his hand on the boy's shoulder and said, "Son, you are brave and headstrong. I understand your anger, for I was once like you. As your father, I will tell you the truth. There are problems all around the world. The poor are oppressed everywhere, even in America. You are my son, but you are also a son of Italy. It is your duty to make this godforsaken land a better country. You must work from within. This is not a job that can be done from America."

He again offered Artemio the water; this time the boy drank. "I know what you are capable of. You are a smart boy, you can analyze problems and find solutions. I see great things in your future. You will bring people together. With this gift you will achieve much in your lifetime." Rafaello took a deep, labored breath. "First you must attend the university and study hard. This will discipline your mind." He looked up at the road and shook his head, then continued. "In your life there will be much adversity. It is only with a fierce determination that you will be able to overcome these challenges."

Artemio took his father's words to heart. He knew from this point on the direction his life would take. He would work to improve the lives of the downtrodden, unlike Mayor Marchese. He would help build a strong Italy, with a government that worked for the people. His father was right. Why go to America? That country was already great. Artemio would make *this* country great again; he would be like the Romans who built this road.

CHAPTER 2
Air Combat

The azure Mediterranean Sea with its whitecaps contrasted starkly with the flat, tan expanse of the Sahara desert. This was the impressive view every day for the Italian fighter squadron based out of Tobruk. It was serene high above General Rommel's tank battles. At the cruising altitude of 25,000 feet, the cockpit became frigid and oxygen was a necessity. A steel gas canister was stored under the pilot's seat, with rubber tubing leading to the face mask. The compressed oxygen had to be used sparingly on these long escort missions. Below Captain Artemio Battaglia's plane were the twenty German JU 88 bombers he was shepherding to their target. Behind his own plane were his two wingmen. He looked starboard and saw his German counterpart, Klaus Meyer, and his wing of Messerschmitt fighters. Artemio grinned, knowing how much the Germans did not like Italian pilots, thinking them inferior. But Artemio was fearless in battle, and even the most arrogant of the German fliers accorded him a grudging respect. Captain Battaglia had all the attributes of a good fighter pilot: he was independent, motivated, and highly intelligent. He did not shrink from combat; in fact, he sought it out. Artemio enjoyed conflict, the challenge of man against man, competing to accomplish opposing goals. When faced with adversity, his pulse would quicken and he felt alert, ready for anything. He channeled fear into performance. This is also what made him a good athlete. He never forgot the cheers he'd heard at his high school soccer field as he kicked the ball past the goalie. He likened shooting down planes to scoring goals. The anxiety he did feel about this war was subtle. He would never admit it to anyone, least of all himself, yet he was plagued by an inexplicable feeling of uneasiness, as if there were a purpose or mission he was not trained for, was not even part of, yet must not fail at.

Suddenly radio silence was shattered. He heard the bomber crews yelling in panicked voices, "Hurricanes! Hurricanes! 6 o'clock low!" From underneath and behind the formation, Royal Air Force pilots opened fire on the bomber formation. The crews of the lumbering twin-engine bombers were not able to defend themselves well from this angle of attack. The formation started to break apart as the first of the JU 88s went down in flames. All the Axis fighters banked hard and dove down to dogfight the Hurricanes. The English fighter pilots were as tenacious as their national bulldogs. Their little island in the North Atlantic was under siege by the Nazi Third Reich; the British soldiers in Egypt understood that their fight in this remote land was to save Mother England. Every German killed here in the desert sand was one less in a landing craft on the white beaches of Dover.

Artemio did not make the same mistake other Italian pilots were making, flying the slower but more agile Macchi fighter like a German Messerschmitt. He had instructed his wingmen in a fighter tactic that he found to be effective against the British. The Hurricane was originally designed to be a biplane with wood, metal and canvas construction. During production it had been updated to a monoplane. The poor reconfiguration meant that the Hurricane was not as maneuverable as the Italian Macchi.

Artemio checked to make sure his wingmen were in position as they followed him into the dive. He lined up his first target. The enemy had the red and blue circles of the RAF on its wing. This Englishman was also a top gun, with wingmen of his own. The three British pilots had just finished a successful pass on the German bombers; they would be euphoric, having scored a kill, which is when tunnel vision takes over. Sure enough, the Hurricane pilots didn't see the three Macchi fighters coming down out of the sun. Artemio took the safety off his machine gun button atop the control stick as the enemy plane began to line up with his sights. He tried to calm himself, to merge man and machine into a single unit. "Come on, baby, come on, a little more...." Gently his gloved thumb depressed the trigger. The Italian fighter plane shuddered as the twin .50 caliber machine guns fire a six-second burst. Black smoke poured out from the leading British Hurricane's engine compartment.

"I got you, Englishman!" Artemio yelled through his adrenaline high. Now training took over and he immediately banked his plane hard. "Climb, come on, climb baby, you can do it!" He felt the nose start to point skyward. The force of the plane pulling forward and pressing him into his seat was exhilarating. This feeling is more compelling than the fear of being killed in battle. It is like a talisman that offers protection. Being the vanguard of the attack, guarded by his wingmen, gave Artemio a sense of order and safety in the presence of chaos.

In all the Fascist forces of air, armored corps, and fleet navy, there was a shared feeling of power among well-trained men, moving as a great formation in their war machines, with the ability to follow any order and the endurance to never quit. This emotion of invincibility was invigorating; it fortified their souls.

Artemio's euphoria was interrupted by a crack of static in his radio earpiece.

"Nice shooting, Captain, now get the hell out of there!" yelled his number one wingman, Lieutenant Mario Piaggio.

I am trying to. The plane soared upward as he pushed the throttle forward. Captain Battaglia could feel the blood leaving his head. He was on the verge of blacking out. He hoped that the Hawker Hurricane he'd just shot down did not have a good wingman.

"Bank! Bank hard! There's a Bandit on your tail!" This from Lieutenant Gitano Ricchetti, his number two wingman. Gitano's task was to sweep away enemy planes that tried to attack his captain from behind. Now Artemio knew that the British pilot he'd shot down had better wingmen then he did.

"Damn it, get him off me, Gitano!" he shouted into his throat microphone. Too late. Artemio felt his plane absorb the peppering of caliber .303 British machine gun bullets. He banked as hard as he could to escape the arc of the gunfire. Artemio looked to his port side and saw red tracer fire from Gitano's plane hit the British wingman's Hurricane. An explosion of flames followed, and the Allied plane dropped quickly into a tailspin. Gitano followed his victim down for several thousand feet. Artemio craned his neck to see if the English pilot bailed out, but either he was too injured or the plane was too mangled. It didn't matter. Just another pilot who could not escape his fate. The Hurricane went all the way to the desert floor and crashed, no parachute seen.

On Gitano's return, all three planes fell back into formation. Artemio, as flight leader, reduced air speed and altitude to 10,000 feet over the hot Sahara desert. He set a bearing to return to base. Gitano announced over the headset, "I got that *Brittunculo*. Your 6 o'clock is clear, Captain." Artemio heard remorse in Gitano's voice. This was the first man his wingman had ever killed. Gitano did not have the traits of a warrior; he was a good-hearted soul. He had no business being up here with these cutthroats. Artemio radioed a coded message to Klaus Meyer that he was out of the fight. Damaged by gunfire, *Contessa* was not responding properly.

Pilots mostly name their planes after women they have known. Artemio used a pet's name.

After several minutes on the new heading, he checked his instrument panel and called to his wingmen through the radio, "Something's wrong. I can't hold my rpms and I'm losing altitude."

"I'm looking under your plane, *bambino*, and a black mist is coming out. I think your oil cooler was hit," Mario informed him as he did a mid-air inspection. Artemio smelled the hydrocarbons burning on the exhaust grill. A hole of that size would mean a forced landing somewhere in Egypt. His thoughts were a roiling mix of hatred for the English because they were well-trained pilots, and disappointment in his own wingmen's performance. Now he would have to survive behind enemy lines, in the desert.

"Captain, you are now officially an ace," Mario added, trying to cheer him up in this difficult situation. "That Hurricane you just shot down is your fifth kill." Mario was a party man, a good Fascist. He liked Artemio, but he wanted the promotion to captain, and it didn't matter who he stepped over to get it. It was only fitting, only proper that he should represent his influential family in the skies.

"I hate to break up this party, *ragazzi,* but I'm losing altitude. I'm not going to make it back to Tobruk." Artemio tried to speak with bravura, but it was a struggle to keep the quaver out of his voice, and he did not entirely succeed. He fought back the panic that gripped him. He had thought he was long past such weakness. Since Mussolini and Fascism had taken over, all Italians felt more confident and in control of their future. Now Italy was a world power with colonies. They looked at Africa as their own Manifest Destiny. If they were strong enough, they could take what they wanted. Now all Artemio wanted was to survive. He gently pushed the throttle forward to increase the rpms, with an eye on the engine temperature.

After going through flight school together, the three young men had deployed to the same fighter squadron in Libya. Artemio knew he had better leadership qualities then Mario or Gitano; he had been first in his class at the aviation academy, Airbase Foggia. He had deserved the promotion to captain, based on merit. This was rare in Fascist Italy, where most advancement was based on family status or bribes. Mario had been bitter, and Artemio knew that back in Rome Mr. Piaggio was pulling strings for his son. The Piaggio family owned several factories that manufactured parts that kept the war effort going; consequently, his word carried a great deal of weight. But pilots needed the best leaders if they were to succeed in shooting down British flyers, and even the Piaggio influence could not alter that reality.

Artemio had distinguished himself by developing a method for out-maneuvering British fighter planes, which he'd demonstrated successfully after a heated argument with Captain Klaus Meyer. This was no friendly rivalry between the Luftwaffe and the Regia Aeronautica. Meyer was a heavy drinker and a racist. Some nights, when he got drunk at the officer's bar, he would say that Italian pilots operated below the standards set for German pilots. The proof of this, he claimed, was that in North Africa there were more German aces than Italian. The undeniable truth of this bothered Artemio, so much so that he'd set himself to solve the challenge the German captain presented.

"Turn north by northwest. That will get us back into Libya," Mario said somberly. He wanted to be flight leader, but there was no honor in this type of advancement through the ranks. In spite of his ambition, he was deeply concerned for his friend.

"I don't want to go down in Egypt, not on the English side of the line," Artemio said, more to himself than to his wingmen. "Come on, *Contessa*, old girl, get me home." He glumly patted the instrument board as if it were his beloved donkey.

He remembered how upset he had been when he first got his orders for Libya. The moment his eyes read the telegram, disappointment must have showed on his face. His girlfriend, Donatella, had seen the look, and she'd come over to console him. She'd told him it didn't matter where he was sent, only that he come home in one piece. Her family had political aspirations for him, but first he needed to become a war hero. Artemio had other ideas; he had hoped fighter command would send him to a European deployment. He was a young man looking for adventure, with fantasies of being stationed near Paris or Barcelona. He wanted excitement, just like the propaganda posters promised: touring with his motorcycle across the vineyards of Spain or along the Seine River, to see the view from the top of the Eiffel tower, or to swim in the Atlantic Ocean. The desert was a stark contrast to those dreams, desolate and inhospitable, like getting a tour of duty on the moon.

Gitano's voice in his earpiece recalled him to his predicament. "I will radio your position in when you land. We will get a reconnaissance unit out here to pick you up, Captain."

"Yes, but wait until you're closer to Tobruk. I don't want the English to get to my location first," warned Artemio, not wanting to sit out the war in a British POW camp. His mother would worry herself to death. Then realization struck him: he could die of thirst before *anyone* found him. All pilots know that whoever picks you up will have water. In the desert water is the difference between life and death, and English water tastes just as sweet as Italian water when you are mad with thirst.

The oil pressure gauge was going into the red zone. He tapped the glass cover of the instrument dial with his index finger in hope that a miracle would change the reading. Artemio started to drop the altitude of the plane and let out the flaps to slow it further; he did not want to be too high if the engine started to seize up and stall. He could see only loose sand below as he descended—a hazard that could flip a plane if the wheels submerged. The airfield at Tobruk, and most of coastal Libya, was hard packed sand and rock, but he was still over the Sahara desert. He was not getting a good feeling about this location.

"I'm putting down my landing gear, Lieutenant Piaggio, and I'm passing command of this mission to you."

"Yes sir, Captain!" Despite his concern for his friend, the excitement of getting his first command was evident in Mario's voice. Gitano tried to lighten the mood. "Artemio, you will be having espresso with us at breakfast tomorrow."

"I hope espresso, not bangers and black pudding," Artemio replied with gallows humor.

Artemio floated the damaged aircraft gently down. The two wing wheels touched the sand and slowed the Macchi, then the smaller trailing wheel sank and dragged. When the plane came to a stop, Artemio cut the ignition and unhooked his safety harness. He opened the Plexiglas canopy and stood in the cockpit. Both of his wingmen flew low directly over his plane. Mario, the more flamboyant pilot, dipped both wings, the universal sign of salute. Artemio waved back as they flew off at full throttle to return to home base.

Now the feeling of being alone in the vastness of the hot desert gripped him. He busied his mind with details to avoid feeling terror. He had lost the security of having the whole Fascist empire around him. When you have been taught to be a cog in a machine, there is a feeling of abandonment when the machine is not there. Now he was just a man.

He surveyed the cockpit and checked his equipment. Radio operational, flight maps, compass, pencil, Air Force issue Beretta pistol, no food, no water. He climbed out of the cockpit and walked on the camouflage-painted wing. The dark yellow base color with the grey-green mottling pattern was specific for operations in the colonies, meant to blend an unnatural machine into the natural environment of the desert. When he reached the end, he jumped off onto the ground. His flight boots sank three inches among the fine granules. Walking around the plane, he assessed the damage. Unbelievable! Twenty-six bullet holes had hit the engine and cockpit, but it was only that one fatal bullet entering the oil cooler that killed *Contessa*. *What luck!* he thought sarcastically. Scanning the horizon, he saw a flat wasteland as far as the eye could see. The view for 360 degrees was sand meeting blue sky. "This is going to be a long wait," grumbled Artemio. He sat underneath the plane for its shade. Even out of the sun, the sand cooked your skin. He started to sweat profusely, but his training told him to leave the flight suit on, no matter how hot it became. The material was a protection from the sun's rays.

Artemio looked at his watch; hours had passed. The heat was starting to affect his composure. Suddenly, the radio cracked with a burst of static. "Sidecar, come in. Sidecar, this is Motorcycle, can you hear me? Sidecar, are you out there, old boy?"

"English!" Artemio hissed under his breath. He jumped to his feet, drew his pistol, and searched the horizon. It was so hot the air shimmered. No dust trail anywhere on the ground, no activity in the sky, not even a mirage. *Mario and Gitano must have landed by now. They would have sent out a reconnaissance unit. Maybe we have one in this area already.* Obviously, the British did; perhaps they were searching for the pilot Gitano had shot down. The English were better at spying and intelligence gathering than any other European power; probably because they were an island off of Europe. The separation of the English Channel made them need gossip like an old biddy missing a Mahjong game.

Looking down, he saw the Beretta pistol and grinned. "What am I going to do with this thing?" he said out loud.

He lay under his aircraft, thinking, *In a few more hours, in this heat, with no water, I'm going to go crazy. Why would Command give us a useless pistol, but no water or food?* As the heat started to affect his mind, thoughts drifted back to his boyhood days. The family was hungry often, but never thirsty. They drank cold, running water right out of the stream. He had never known dehydration like this. When the hunger was bad, his mother would go out into the high mountain meadow and pick young green leaves from the field, arugula and dandelions mostly. She served them with olive oil, vinegar, salt, pepper, maybe a tomato from the garden if one was ripe. The desert, by contrast, was austere, a wasteland. Nothing could live out here. From the time he'd arrived in Libya, Artemio had felt an aversion to the desert; now he despised it. He missed his mother and father, he missed his home and the cool mountain rains.

"I hate the desert!" Artemio screamed.

Screaming had been a mistake. His throat was painfully dry. He closed his eyes and lay still to conserve energy.

The airbase at Tobruk was made to be like a small Italian city. You could buy that day's Roman newspaper. The radio played opera, with frequent breaking news bulletins of how well their armed forces were performing in Russia. The base had paved roads that were full of Fiat cars and trucks. An Italian engineering regiment was building a railroad from Benghazi to Tobruk. In the officer's bar, you could meet diplomats and sailors whose talk was always of Italy and the girls back home. They would toast with Italian wine,

Campari or grappa, while smoking Italian cigarettes. They would say, *See you in Venice, ... Rome, ... Milan*, or whatever city was under discussion, as if it were only a ride on the autostrada away. Libya had been a colony of Italy since 1911. Tobruk, a coastal city, was a valuable supply base with a deepwater port. Large freighters from Europe could restock provisions—a war in the desert needed everything transported in. Yet the more they tried to make North Africa seem like Italy, the more homesick everyone felt.

The indigenous population of Libya had to be subjugated. That is what mother countries do to their colonies. How else could they extract the raw materials and cheap labor that was needed? Tobruk, being a desert fortress, had a barbed wire fence and a minefield. No one ventured past the heavily defended perimeter. There were machine-gun emplacements and guarded checkpoints to regulate movement in and out the citadel. It was like that wire was the end of civilization. The Arabs lived on the other side of the wire and were not allowed in. The Untouchables—no one ever spoke of them, but everyone knew they were there. He wondered how these people managed to survive in this hellish place, beyond the wire.

This godforsaken desert could be my grave, Artemio thought. *The flight suit is full of sweat, and I am beginning to stink. This lightheadedness is from the dehydration. I will need water soon to stay alive. What if I am dead already? No, I must be alive, I can smell. But I think you would have your senses in the afterlife. Wouldn't you? Death wouldn't be like this; it would be hell. Is this hell? No one will ever find my body. How will my mother take the news when they tell her I am dead?*

A voice coming from around him said, "Has any pilot ever been downed in the desert and rescued before?"

Artemio jumped to his feet and looked around, pointing his gun; there was a tremor in his right hand. "Who's there? Identify yourself," he demanded. He held on to the fuselage to steady himself. "I don't see anyone, only desert." Exhausted, he collapsed back down, confused and scared. "Okay, now I'm hearing things."

"Have you ever met another pilot that was actually rescued from the desert?" the voice asked again.

He rubbed his eyes, looked around quickly and croaked, "Who... who is there?"

"Did you ever meet anyone that was actually rescued from beyond the wire?" the voice repeated a third time.

"No." Artemio answered quietly, embarrassed that he was talking to no one.

"What did you say? I couldn't hear you," the voice said loudly.

"No, I never met another pilot shot down and rescued from the desert," Artemio said, thinking, *I am having an auditory hallucination.*

"Oh, there probably were some pilots rescued before you arrived at Tobruk," the voice said coyly.

"I have been stationed at Tobruk for four months, and was at Tripoli for a year before that. My squadron has been in combat every day. I have never seen anyone come back in through that wire." Even as he spoke he was thinking, *Why am I even having this conversation? Am I going mad? I don't think I'm talking out loud; my throat is too dry to speak.*

"Come now, Captain, are you saying the vaunted Regia Aeronautica does not even look for its own downed pilots?

Would they abandon their own?" The air was heavy with silence. "We are talking about the same Air Force that pioneered the poison gas bombing of civilians." The voice slyly corrected itself, "Oh, wait, you participated in that mission, didn't you?" Then it inquired in a judgmental tone, "At ten thousand feet, do you see the suffering below you? Children with their hands on their throats, gasping for breath. Men watching their families die in front of them, the last sight before they go blind."

"I don't know, I just... I don't know," stuttered Artemio as he cried, but no water travelled down his cheeks.

"Admit it! The truth shall set you free." The speaker laughed at the airman lying on the sand. "Do you even want to live?" The speaker was a trickster. It was like being cross-examined by an attorney who was trying to get a confession at a murder trial.

"Yes, I want to live!" Artemio shouted through his sobbing.

"Things look grim for you."

Artemio did not answer. He was too ashamed of himself.

"Death out here is a horrible way to go. No fitting end for a man." The voice said that like it was speaking from experience.

"Who are you?" Artemio demanded.

"It doesn't matter who I am."

"Are you my conscience?"

"No. I am definitely not that." There was silence, then the voice continued. "You have a pistol, I see. Planning on fighting all of General Montgomery's forces with that little thing?" it demanded sarcastically, then added, "Why would fighter command give you a pistol you could not use?"

"I don't know. It's just a pistol," Artemio said dejectedly, as he rubbed his sandy brow with the back of the hand still holding the gun. He hoped the demon inside his head would leave.

"I was there when the two police officers came upon your beautiful little Contessa," the voice said.

"What?! What are you talking about?!" Artemio snapped back. He tried to jump to his feet, but staggered, then fell onto the burning sand. He wanted to see who was taunting him.

"Come on, Artemio, we both know it was your fault!" the phantom voice insisted.

"No, it was not my fault!" he wailed like a child.

"Yes, it *was* your fault. Your father told you to walk the donkey in the grass, off the road," the voice said. Artemio felt it probing his mind.

"Yes, he did, but I...." Artemio could not finish.

Then the voice changed, as if another entity were speaking.

"I shot your donkey in the head, then got back on my motorcycle and laughed at you and your useless father."

"You are the Devil," Artemio sobbed.

"No, I am your friend," the first voice was back. There was a pause. "I am here to show you the way out."

He rolled in the sand, as if to get away from the voices.

"Artemio, you have a loaded gun. You are a proud officer in Regia Aeronautica. They gave you that gun for a purpose. It is your duty, to the King of Italy, to Benito Mussolini, and to Fascism, to shoot yourself."

"What?! Never! It is a sin against God to do that," he answered back in a tone of revulsion.

"God? Ha! You don't even believe in God."

"I know I don't pray enough, or go to church. I am not a good Christian by those standards. But I can tell you this: I counted 26 bullet holes in that plane and not one of them hit me. The oil cooler is right under my seat! I believe God saved my life for a reason. If I commit suicide, I cannot get into heaven." Now Artemio spoke confidently. He knew who his adversary was.

"Can you get into heaven after murdering five men, *Ace*?" the Devil asked cynically. Artemio became indignant. "It is not murder! Those men were fighter pilots like me. We all know what can happen to us when we climb into that cockpit. Those airmen were given a fair fight; I won. If conditions were different, I could have crashed and burned instead. They were trying with all their skill and equipment to kill me!"

"That is your argument, counselor? Self-defense? Many have tried that one before on your God, and they didn't like the judgment. Don't you know all man-killing-man is wrong? You should have read the Bible more, Artemio." The voice waited, to let his prey stew. "If you had, you would remember God's wrath at Cain for killing his brother. God said, 'Your brother's blood is crying out to me from the sand.' You Christians always forget that your God is a vengeful God."

Artemio had to muster all his strength to answer back, "No, my God is a loving God."

"Why do you say that? Did you get a warm fuzzy feeling when you saw the Last Supper mural in Milan? I told Leonardo that people would misinterpret their emotions when they saw it."

"You were there?" Artemio asked, puzzled. *Was the Devil there when I was looking at the mural? Was he there when*

Leonardo da Vinci painted it? Was he there when Jesus was having the Last Supper?

"I am everywhere, all the time," laughed the Devil.

"Yes, you are Judas Iscariot, the betrayer!" Artemio said to his tormentor.

"Thank you. So kind of you to remember. That was one of my finest performances," the Devil said, like a conceited actor.

Artemio's fingers gripped the sand as he made a fist. "When I was a little boy, on Sundays my mother took me to church. We had catechism after mass. The priest spoke of Saint Anthony who lived in Egypt. He was a desert monk."

The Devil recoiled at the name of the saint and cut him off quickly. "He also died in the desert. In the sand, not far from where you are lying now."

"Yes, but while he lived, he fought you."

"Not really. It was a feeble attempt." Satan did not like the way the conversation was going. He was getting annoyed and said gruffly, "Wouldn't you like some cold water now, Artemio? All you have to do is obey me."

"Saint Anthony put on armor and fought you like a gladiator," Artemio answered.

"There is no armor here, Artemio. This is how it will end for you. Put the pistol in your mouth and pull the trigger!" The Evil One sounded furious.

Suddenly, the radio announced, in the Italian language, "We can see his plane and we are approaching it." The fiendish voices subsided, and calm came over Artemio's body. He felt limp and weak as every muscle in his body relaxed.

The recon team found him lying on his back under his airplane, dehydrated and unable to move.

CHAPTER 3
Desert Rescue

"Hey Captain, wake up! This isn't a resort in Monaco. We have Englishmen everywhere looking for you!"

The shout came from a tall man wearing a khaki tropical uniform with a pith helmet, standing in a desert reconnaissance vehicle. Artemio could not move; all his muscles were flaccid. He lay supine under the fuselage, face up and arms out to the side under the wings, as if he was on a crucifix. Artemio was certain he was in one of Dante's inner circles of hell. The desert light was blinding, but he heard everything around him.

"Paolo, Giovanni, get that man off the desert floor and get water into him. Be careful, he may have broken bones."

"*Si, Padrone.*" The two men acknowledged the order and jumped off the AS-42 desert patrol vehicle.

"Is he alive?" Sergeant Major Niccolo Sansone peered out from under the brim of the large tan helmet. He was a pragmatist.

"Yes, but he is dry as a raisin," Paolo answered. He wore a dirty and tattered sahariana jacket and a soft fez cap.

"Giovanni, any bullet holes in him?"

"*No, Padrone.* He's good, just sun exposure." Giovanni was the medic, but only by default. He had taken care of sick animals and delivered calves on a ranch. Lately he was getting a lot of experience stopping bleeding, packing wounds, and keeping men alive.

"Lorenzo, keep an eye to the sky." Sergeant Major Sansone was nervous because he knew they should not be out in daylight. Strategy was his forte; as long as he could outsmart the British he could keep his men alive.

"Yes, Sir," answered Lorenzo, who operated the 20 mm Breda machine gun. He was their anti-aircraft gunner, the only man in the Recon Scout Battalion to have shot down two enemy planes, both times while being strafed. This was quite an accomplishment; usually land vehicles lose the battle against an airplane.

"I can smell Englishmen everywhere. They want our little Ace," said Niccolo with a healthy dose of paranoia.

"*Padrone*, should I take out the machine guns from the sick bird?" asked Eduardo. He was Sicilian and had been in desert recon teams for years. Niccolo relied on Eduardo to keep the crew together. Furthermore, there is a market in the desert for guns and gasoline. It was common for this recon team to barter with the indigenous population for intel.

"No, you old fox, you will have to scavenge for parts another day. We are not even going to blow up this plane. We have to get out of here fast. I can feel the enemy breathing down my neck," said Sergeant Major Sansone. "Paolo, Giovanni, get him in *Il Mulo,* now!"

Il Mulo, the mule, was the nickname the crew affectionately called their patrol vehicle. The modified armored truck had oversized tires, a powerful 6-liter gasoline engine, and four-wheel drive. Everything the team needed for life here in the desert was provided by *Il Mulo*: reliable transportation, water, food, shade, armored protection and firepower.

As Artemio's vision started to return, he could see blurry images around him. He was in the three-sided metal compartment of a desert recon vehicle, lying on blankets, getting a bumpy ride. A canvas canopy was keeping the sun's rays away from his skin. His eyes focused on the bearded man pouring water into him.

Giovanni smiled at him with yellow, cigarette-stained teeth. His beard was black and dirty, like the hair on his head.

"Captain, we saved you from certain death back there," he said. "Drink more water." After seeing to it that his patient took a small gulp, he asked, "What is your name?"

"Captain Artemio Battaglia, of Regia Aero—"

"Okay, Captain, I know who you are. I don't need a full resume. We got orders to find you," Giovanni cut him off.

"Then why did you ask?" Artemio asked, disoriented.

"To see if your mind is here, or still traveling. You know, in the desert without water, the mind can wander into a nether world, meet strange beings, go to strange places. It has happened to me." Artemio looked into the man's hazel eyes, to see if he had a deeper knowledge, if this man had encountered the voice also.

Lorenzo yelled from his gun position, "The only strange place you were ever in, Giovanni, was a Benghazi whore house!" The rest of the crew laughed.

Giovanni frowned at the men's immaturity. "Trying to find someone out here is truly like trying to find a needle in a haystack. God is with you today, Captain."

Artemio was thinking the same thing, remembering all those holes in his plane made by bullets that missed him. Then these arid angels arrive with water at a critical moment.

"This is the kind of work I enjoy," the medic continued, "being a savior. It is better than being a killer. A lot of what we do is gruesome." A strained look came over his face. "I don't like pulling dead bodies out of tanks, or disassembling equipment with body parts on them, baked in the sun." Just the talk of this work made Artemio nauseous. Giovanni got to his feet and stuck his head out of the canvas canopy and yelled, "*Padrone*, he is awake and talking."

"*Buon giorno*, Captain," Niccolo said, as he made his way over to Artemio and looked under the canvas tarp. "Are you enjoying the ride this beautiful day, complements of the Italian Army?"

"Are you the commanding officer of this crew?"

"No, our CO died three weeks ago in a night engagement with a British patrol, I am sad to say. My name is Sergeant Major Niccolo Sansone, the 1st Reconnaissance Gruppo, 3rd Battalion, based out of Bir Hacheim." He had a wrinkled face with leather skin, the face of a man who has been in the desert too long. Fatigue showed on his brow, and the crow's feet around his eyes were premature for such a young man. They were from many long hours of squinting into the sun; he was always looking for the airplane that could kill them.

"Tell me, Sergeant Major, why does everyone on this vehicle have a beard? It is against Army regulations, is it not?" In the Air Force, every man was well groomed and shaven, part of daily hygiene. These men looked unruly and insubordinate to Captain Battaglia, and he did not appreciate their lack of access to running water.

"Army regulations!" Niccolo laughed. "Army regulations out here in the Sahara will get you killed!" The Sergeant Major was a man who made a meticulous study of what worked and what failed in the desert. Only success was repeated in this outfit.

Giovanni added, "If we know an Army regulation, we do the opposite. That is how we have managed to stay alive this long."

Paolo could not see Artemio because of the canvas drape, but had heard him speaking. Now he spoke up and said, "I don't like this one; he is going to be trouble for us. We followed orders to get him. This is crazy, to be in Egypt during daylight. I am sure only evil will come of it."

"Shut up and watch the sky, Paolo," Niccolo yelled without turning to look at him. Paolo had been born in southern Italy near Calabria. He never knew his father, who had ran off soon after he was born, leaving his mother to raise four boys on her own. Over the years, several men had lived in the house with Paolo's mother, but none of them were father figures. Paolo had had an unhappy childhood: growing up in the streets, begging instead of going to school. He could not even speak the Italian language; he only knew the Calabrese dialect.

Artemio noticed the medic was wearing a light khaki tropical tunic with a green European issue field cap on his head. Some of the other men wore the *camiciotto sahariano* jacket with short pants. Eduardo had the one-piece blue jumpsuit that armored units were issued, with a diagonal, across-the-chest ammo belt and pistol holster. Not a single uniform matched. In the Air Force, uniforms and rank are highly regulated. The men of Regia Aeronautica took great pride in their dress, especially the wealthy men, who individually purchased their tailored uniforms. *This is a very disorganized group of misfits,* Artemio thought. *I hope they are capable of getting me home.* "Giovanni," asked Artemio, "what is your job on this vehicle?"

"Job?" He sounded as though the question was absurd. "We have no jobs. This is a small ship in a very large sea. Each man must perform all functions, or the ship will sink. Right now Eduardo is driving; he will get tired, and maybe I will drive. When the enemy appears we all become gunners, even you, fly boy."

Artemio understood that they were like the vulnerable nocturnal field mouse he used see on the high bluffs back home: the scared rodent who is so hungry that it must venture out during the day to find food, only to be killed by a stronger, more dangerous hunter—the hawk. Out here in the desert, airplanes were the more dangerous hunters.

"Giovanni, do you already have our guest manning weapons?" demanded Niccolo. He often used humor and wit instead of just barking orders; that was his leadership style.

"*Padrone*, I was just explaining to the Captain how every man must fight on this vehicle."

Niccolo laughed and said, "Yes, our Ace can use his Beretta pistol to shoot down more English planes." The whole crew laughed. Artemio knew he could make a scene about the laughter at his expense. As a captain he was the senior officer, but he understood that there was a different type of discipline going on here. He decided to take some ribbing to endear himself to the crew. Besides, he was grateful to them for saving his life. Artemio understood that rank alone does not make a true leader. He saw that the sergeant major was more than just these men's commander: he was their only ticket out. They needed his experience and direction to get back to Italy alive. Artemio asked, "Sergeant Major Sansone, where are you from?"

"I come from the city of Bari."

Artemio had noticed that the sergeant major's accent was from the south. If he spoke in his dialect, no one would understand him. Italy was like the tower of Babel, every city speaking differently, but Mussolini had been very strict about his "One nation, one language" policy.

When Niccolo spoke, he gestured with his hands, moving them with big arcing patterns. This much anyone could see, but with the strange clarity of his recent ordeal, Artemio saw more. He perceived that this man had a gentle soul, but his eyes had seen too much pain, and his mind was at its breaking point for endurance. He had an obligation to keep these men alive, and it was wearing him down as the task became harder. Artemio understood that a man formed bonds with men under his command, but there was also a barrier—there had to be. The sergeant major had crossed the line: he cared too much for his men. As Niccolo began talking of Bari, his memories were taking him to another place, a better place. His mind was escaping from this desolate wasteland to an oasis where it could heal.

"I miss Bari very much. My father had a fishing boat and we would go out all day on the Adriatic Sea. The water would be cool and blue. There are no troubles on the sea, only here on land. I think back to those voyages on the calm water; they would last for hours. My father and I never spoke much. I want so badly to get home and be again on that boat, to talk to my father, to tell him what I have learned. To tell my father I love him," he said wistfully.

"Now he is the captain of *this* boat," Lorenzo interjected into the silence that followed. "And we fish for men like you, Captain." The crew all smiled.

Artemio admitted, "I have never traveled to Bari, although I did know a girl from Bari when I was at the University of Milan."

"Ah, Baresi women are the most passionate women in all of Italy," Niccolo said, longing to be back with one. Then he added a cautionary note, "This is not always good. You see, if you cross Baresi women, they have been known to kill unfaithful husbands, like a black widow spider."

Artemio smirked, "Then it is a good thing that I never got into her web."

"What about now, Captain, do you have a steady girl?" asked Giovanni.

"Yes I do, a Roman girl."

"I have never known a Roman girl," replied Niccolo. His facial expression revealed that his brain was reviewing all the girls he had known in his life.

"Do you have a picture, Captain?" asked Giovanni.

Artemio reached for the pocket of his flight suit near his heart. "This picture was taken soon after I met her in Rome." He handed the picture to Giovanni as if it were gold. He was very proud that he had such a beautiful girlfriend.

"*Che bella*, what a catch," Giovanni said, as he passed the picture around to the rest of the crew. It drew whistles, and some rude remarks, as the men admired the image. Artemio's thoughts went back to the moment he'd met Donatella, remembering his attraction and desire to be with her. His speech had failed him; he'd barely managed to get out a "*Buon giorno*" when introduced to her. Donatella had been a 21-year-old fashion model trying to break into the movie industry.

"How did you meet this Venus, Captain?" asked Niccolo jealously.

"At a photo shoot in Rome. She is a model," Artemio explained. The men broke out in more whistles and catcalls. Niccolo repeated his question. "I still don't understand. What is she doing with *you*?"

"We filmed a newsreel, about how the Air Force was getting a new advanced fighter plane. They asked a few cadets to volunteer, so I did. Part of the newsreel showed how airmen get beautiful girls. It's all propaganda, you know, to entice recruits to join the Air Force, or so I thought. The model that they assigned to me was Donatella Capoletti. After the filming I asked her out, and she said yes."

"A Roman named Capoletti, this name is familiar to me," Niccolo thought out loud.

"It may be familiar to you; her father is a general in the Air Force."

"*Ma che*, did you step in it! A fashion model girlfriend, and her father is a general," Lorenzo said in a tone of disbelief.

"The guy just crashed a plane and doesn't even have a scratch. Lucky for him! If his face had scars, how long do you think that fashion model would stay with him?" said Eduardo from the driver's seat.

"Okay everybody, siesta is over. Lorenzo, stop drooling on that picture and give it back to the Captain. Everybody at their posts and eyes to the sky," ordered Niccolo.

It was a long journey back to Tobruk, with only the drone of the truck engine to mark the passage, but Artemio was starting to enjoy the company of this disheveled group of outcasts. They didn't know the difference between a Fascist and a Communist, and didn't care. They didn't know why the British were trying to kill them or why they were ordered to kill Englishmen. The crew of *Il Mulo* just wanted to survive the war, to get back home to Italy. They didn't care how the war ended, who won and who lost. Artemio knew he could never be one of them. He felt it when he mentioned his alma mater, the University of Milan, one of the most prestigious schools in Europe. The men of this crew had little education. They were enlisted men, all drafted; he was an officer. There would always be a wall between them.

"Tell me, Sergeant Major, if your CO died three weeks ago in a firefight, why has Division not assigned you a new one?"

Giovanni answered before Niccolo could speak. "Because Command cannot find anyone who could do a better job than our *Padrone*."

Paolo added, "They cannot find anyone stupid enough to ride with us." This got dirty looks from the crew.

Eduardo yelled to Niccolo, "*Padrone*, we are at a quarter of a tank of fuel. Should we stop soon to fill up?"

"No," Niccolo called back. "I want to keep going till darkness. Night is the best cover; then we will refuel."

"*Attenzione! Attenzione!* Aircraft at 2 o'clock in the sun!" yelled Lorenzo. He had the best vision of the crew. He could spot the enemy, get them in his gun sights, and kill them. He was the rare breed of man that every army wanted, and the army that had the most of them would win the war. Lorenzo did not speak much. He was not proud of his ability. He rarely thought about life or death, he just did his job skillfully. The men in *Il Mulo* were thankful to have a comrade like Lorenzo protecting them.

Niccolo shouted orders while looking through his binoculars. "Battle stations! All hands on deck!"

"Is it British or is it one of ours?" Paolo asked nervously.

"It doesn't matter; even our *paesani* will shoot at us. They will just assume that we are British, as we are here in Egypt," said Niccolo.

"Fratricide," Artemio said grimly, as he came out from under the canvas. He knew that was every pilot's fear. Killing your own men is a horrible tragedy.

Giovanni, surprised to see the Captain standing, yelled, "The winged warrior is on his feet!"

"Give him the 6.5 light machine gun," said Paolo. "Every man shoots."

"Put a helmet on that precious officer's head of yours, Captain," suggested Lorenzo.

Niccolo, still glued to the field binoculars, said, "He sees us; he's banking toward our position." Then he spoke with the voice of command. "Paolo, Giovanni, load the 20 mm cannon and break out more ammo. On my orders, Lorenzo, open fire." His voice changed slightly with disappointment. "Shit, it's a ground attack Hurricane. I can tell by the modified wings that it has four 20 mm cannons of its own. Wait, Lorenzo, *aspetta*, wait... fire... now!"

A large explosion rocked the vehicle as the Breda model 35 anti-aircraft gun discharged. There was a flash at the end of the long barrel and the smell of cordite. Then another, and another followed rapidly, seconds apart. Lorenzo was fixed on his target like a major league batter not taking his eye off the ball. Giovanni and Paolo reloaded the cannon with a fresh magazine full of high explosive shells. Their movements were quick and precise. Artemio was amazed by the way these misfits suddenly transformed into a well-coordinated machine functioning flawlessly. Niccolo's loud commands could be heard over the cannon fire: "Fire all weapons!" Artemio could see the black speck of a plane against the blue sky background in his machine gun sight. As his finger pulled the trigger, the wooden butt stock of the light machine gun banged into his shoulder. It was difficult to keep the weapon steady in full automatic fire. The black speck grew in size as it approached. White flashes started to appear on the leading edge of its wings, as it fired its own cannons. All the men in *Il Mulo* were firing guns at the enemy plane simultaneously. Brass shell casings of every caliber flew around the reconnaissance vehicle and bounced on the deck.

Artemio understood what that British pilot was enduring. Ground attack pilots were different from fighter pilots. Their cockpits were armored to protect them from small arms fire. This gave them a false sense of invincibility. A fighter pilot is like a fencer. Each man spars with his foil and parries each thrust—it is a deadly ballet which eventually yields one clear victor. Ground attack pilots are more linear. They focus in on their target and do not deviate from the flight plan. These men fly directly into the maelstrom of steel coming at them from below to deliver their payload of death. These pilots are bullfighters, locking eyes with the bull. They must have confidence and fortitude of mind as the horns of the bull charge toward them. The matador waits for the right moment, holding the hidden sword as the bull thinks he will do the killing. The enraged beast lifts his head before the goring; at this moment the neck is exposed. The skillful matador drives his sword into the fleshy part, past the collar bones and into the heart for a clean kill.

At that moment, the British aircraft fired all of its 20 mm cannons at once into *Il Mulo*. The sound of the multiple explosions hurt eardrums, and all around the armored vehicle sand flew into the air. This blinded Artemio, but he continued firing his weapon until the magazine was empty. The platform the men were standing on jolted, and they fell to the floor. The barrage from the Hurricane was withering. The only thing a man without a weapon could do was to crouch on the bottom of the vehicle and pray for the nightmare to end.

As the plane passed over, the Italians got up and watched as it climbed away from them. The airplane's engine gave out a loud, deep roar at full throttle. Artemio saw then that the plane was hit; the matador had been pierced by the horns. A black trail of smoke flowed from the engine. The crew watched as the injured bird tried to fly away from them. It is a macabre sight to watch another man die; they could not turn their heads away. Artemio reflexively started to think like a pilot in trouble. *Climb, you have to get more altitude, full throttle. Pull back on the stick, then level the wings.*

If you do not succeed at killing a man in the desert, he will track you in the sand and seek revenge. The more austere the environment, the deadlier its inhabitants, like the Egyptian cobra. All pilots know the rules. What was unknown was how many downed pilots were turned in as prisoners of war, versus those summarily executed in the field. People who have been the victims of aerial bombardments are not hospitable to the man in a parachute. This pilot wanted as much distance between him and the recon group as possible. Unfortunately for the Englishman, it was not his day. The engine stalled. The men watching the plane heard the engine sputter, then start up, then go silent.

Heaven Cries

Artemio was going through the in-air restart procedures in his head, the very maneuvers the Englishman in the cockpit was trying to accomplish, to no avail. In total silence they watched the plane go nose first into the desert floor. The reconnaissance men could see the red ball of flame, and a second later they heard the crash and following explosion.

No one in the armored vehicle said a word. The Italians knew it could easily have gone the other way. The matador could have been victorious. This Englishman would have celebrated at the squadron bar, with the other pilots congratulating him and buying him drinks. They would have lit his cigarettes and patted him on the back, then laughed and told stories about women back in London. The desert floor would have held the wreckage of an Italian reconnaissance vehicle on fire, bodies littered around it. Each man had a vision of his own death, based on his recon experiences of previous battlefields. Naked bodies stripped by local Arabs, lying in contorted positions. No one to bury them as they lay on the hot sand with only the flies as mourners. Artemio wondered, *Is it chance or is it fate? Is there some omnipresent power that controls these events?* Young soldiers who have survived a few battles say it is their skill and training that keeps them alive. More experienced warriors who have seen much combat will tell you that there is divine intervention.

The stillness was broken as Paolo yelled out, "Eduardo, Eduardo!" Paolo was standing outside the vehicle, leaning over Eduardo's lifeless body. A piece of shrapnel from the fighter bomber's cannon shell had gone into his neck.

"Oh great Allah, he is dead!" Paolo cried.

The rest of the crew came over to see. Eduardo was slumped over in the driver's seat. He still had his finger on the trigger of the Revelli 8 mm medium machine gun. The top half of his blue one-piece jumpsuit was soaked with blood. Giovanni took off the man's helmet. He grabbed Eduardo by his hair and lifted his head. Examining the gash across his neck, Giovanni said grimly, "At least he died quickly."

Men who see death often still feel sympathy and remorse for a fallen comrade. They wrapped Eduardo's body up in a tarp and placed him where Artemio had been convalescing before the battle. Niccolo gave new orders. "We have no time to bury him or pray for him. That pilot radioed in our position. Unless you boys want to meet his friends, we've got to get the hell out of here. There is two hours of light left. Giovanni, you drive. Lorenzo, eye to the sky."

The reconnaissance vehicle continued west into Libya. They watched the sun set in front of them, the beautiful red orb sinking behind the earth and leaving blackness in its wake. Nighttime was still oppressively hot, but peaceful, with no chance of an aircraft spotting them. In nautical twilight the sun is below the horizon, and ground targets breathe easier. With the darkness they stopped and refueled *Il Mulo*. No one was allowed to smoke during refueling, and red lenses were used on the flashlights. Artemio took advantage of the respite to ask Niccolo, "The night action with the British that killed your CO, how did that come about?"

Niccolo looked at Artemio for a long time, considering whether or not he should tell him. With Eduardo's death the mood on *Il Mulo* was somber. Then he said quietly, as if he didn't want anyone else to hear, "We listen to the radio for British voices. They always talk too much, and the

Australians are even worse. The British we can understand, the Australians just speak gibberish. That night the radio was completely silent and we thought we were alone in the desert. We came up behind a solitary English tank moving slowly in front of us. I told Lieutenant Calzetta we should be further back, for stealth reasons. We followed protocol and radioed in the coordinates, so at first light you boys in the Air Force could destroy the armored vehicle. The proper thing to have done would have been to shadow them out at 2,000 yards. The Lieutenant insisted on closing with the tank to read its regimental markings. Calzetta was a boy from the Veneto. He said his family could trace their heritage back 500 years to Venetian spice merchants. He was a rich kid with a good heart, but not tough enough for the desert of North Africa." Niccolo was silent for a moment, then continued.

"We matched their speed, about 15 miles an hour. It was a Sherman tank, one of the new ones that the Americans build and give to the British Army. The Lieutenant ordered the crew to battle stations. We were 200 yards behind the tank. The distance was really too close for safety." Niccolo swallowed hard and continued, "While preparing battle stations, Paolo, loading a machine gun, accidentally discharged it, firing several rounds into the tank's turret. This noise gave away our position while only scratching the American steel."

Niccolo could not go on, he was too choked up to speak. When he regained his composure he continued. "The tank stopped, so we stopped as well. Everything went quiet; except I heard the Grim Reaper standing beside me laughing. We were directly behind the tank. Suddenly the turret of the immense monster began to turn around. I sat in this very reconnaissance vehicle and started to pray to a God I have not spoken to since I was a little boy. That Sherman's 75 mm barrel pointed right at my head, and I knew there were only seconds left to my life. I asked God to forgive all my sins, for the men I have killed in anger and the hapless men who died following my orders."

Artemio knew then that the sergeant major had been in combat too long and was ready to snap. Both his hands were trembling; he reached out and held the truck's door to stop the shaking. Artemio thought of his own mental fatigue, and the voice he'd heard back at his plane, and realized it is common for men under this much stress to lose it. "What happened next?" he asked the sergeant major.

"Lorenzo happened next," Niccolo went on more stoically. "He started firing 20 mm armor-piercing shells into the engine compartment of the tank. The armor on the back of a Sherman is thin. The fuel tanks caught fire, and then the whole tank was ablaze."

Paolo pushed past them with a full fuel can in each hand and added to the conversation, "The Germans call those tanks Tommy cookers."

Niccolo's face turned red with anger. "You son of a bitch! I told you never to say that around me again!" he yelled.

"But *Padrone*, everyone says that about those tanks," Paolo said apologetically.

"I don't give a damn what other people say. If I hear you ever say that again, I will leave you in the desert to die!" Niccolo said furiously and walked away.

Giovanni, who was watching and listening to the conversation, finished the story for Artemio.

"The Englishmen could not get out of the tank. We heard their screams for minutes as the fire consumed them.

Eventually the ammunition exploded. This blew the commander's hatch and his body 50 feet into the night sky."

Artemio now understood why it was hard for Niccolo to retell this story. "What happened to Lieutenant Calzetta?"

Giovanni continued, "When the fire started, the Lieutenant was so upset that the men were burning in the tank he jumped off *Il Mulo* and ran to them. He thought he could pull them out and save them." He shook his head, "The Lieutenant did not understand war in the desert. He was idealistic."

Paolo added, "The one thing I have learned about the desert is, never get out of *Il Mulo*. She gives us life and protection."

Giovanni raised his hand to Paolo and said, "Shut up and refuel the truck." He turned back to Artemio and took up the tale. "The Sherman tank was not alone. It was part of a larger tank column. The British long-range desert group was escorting these new tanks under the safety of a moonless night to their future front line positions. The Special Air Service troops attacked us with their Chevrolet trucks as if they were banshees; they flew over the sand ridge. I actually saw the wheels in the air."

Paolo injected, "They were mad as demons flying out of hell."

Giovanni looked at Paolo as if he were about to curse at him, but did not. "Calzetta was half way between the tank and our position when he saw the SAS trucks. I observed the Lieutenant with the flames of the tank behind him; I saw him turn back to us and try to run. His face had a look of horror I will never forget, the knowledge of certain of death, a second before death arrives. He was mowed down by a Vickers machine-gun."

Artemio imagined this night engagement gone awry. "How did you get away?"

"Eduardo drove us into the soft sand while Lorenzo fired the Breda gun nonstop behind us. He knocked out the first two trucks quickly. Our Lorenzo is a one man wrecking crew. We lost the rest of the Long Range Desert Group in the fine sand. That is why *Il Mulo* has fat tires. Their trucks got stuck and could not follow us. Eduardo knew this would happen."

Just then Paolo yelled to the group, "*Il Mulo* is fully fed."

The men got back into their refueled patrol vehicle and continued, Niccolo tracking their location by the stars. At a precise time, he took readings of two known stars with a special transit called a theodolite, then used tables from the Regia Aeronautica—a rare collaboration between Army and Air Force—to convert readings to exact latitude and longitude. It was the only way to navigate at night in the desert or at sea. They had a set location to reach, a rendezvous point frequently used by the recon group.

"I liked Eduardo very much. He was a good man. He did not deserve to die like that. When we get to Haadi's tent, I will give him a good Muslim burial," said Paolo, almost in tears.

"What are you talking about? Eduardo was not a Muslim," said Lorenzo.

"He deserves a proper burial, and the one I give him will be the best he's going to get," said Paolo. It was clear Paolo got upset about death in the desert and the way that bodies are just left on the sand, like that of Lieutenant Calzetta.

Giovanni told Artemio that Paolo had been born a Catholic in Italy, but he had been raised by a non-religious mother. He'd converted to Islam during his time in North Africa, after almost dying at the first siege of Tobruk in

January of '41. He had been stationed at a listening post outside the wire during a British artillery barrage. They observed an Allied advance, but their phone lines were cut and Paolo drew the short straw to be the runner taking the information back to headquarters. In less than a minute after he left the protection of the bunker, a direct hit from an artillery shell landed on the observation post, killing everyone inside. Paolo saw his friends die and wondered why he had lived. Haadi, a Muslim nomad, told Paolo it was a sign from Allah that he would be protected if he converted to Islam.

The truck rumbled along the deep basin floor in total darkness. Niccolo broke the silence with what sounded like a eulogy, "Nobody could field strip damaged vehicles in the open desert like Eduardo. It did not matter the make or model. I have seen him field strip Axis and Allied airplanes; trucks, tanks, he could do them all, and fast," Niccolo said wistfully. "He could have had both heavy machine guns out of your Folgore, Captain, in fifteen minutes flat."

"Wow, my ground crew back at Tobruk is not that fast." Italian mechanics are an inconsistent bunch, he thought. There were several he would not let near his plane.

"He learned that skill in America," Giovanni said.

"What?" demanded Artemio in disbelief.

"Yeah, he lived in Brooklyn, New York, for five years," explained Giovanni.

"Really? He never told me," said Lorenzo. "Or maybe he did; I never understood that Sicilian language."

"Yes, he explained to me that he and a friend would get orders to steal a car, or just certain parts. Eduardo worked for a criminal gang. They told him what they needed in the morning and he would deliver it to them that night. This gang was a very dangerous, organized unit," said Giovanni.

"Like *Mafiosi*," Lorenzo interjected.

"Yes, they were Mafia," Giovanni agreed. "Eduardo got into trouble with the gang's leader. He borrowed money from him and then lost it gambling. It was an amount he could never repay. So he fled back to Sicily and joined the Army to get away from this *Cosa Nostra*. About a month or two after getting assigned to North Africa, he gets a letter from his mother in Brooklyn. The letter said that the *Mafioso* leader was murdered by one of his own men over a girl. His mother went on to say that now it would be safe for him to return to America." Giovanni shook his head in sadness and continued. "That's the bad luck he had. Poor Eduardo thought Libya would be safer than Brooklyn. When things changed he could not get back home."

Artemio could see the irony of this story. The hit taken out on Eduardo in Brooklyn by a now-dead Mafia chieftain had set in motion a series of events that would end with a British pilot killing him in the desert. *We are all in Fate's web.*

Artemio admitted to the crew, "I have an uncle in America. My father's brother left for New York before I was born. We get letters from him now and then. He says he loves America and would never come back to Italy. He started as a *camariere,* and now owns a restaurant in Manhattan."

Giovanni and Niccolo both said they had family in America also.

"That is amazing that the three of us, and Eduardo, have a connection with America," said Artemio, surprised.

Giovanni said, "I have family in Boston, and they love living there."

Artemio followed with, "My uncle Bruno lives in the Bronx. He takes a train underground and it travels under a river to get to his restaurant."

"He must be Baresi," Niccolo interrupted.

"No, Piacentino," corrected Artemio.

"But the letters from my family say that the Bronx is full of Baresi people. They deliver ice in the summer and coal in the winter. No one else is allowed do that work but Baresi people; it is like they have their own *Mafia,* too!" All the men smiled half-heartedly, still feeling the sadness of Eduardo's passing.

Niccolo continued with a different tone to his voice, "Captain Battaglia, are you a good Fascist?"

"Yes, I am, Sergeant Major." This question was a strange one to ask and had deep ramifications if not answered correctly, or if taken out of context. "Why do ask?"

"This talk of how good it is in America is rank internationalism. It is defeatist to say you have family in America, to preach that it is better than Italy."

The men became quiet and stared at Artemio. Niccolo was no Blackshirt, nor a Mussolini-loving ideologue; he was angry at the system. He was playing devil's advocate, because it was the system that had sent them to fight in the colonies, the system that had killed Eduardo. Nevertheless, Artemio had to be very careful; any man can report an officer for anti-Fascist speech or defeatism. Artemio's face changed as he gave him a look of indignation.

"Are you questioning my loyalty to king and country, Sergeant Major?" he said forcefully. "I'll have you know that as a fighter pilot and squadron leader, I have been on many tactical missions that are still classified, and I have done more for Italian victory in this desert than you could ever imagine."

But the man's query sparked an internal interrogation. Artemio had never asked himself, how much of a Fascist was enough? He had talked to Blackshirts and always thought their brand of Fascism was too extreme. Beating up people who didn't agree with you, or incarcerating them in re-education camps, were tactics that were too brutal. There was a time in college when he had considered himself a devout Fascist. His time in Rome with Donatella's family and their power had started his questioning of the Mussolini government's authority. Was it degenerating into the oppressive Italian government of his childhood? After months of continuous air sortieing in North Africa, fatigue was affecting his decision making. He did question his own loyalty, but the men on this mission must not know that.

Niccolo reared back physically, as if he'd stepped on a scorpion, and said apologetically, "No, sir, Captain, but I thought you were idealizing America. Perhaps even at the expense of our Axis forces."

Artemio leaned forward and was in Niccolo's face when he said, "Let's get one thing straight, Sergeant Major: no one cares what you think." He held his index finger in the air. "You have one task, and it is vital to the war effort, which is to get me back to Tobruk. I am sorry about Eduardo, but you have a mission, and if every man on this truck has to die to complete it, then so be it! I will drive this damn thing back to base alone with all your bodies piled up on Eduardo's if I have to."

He had to lay down the law to the crew. It had been insolent for them to even ask questions of him. These things started with joking and becoming too friendly. He had to pull rank on them. Artemio knew if he did not appear to be a strong Fascist leader, word would make its way up the chain of command. He did not like being authoritarian, but this was how one must behave in the atmosphere of Mussolini's Italy. What had happened to the early days of the movement, the fraternalism, when all men rolled up their sleeves and worked together? It had been reduced to looking over one's shoulder to see who was informing on you.

Niccolo looked down subserviently. "Understood, Captain." He got up, turned around, and under his breath said, "These officers are all bastards."

Then loudly he gave commands. "Giovanni, set a course, north by northwest. Paolo, get me the star maps and the theodolite. We have a squadron back in Tobruk that is looking for its missing ace."

CHAPTER 4
Arabs

Il Mulo lurched to a stop. Artemio awoke from a shallow sleep as his head hit the main gun mount. He rubbed his bruised forehead, disoriented for a second. The truck exhaust fumes revived his memory of the present situation. Artemio lifted himself to his knees and prepared to curse someone's poor driving. He peered forward to see Giovanni fighting with *Il Mulo's* transmission and doing some cursing of his own. Niccolo was looking at star charts and plotting their location. Then the sergeant major changed his view from celestial to terrestrial, looking straight ahead through binoculars into the darkness. The sky held enough light to make out geometric shapes. He said, "I am sure those are the tents."

Giovanni said in amazement, "I don't understand how you know all of this astronomy. I've been working with you for many months, and all I know is we're facing north."

"Gio, my friend, it is your job to keep me alive, and it is my job to get you home."

"Sergeant Major, is that Gabr Saleh?" Artemio asked.

"No, Captain," whispered Niccolo, turning back to him. "This is the rendezvous point. It is ten miles south of Gabr Saleh."

Heaven Cries

At the turn of the 20th century, Italy divided the colony of Libya into three administrative zones. Cyrenaica was the eastern-most part of Libya, bordered on the north by the Mediterranean Sea and on the east by Egypt. Tripolitania was northwest, bordered by Tunisia; Fezzan in the southwest was bordered by Algeria. Fifty-thousand Italian peasants lived and worked in these three zones, growing cereals, fruit trees and grapes for wine. These products were all sent back to mother Italia.

"Are you familiar with this area, Captain Battaglia?" asked Giovanni.

"Yes. When I was first deployed to Libya I did aerial reconnaissance. My wing men, Mario and Gitano, would watch for British fighters, while my mission was to collect photographs of English installations and troop movements. I would fly east along the coastal road into Egypt, where the threat would be enemy planes from the island of Malta. Later, I would turn south and fly my mission. The return to base was never the same route, but sometimes it was northwest over the Sahara desert, flying over Gabr Saleh. If the English noticed a set flight pattern, they would send up fighter planes that would loiter, waiting for you."

"The work sounds dangerous. Was it?" inquired Niccolo.

"Yes, but I miss it. I love flying. Below you is the barren emptiness of the desert. In a single seat fighter plane with only the drone of the engine, you are truly alone. Flying in the clouds is liberation. Freedom from the gravity of earth is as close as I have come to escaping the emptiness of existence." The foot soldiers did not understand, but they could feel how much this pilot needed to fly. When he spoke again, Artemio's voice was subdued. "Intelligence gathering is not like aerial combat. The photo reconnaissance missions all went uneventfully. I never had any British interference, simply pressed a button and the camera did the work." He thought of those days as his halcyon days in North Africa. He had drunk less and slept better. That had all changed after meeting the German pilot, Klaus Meyer, who had convinced him his only chance for advancement was through combat and kill counts. He had wanted to prove to Donatella that he was worthy of her, and of her family. He'd thought the sacrifice would be worth returning home a war hero. He had believed that once, but after continuous combat, the atrocities and the loss of friends, he was tired of the fighting.

"Our actual contact point is at an oasis maintained by an Arab named Haadi. He is a desert wanderer, much like Mohamed himself," stated Niccolo.

Giovanni added, "Though I don't think Mohamed hated the English Empire as much as Haadi does." Both men in the front seat laughed at that joke. Niccolo then commanded Giovanni to send the signal: three quick flashes of the spotlight, followed by two slow. They waited, and a signal came back from the group of tents: four quick flashes.

"That's our cue. *Andiamo,* let's go," Niccolo said excitedly. Giovanni banged the stick shift into first gear. With a lurch he drove *Il Mulo* forward, without head lights, to the cluster of tents. A dim glow appeared at the opening of the largest of these, its tarp held open to allow the vehicle to pass. Once they were inside, a lanky figure wearing an Arab pleated cap on his head, sandals, and a loosely flowing, long, black smock, a *galabiyya,* closed the canvas tarp behind them, completely hiding the reconnaissance vehicle and its crew. Two small kerosene lanterns illuminated the tent with a faint, yellow light. The crew members who had been lying down in *Il Mulo* began getting up and grabbing their gear.

The lone figure approached Niccolo and said, in perfect Italian, "*Ciao, amico mio.*"

Niccolo answered back, "*As salam aleykum,* Haadi."

The Bedouin's response was, "*Wa aleykum as salam.*" They kissed each other on both cheeks.

Lorenzo leaned towards Artemio's ear and whispered, "This is how we survive out here. The Bedouin have many formal customs. Just follow our lead. Whatever you do, don't talk to the women."

Their host stood as straight as a young man, but his long beard was more grey than black, and his brown skin had a leathery appearance from sun exposure. The sergeant major was telling Haadi that Eduardo had been killed in combat. The nomad's face saddened behind his long beard, and his eyes filled with tears.

"We have lost our brother," Niccolo said mournfully.

"This is terrible news," Haadi said, grief-stricken. "Eduardo was my brother as well."

"We will all miss him," Paolo said, after he and Haadi exchanged greetings and embraces. "We must give him a proper burial. I shall wash and shroud the body. Do you have any clean, scented water, and a white cloth for the *kafan?*"

"Yes, of course. I will send Jamal to assist you."

Haadi turned back to Niccolo and asked, "How did this misfortune happen?"

"It was English bombs dropped from the sky on us," Niccolo replied.

"That is no way for a brave man to die! May Allah strike all the cowardly English soldiers blind!" Haadi declared, gazing upward as if it were a prayer. He then looked back at the men with a puzzled expression. "I am confused, now that I see everyone. You are a crew of five. With Eduardo dead you are still a crew of five?"

Niccolo stepped forward, put his hand on Artemio's shoulder and said, "This is an Italian airman shot down by the British. We picked him up in the Egyptian desert, and we are transporting him back to Tobruk."

"Ah," Haadi nodded, "He is the Italian fighter ace!"

Every man stopped in his tracks, astonished that their secret was known. The Italian men's eyes darted around, and the air in the tent was thick with tension.

"How did you know that?" demanded Giovanni. The Bedouin smiled and crevices appeared in his brown skin.

"The British Long Range Desert Group was here, four hours ago."

"SAS this far west?" Niccolo asked in amazement.

"Yes, four attack trucks and two supply trucks filled with fuel cans. The men who questioned me wore white keffiyeh on their heads." Only the most ardent SAS men had adopted the keffiyeh, a traditional male Arab headdress worn for protection from sun and sand.

"What should we do, *Padrone*?" asked Paolo in a terrified voice.

Niccolo thought for a minute, then said, almost to himself, "They are on a patrol circuit." He turned to Haadi and asked, "What direction did they take when they left here?"

"North."

Niccolo made some calculations in his head, all the while staring at his watch. "We can stay here for some time, maybe 12 hours. We will eat, bury Eduardo, and sleep a little. When darkness returns we will move out." He looked at Haadi and politely said, "With your permission, of course." The Arab nodded his head in agreement.

Paolo turned to Artemio and got right up into his face. "What is so special about you? Now we have the British army and the RAF coming down on us!" Dislike was plain in Paolo's voice and his stance was threatening. Artemio braced himself for a fight.

He answered back just as forcefully. "I am just an Italian fighter pilot who got shot down, that is all."

Haadi put in, "The British Special Air Service commander told me that you made ace in one week. That's five planes you've shot down in seven days. I think they want you dead for a good reason, young airman."

Niccolo looked surprised as he scratched his brow and said, "You told us you've been flying in North Africa for over a year. How did you get five kills just this week?"

The entire crew was facing Artemio now; he felt their eyes on him. He did not like being questioned this way. However, they were risking their lives for him. He felt he owed them an explanation.

"I developed a technique of air combat which uses the advantage of our Macchi fighters' ability to turn tightly. Our fighter planes are thoroughbred race horses, but the Germans make us fly them like draft horses. The Folgore has superb agility with finger-light handling; the Hurricane fighters are as graceful as furniture moving vans. This is the week I started testing my theory. My wingmen and I have flown every sortie we could out of Tobruk. We have made kills on every mission."

Lorenzo asked excitedly, "So with this new strategy we'll win the war and go home soon?"

Artemio would have liked to say yes, but honesty compelled him to answer, "I do not know. My technique may not work against their newer and better Spitfire planes. The British are now confident England will not be invaded, so they are moving their Spitfires to the Island of Malta. I have spoken to our pilots who have encountered the new planes, and they say these fighters are faster and more maneuverable than the older Hawker Hurricanes."

The Reconnaissance crew fell into a melancholy as they assessed the situation. They saw this man they'd found in the desert in a new light. This pilot was a valuable asset for the war effort and must be carefully delivered back to Tobruk, as swiftly as possible. But their exhilaration turned to dread at the prospect, knowing how difficult the mission would be, knowing the British would stop at nothing to get him, and not just any British soldiers—these were SAS men.

"Eduardo is dead because of this man, and we will be next!" Paolo yelled, making a fist.

"Shut up, Paolo! Go refuel *Il Mulo*!" Niccolo ordered. He pointed to the supplies coming off the truck and instructed, "Leave five jerry gasoline cans and the British weapons we confiscated with Haadi. Do not forget, you are on report for accidentally discharging that machine gun," Niccolo added. "If I hear another word out of you about this Captain, I will see that you are court-martialed in Tobruk. The Germans will put you in front of a firing squad."

Haadi, wishing to reduce the tension, interjected, "Let us all calm down. Niccolo, thank you for the gas and guns. Paolo, my son, in my house there can be no violence among guests. My son-in-law, Jamal, will help you with Eduardo's body. We will bury him according to our faith, but first we must wash our hands and eat."

"*Io fame*, I'm starving," announced Giovanni.

"My wife Fahima has made you all a good dinner," Haadi said proudly.

Paolo and Jamal stayed behind to finish up the work. The other men walked outside into the cooling night air and made their way toward another large tent silhouetted against the starry sky. Haadi lifted the draped doorway with one arm so his guests could enter. Three women were in the tent, cooking and preparing the meal; all three had their veils down. Upon seeing unfamiliar men they quickly fastened their veils so that only their eyes showed. They were not introduced. Attention was not paid to them. They were to cook and serve the meal, yet the men were to pretend they did not exist.

The oldest was Haadi's wife, Fahima. She wore black and white sheer cloth draped over herself in many layers, and her head was fully covered. Artemio thought she looked like a Catholic nun. The next oldest was Madihah, Haadi's daughter and Jamal's wife. She was about 25 years old and wore a very elaborate yellow headdress that became part of her robes, like a hooded cape. Some of her long black hair could be seen around the hood. The younger daughter was 18 years old; her name was Kaheesha. She was unmarried and the prettiest of the three women. She wore loose yellow pants with a pink flowing dress, and over that, a red robe. On her head was a simple embroidered kerchief which showed her slim neck. Her long, jet-black hair lay on her shoulders, and as it moved it revealed large gold hoop earrings. All three women were barefoot; multiple rugs made up the floor of the tent.

The men sat on pillows in a circle and discussed events of the day. The food was served to them by the women as they came out of the cooking area. All three women placed appetizers in the middle of the circle. Kaheesha lowered a bowl in front of Artemio. The two of them stared into each other's eyes a second or two more than was appropriate. He watched her walk away; she was the most intriguing girl he had ever seen, exotic to a boy from Piacenza, especially with those clinking gold bracelets on her ankles.

Appetizers consisted of bowls of hummus, tabouleh made with parsley, mint, and bulgur wheat, and dates. The regular crew of *Il Mulo* were comfortable using the local technique of grasping pita bread between the thumb and forefinger of the right hand, then picking up tabouleh and bringing it to their mouths. Artemio slowly brought some to his mouth, but then dropped it on his lap. The entire circle grinned as they watched him struggle.

"Hey, Captain, are you having trouble eating?" asked Niccolo.

"This is more difficult than learning how to fly," joked Artemio. All the men in the room chuckled. He turned his head to look at the back of the tent to see if Kaheesha laughed. She did.

Dinner was served in a very large pan: goat meat on a bed of couscous. By now Artemio had mastered the knack of pita bread between the fingers; however, he still wished he had a fork.

"What spices am I tasting?" Artemio asked Kaheesha. She turned her gaze away from him, not answering, and walked back to the other women. Haadi turned and yelled to the back of the tent to ask his wife the same question in Arabic. She answered him back in the same language. This struck Artemio as strange, because it was clear that everyone in that tent spoke Italian. Haadi translated for Artemio, "Saffron, paprika, and cinnamon."

Now Artemio remembered that speaking directly to the women was not allowed; it could only go through the husbands. He looked over at Lorenzo, who rolled his eyes as a reminder to leave the women alone.

The conversation for most of the evening centered around the war. Haadi had a good command of geopolitics. He predicted General Rommel would drive the Africa Corps through Egypt, then past Palestine and into the oil fields of Saudi Arabia.

Paolo said gloomily, "Allah protect us. we will never get out of this country. We will surely all die here in the sand."

Niccolo added, "It does make sense. After our armies win at Stalingrad, they will turn south to the Caucasus oilfields."

"Yes," agreed Haadi. "A mechanized force must have oil to live; it is their blood. The Africa Corps will link up with General von Paulus's Army Group South, in Iran. The Shah is already a big supporter of Hitler and Mussolini."

Artemio added, "I heard on the airbase radio that Axis forces now control the entire Black Sea and the Crimea. The Russians are retreating into the Ural Mountains." He turned his head to look where the women were gathered to see if Kaheesha was looking at him. Their eyes met and she turned away quickly. Kaheesha then spoke in Arabic to the women. Whatever she said made them laugh loudly.

Haadi yelled at the women in Arabic, "Please lower your silly voices! The men are having an intelligent conversation over here." His wife Fahima answered back, saying something in Arabic that made Haadi laugh so hard his beard shook. The Italian men were curious about what was causing such a commotion. Haadi saw the questioning expressions on their faces and explained, "My young daughter cannot stop looking at your captain. She has never seen a man without a beard, and hands as soft as a woman's." With this comment translated into Italian, the whole room except for Artemio was laughing.

Mint tea and sweet almond and sesame balls were served for dessert. The women never sat or ate with the men; they had to stay in the back of the tent. Paolo and Jamal did not linger. They went to prepare Eduardo's body for burial. When the dessert and tea were finished, Jamal re-entered the tent and asked everyone to come out for the funeral prayers.

Haadi, who had worked in a mosque in Benghazi when he was younger, read the prayers. As is traditional, he stood in front of Eduardo's body, facing away from the others, and prayed silently. Outside in the desert there was only the starlight; each man was alone in the dark, with his thoughts and prayers. When Haadi was finished, he turned to the mourners. The walk back towards the dinner tent was solemn. It is at times like these that people consider their own mortality.

A strong hand grabbed Artemio's shoulder from behind, and Haadi murmured in his ear, "Come with me, young airman. I have to speak to you." The two men peeled off from the group and entered a small tent north of the compound.

"You may not know the ways of Islam," Haadi said. "Sit here and let me tell you." That same strong hand pushed Artemio onto the floor pillows. "Our women are sacred. You may not look at them or talk to them. I saw the two of you, giving each other glances over dinner. I should have said something then. My daughter is young and impressionable. She knows you are a great warrior and an aviator. Her life force is not meant to be with yours. Kaheesha is fair and fragile; she writes poetry. I have nothing against you personally, but I know your destiny. You will become a great man, one whom nations will listen to, a counselor, not a warrior. This will take you far from the Sahara desert."

Artemio had mixed feelings about Haadi's premonition of the future. What did he mean, a counsellor, not a warrior? He answered Haadi with a question. "Why does Islam treat its women so poorly, as less than men? I understand that women are different from men, but doesn't God love both equally? He made men with certain strengths, and he knows our weaknesses. He made women to complement us. They have strengths we do not. We come together as one, and together we are better than each other separately."

"You are an idealistic young man. A woman, if she ever gets leverage on a man, can destroy him."

Artemio thought of Donatella, her sexual power over him, and her influential family. Haadi's words did resonate, but he loved Donatella and wanted more than anything in the world to build a life with her.

Artemio, struck by the awkwardness of the discussion and wishing to get back to his crew, decided to pay Haadi a compliment and walk away, as some men do at cocktail parties.

"Haadi, I am very impressed by your knowledge of world politics, geography, religion, and life in general." Artemio smiled and was about to stand.

"Do you think I am a camel jockey, or that I grew up in a tent with goats? I did not always live here," Haadi said defensively, his finger twirling in the air, indicating the tent and its contents. "As a young man I was in training to be an imam in Benghazi. From there I was going to study in the city of Mecca."

"What happened?" asked Artemio, surprised by Haadi's vehemence and the change in his circumstances. He stayed seated to listen to the explanation.

"The Devil intervened." Haadi made a grimace, then said, "No! I must stop myself from saying that. The truth is, I was a weak man." He looked down at a pillow as he began to tell the story.

"When I was a young man growing up in Benghazi, I loved the mosque and studying Islam. Everyone thought that I would progress and become a great imam. Some of my duties at the mosque were to distribute food and clothing to the poor of Benghazi, mostly widows and orphans.

"There was a woman on my route to whom I would make a weekly delivery. I don't know how she got on the list; she was married with no children. I would stop by and leave food. She always wanted to talk, usually about her husband, how he was mean to her and beat her. Sometimes she would make me coffee and insist I have some with her. Things started to get inappropriate when she touched me. I should have stopped it, but I felt something stir inside when our hands held. This behavior was wrong and I knew it. As the weeks went on she would become more and more bold. On one visit she was wearing Western clothes and makeup. We embraced and I lost control of myself. I do not want to say that we made love, because this was not love. It was animal passion that physically felt exhilarating. I realized I had no power to stop this. Week after week I went back. I was a slave to her female influences. I hated myself. There was something wrong with her mentally; she needed sexual gratification from many men. There was a devil inside her that made her debase herself and destroy the men around her." Artemio could see how distressed Haadi was; his hands shook as he spoke.

"Her husband suspected she was cheating on him. He came home early from work to find her in bed with another man, and he killed her. There was an inquiry; I was asked about my visits to her. The affair was found out by the religious authorities. It was covered up to protect me and the reputation of the Mosque, but my ambitions and future were over," Haadi said heavily.

"I am sorry."

"Don't be sorry for me. I tell you this story so you may learn from my mistakes."

Haadi shifted his body on the pillows so he was facing Artemio, then asked, "Tell me something I do not know. How are you able to kill so many English airmen?"

Artemio turned to look for the exit, wishing to leave. He was uncomfortable talking about this skill. How can you be proud of the fact that you are a good killer? Once again, he longed for the days of surveillance.

But Haadi was insistent. "Where was this ability obtained?"

So he told Haadi about the officers' airfield bar at Tobruk, and how Italian and German pilots would drink after missions. He'd made the acquaintance of a German Messerschmitt pilot named Klaus Meyer.

"Klaus was a big mouth. No one would drink with him unless he was buying."

"So this big mouth taught you how to shoot down British planes?"

"No, he explained to me how the Germans use their Messerschmitts to shoot down British fighters. I copied German tactics exactly and almost got killed. The Italian Macchi fighter is not as fast as the Messerschmitt in a dive, but it is more maneuverable in tight combat. I developed an approach that is suited to Italian strengths and applied it to the British Hurricanes' weakness." Haadi was looking intently into his eyes. It made Artemio uncomfortable. "Why are you so interested in air combat?"

Haadi smiled and said, "I just like to hear stories of Englishmen being defeated."

"What is your problem with the English?" Artemio was curious. Haadi seemed to feel strong hatred for the English beyond the impersonal enmity of war.

Haadi's face lost the veneer of friendliness.

"I assume you Arabs hate all Christian European soldiers in your country," Artemio ventured.

"We know that Christian armies come, and then later depart. We Bedouin people do not concern ourselves with European wars. The great dilemma for our people is the League of Nations and their Balfour Declaration. This allows Britain to support unrestricted immigration of Jewish settlers into Palestine. This will be a long term problem for Arab people."

"The English will never relinquish Palestine. They have not liberated a colony since King George the third lost America," grinned Artemio.

"It is not English governance we are against. The growing population of Jews in Palestine is the problem."

"Haadi, I have to tell you, from what I have seen as a European, the Jews need a homeland. America and England have quotas on how many they will take, and it is insufficient. Russia takes a lot, but still not enough. Hitler cannot expel them all from the Reich; they have no place to go. I am told the Nazis will turn their work camps into extermination camps. That is their final solution. The Jews must have a safe haven like Palestine."

"The history of the Jews has been exodus after exodus; today is no different," Haadi replied. "Please do not export your Christian problem here to us. Jerusalem is a holy city in Islam, because of the Dome of the Rock. This is where the prophet Muhammad ascended into heaven accompanied by the angel Gabriel. We cannot let this place be overrun by infidels."

"The Jews only wish for a sanctuary to live; they will not interfere with your practice of religion."

"The Romans ruled Palestine and have left; the Turks have ruled and have left; and the English will leave also. The Jews here now will never leave. They believe that God promised this land to them."

Artemio thought for a moment then said, "A man here in the desert recently reminded me of a holy story that all three religions believe. It was the story of the brothers Cain and Abel. After your death, don't you think Allah will ask you how you treated your Jewish brothers?"

"Jews are not my brothers!" Haadi spoke vehemently.

"Abraham was told to bind his son Isaac for sacrifice, which was an important part of Jewish history. Isaac is also a prophet in Islam. He had a brother, another prophet, called Ishmael, who became an ancestor to Muhammad. Arabs and Jews are brothers, even though you deny it." Artemio could not understand how both the Arabs and the Jews could miss their connection with each other. How could they refuse to see that? He saw it clearly, and it seemed to him suddenly that if one race were to perish, the other would also die, like conjoined twins who only too late realize that they both share major arteries.

"What man reminded you of this story? Was it the voice in the desert?"

Artemio's face turned white, and he was struck speechless.

Haadi went on forcefully. "After a year of military obscurity, you develop a war-winning strategy to kill large numbers of your enemy. You are shot down and crash land in the desert, with no water, yet you are in perfect physical condition." He waved his hand up and down Artemio's body as if to medically scan him. "Someone or something is protecting you. I know who you met in the desert! I have met him, too."

"I don't know what you're talking about!" Artemio denied as he got up off the pillows. Haadi grabbed his wrist to prevent him from walking away.

"I know you tried to fight him, as I did, but you failed. When I look into your eyes, I know you have met him. He has left something. I can see the devil has left a splinter inside you."

"Get it out of me, Haadi. How do you get it out?" yelled Artemio, as his limbs started to twitch uncontrollably.

"This is why I told you of my former life in Benghazi." Tears were forming in the nomad's eyes. "That woman left a splinter inside of me also. The point of my story, Artemio, is that no one can get it out of you. No one can get it out of me. There is no surgery to lance this abscess. If you ignore it, the hate will grow, the wound will fester. Eventually it will overtake you, and you will become a monster."

Artemio was frozen in panic as he listened.

"In this realm, we must deal with other dimensions. There is but one eternal conflict. History shows us that an enemy can become a friend; these are the fickle winds of war. The English are your adversary today; they will be your ally tomorrow. On a different level, one that is deeper, more concrete, a struggle exists between good and evil. This enemy lives inside you and he can never be completely defeated." Haadi let go of his wrist and said, "Now you know your *jihad*, your holy war against the Adversary. The Evil One, like a maggot in a wound, has bored inside of you. He will always be present. There will be daily combat for your soul."

Shaken, unable to speak, Artemio stumbled from the tent and went in search of the others. Whatever the old man had said about what he would become, he was a warrior now, and he had to rejoin his unit, rejoin the fight. But would he be doing the Devil's work?

CHAPTER 5
Blackshirts

Leaving the collection of tents and Haadi's extended family, the recon team continued their peregrination, like nocturnal creatures scurrying across the desert floor. Niccolo was looking at his star charts to configure a solution that would get them back to Tobruk.

There had been many nights when Artemio would look up at the stars and wish he could navigate like Christopher Columbus. The idea of being on a boat as it is pushed by the wind, the spray of salt water in his face, felt like an indulgence. What a life that would be, exploring new lands and learning about the local people. It would be liberating to leave all the Old World problems behind.

Artemio's thoughts turned to other starry, winter nights, when he was a student. he would walk across college campus to the rathskeller, a cold, dry breeze in his hair. The heavy wooden doors of the pub, when pushed open, were like a portal into another dimension, and entering was to cross over from one reality to another. This is where students came to drink, eat, talk politics, and complain about their professors. Even the descent into the cellar changed one's perspective. The narrow stairway had stone walls on both sides, barely shoulders' width, dark and with an acrid smell.

If another student was coming up the steps, both would have to press against the walls to pass one another, and one got an uncomfortable feeling of claustrophobia. Then the basement opened up into a large, poorly lit hall with gothic ceilings. The music was performed by a local band. This was the hang out for the college bad boys. There was loud talking, laughing, cheap beer and smoke-filled air. Now, standing under these stars, he remembered the night everything changed....

Artemio saw his roommate Mario across the room, sitting at a table alone. A rare to sight, for him not to be among a myriad friends. Mario was a good looking boy, even without the expensive clothes he usually wore. His parents, industrialists with close ties to the Fascist regime in Rome, had sent him to the finest private schools money could buy.

"*Buona sera,* Mario."

The boy looked up from the table with an uninterested expression, and said nothing.

"Where is Gitano?" asked Artemio, looking around for their other roommate.

"I don't know where he is. He is probably chasing that redhead he's always pining over."

"You mean the one you went out with Wednesday night?" Artemio said, with a disapproving frown.

"You knew about that?" Mario said, surprised. "Hey, don't tell Gitano. You know how sensitive he is."

"Mario, have you seen him in here or not?"

"He's a big boy; he can look after himself."

"Oh, you're a great friend. You know Gitano; if he's not careful someone will sign him up for a tour of duty in Spain."

Mario laughed, knowing full well that that could happen, then asked, "Am I my brother's keeper?" He looked straight at Artemio; he was not smiling. Then he added, "Why don't you be a great friend and refill this pitcher with beer."

Artemio gave him a disgusted look and said, "Yes, you are your brother's keeper. You should have learned that lesson by now." He took the empty pitcher and walked to the bar, the whole time scanning the rathskeller for his other friend.

Gitano was a skinny lad, almost girlish with his long, light brown hair. He had a prominent Romanesque nose too big for his face. Of the three of them, he was the one who did need to be watched over and kept out of trouble. Mario and Artemio would often talk politics and show everyone what good Fascists they were. Gitano would keep up his end of the conversation, but with no real emotion. His family were poor farmers from the south of Italy who had either been forced or persuaded to emigrate to Libya. Gitano did not talk about it much. His family had been sent there in the 1920s as part of the national policy of living space; the Germans had the same program, called *Lebensraum*. Gitano had been born in Libya, and according to his birth certificate he was Libyan, not Italian. But the Italian government, as a benefit, provided free college education to the children born to these émigrés, if they had above average achievement.

Artemio was also a scholarship kid, but his scholarship was fully academic, based on outstanding grades in math and science. All three boys were very proud to be students at the University of Milan. Although the University of Bologna boasted of being the oldest institution of higher learning, the University of Milan was ranked as Italy's premier university. Their professors often told them that Fascist schools produced the best and brightest of humanity, the cream of the crop.

Artemio walked across the crowded room, looking at all the faces, but he did not recognize anyone. He felt like a stranger this evening; people were laughing and drinking as usual, but things did not feel right to him. He felt at a distance from everyone in the room, even more than usual. As he approached the bar he saw the lone bartender frantically preparing drink orders. Artemio waited his turn in the queue. For the first time he studied the wood counter. Even in the poor lighting he could see the rich dark brown walnut with a magnificent large grain, very finely sanded and covered with a thick, clear lacquer. It must have been a large, old tree to give up this exquisite piece of lumber. It was a shame the tree had had to die to create this beauty, but the result was an expression of man and nature merging, producing an object of high art.

Artemio's thoughts were interrupted by a rude man in uniform who had been hiding in the shadows of the bar and moved to Artemio's side quickly. He was wearing a black woolen cap and a matching black shirt with pins on the lapel. A black leather Sam Browne strap went around his left shoulder and attached to his waist belt. His face seemed friendly with a big smile, but for some reason Artemio did not trust this stranger.

"Hey, fella, have you heard about the war?" The man in black garb yelled to Artemio over the music.

"Refill on the pitcher, please," Artemio yelled to the bartender, without looking at the intruder.

The insistent man repeated the question, only louder, "Hey, fella, have you heard about the war?" A chill went up

Artemio's neck; he knew he was going to have to talk to this tenacious fellow while he waited for the beer.

"No, what war?" Artemio answered loudly back.

"Our war in Spain," the Blackshirt yelled.

Artemio watched the amber liquid slowly slide down the inside of the tipped glass pitcher as the bartender filled it, then said aloud, "I heard that the Spanish are fighting each other in a civil war, but that's not our war."

The pitcher with its foamy white head was finally presented. The bartender placed it on the ornate wooden bar. Artemio threw down a few lira coins and tried to get away from the Blackshirt. The annoying man took a step forward and grabbed Artemio's arm, which almost spilled the beer.

In a lower, more authoritarian voice he said, "Italy is a world leader now, thanks to our illustrious leader, Benito Mussolini. We must influence world events. This conflict in Spain is fascism versus communism." Having gotten the college student's full attention, he continued. "Italy and Germany must crush the Reds wherever we can find them."

Artemio, angered, answered back, "Let the Spanish settle their own problems on Spanish soil. Many Italians still live in poverty. There are Italian children that don't go to school and have empty bellies when they go to sleep at night. These are the problems our illustrious leaders should be working on!"

The two men were now glaring at each other.

"You do not understand what is at stake here. The USSR is a red stain on the white linen of Europe. We cannot afford another Communist foothold, especially in the West. Could you imagine a Communist Spain? It would be like a vice grip squeezing Italy and Germany until we are crushed and drained of our life!"

Not wanting this to escalate any farther, Artemio pulled his arm free and said, "I've got to get this beer back to the table. It's getting warm."

"Wait, what is your name?" the Blackshirt inquired.

"Artemio."

"I see you have a table with your friends. Is it all right if I sit with you? I will explain to you why Italy has important business fighting communism. The next round of drinks is on me." He gave an eerie smile. "And I will tell you of our adventure in Spain." Artemio could see this man was trouble. A queasy feeling was overtaking him.

"No, that is not a good idea. After I finish this beer I'm leaving to study for a test in the morning."

Artemio made his way back to the table and saw that Gitano had arrived.

Mario looked at him and said, "Hey, where have you been? You took a long time to get that beer. Look, our prodigal son has returned." He pointed to Gitano.

"Oh, I got detained. It was that Blackshirt at the bar." Both his roommates turned to look.

Gitano said heatedly, "You cannot even buy a beer around here without being bothered by these thugs."

"You mean you haven't signed up yet for their 'big adventure' in Spain?" Mario asked sarcastically.

"It's not funny, Mario. A lot of guys are signing up, and they don't even know the difference between a Republican and a Loyalist," said Gitano, looking around to make sure no one was listening to what he said.

Artemio, now annoyed, said, "Come on, Mario, even a good Fascist like you must admit, we would all die for Italy, but it is crazy to die for Spain."

Mario's face changed; he became angry and said, "Neither of you understands world politics. Times have changed. Now a country can be strangled by outside forces, like the League of Nations and their sanctions." He looked at the roommates. "Who runs the League of Nations?" Mario paused, then answered the question himself. "Britain and America. What a joke! Britain has more colonies in Africa than we do, but they put sanctions on us. We have the same policies as they do, but we are honest about it, while they are hypocrites. They see us as their competition for the big land grab in Africa." He shook his fist as he spoke. "I say the League of Nations can shove their sanctions. We must be strong and independent. If we need living space, or raw materials for our factories, we must take it, just like the British do!"

Gitano, not wishing to disagree with Mario, calmly said, "You and I both listen to all of Mussolini's speeches, but you memorize them and repeat them back verbatim."

Artemio added, "I don't like the Blackshirts telling me that I don't understand. I may disagree with them on policy, but I am as good a Fascist as any one of them. The difference is, I think about things and draw my own conclusions. The Blackshirts just repeat Fascist dogma. They are all emotion and no intellect."

Mario became enraged, pointing his finger at Artemio and shouting, "Okay, Mr. Intellectual Elitist, what Fascist dogma do you disagree with? Italy got screwed at the Treaty of Versailles. We were victorious in the Great War, took heavy casualties, and they gave us nothing for it. Or do you disagree that the decorated war hero Benito Mussolini reduced the terribly high postwar unemployment? He did that by stopping the strikes and jailing the Communists. We now have Ethiopia as a new colony in Africa, thanks to the

Fascists and our great Army and Air Force. So just what do you disagree with?"

The boys knew to deny any of these facts would lead to banishment from the party. They were effectively silenced. But Mario was agitated and loudly continued his diatribe.

"Before Mussolini, the Northern European countries would spit on Italy. Now that our soldiers win on the battlefield, and our industrial output is higher than theirs, they respect us."

Stung, Artemio repeated, "Respect? Is that what this force of arms is about, respect? Italy should send its young men into Spain to fight, bleed, and die so France and England will *respect* us?"

Mario turned on Gitano and demanded, "And what do you have to say for yourself? Are you as misguided as our roommate?"

Gitano stuttered and said, "You, you must admit, Mario, there are extremists in our party. Even here at the University some professors are worried about losing their jobs just because they are Jewish."

Artemio took a sip of beer and injected, "Dr. Ibrahim told me if they get rid of all the Jewish professors, the math department will be cut in half. That would hurt our school's prestige."

Gitano, emboldened by his second beer, added, "The beating and jailing of trade unionists is too much. They should have some say in their work environment."

Mario was not backing down. "What the hell do you know, Gitano! You are always soft on the Commies. My father's factories were shut down for three months because of those bastards. We almost lost everything when the banks called in the loans. My family didn't have any more money.

Bankruptcy would have been inevitable if the Blackshirts hadn't broken up the strike with force. They also explained to the bankers that they had to wait for their money. This helped everyone. My family remained solvent, our employees went back to work and got paychecks, and the banks were repaid their loans. If there was ever an argument for breaking heads, that was it."

Gitano pressed his thumb and fingers together and waved his hand in the air, exasperated, "*Madonna Mia!* Mario, you don't listen to anyone!" He did not want to continue the conversation any further. He was uncomfortable talking about Mussolini in a crowd; he might get denounced as a traitor. Because his parents had been relocated and he had not been born in Italy, he always feared deportation. Artemio, also disgusted with the argument, stood quickly to leave. Suddenly the room started to spin, faces laughed at him, and the beer felt like it would come up; he grabbed his chair to stabilize himself. "I need a walk out in the cool night air," he told his roommates.

Stepping out the doors of the rathskeller, like closing the back cover of *The Divine Comedy*, was returning again to the ordinary world. He adjusted his coat, the cold air of autumn clearing his head. He walked along the cobblestone streets of his newly adopted city. Milan was everything Piacenza was not. Milan had all the allure of the big city that a young man could want. It had a new, thriving fashion industry with beautiful girls working as models, and a great nightlife, with numerous bars, cabarets, and restaurants. The streetcars ran all night. Milan also boasted an internationally winning soccer team. It was a city full of multinational businesses and had an energetic, cosmopolitan feel. Milan also had better weather than his home town of Piacenza, even though they were only 50 miles apart. The winters of Piacenza were bitterly cold and foggy.

His thoughts turned to his aging mother, and he wondered how she was getting along. The cold, damp weather wreaked havoc on her lungs every winter. Rosa was alone now, his father having died the previous year. He remembered sitting at the bedside as his father passed. The last moments of life had been a struggle for his father. Artemio had held him, telling him that he always loved him, but now was his time to let go, and they would all be together in heaven.

The walk back to his dorm room along Via della Spiga filled his head with many thoughts. He looked up at the old city wall, fascinated by how the big stones fitted together so well. He imagined great craftsmen putting this wall together. What had they been like? In the moonlight the stone gave off an enchanting red-yellow hue. Such a great effort had gone into building this huge rampart with its massive stones: the manpower, the money, and the time. What kind of people would build such a wall? At one time it had encircled the entire city; had it made the people feel safe and secure? He knew that the Duke of Milan, who had built the castle and the city fortifications, had been defeated in combat by the French and had been exiled. At the same time, Leonardo da Vinci left Milan and went to Paris. Was all the time and money wasted? Had the wall served its purpose, or was it a giant monument to the folly of man? *Is my country today spending too much time building castle bastions, only to have them knocked down by something we have no knowledge of yet? Fascism is like these big stone walls. It gives the Blackshirts, the politicians, and the average*

Italian a feeling of safety and security. What if, like these walls of Sforza Castle, they can be defeated?

The night air tingled in his nostrils. There was a distinct odor of burning garbage in the distance. This time of year in Piacenza people burned pinewood, which had a pleasant smell. He was walking in an area of Milan where the wall was destroyed, where only rubble remained. This was a low-rent part of town; a lot of criminals, homeless people, and prostitutes lived here. He heard a disturbance on the other side of the wall and climbed the loose stones to look. He saw a man on his knees. There were four or five paramilitary men standing over him, hitting him with clubs.

Artemio became enraged at this sight and yelled, "Hey, you, leave that man alone!" He scrambled over the broken stones of the fallen wall.

All the men turned toward the sound of Artemio's yell.

When he reached them he demanded, "What is going on here?"

"He is a dammed Communist," one voice out of the darkness said.

"So he is a dammed Communist. Did you have to turn his face into bloody chopped meat? Leave him alone now," commanded Artemio. He brushed by the men standing in front of their victim. Another figure in the action squad reached down to his belt and put his hand on a pistol where it rested in his leather holster. Artemio bent down to help up the beaten man. As he leaned forward, a Blackshirt lifted a baton to hit Artemio on the head. Quickly, as if he had the hands of a magician, another man from the back of the group grabbed the cudgel and stopped the motion.

"I know this kid. He's from the University," the fast-handed man said authoritatively. Artemio, realizing he was known to one of the men, looked up to see who was speaking. He recognized the *Squadristo* as the man from the rathskeller who was trying to buy everyone beers. The two men's faces were uncomfortably close. In that alley with only the light of the moon, Artemio was able to see things that he had not noticed before. The face of the Blackshirt from the pub had pock marks from old acne scars. Among these men, he held himself with an air of authority. There was no smile now. The Fascist band all had matching uniforms: black shirts and woolen black berets with the special badge of the unit, marking them as a detachment of Milan's famed Black Brigade Legion. The people of Milan had been the first to embrace Fascism and Mussolini, and Milan had the largest Blackshirt regiment. This was odd, considering that northern Italy also had the largest population of Communists. Everything in Italy was a contradiction.

"Lieutenant Scarafaggio, why do we leave this one?"

"Shut up and follow orders, Gazzola."

"Is this what you do to Communists?" Artemio asked indignantly, holding the beaten man.

"You should see what we do to them in Spain. There we have tanks, planes, and machine guns," Scarafaggio said smugly. He turned to look at his men and they all nodded in agreement.

"We have no need for those things here. This is Italy! We have laws, courts, and basic human rights!" Artemio said this as if Italy were the birthplace of civility. For a very long and strained few seconds the men stared at Artemio while holding weapons. He then added, trying not to let his voice crack or show fear of any kind, "I am taking this man to a hospital now." He backed away slowly, dragging the injured man.

"Be careful of your actions, Artemio. I know you now, and I will be watching you," Scarafaggio said ominously.

At a safe distance Artemio picked the man up off the ground. The man's body was thin in his baggy clothes, yet it was still a struggle to lift him. Artemio put one of the man's arms around his neck, while one of his own arms wrapped around the man's waist. They stumbled down the street. Artemio realized he did not know where he was. He just knew he had to get away from those goons. The hospital was close to the University, on Via San Barnaba. After a few blocks of dragging the limp body, the neighborhood improved and more people were on the street. Artemio was exhausted and could not go any farther. They came to a well-lit café with outside tables. Artemio lowered the injured man into a chair, his body slumping over the table. Artemio called to the waitress and commanded her to bring him a towel, water, and some ice. She came back quickly with the supplies.

Upon looking into the man's face, the waitress exclaimed, "Oh my God, what happened to him?"

"I don't know what happened. I didn't see anything. I just came up on this man lying in the street." Even after telling members of the National Fascist Party that Italy has basic human rights, Artemio still knew enough to conceal the truth about his involvement in this evening's paramilitary activity.

The stranger had a matted, black beard that was full of blood and road dirt. Artemio gave the man some water to drink, carefully, a little at a time. The man choked and coughed as he drank, but the water did seem to revive him.

Artemio said, "Easy, easy now," just as if he were talking to a donkey back on San Giorgio mountain.

The stranger finally spoke.

"Thank you for what you did back there. I know they were going to kill me."

"What did you do to those guys that would get them so mad that they wanted to kill you?"

"It is not an action that enrages them, it is a philosophy. Their anger comes from the knowledge that all men reject being oppressed. Fear and intimidation are their weapons. That is enough for most. For men like me, they have another level of punishment," said the man. He looked like Rasputin, the czarist monk.

Artemio made an ice bag out of a napkin and placed it on the man's jaw, which was starting to swell. Then he asked, "What is your name?"

"Do you really want to know my name?" the man answered back. "You are already in a lot of trouble for helping me."

"I will tell you my name," Artemio said, to show the stranger he felt no fear.

"I already know your name. It is Artemio, and you are a student at the University. You see, I was listening even while I was being beaten." Artemio frowned at the thought of the beating. The bearded man continued, "It would not be polite for me to refuse someone who did so much for me tonight. My name is *Il Volpe*."

The Fox. Artemio was speechless, not knowing what to make of this *nom de guerre*. Finally he said, "You must hide for a while. The Blackshirts will still be looking for you."

"I know. I'm leaving for Spain, to join the Republican International Brigade. You should come with me, Artemio. It will be a great adventure. The Russians will teach us how to drive a tank and clear the jam of a Maxim machine gun."

Artemio did not look interested, so he added, "Don't forget Spanish women, eh?"

"I was already offered that adventure tonight, but for the other side," mused Artemio.

"You are a moral and freedom-loving man, Artemio. You have no business with those Fascist pigs." Artemio liked the kind words this man said about him, but he had to explain further.

"Yes, I am moral, which is why I cannot go to Spain. The killing of people just because they think differently turns my stomach. I believe that the Spanish civil war will be a crucible that will not end with peace. It will only forge new weapons that could destroy all of Europe." He continued to wipe *Il Volpe*'s blood from his head and neck. "Red, Black, it doesn't matter. I work here, from within, to extinguish the fires."

Il Volpe proclaimed, "Comrade Stalin tells us that there will be a global conflict. All the great powers will be drawn in and falter, and this is when International Communism will begin."

"I would not make a good Communist," Artemio replied. "I do not believe the world must be destroyed in order to save it."

"Someday soon, Artemio, when you are sick of the fighting, you will realize it is the idle rich who run their war factories for profit only. They are the enemy, here as much as in Spain." Artemio thought about Mario's family and how their factories made war materiel. The Piaggio family discussions revolved around the suppression of workers' rights and communism. But surely, there must be a center point, some common ground, around which all people could rally?

Heaven Cries

Il Volpe tried to get out of his chair and get to his feet, but he was in such a weakened state that he fell back. This only gave him more determination. With his arms on the table he forced himself up and to his feet. Like a wild animal being birthed in the woods, he struggled for life, even though the odds were against him. He started to walk away, but turned to Artemio and said, "I will not forget your name. I owe you a favor. However, you, Artemio, should never mention my name to anyone." He walked slowly off into the night.

The waitress returned and said, "Where is your friend?"

"He is not my friend. I told you, I just found him along the side of the road, and he needed medical attention," Artemio responded, not wishing to be associated with him.

"You did all of that for a stranger?" she said, impressed by this young man's generosity. "Let me get you an espresso on the house."

She returned a few minutes later with the owner of the café. She pointed to Artemio as she handed him his coffee and said, "This is the man I was talking about."

The owner was an overweight, balding man dressed in a white cook's uniform. He wiped his hands on a dirty white apron and said, "Let me shake your hand. I grew up in a religious family, but in this sinful and modern age I lost my religion." He gave the waitress a look like he wanted her to leave, which she did.

"My wife is at home taking care of our sick daughter, who, the doctors say, will not live much longer," he continued. "My wife cries every night. We are both sick with grief. I do not know how to console her. Tonight I will go home and tell her not to worry about the problems in our life, because I have met the Good Samaritan." He looked at the floor as if he were bowing. "I think I will start to pray again. Thank you so much for what you have done."

Artemio felt unworthy to be called the Good Samaritan. However, he did see that the owner felt better about life. He smiled at the man.

"I just did what any good Italian citizen would do."

"Maybe you did what any good citizen should do, but your actions tonight, unfortunately, are far too rare," the owner said sadly, mourning for civilization.

Artemio drank his coffee by himself and reflected on the solemn events of this cold evening. The warm espresso felt good in his hand. He looked into the demitasse cup and saw the bitter black liquid separating from its brown foam. He realized the world was getting more polarized and violent. Things were not as simple as life had been on the top of the mountain in his youth. Since Mussolini's march on Rome, Artemio had thought that things in Italy were getting better. Tonight had proved this was not the case. Even the best laid plans of men can become perverted. As winter closed in, the nights would grow darker and colder; so, too, would all of Europe.

CHAPTER 6
Graduation

Sand blew into Artemio's face, like the sharp facets of a million diamonds scraping his skin. One more benefit to a bearded face, he thought. The wind speed picked up, and breathing became more difficult. He wrapped a cloth around his head for protection and watched the reconnaissance men setting up poles and lashing tarps as a full-blown sandstorm swept over the camp. What should have been morning showed no sunrise in the east. There was nothing you could do when these storms hit except button up. With the truck fully secured, the men hunkered down amongst the cargo and prepared to weather a long tempest.

He'd come a long way from racing in Mario's Alpha Romeo to lying down in this armored truck between a cannon and a machine gun, a rolled up knapsack for a pillow. He remembered how the accelerator pedal on the car had been so responsive to the pressure of his foot. The tires held the road like the rubber was melting into the pavement. The best part was shifting the racing transmission and listening to the powerful, straight eight-cylinder engine roar....

After their graduation ceremony in Milan, Mario let him drive the Alpha.

"Will you slow down? You're diving like you're in the Targa Florio!" yelled Mario from the front passenger seat.

"Am I driving that fast?" he said, grinning ear to ear.

"Can't you hear the girls screaming behind you?" Mario laughed.

In the backseat were Olympia, Mario's longtime girlfriend, and her schoolmate, Gabriella. Olympia's father owned the largest bank in Milan and was a close personal friend of Mario's father. Since the two men had a son and daughter the same age, it had seemed natural to push them together. Olympia was a wild girl whose parents always gave in to her excesses. Her friend Gabriella was the opposite, a shy girl who did not talk much. Her clothes were simple in comparison to those of Milanese women of means. Her father was probably a craftsman, or in some kind of trade.

They drove out to Parco Sempione, a favorite park in the area, originally designed as an English garden. It had wide grass lawns bordered by roses, chrysanthemums, and peonies. They left the car and the four of them strolled together. Artemio was so infatuated with Gabriella that he didn't notice when the other two walked in a different direction. Gabriella's hair was a striking jet black with a shiny luster and a long, waving curl. She had big, dark eyes that opened to her soul. They walked past many varieties and colors of roses, talking about their lives. She told him that she played soccer for her school team and that she liked to coach the younger girls. He had also played the sport in high school and been the leading scorer on his team. He thought to himself, *She would make a good striker: she is tall and has long, muscular legs.* Her politeness made her seem out of place among the aristocratic Milan families. Her father was successful, but not enough to be one of the city's elite, so not many well-to-do families would approve of a courtship between their son and Gabriella. She, and all people of the lower financial strata, could feel the rift. Artemio thought she was sweet and liked her manners and poise; they were refreshing. He didn't fit in with the gentry class, either—a boy from San Giorgio Mountain with no inheritance.

"Olympia tells me that you are from Piacenza. Is that true?"

"Yes. I was born there, but I don't feel like that is who am," Artemio said, thinking back to his life with his parents on the top of the mountain and feeling slightly embarrassed for his meager beginnings.

"If you are from Piacenza, you are from Piacenza. It does not mean any more than that," she said, as if teaching him to be proud of who he was.

Artemio was relaxed and enjoyed talking with her. He never felt he had to be on his guard, or must say the politically correct thing. In Fascist Italy, Artemio knew, if you wanted to climb the ladder of success, you must know the right people and say the right things. If you were liked, you would be invited to the "in" parties and would be recognized in the future. Gabriella, pretty as she was, would hold him back in his social advancement. And yet this young woman had an inner sense of things. She understood people and had a kind, caring soul. She was a typical Italian: bright, and hard-working to a certain point. She has a desire for a good life, but no high ambitions. She dreamed of getting married and settling down with children. The man who married her would enjoy the common pleasures of life each day, making love to a proud, strong woman who was a loyal wife and a good mother to his children. But Artemio wanted more than the sort of life his parents had known; he was ambitious and yearned for a grander stage.

When they got to the restaurant after their walk in the garden, the street was full of double-parked cars. Men were running back and forth, trying to valet the sudden rush of arrivals. Mario's father was always throwing big parties for business associates and politicians and used this hall often. The restaurant was a two-story brick structure, with the bar and main dining room on the ground floor. The upper room was where the Piaggio private parties always took place. It had several windows overlooking the street, and running parallel with the window was a long dais that held the table for the guests of honor. Small round tables were dotted around the rest of the room. Artemio chuckled to himself; from the smaller tables, a guest's perspective, it looked like a renaissance painting—a Florentine idealization of reality.

Mario sat at the main table between his parents. Fellow graduates and guests of honor, Artemio and Gitano took their places to the right of Maximo Piaggio, Mario's father. Aunts and uncles took the rest of the seats on the long table. Mr. Piaggio was dressed perfectly for the occasion, wearing a tailored blue pin-striped suit with spats shoes. The jacket pocket had a seemingly endless supply of Cuban cigars that he would hand out to all the men. Maximo turned to Gitano and said, "I am sorry your parents could not make it today for your graduation. They would have been invited to our celebration here tonight."

"Thank you for their invitation, sir, but they cannot leave the farm collective in Libya," replied Gitano.

"Is it an expensive trip from Libya?" asked Mario while adjusting his tie, not looking at Gitano. He hoped to cause him embarrassment over the fact that his parents could not afford to travel.

"Yes, it is."

"And I'll bet it is very difficult for Italians to get back into Italy once they've been relocated to a colony," Mario said loudly, watching Gitano's face and neck redden. "You must be very proud of your parents for doing their duty to Italy," Mario added, in a sarcastic tone.

Mrs. Piaggio inquired, "Artemio, is your mother feeling any better?"

"Yes, and thank you for asking. She had a bout of pleurisy and was in the hospital for two weeks, but now she has been discharged and is recuperating slowly." He felt guilty about not visiting her in the hospital.

A quiet pause overtook the conversation. Then Gitano turned to Artemio and whispered, "Are there any politicians left in Rome? Because I think they're all here."

Artemio laughed and said, "The money is made in the north to pay bribes in the south."

Maximo was an experienced host. He never sat for a long period of time. Soon he was circulating around the room, making people feel welcome. By contrast, Luigi Mercati, the chairman of the board at the Bank of Milan, stayed at his table. People waited in a receiving line to pay their respects to him, as if he were the Pope, or a Mafia chieftain. Mr. Piaggio was a natural at shaking hands, patting backs and telling jokes. Cajoling people to get what he wanted was a skill perfected over years of dealing with civil servants, politicians and bankers. This method reduced bureaucratic red tape, such as making a problem easement go away on a construction site, or getting a permit that your competitor will never get. Piaggio factories were being built all over Italy.

Artemio had also left the table and was standing by himself, drinking his Negroni cocktail, a bitter aperitif. He looked out the window, appreciating the high clouds which were turning a reddish hue in the sunset. He was daydreaming, soaring through them like a bird. Maximo came up behind him and put his firm hand on his back. "My son tells me you boys had a great academic year and have a good class ranking."

"Yes, we do, Mr. Piaggio. We worked hard, and it paid off." Both men knew Mario's good grades were a result of his roommates tutoring him in every class.

"And I understand that you are good Fascist," the elder Piaggio said loudly on purpose. He looked around the room, expecting many to hear it.

"Yes, sir. I think Benito Mussolini is a great leader for our nation, both as a warrior and a statesman."

"Now that is high praise. Do you know that *Il Duce* has personally helped me deal with many of my labor union problems?"

"Yes, Mario mentioned it once," Artemio said cautiously. He did not want to tell Maximo that his son told everyone who would listen that *Il Duce* was a friend of the family. Artemio was feeling awkward with these political topics, which were really just pronouncements of party loyalty. He continued anyway, because he thought it was proper. "Our economy is great because of the strong hand of Benito Mussolini on the wheel."

Mario's father now put his arm over Artemio's shoulder, then leaned in and spoke in a much quieter voice, "Mussolini keeps pressure on the Commies, that is true. Always remember, Artemio, it is men like me who make our economy flourish. Businessmen employ large numbers of people in their factories. These workers are mostly rabble. If they did not have jobs, they would become troublemakers. The last thing the government in Rome wants is rioting in the streets." Artemio did not know how to respond; being quiet and attentive seemed to be the right way to play this.

Mr. Piaggio continued, "Look at the anarchy in France and Britain. They are paralyzed by wildcat strikes. The Communist Party in those countries is too strong. They act like a cancer and will drain the life out of their victim." He took a puff from his cigar and blew a smoke ring while looking up at the ceiling. "The other great economy in Europe, after ours, is Germany. Hitler copied all of Mussolini's strong-arm tactics to suppress the labor unions; the only difference is, he calls his goons Brownshirts. The Germans, however, always overdo everything. This thing with Kristallnacht was too much." He shook his head and added, "A messy business."

Artemio was fascinated by the wealthy entrepreneur's gold watch and diamond ring, but tried to follow the economics lesson.

"Look at even the great America, with their president Roosevelt: they cannot get out of their economic depression. This is because Roosevelt is soft on the unions. I think he is a bit of a Communist himself! He does not have the will to be a street fighter like Mussolini." In his expensive silk suit and greased-back, thinning hair, Maximo had the eyes of a carnivore. He looked up and scanned the room again for any who might be listening to them. He then dropped his head, almost against Artemio's face, and in an even a lower voice said, "Personally, I think Mussolini is an idiot. Do you ever watch his speeches on the newsreels? His body language and facial expressions are asinine. The man looks like he is a tragic character in a Marx Brothers movie. But I will keep supporting him, and his Fascist thugs, as long as they keep the conditions right for economic growth, and, of course, profits!"

Artemio took another sip of his red Negroni, in which most of the ice was now melted. He maintained eye contact with Mario's father, but did not reply. This wealthy factory owner was a sly man of much power. He could afford to be reckless with his thoughts. Artemio knew that, as a young man with no political connections and no money, he had to keep his ears open and his mouth shut.

"You are my son's best friend, and I see what he likes in you." This loud pronouncement was like the period at the end of a sentence, signaling that the conversation was over. Maximo's piercing eyes, like those of a predator, looked up and scanned the room until they caught the next person he wanted to speak to. He gave an insincere smile as he loudly said, "Senator, good to see you! How was your flight in from Rome? I hope my plane had enough champagne this time?" and he quickly walked away from Artemio.

The crowd was getting hungry, and the afternoon feast was about to begin.

"Hey, Gitano, were you listening to the maître d' explaining the menu? I'm sure you're not used to the traditional food of northern Italy. Here in the "white belt" we eat a lot of rice, butter, cheese and cream," instructed Mario, as though he were a professor at the university.

"Polenta! Don't forget polenta," interjected Artemio. The menu was classic for Milan and the Lombardy region. The antipasto was *bresaola*, an air-dried fillet of beef, with shards of Parmigiano Reggiano cheese over arugula salad leaves. Next came the *primo piatto* of risotto with porcini mushrooms, followed by *cotoletta alla milanese*: a delicate veal chop, hammer pounded to tenderize the meat even more, then dipped in breadcrumbs and sautéed in butter. The next course was *formaggio*: Gorgonzola, a blue veined cheese, served with slices of pear, walnuts, and honey drizzled over the top. Dessert consisted of *panettone*, a yeast cake made with eggs, saffron, raisins and dried candy fruits. The dessert was served with a glass of *prosecco*, a sparkling white wine from the Veneto region.

Artemio looked around the room as everyone was eating; he saw people talking, planning their futures. He felt detached from the room, not really part of the crowd. The Piaggio family had told Gitano this was how people ate in this region. Artemio's family was also from the north, but his father did not own factories. Their diet rarely included meat, except on Sunday. Breakfast consisted of a cup of espresso with dry toast from last night's bread. Lunch was a salad, usually dandelions. A magnificent dinner for them would be ravioli stuffed with spinach and homemade ricotta cheese. Artemio looked over at Gitano and saw him talking with Mario's mother. He saw the poor boy from the south, a farmer's son, who had never eaten better than today. How many Italians were eating just a bowl of pasta and beans, or polenta, for the day? A feast like this was only a dream for most. *This is a social injustice that must end,* he thought. *If only the rich could see how connected they are to the poor. Without improvement in the lives of the poor, they will lose hope. That is the ground the Communists need to sow their seeds of revolution.* Somehow, in the United States they were able to do better. His uncle Bruno wrote in his letters that every American ate meat regularly: hamburgers, pork chops, chicken. Artemio dreamed of trying a five-cent hot dog at Nathan's in Coney Island.

When dessert was over, the men went downstairs to the outside bar, where they could smoke their cigars and drink Sambuca Al Fresco. The women remained upstairs; it was their time to gossip. The ladies loved to talk about other women who were not present. A favorite topic was who was having an affair, and did the spouse know.

Artemio sat outside with the men, enjoying his drink. He felt very relaxed and was completely enjoying the moment, his earlier concerns over injustice forgotten. As he looked out onto the street, feeling the alcohol creeping into his head, the telephone poles on the sidewalk were like cypress trees forming a long, continuous line along some Tuscan driveway. As the sun started to set, long shadows from each of these poles were slowly moving toward him, like thin daggers. A radio mounted on the wall played the music of Giuseppe Verdi. The lovely melody gently filled the room and spilled out onto the street. The discussion among all the men had centered on the Italian colonies in Africa and how proud they felt about their powerful country. The other Europeans were fearful and jealous of them. Italy was at last the equal of the French and the British, and they owed it all to Benito Mussolini. Nowadays conversations about *Il Duce* always seemed to include the warming relations with Adolph Hitler. Italians would say, "If all of Europe is afraid of Hitler, he is good to have as a friend." The occasional rebuttal was something like, "It is a terrible thing, the way he treats the Jews," or "How can you be friends with people who think they are the master race?" The discussion always ended with, "Mussolini is smart. He has gotten us this far; he will know how to manage Hitler and the Germans."

Heaven Cries

The opera music stopped suddenly and a stern, male voice came over the radio. "Attention, attention! This is a news bulletin from Rome. At 7 o'clock this morning, a combined air and sea assault from our brave men of the Italian Navy, Army and Air Force was launched against the belligerent country of Albania. The Italian people and its armed forces had no choice but to invade Albania when it threatened to cut off shipments of raw materials. This action comes after months of our beloved *Il Duce* demanding that the Albanian government and its people stop mistreating the Italian minority population living within their borders. More news of this invasion will be reported as it becomes available. All Army reservists are to report to their bases." The men in the room looked at each other with blank stares for a second or two. Then, as the shock subsided, people started yelling, "It's war! It's war!"

Gitano's voice trembled as he asked, "What are we going to do?"

Mario, enraged with adrenaline, shouted, "We will go to war and fight those bastards!"

Mr. Piaggio spoke with a much cooler head. "Everyone calm down. We don't know all the facts yet. Let's not do anything rash before we know what's going on." The local officials and politicians in the room quickly got their coats and made their way to the parked cars and taxis. This created a feeling of uneasiness, as the others seemed to wonder, *Where are they going? What do they know?*

"We must get back to the university and see what our classmates are doing," said Artemio. That moment he saw Gabriella running down the stairs to look for him. Her eyes met his for a second and he could see the worry in them. He should run to her. He wanted to, but Mario grabbed his arm and pulled him out of the restaurant. The three young men made their way to an electric streetcar. The bell on the well-used conveyance was incessantly clanging because people kept crossing the tracks. Some confused people were just standing in the way as the car approached. As the tram rolled deeper into the city center, it became impossible to continue. The streets were filled with hysterical people. Milan had changed; its people were in crisis. Since the Spanish Civil War and the destruction of Guernica from the air, people who lived in big cities were fearful of being bombed. Artemio could feel the change; it was palpable, like a pulse. Everyone felt a fear of the future.

The streetcar came to a stop in a piazza that was mobbed with unruly people, some of them drunk. It was clear that in a few hours the police would not be able to control this crowd. Mario turned to his friends and said, "I'm joining the Air Force!"

Both boys, befuddled, answered back, "What?"

"Yes, that is what we must do," insisted Mario.

"You're crazy!" Gitano shouted.

"No, I'm not crazy. We've talked about this before. The Army and Navy would not be right for us." The three of them used to joke that, in the hierarchy of intelligence, the lowest level of military service was the Blackshirts. The Army was only slightly better, then came the Navy. The smartest, and also the most difficult to get into, was the Air Force. But that was an abstract dorm room discussion, never meant to go this far.

"This is the time for all good men to act. Now is when Italy needs its sons. I have spoken to Galeazzo Ciano about joining the Air Force, and he agreed with me."

"Do you mean Foreign Minister Ciano, *Il Duce's* son-in-law?" asked Artemio.

"Yes, he is a friend of mine. He was a highly decorated pilot in the fighting over Ethiopia." Mario continued, "The Air Force will accept us; we have graduated from Milan University. Our professors taught us that we are the best of the best. We are the elite of our generation."

Artemio knew he was right. There are times when ordinary men must take extraordinary actions. The three boys, and a few other classmates, went to the Air Force recruiting office and enlisted.

As the boys were leaving the building, they were talking and laughing among themselves. Artemio bumped into a man walking in the street. They both stopped and looked each other up and down. He quickly recognized by his uniform that the man was an officer in the Black Brigade. This soldier was wearing a black cotton shirt with light khaki trousers. His black hat was a *beretto di campagna* and had the unit markings of the Red Fasces badge. He wore a black leather belt prominently displaying the holster with his Beretta pistol. Artemio's mind was taken back to the night he saw *Il Volpe* the Communist being beaten. It was this man and his goons who had done the trouncing.

Mario spoke first. "Congratulations! When did you get promoted?"

"Thank you, but I am not at liberty to discuss any of the internal workings of our organization," replied Scarafaggio, who was in a permanent pose of attention. "Have you heard about the invasion of Albania?" he asked, with no expression on his face.

"Yes we have, and we all signed up for the Air Force," Mario proudly announced.

Scarafaggio was disappointed in their choice. "You boys have made a big mistake; the Air Force doesn't see any action at all." Then his face lit up with excitement. "We have a Blackshirt division involved in the invasion right now. Blackshirts were the first on the ground to fight, even before the Army! We're going to teach those Albanian pigs and their Gypsy cousins what a Fascist boot on the neck feels like." He said this with hatred. "I'm sorry; I must get going. I have much work to do for future operations." He walked away, body erect, almost marching.

Emilio, one of the classmates who had also just enlisted, said, "I heard that the Blackshirts have been fighting very aggressively and bravely in Albania, but that they are taking heavy casualties, much higher than the Army."

"It was good to see Scarafaggio again," Artemio said with a smirk. Then he added, "After talking to him I realized we made the right decision by going into the Air Force, not becoming Blackshirts."

"Well, the only thing to do now, men, is to get drunk," said Mario.

"Yes, I'm going to drink to forget what I just did," agreed Gitano.

Roberto, another classmate, said, "If the Albanians don't kill me, my mother will!"

The group found themselves at a nightclub in the business district of the city. They told the club owner that they had just signed up for the Air Force, and he gave them free drinks all night. They were unsure of what they had just gotten themselves into; however, each one of them refused to show any sign of trepidation. With their male bravado and alcohol, they remained calm and stoic. At one point Artemio was looking for Mario when he saw him at the bar. He was talking to a beautiful young lady with long, straight red hair. As he walked toward them he noticed she was dressed very provocatively. Her tight skirt clung around the curves of her buttocks. With all the office buildings around, Artemio assumed she was a secretary. Mario always found the pretty girls in any room. He was sure his friend was feeding her a story about how dangerous his life in the Air Force was going to be. Suddenly her right hand came up off the bar and slapped Mario in the face. With a look of scorn, she got off her stool, took a second to stabilize herself in her high heel shoes, and marched out of the nightclub.

What did he say to her? Well, Mario has that effect on a lot of people, thought Artemio. He approached Mario, now alone and staring into his drink, then climbed onto the same high stool the secretary had been on.

"That didn't go well."

"Women come and women go," Mario answered, with slightly slurred speech.

"They are not streetcars. You should pay them a little respect."

Mario continued to stare at his drink in silence.

"You know, I have seen Scarafaggio before," Artemio said, changing the subject.

"Yes, I know," said Mario, in a bored tone. "We've all seen him around the rathskeller, trying to recruit naïve young freshman into the Squadristi Legion bound for Spain."

"No, I mean outside of school. I saw him and a group of his nationalist Fascist party thugs beating up a Communist by the city wall. It was horrible what they did to this man's face. They held him down and beat him. I am pretty sure they were going to kill him right in front of me."

"Really?" said Mario, as he turned to look at him, interested in this story.

"I walked over to them and told them to leave the man alone. I thought for sure I was going to get a serious beating from those guys."

"You're crazy, my friend!"

"I told them what they were doing was wrong. In Italy, we must be bound together for the common good of our country. We must care for each other; even the weakest among us is still a proud Italian citizen."

"Is there more to that speech?"

"No. Then I picked up the badly beaten man and dragged him away from those thugs."

"Listen to me, Artemio, that is stupidest thing you could have done. Those guys are not the police; they're not the Army; they are special action squads that answer to no one. You could not go to the police if you had a problem with them. The police are afraid of the Blackshirts. Do you understand how powerful they are? You are alive only because Scarafaggio didn't feel like killing you that day. This is the real world, not the ideal fantasy you have created in your head about how all men are created equal. Go to America if you believe that crap. In our future, things could get very dicey. You better stay close to me, and I'll try to keep you alive."

"You don't have to tell me how dangerous these times are. But does that mean we have to change our concept of good and evil to fit the Fascist party's definition? If good men do nothing, then darkness will only grow. You are right that Scarafaggio and his kind are very difficult to deal with now, but this is the time to rein them in. If we wait longer and they grow in power, there will be a point where your father's money will be of no use to you."

Mario didn't like other people talking about how rich he was, even though he bragged often about it. He looked like he might hit Artemio. Instead he got up off the stool and walked away.

Artemio knew he had crossed the line, but both men had said too much. Alone, he left the bar. He walked aimlessly for several blocks, having no place to go. He was lost. Most of the insanity over the invasion of Albania had died down by now. He walked up to an old church with brownstone masonry. It had uneven steps that led to intricately carved brass front doors. He decided he would light a candle for his sick mother and to the memory of his dead father. When he pushed on the green oxidized copper handles, they would not budge. *How strange is this?* thought Artemio. *A church is never locked.* He leaned to the side and rested on the banister to read the plaque of the church: Santa Maria delle Grazie.

He walked down the broken marble steps back to street level. Turning the corner of the medieval stone building, he found a doorway below street level, which had been the ground floor 500 years ago. He stepped down to the side door and pushed on it. The door creaked as it opened. The room beyond had a sick, musty smell, like mold. By the light of several candles he could see tables and chairs lined up around the room. Artemio walked to the front of the room to light a candle, then stopped. On the wall was the most magnificent painting he had ever seen in his life. It was a fresco of men eating at a table. The work was old and poorly maintained, faded and with flaking paint so that the underlying wall showed through. He stared at it and realized that this must be *The Last Supper* by Leonardo da Vinci. The mural had cracks running through it from water damage. He strained his eyes in the faint candle light to make out the details. Jesus was in the middle with six apostles on either side of him. Artemio started to feel a warmth come over his body and a relaxation in his muscles, a pervasive serenity. His nose detected a sweet, heavenly scent that overpowered the smell of mold. There was Judas the traitor clutching his 30 pieces of silver, the one who betrayed Jesus with a kiss. He was clearly an agent of the Devil. Strange feelings, intuition rather than knowledge, came over Artemio as he gazed in the dim and flickering light at the damaged mural. It was like another sense, an understanding that there would be betrayal in his life. The warm feeling was getting stronger. He focused on St. Peter in the picture and felt a closeness with this figure. The apostle held a knife in his hand. Could this mean he was to be an avenger, a slayer of evil? Artemio felt a new confidence and strength inside himself. He was no longer unsure of his future. He didn't know what the Air Force had in store for him, but his feelings of dread and worry were fading away, replaced by optimism. He was prepared for his new life and ready to embrace it.

CHAPTER 7
Rome

He awoke from a dream to find he was living a dream. Her eyes were deep blue and looking right into his. Her full lips moved, with the magnificence of celestial bodies.

"Are you still sleeping?"

Artemio was sure now that he was conscious and this was reality. This dream girl was Donatella Capoletti, the part-time model, part-time actress, the one from yesterday's newsreel propaganda filming.

At their introduction Artemio had been overwhelmed by her beauty, but had tried to play the cool, reserved fighter pilot. She was the same age as Artemio, but her life experiences were very different. She grew up living the good life in cosmopolitan Rome, oldest daughter of an influential father. Her beauty made it impossible to look away. The fashion industry only intensified what was already there.

He had been surprised, when he asked her out, that she said yes. His fellow pilots, Mario and Gitano, had also paired up with actresses from the back lot shoot. The evening started out as a group having drinks after work, but soon Donatella's eyes were wandering around the room. She was looking bored by her second glass of French champagne.

Artemio had realized he had to act fast or lose her. When he asked if she wanted to leave, a brightness lit up her face.

"I know of a wild party happening at the Spanish Steps, but I don't think the others are right for it."

The two of them left the bar. The first thing Artemio had done when he got to Rome was to buy a second-hand motorcycle. After several failed kick starts, Donatella got on the back of the loudly sputtering machine. She yelled directions into Artemio's ear as she held him tight around his waist, and her knees gripped his thighs so her high heels would not touch the hot exhaust pipes of the motorcycle.

Just four days ago, the three boys had graduated from a rigid military flight school at airbase Foggia in the south of Italy, and their commanding officer had ordered them to go to Rome. Regia Aeronautica was falling behind in recruiting young men for the rapidly expanding Air Force. Newsreels of young, good-looking men in uniform getting beautiful women to swoon over them boosted enlistment.

The best of the Italian film industry was employed in this endeavor. Artemio had trained for air combat in a past-its-prime frontline fighter plane, a slow-moving Fiat CR .32 biplane with a single archaic radial engine, an open cockpit and no oxygen. For the propaganda film clip, though, the Air Force donated their most modern fighters: Macchi C.202. The three boys did not actually fly them, however; they only sat in them while a movie of blue sky and clouds played behind them as the backdrop. Another camera crew filmed the stage action. The ground scene was a city street, really a back lot in a film studio. From the scripted lines to the perfect lighting and make-up, everything was artificial. Although typical of Madison Avenue advertising, this sham was a tool of politics. The Fascist regime in Rome was falsifying everything, from bogus battlefield victories to fabricated economic statistics. Mussolini himself seemed artificial, a bad actor. He lied to Italy, and Italy loved him for it.

The only reality that Artemio cared about was Donatella. He knew she would be difficult to handle; he would have to be at the top of his game, all the time. Her family, the Capolettis, had been leaders of Italian military forces for several generations. Her father, Enzo Capoletti, had been the first in the family to enlist in the then-new Italian Air Force and had gone on to become a highly decorated World War I ace. After the war he'd grown disenchanted with the government and how veterans were treated. He'd met a young Benito Mussolini, a wounded war veteran, and they'd become good friends. Benito had been amazed at how gorgeous women were attracted to fighter pilots. Pilots had an élan about them that intrigued Mussolini. Through their relationship, Enzo became a Fascist Air Force general.

Naked, Artemio got out of bed and walked to the bathroom. In the living room, he tried to find the pieces of his uniform that were strewn around the apartment: underwear on a chair, his tie around the neck of a Centaur statue; then he noticed Donatella wearing his Air Force issue shirt. She was looking out the window. He quietly walked up behind her and put his arms around her waist. She was pleasantly surprised and melted into his arms. He sank his face into her long blonde hair and smelled her scent. She placed her arms over his and said, "Make coffee for me. I need coffee."

"Yes ma'am," he answered. "Shall I make an egg for you?"

"That would be great if I had any eggs."

What do you have? I can make anything," Artemio said confidently.

"My icebox is empty. I am afraid I'm not much of a cook."

"You are a young, thin fashion model; why should I be surprised?" asked Artemio. "We will go out for breakfast." He thought for a moment. "Do you think my motorcycle is okay where I left it last night?"

"Oh *Madonna*! We are lucky to be alive. You were so drunk, we should never have been on two wheels!" She said this as emotionally as if trying out for a part in a movie.

"*I* was drunk! I had to carry you up three flights of stairs! When we got to the top I noticed one of your high heel shoes was missing. I had to stumble all the way down to the street to get it." They both started laughing. When their eyes locked, Artemio leaned in and began kissing her. Donatella wanted him, too. He had no control of himself; he obeyed her speechless commands. His tongue entered her warm, wet mouth; her neck went back, allowing his entry. Artemio picked her up, as he had the night before, and carried her back to the bedroom.

Donatella had a small one-bedroom apartment on the third floor of a very old but well maintained building on Isola Tiberina, an island in the Tiber River. It was a bohemian neighborhood, populated by unknown actors, playwrights, and artists. There was no elevator service, but the view from her windows gave a wide panorama of Rome. Artemio looked out the windows and saw the river winding toward Castello Sant' Angelo, with its crenellated walls, where the popes sought refuge when threatened; it had underground passages to the Vatican.

He looked at Donatella's perfect nose and saw a few freckles on her skin. They enjoyed their coffee in silence. Artemio announced unexpectedly, "Let's go to the Vatican."

"Why would you want to go there?" she asked, surprised. Looking at him suspiciously, she demanded, "Are you religious?"

Artemio took a sip of his espresso, exhaled slowly and said, "I think so. I believe in God, or a higher power that created all of this." With his hand he made a waving motion.

Donatella's voice changed and became less playful. "Everything you see here was created by Romans. For thousands of years we built things. Romans created this city, the Vatican, and this apartment." She paused, and Artemio could see the passion in her eyes. She added, "Romans even created me!"

"Well, if the Romans created you, then they are the greatest artisans the world has ever known."

She smiled at that compliment, and her blue eyes became even brighter. Artemio continued more seriously, "I thought everyone in the Fascist party was a good Catholic." He blew into his demitasse cup of hot espresso. "Mussolini made Catholicism the official religion of Italy, and it now must be taught in public schools. He even gave the land of Vatican City to the Pope."

"My dear Artie, religion is but a means to an end. Karl Marx wanted to overthrow governments, and since religion supports the government, he had to liberate the people from their religion. You know he said religion is the 'opiate of the masses'. He was right about that. Now the contrast is this: *Il Duce* doesn't have a pious bone in his body, but he wants the allegiance of the Pope. His dictate shows the Catholic people they must choose fascism over communism."

"Donna, does that make you an atheist?"

She was annoyed by the question. "My family has fought Italy's wars for as far back as anyone can remember. On the land, sea, and now even in the air. No one came home and said God helped them or intervened in anyway." She looked at him, at his disheartened expression. "Arty, I tell you this: as a Fascist soldier, you must be strong and depend on no one. You are a new Roman Centurion. Like those before you, from the icy Rhine of Germania to the burning desert of Arabia, be independent and always maintain the initiative, or you will not make it home." A heavy silence descended on the conversation.

Donatella then spoke in a cheerful tone, "So you want to go to Saint Peter's Basilica."

"Yes."

"This is good, because you can confess your sin."

"What sin?"

"The way you ravaged me last night. You were an animal in bed." She laughed out loud. "No amount of Hail Marys can cover that."

He sheepishly smiled at her as he remembered the best night of his life. "No, I want to see the *Pietà*. My father said that Michelangelo's sculpture is of Mary presenting the dead body of Jesus Christ to all of us. He told me it was very emotional; he cried when he saw it."

"Okay, *turista,* I will take you there, but then I want to picnic at Villa Borghese for lunch."

They left her narrow three-room apartment and walked onto a dirty cobblestone street. Crossing over the Ponte Fabricio to the east side of the Tiber River, he held her hand as she smiled at him. They strolled past Rome's 16th century synagogue, and Artemio admired the old structure.

Donatella looked up and said, "Some of these decrepit buildings have to be demolished. Mussolini has plans to clean up the Ghetto. He is so busy now I don't think he will ever get to it." Artemio thought of some of the ancient Roman ruins at the Forum that were just piled blocks of marble; no one wanted to 'clean them up'. Artemio felt this plan could be a euphemism for something more ominous.

Along the Via Veneto they came to the old Roman wall and passed through it at Porta Pinciana. The Vatican with all its art and history was everything Artemio the traveler wanted to experience, but Donatella found it tiresome and soon demanded they get lunch. Once in the Borghese Gardens, they laid out a blanket on the grass. The sun was bold in the cloudless sky, but a cool breeze came down from the seven hills. The lawn held a few other quilts with young lovers, like boats on a tranquil lake. Artemio looked inside his panino as if it would reveal hidden knowledge and declared, "This is the worst prosciutto I have ever eaten."

Donatella took a bite of her sandwich. "There is nothing wrong with this prosciutto."

"It's not as good as Piacenza prosciutto. This is too salty."

"Artie, this is Roman prosciutto; stop complaining. Our prosciutto is different, that's all. Truth be told, I find yours bland." She looked at him with a devilish smile and said, "I hope you don't turn out to be as bland as your prosciutto."

He did not look at her but only frowned. He put the sandwich back into the butcher paper and said, "Donna, I want to spend every minute of my life with you." He paused, then added, "But I can't. I will be assigned to a posting in the next few days. I may be gone a year or more; I might even be killed."

She rubbed the back of his neck as they sat side by side, Artemio felt as though she was the only other person on the planet with him. "I know you will come back to me and be a great Italian war hero. We will all be proud of our flying ace, just like my father."

"I am not like your father. I don't even want to fight. I want to live in a house and wake up every morning to your beautiful face." He thought of how his parents had lived. It was a simple life, but they always had each other.

"We will have that someday, baby, but first you must earn a good military reputation so we can be a power couple with the gravitas to be invited to any party in Rome."

He felt he wasn't getting through to her. "I don't want to go to parties, especially not tonight. Can we stay in your apartment, just the two of us?"

"No, Artie, I told you there is a big affair tonight at Piazza Venezia. Massimo, the movie director, will be there. All of Rome's film industry will turn out for this event."

"I don't feel like going. I drank too much last night."

"Artie, I have to go, and I need a soldier on my arm for the paparazzi. Please come with me." Artemio thought, *Any soldier will do?* Feeling threatened that someone else might take his place, he agreed.

"Oh, thank you so much!" She leaned in and gave him a peck on the lips. "For being such a good boy, I have a reward for you." She let the last words linger in the air.

"A reward?"

"Well, I was going to tell you after the party tonight. But since you're so glum, I will tell you now. Daddy has arranged a seaplane to take us to the island of Capri. Isn't that great?"

"Wait, the General has arranged military transport for his daughter to go on vacation?"

"Not just me; you're coming too, silly."

"Won't the Air Force need that seaplane for patrol or something?"

"You are such a child sometimes. Regia Aeronautica has plenty of seaplanes on patrol. This is a perk of being a general. I think my father got the plane for you, Artemio."

"Me?!"

"Yes, he wants you to see the benefits of being a Fascist and a friend of the Capoletti family. He may call on you someday for a favor. He needs to know if you are a man who can be trusted."

I will never understand Romans, Artemio thought to himself. *I would move heaven and earth for Donatella. The only repayment I would ever want is to hear her laugh or touch her face.* But this was not how Romans did things. They routinely mixed politics with pleasure. They had a need to control, so much so that the control became the pleasure.

The plane flew low over the tranquil island of Capri. From the air you could see how the entire bay of Naples was an ancient water-filled volcano. The mountain peak on Capri was just part of the volcano's rim. From its crest the land sharply tumbled into the Tyrrhenian Sea. The three-engine plane with its twin floats taxied on the water into Marina Grande. The loud military machine, half plane, half boat, reduced its throttle as it passed the rocky breakwater. Hydraulically powered wheels descended from the pontoons, and the pilot revved the engines for the power needed to climb the steep ramp of the port. The lumbering goliath discharged its passengers on dry land. The smooth landing did nothing to soothe the turmoil Artemio felt.

Donatella, trying to get him out of his foul mood, playfully said, "What would you like to do on the island, my little *turista*?" Artemio did not answer, just sulked.

She was tired of sweet-talking him. "Honey, you're upset over nothing, I told you, Massimo and I were discussing his latest film project, and he doesn't have any cast yet!"

"You were gone for over an hour, and I could not find you anywhere. I was worried about you."

"Oh, that is so adorable, *amore mio.* You do not have to worry about me. I was born in Rome; I know my way around the streets and the people." As they walked along the shops at the seaport, passers-by on the sidewalk nodded hello.

"Where I am from, when two people go out together they stay with each other."

"Really? Well, I am not like that. I like to circulate around the room and be with many different people. I get so bored talking to just one person at a party."

Artemio could not get her to see his point. "Like you were so bored, you and your girlfriends took your clothes off and jumped into the Treve fountain?"

She smiled at her recollection of that event.

He was irritated. "It is not funny. If I hadn't gotten forceful with the police and pulled rank with my uniform, they would have arrested you all."

"You're so dramatic today," she said, giggling at his anger. "You know, Massimo told me he would add a scene like that in his next movie."

"I am not being dramatic, Donna. You drink too much every night. It is a nonstop party with you." As Artemio looked out past the harbor, his eye caught an old Italian Navy cruiser putting out to sea from the Naples seaport. Thick, black smoke was billowing from the four smokestacks of the antique ship; all its coal-fired boilers were at full steam. He thought to himself, *I can't believe men have to go to war, fight, and die in a dinosaur like that. One torpedo from an airplane and all hands would be lost.*

"I didn't think you were the jealous type, Artemio. It is not becoming in an officer."

"I did not think I was jealous either, but I am crazy about you. I think I'm losing myself in you." He held both her hands and looked into her eyes. "I don't think you feel the same way about me."

"Artie, baby, these are tumultuous times. You are not a boy living on that mountain anymore. The whole world will be at war soon, and you will be posted far away. I have my film career that I am trying to get started. It is all too crazy to be getting serious now." She turned her gaze from him. "I really like you, but I need my freedom too." She frowned, then looked back into his sad eyes. "Yes, I like going to parties and drinking. I flirt too much, but I always come home to you. You make me roar like a lioness in bed." She put her head on his shoulder as her arms hugged his waist. Artemio remained quiet, enjoying her body against his; he craved any affection she gave him. They walked for a while up the hill, away from the port, immersed in their own thoughts. Donatella stopped, turned to Artemio and said, "This is my car."

"Wait... What? This is your car? Are you kidding me?!" he said in disbelief. She gave him her minxish smile and threw him the keys. They both jumped into the red two-door convertible, a 1935 Jaguar. The enamel of the paint was so rich and thick it looked wet. Artemio turned the ignition and the engine thundered to life, each cylinder firing as a chamber of its heart. This thoroughbred horse wanted to run.

The warm ocean wind blew back his military regulation haircut. When he looked over at Donatella he saw that her kerchief kept her hair in place, though the long silk scarf she was wearing around her neck flowed in the torrents of air. She had on large, white-frame sunglasses that contrasted with her ruby red lipstick. The roar of the sports car's engine mixed with Donatella's laughter as they took each hairpin turn. His heart rate quickened and his pupils dilated with each gearshift and squeal of the tires, as the coupé barely held the edge of the mountain road. Beyond the curb was a thousand-foot drop to the deep blue Mediterranean. The closer he brought them to danger, the more excited she became. She encouraged him to risk, to push, to grow. Donatella had done it again. She was able to make him feel more alive than ever before. He could not stay mad at his Roman goddess. She was perfect. Or was she?

At the highest peak the pavement ended. There, rising up out of the earth, was a large portcullis in a fortified gatehouse. The adjoining high masonry wall went along the top of the mountain and then descended down it. It was ancient; it had been used in the defensive armamentarium of several kingdoms and potentates, the Capoletti family being only the most recent. It was clear the design was to keep the right people in and the wrong people out.

Donatella, drained by the excitement, said, "This is the end of the road. Leave the keys in it. A man will take it to the garage." The gate opened and a servant came out to greet them. He was in his 50s and slightly overweight. She introduced him as Peppino, the head butler. "He has been with our family since before I was born."

The man with the pencil-thin mustache nodded in respect and said, "I hope the plane flight was comfortable. Sometimes you can have unstable weather. If you would like a carminative, just ask."

"No, thank you; the flight was pleasant enough," replied Artemio, as he thought about the argument he'd had on the plane with Donatella. Another man, the valet, took the luggage from the trunk and brought it inside.

They passed into the courtyard, which contained palm trees, bougainvillea of different colors, and flowering cactus plants. Donatella put her hand into Artemio's as they walked. Peppino, following behind them, got the message: one room.

The main house was expansive, with marble columns and mural-painted walls interrupted by alcoves that housed alabaster statues.

"*Mamma Mia*, is this your house, Donna? It's huge!" Artemio said, craning his neck as he looked around.

"It has been in my family for centuries. We don't know when the family actually acquired it. The foundation has been researched by archaeologists at the University of Rome, and they date it to Emperor Tiberius. His fortress started at the harbor where the seaplane landed. This house was built on the outskirts of his Villa Jovis palace."

"I'm impressed by this house, and your family's wealth. I did not know any Italians lived like this."

"Italians, no; Roman Fascists, yes. I show you this, Artie, because I will be waiting for you, when you get back from the war. You can live like this, too, with me at your side. Tiberius is not cold, dead history. The Roman Empire is alive today, and we are the new emperors. It is your time to conquer, to take what is yours, for the glory of Rome."

She was seductive and he liked everything he heard. He could not stay mad at her flirtatious ways. He could overlook the continuous parties, the endless martinis. He was attracted to her lavish lifestyle; he wanted it all. His head was spinning. Was it a sellout of what his father told him on the mountain, to fight for justice and equality for all Italian people? Is this what he had wanted as a student in Milan? Was this the Fascist reward for beating up Communists in the street? In his life, would he choose to become the Good Samaritan, or Pontius Pilate?

Artemio came up for air and treaded water in the cool, blue Mediterranean Sea. After the rigors of basic training and flight school, he was in good shape. He was sure this was where the gods of antiquity must have lived. He had swum far from the boat, and Donatella was waving him back, like his personal lifeguard. The sleek craft had twin outboard engines, and the dark brown, natural teak wood from Southeast Asia provided a contrast to the sapphire sea. The boat was in a turbulent spot and rocked violently from side to side. Donatella was standing in the back in her white, two-piece bathing suit, holding the rails to stabilize herself. He thought she was the most enticing woman on earth. At that moment he wished he were a sculptor; he would spend the rest of his life studying her every curve and contour. She would be his only model, and he her dedicated artist.

"Armando wants to take us to the north side of the island," Donatella said as he swam close to the boat. Armando was the captain of the boat today. He worked for the Capoletti family in various capacities. Mostly he babysat Donatella. As Artemio climbed the ladder, he read the appellation on the stern in gold paint: *Gelosamente,*

Jealously. He smiled, thinking, *Being on this boat, in Capri, with a fashion model, 'jealously' will be how everyone else sees me.*

She handed him a dry towel with one hand, steadying herself with the other.

"I like it here. The arched stones jutting out of the sea seem so primeval. These were here before mankind," Artemio said. He felt a tranquility, a peacefulness, in this place, even with the turbulent sea.

"It is called the rocks of Faraglioni. The water is uncontrollable in these shoals," yelled Armando above the noise of the motors, as he pushed the throttle forward, defending the boat from each wave's attack. *It seems these Romans are uncomfortable around things they cannot control,* mused Artemio. Sitting in the back of the pleasure craft, he watched the captain struggling. Armando wore a tight tank top shirt with blue nautical stripes running across it that accentuated his muscles. *A fight with this guy could be a real challenge,* Artemio thought. In spite of the captain's manipulation of both throttles and the wheel to navigate between the high swells, a rogue wave got through and hit the boat. This knocked open the cabinet door under the boat's wheel, exposing a fully automatic Beretta machine pistol. The gun was mounted to the wall and had an extended 30-round magazine jutting out of the pistol grip. Artemio turned to Donatella, who saw the same thing, and asked, "Armando needs a gun here?"

"Armando always has a gun," she answered from under her big floppy hat. Her right hand held it on her head so it would not blow off.

"If there is one place on earth where you do not need a gun, it is here. This place is paradise."

Donatella turned from looking at the sea to looking into his eyes, "Satan enters paradise often. Wasn't Eve tempted by the serpent in the Garden of Eden?"

He was taken aback by her response, then she added, "Vladimir Lenin stayed on the Island of Capri many years ago as a guest of a big Communist sympathizer."

"I did not know that," Artemio said, surprised.

"Arty, even Tiberius had his Praetorian Guard to protect him on this island," she said in the tone of a condescending teacher. He thought that was a bad example. Emperor Tiberius went mad with power and was killed by his own Praetorian Guard.

Armando pulled the throttle back and slowed the boat as they approached their next destination. He stopped the boat and weighed anchor in front of an opening in the rocks. As the waves hit the ancient volcanic basalt, the opening would disappear. When the water retracted, the entrance could be seen again for only a few seconds.

Donatella got up from her seat and said, "Let's swim in."

"Why, what is in there?" he asked fretfully.

"I cannot explain it to you, but I can show you."

They both jumped off the boat's railing, hand in hand, and let the cool blue water envelope them. As they came to the surface, the water had a strong chop. Waves crashing into the rock wall created a white foam. They swam to the cave's orifice. Donatella informed him, "We have to time this just right. When the water is receding, you can see the hole. If you wait until you can see the entrance, it's too late to go, and you will be pushed up against the rocks." Artemio was not comfortable with this; he did not want to have to explain to her father or Armando if she got hurt. She was such a risk taker! But he would have to do this if he wanted to be with her. That was the type of girl she was. Donatella needed excitement all the time or she got bored. He would have to demonstrate his bravery today.

She continued, "When a big wave is going in, you follow it. As it smashes against the cliff, dive low and swim hard against the current, and the next wave will push you into the grotto." Artemio's stomach started to turn inside him; still, he had to do this or his girlfriend would lose respect for him. Without another word, Donatella was off, swimming after the next high surge. He saw her go under the water, and then never come up. He turned around to see if her bodyguard was watching these events. Armando was standing on the bow of the boat looking right at him, and both men were thinking the same thing: You better go get her! He saw a roller moving towards him and turned to catch it.

He felt like an Olympic swimmer using powerful scissor kicks to maximize speed. As his wave crashed against the jagged rocks, he took his last gulp of air and dove down like a dolphin; then, still swimming forward, he struck upward. Artemio's lungs almost burst before he reached the cool, sweet air of the subterranean vastness.

Entering the Blue Grotto was a surreal experience. Artemio was struck by the complete silence of the space. The cave had no artificial light, and no direct sunlight reached it. The indirect light that filtered through the water filled the enclosed cavern with a deep, cobalt hue. He was awe-struck. As he looked around, his eyes fixed on another human form. It was Donatella, grinning at him, her long, wet blonde hair floating and swaying on the surface of the water.

"You're crazy, you know that? You're crazy!" he yelled, wiping the water from his face. She broke into laughter, seeing his vulnerability, like a little boy, and the loss of the cool, competent pilot. She swam to him and hugged him around his neck. He kept them both afloat by treading water. She rested in his strong arms and whispered into his ear, "You will never forget this, and you will never forget me." He knew no words could ever be truer.

Later that afternoon, as they returned home, passing through the gatehouse of Villa Jovis, Donatella suggested, "Arty, let's have drinks on the veranda before dinner."

"I would like that; it would be a perfect end to a perfect day."

Peppino came running when he saw them. His pear shaped body waddled from the main house to meet them. He was gasping for breath as he said, "Signore Battaglia, a telegram from Rome came for you. Excuse my interruption, but I thought it might be urgent." Artemio and Donatella looked at each other and their hearts sank. This telegram ended their time in Capri. He took the telegram from the butler and just stared at his typed name on the paper.

"Hurry, open it! Don't you want to know where you're going to be posted?" she said, like a child with a wrapped birthday gift. He looked into her face and had a million more things he wanted to tell her. He wanted to talk about their future together, how much he missed his mountain home, how much his mother would love her. Marriage. Children. None of that mattered now. He begrudgingly opened the telegram. It read:

LIEUTENANT ARTEMIO BATTALGIA THE KING OF ITALY AND IL DUCE BENITO MUSSOLINI ARE ASSIGNING YOUR

SQUADRON OF THE REGIA AERONAUTICA TO THE AIRFIELD IN TRIPOLI LIBYA STOP YOUR LEAVE IS TERMINATED AT ONCE STOP RETURN TO YOUR BARRACKS STOP GOOD LUCK AND BRING GLORY TO ROME STOP

His arms fell to his side, almost dropping the paper, and his head lowered as he mumbled, "Libya." It was the sort of reaction one would expect to a telegram announcing a family member's death. Donatella grabbed both his arms and said, "There is nothing wrong with that. Libya is a fine posting!"

"Africa is the one place I didn't want to go," he said sorrowfully. Peppino turned and discreetly left, like the good servant he was.

"Artie, stop acting like this." She thought for a moment and added, "The truth is, outside of Rome, the whole world is a shit hole." This was not cheering him up. She tried another angle. "It is all part of the Axis plan, a parallel war. The Germans in the north fight westward, and we Italians in the south also fight westward." He continued to stare at the telegram, hoping the ink on it would change. "You have to do your duty for your county. It is only for a year or so, and then Daddy will get you back here to me."

"It is more than that, Donna. I love to fly, and I am the best pilot in the squadron. But there is something about the desert; if I go there I will not return. I don't want to die in a barren wasteland."

"Arty, we can make your assignment as easy as you like. We can have you fly a transport plane or do reconnaissance missions." Her voice became stern. "But you have to go!"

"I know. I know. I will do my duty. It is just that I always saw myself in combat, flying over farms and hamlets in Europe, green and alive with trees and people. If you get shot down, you can try to make it back to your own lines on foot. The desert is not hospitable to a downed airman; it is a death sentence."

"Don't think about that. We would never let that happen to you. Go clean up and get ready for dinner. I will make arrangements for the seaplane to pick us up in the morning."

CHAPTER 8
Walls of Tobruk

Il Mulo turned onto the coastal road, officially named Via Balbia. The Axis soldiers just called it "the way to the front", because traveling east led to the English lines. The evening sea breeze was refreshing as it blew over Artemio's sunburned skin, providing respite from the oppressive heat. This thoroughfare was the only permanent, man-made construction from Tobruk to Al Alamein. Italian engineers had used steam-powered rollers to crush the ancient coral and pack it down to form a roadbed that was only inches higher than the desert floor.

Traveling on this single artery at night was treacherous. The reconnaissance crew saw trucks, tanks, officer staff cars and vehicles of every description moving in both directions frantically, like two black snakes slithering side by side. The twilight was darkening, with only a waxing quarter moon in the sky. All the vehicles had to maintain strict light control, driving with their headlights blacked out. These rules were enforced by a band of feared German military police nicknamed headhunters.

Niccolo, uneasy, said, "Something's up. I have never seen this road so full of traffic."

"There must be a big military operation in the works," guessed Giovanni.

"Everyone's acting crazy, all in a hurry. Don't they know they'll just have to wait at the next checkpoint?" said Paolo from the back.

At every mile they passed a manned 88 mm anti-aircraft gun aimed upwards. Men with binoculars and range-finding equipment stared up into the night sky, on high alert. These positions were semi-prepared open pits. The gunners called these perfectly round, excavated holes in the sand, whose four-foot-high walls were reinforced with concrete, "kettles". Small underground rooms were dug projecting off from the circle to house ammunition and living quarters for the Luftwaffe men. To Artemio's right was the Mediterranean Sea, and small patrol boats plied the inlets. A searchlight would be activated for a few seconds, then quickly extinguished. This illumination would help the skipper avoid rocks or semi-submerged wrecks. The fear of being targeted by English submarines kept lights to a minimum. If an enemy's surface ship was discovered by one of these little wooden patrol crafts, they would radio the coastal artillery information like grid position, heading, and speed, rousing these giants from their slumber. These guns could not be seen from the road, as they were positioned a mile or more from the beach. Having calibers of 150 and 210 mm, these anti-ship batteries could launch an armor-piercing round fifteen miles to sink any size ship, even as big as a dreadnaught. The barrels of these guns were housed deep in rebar-impregnated concrete encasements, to protect them from counter-battery fire.

A line of BMW motorcycles came up from behind and started to pass the recon crew, the lead motorcyclist signaling with his right arm that they must pull off the road. Giovanni cursed in Italian, but followed orders. German military police were not a group to be trifled with; they, like the Nazis, were held to a different standard. This security force had the authority to arrest, interrogate, and shoot anyone they thought a threat to fortress Tobruk. When *Il Mulo* came to a stop, the motorcycles positioned themselves in a semicircle. Three of the four BMWs had sidecars, each holding an additional German soldier pointing an MG 34 machine gun in their direction. The motorcycle men wore helmets, goggles and leather gloves. A thick dusting of sand covered these road warriors, providing camouflage they did not appreciate. A staff car drove up and pulled off the road in front of them, then two liaison officers, a German and an Italian, exited the car and walked over to the men.

Niccolo was the first to speak. "Easy boys, we're all on the same side here."

The German commanding officer spoke, also in Italian: "Papers!" and held out his hand. His uniform was perfectly fitted to his slim physique. After spending three days with the bearded, foul-smelling crew in the truck, Artemio was impressed by this smartly dressed gentleman. Around his neck he wore a gorget, one of the distinctive accoutrement worn by the German military police. The shiny aluminum plate dangling from his neck had an embossed eagle holding a swastika.

"Where are you coming from?" the Italian officer demanded, while the German officer scrutinized their documents. All the men on the truck recognized the distinctive Roman accent.

"We were in Egypt on a two-week reconnaissance mission, and then we were ordered to pick up this downed pilot," Niccolo reported, as he pointed with his thumb and closed fist to Artemio behind him.

"What is your name and unit?" the German officer demanded of Artemio.

"I am Captain Artemio Battaglia of 1st Stormo, 6th Gruppo, Fighter Squadriglia."

"Then you are based here at Tobruk," stated the Italian officer.

"*Si*, yes," said Artemio.

"When were you shot down, Captain?" the German asked, now staring through his wire-rimmed glasses into Artemio's face, trying to detect a lie.

"Three days ago, on a bomber escort mission into Egypt."

"Then you haven't heard. We are on a heightened state of alert. There have been intelligence reports that an attack on Tobruk could happen at any moment," said the Italian officer, trying to be as formal and cold as his German counterpart.

"How can we be attacked here? We saw the main British attack force massing for an offensive, but that was way back at Al Alamein," said Niccolo, dumbfounded.

"The plan is thought to be a full-scale raid by air, land, and sea to capture and hold Tobruk until regular forces can relieve them. These Special Forces troops will not be wearing their British uniforms, and they will speak both German and Italian." The Italian officer's face had a grave expression as he explained.

"Get back to your headquarters units now and await further orders," barked the German officer as he handed back the crinkled papers to Niccolo. He then did a very formal about-face and marched back to his open-top car. The German soldiers standing around the truck lowered their submachine guns and got back onto their motorcycles, while their fellow soldiers in the sidecars kept their machine guns trained on the reconnaissance men.

"Do as he says. I've seen this unit shoot Italian soldiers on this road who don't have proper papers," the Italian officer urged in a quiet voice. He seemed more at ease when his German counterpart was unable to hear the conversation. He turned to Artemio and nodded his head, which made his thick eyebrows rise. "I am glad you are okay. Your squadron has been using your strategy of air combat with good results."

Artemio was stunned. "You, an army officer, know about it?"

"Everyone on the base is talking about it. You have made all of us Italians proud in front of these arrogant German bastards. *Andatene e buona fortuna*, go now, and good luck."

The men sat in the recon vehicle a minute while the German drivers kick-started their Bavarian-manufactured motorcycles. They used their body weight and all the power of their legs to cycle the twin pistons and ignite the fuel in the cylinders. With the distinctive BMW rumble, the machines drove off, leaving a cloud of dust.

Artemio thought about the Italian officer riding along with the Headhunters. They made the law up as they went along; he was the liaison officer. Did he complain or try to stop them when they shot Italian truck drivers? He seemed like an affable guy, someone you would like to have a beer with, but how could he be complicit with Germans killing his own countrymen? Did the standard for human decency drop so low in this war?

"Giovanni, let's get this movie-star pilot back to his commanding officer. I'm growing tired of having to take care of him," grinned Niccolo.

"Seriously, I must get back to my squadron, now! The first wave of the attack will be to bomb the airfield." Artemio felt a surge of excitement along with pride. He was good at air combat and his men needed him. The idea of flying with Mario and Gitano again made his heart race.

They traveled to Al Aden Road, where another checkpoint was set up. Tobruk was just a dot on a map, but it consisted of a massive complex of bases and fortifications. The plans were not styled on the perfect star pattern of the French General Vaubaun. This was designed by Italians, more as a Renaissance genius would have drawn them: a loose configuration of barbed wire, minefields, and concrete bunkers. Armored units were stationed in open areas of hard-packed sand where defensive tank counterattacks could be launched. The base had two airfields: one was just outside the harbor that held a mix of German and Italian fighter planes and seaplane support services; the second airfield held both fighter escort and long-range bomber groups. The Al Aden airfield was used to bomb Malta and harass British shipping from Gibraltar to Alexandria.

The harbor of Tobruk was a deepwater port, essential to the war. Fighting in the western desert required that water and fuel be resupplied constantly. Both the Africa Corps and British Commonwealth forces consumed large quantities of both, plus food, ammunition, and medical supplies. Tripoli was the safe deepwater port for Rommel; Alexandria was the same for Montgomery. These two generals both needed Tobruk in the middle of their battlefield for sustenance. Artemio could not understand why, with all the goals of the

Axis Forces being met, at least on paper, the Mediterranean Sea was no longer *"Mare Nostrum,"* Our Sea. German and Italian aircraft and ships regularly attacked British shipping. From Libya, Sicily, Crete, and Foggia, a firestorm rained down on the English, yet their naval forces still held sway.

Giovanni slowed *Il Mulo* to a stop behind a convoy of Steyr trucks waiting for the sentries to clear them past the gate. These trucks had air-cooled engines and were perfect for desert operations. They never needed water, never overheated. Eventually the recon group moved up the queue to the guardhouse. A black soldier in an Italian motorcycle uniform asked Giovanni to show his papers. Artemio looked around and saw seven or eight black men who were in the *Polizia dell'Africa Italiana,* standing with their Beretta submachine guns trained on the recon soldiers. The man asking for the papers was clearly a no-nonsense sergeant. These men were veterans of the invasion of British Somaliland. They all wore brown leather crash helmets and coats. A wide, tan canvas belt ran across their waists, with multiple sewn pouches for additional 9 mm magazines. The uniform was strict Italian Army issue, except that tucked into each ammo belt was a long, 14-inch, curved tribal fighting knife. When the ammo ran out, these African colonial soldiers carried on with hand-to-hand fighting.

Artemio was proud to serve with these brave soldiers. The Italian Army had been quick to realize their potential. Though not a racially integrated army, black units fought alongside white ones. The logic of enlisting good fighting men, regardless of origin, was obvious to Italian Fascists. The German Army, on the other hand, could not see past skin color. The Aryan superiority concept would be the Germans' undoing, Artemio thought. Hitler used this philosophy of the master race to indoctrinate young Germans. They were taught to believe that it was their right to conquer and subjugate the "untermenschen"—those who were considered to be sub-human, less-than-men. This made it impossible for Germans to fight side-by-side with black men.

The sergeant at the gate explained to the crew that these papers were old and new ones needed to be issued. Niccolo acknowledged the defect in the papers and told the guard he would correct it. He knew better than to try to pull rank on this sergeant. The men in *Il Mulo* were exhausted; they wished for a hot bath and some shuteye. Just a few more miles to go and it would all be over.

CHAPTER 9
Special Air Service

The reconnaissance vehicle was moving fast and had to brake hard to stop in front of the Headquarters building, sending up a cloud of fine, sandy dust. Artemio was in a hurry to get back to his unit, but he owed these men a formal goodbye and thanks for saving his life. He purposely gave each man a direct look in the eyes and a strong handshake, instead of the more formal Fascist salute.

When he got to Niccolo, the last one, he kissed him on both cheeks and said, "Even though you are only a sergeant major, you are the finest officer in the entire Italian Army. I am honored to serve beside you. I hope we will meet again, after the war." He turned to the rest of the crew, "I consider all you men my brothers."

Niccolo was proud to be singled out for recognition. "You are a special person, Artemio. I do not know what the future holds for you, but I believe it will benefit all of Italy. As for us, the little rodents running along the desert floor? No, I don't think we will meet again." They both felt the strong bond between them. "Now get up in that plane of yours and win this war for us!"

Artemio turned and ran up the concrete steps, making a slapping sound with each footfall of his leather flight boots.

The Headquarters building was made of imported red brick. Two black soldiers in Italian uniforms stood on either side of the steps, guarding the entrance. One, a sergeant, was holding the traditional Beretta submachine gun of police units; the other, a private, held a Breda light machine gun. They saluted him with the right hand up; he returned the Fascist salute as he moved to the closed front door of the building.

He burst through the heavy wooden door, expecting to see a whirlwind of men and papers moving from desk to desk, for headquarters was usually busy. To his surprise, he only saw Colonel Zangari sitting behind a desk, looking through logbooks. The Colonel glanced up briefly and returned to his reading. When he realized whom he'd seen, he looked again and blinked his eyes in disbelief. He jumped to his feet and yelled, "Artemio! My God, it is so good to see you!" He ran around his desk and hugged the young officer. "Everyone here was worried sick about you!"

Zangari, an older, gray-haired man who actually enjoyed doing paperwork, was a highly decorated World War I fighter ace, one of the few men who are perfect for war but are completely lost in life when the combat ends. As soon as there were hostilities in Albania, old Zangari left his wife and reenlisted. He would have been given an office job at some airbase in Italy, but he'd requested Foreign Service; it was what he was good at.

"Colonel, where is everyone?"

"All airborne. A fishing boat in the Mediterranean has radioed in a large formation of heavy bombers coming our way from Malta," Zangari said with concern.

"I know about the impending attack. I need a plane. Do you have a plane for me?" Artemio was so excited he was panting.

"Captain, I am not authorized to give you an airplane. You will have to wait for your CO to clear you for flight duty," Colonel Zangari said, his hand on the young man's shoulder to calm him down.

Artemio opened his mouth and was about to launch an impassioned plea for an airplane when an explosion blew the windows into the building. The concussion of the blast knocked both men and the desk across the room. The two officers were covered with glass shards, stunned and deafened. For several minutes neither man was able to stand. Artemio looked over and saw complete bewilderment on Zangari's face: he was in shock. Carefully Artemio brushed glass from his face and felt warm, sticky wetness. He looked at his hands and saw them red with blood. Slowly, he got to his knees and started to stand on shaky legs. Colonel Zangari stayed on the floor in a fetal position. Dimly at first, and then more loudly as his hearing returned, the sound of machine gun fire replaced the ringing silence; Artemio recognized it as a British .303 caliber. Staggering to the doorway he saw that the door had blown off its hinges. Stepping onto the porch, he saw the two policemen dead on either side of the steps, their bodies blown back against the building.

He looked out onto the airfield and could see British long-range desert reconnaissance trucks moving fast, three men in each vehicle, one driving and two firing Vickers or Browning machine guns. He looked north, across the airfield, and felt the sea breeze in his face, mixed with the smell of cordite. A Chevrolet truck was stopped next to a three-engine Marchetti transport. The parked plane was painted with a camouflage pattern of green, brown and tan, the colors used in the Trans-Mediterranean route between Italy and North Africa. An SAS trooper was arming the fuse of a satchel charge and placing it below the windshield of the plane so as to destroy all the controls and instrumentation needed to fly. He then jumped from the wing back into his truck, and the driver sped off to continue the mayhem.

Artemio ran down the steps and picked up the Breda machine gun from the dead corporal. The man's face and body looked like he was still alive: no bullet holes, no shrapnel punctures, no burns, only blood leaking from his nose and ears—he'd been killed by the concussion blast. He checked the machine gun's magazine to make sure it was full. Back on the porch, he stabilized the gun on the wooden railing. His head was still spinning, his eyes were hard to focus, but he lined up the sights of his gun with the desert truck driver's head and chest. The Englishman had a black beard and was intent on getting to the next parked aircraft. Artemio tracked and centered on the man's face, and slowly depressed the trigger. A stream of copper-jacketed bullets in full automatic fire mode spat from the weapon. The SAS trooper fell forward onto the steering wheel. Then his body slumped to the right, turning the fast-moving vehicle. The truck flipped onto its side, crushing his two passengers. Simultaneously the TNT charge on the S.79 transport plane blew up. A ball of flames rocketed into the sky, collapsing the landing gear. The big bird hit the desert floor and burned.

Artemio ran down the steps, grabbed another magazine and loaded it into the light machine gun. He now had the attention of the English attackers; gunfire started to come his way from a Willy's Jeep with a Lewis gun mounted in front of the passenger's seat. For now, the bullets were going over his head and hitting the brick of the headquarters building. Shattered brick pieces and red powder were falling on him, but he knew it would only be a moment before the shooter corrected his aim. He went down on one knee, shouldered the weapon and returned fire, killing both SAS troopers in the jeep. Artemio knew he had to move for cover—"shoot and scoot." He ran as fast as he could towards a building that was used as a lecture hall, galvanized by the sound of bullets whizzing past his head. Mid-stride, his body pitched forward. Artemio landed on his hands and chest hard, sand mixing with the drying blood on his face. As he fell he was thinking, *What a bad time to trip, in the middle of a firefight.*

He could not get back on his feet. When he looked at his left leg he saw his boot was full of blood: a bullet had gone through his ankle. He had fallen behind a one-sandbag-high walkway embankment that did not offer much cover or concealment, but it was considerably better than nothing. He placed the machine gun over the sandbag and hitched himself forward to look over the airfield. There were many commando teams, British and Australian, shooting and dynamiting fuel tanks and spare parts sheds. The airfield was littered with the bodies of Italian and German security forces and repair crewmen who had tried to fight back. On the south side of the runway he could see a German armored car firing its 20 mm cannon. The gunners were fast and accurate.

Dirt started to kick up in front of Artemio's face; he was taking fire. Peering over the top of the sandbag, he saw the tan-painted grill of a Canadian-manufactured GMC truck that had veered towards him. The vertical metal strips in front of the radiator looked like the teeth of a monster set to devour him. Above and behind the driver was a second man firing a machine gun. He wore a white linen keffiyeh—the Arab headdress the SAS used in the desert. Artemio and the British machine gunner locked eyes on each other. Artemio adjusted his automatic weapon and brought the front and rear sights into alignment, tracking the Englishman's auburn beard. As the truck bore down on him, he pressed the trigger. The gun jerked into his shoulder as it fired each 6.5 mm bullet toward his enemy, but the gunfire seemed to have no effect, even though Artemio knew they should have found their mark. This Englishman was different, even bullets could not stop him. When the magazine had emptied; the gun was useless. He cast it aside and drew his Beretta pistol, aiming it at the oncoming soldier. The SAS trooper had stopped firing his own gun—perhaps it was out of ammo also. The rumble of the engine and the noise of the rubber tires breaking the little limestone rocks in the sand grew louder as the truck closed the distance. Artemio realized the Englishman's machine gun had not run out of bullets, it simply could not aim low enough at the short range to kill this pathetic, wounded Italian soldier lying in the sand. Artemio's left eye was closed, his right eye sighted for a head shot. Under the clean, white keffiyeh flowing back in the wind, the man's face was rugged, good-looking and stoic; then it seemed to blur, and Artemio was seeing the face of the policeman who shot Contessa. The coldness and brutality of a killing action is universal throughout time. Above the front site of the Beretta, Artemio saw the Englishman pull the pin of a hand grenade. It was the type the Americans made, with the pineapple fragmentation pattern. The smoke of the burning fuse blew back in the breeze. The SAS man had a lurid grin as he tossed the live grenade. It traveled through the air in slow motion. Artemio knew if he squeezed the trigger now, the enemy soldier would die instantly.

However, his own life would end in the blast of that grenade. Both men would walk hand-in-hand into the clouds to meet some omnipotent God. When asked, "What are you two men doing here?" how would they answer? As Cain? "I do not know; I am not my brother's keeper." Over the millennia of man's conflicts, God had heard every excuse there is; but aren't they all only variations on that? Perhaps the voice in the desert was right!

As the truck passed by and the grenade fell towards him, Artemio knew he had to get on to the other side of the low sand-bag wall to minimize the shrapnel's damage. He tried to roll, but his left leg would not move; the pain from the wounded ankle was excruciating. Then he felt a push that propelled his body over the wall. Simultaneously he heard, "This is not your time; you are still in my service." That was the last thing Artemio heard and felt before the explosion brought darkness to his world.

CHAPTER 10
Dr. Kurt Bauer

Inside the hospital room, the walls were freshly painted a bright white, but the stucco showed signs of shoddy workmanship underneath. This was a hasty cosmetic repair of structural damage. A military hospital could be a place that delivered dubious health care. "Fix 'em up and get 'em out" places were known to all armies of the world. A strong smell of ether overpowered the paint odor in the room.

Dr. Kurt Bauer was looking at a chart, barely paying any attention to the nurse who was trying to give him a report. "The Captain has been having muscle twitches all night." He flipped another page on the clipboard without responding. Dr. Bauer's thoughts were compartmentalized to track several images simultaneously, one of which was of himself sail-boating on Lake Muritz. He had been chief resident during his medical training in Berlin; attending physicians had asked him for advice with their patients, and all the nurses had flirted with the young, single doctor. But that was a long time ago, before the war. Before the bombing. Now he was only the ruins of that neophyte physician: overweight, bald, and disliked by all the hospital staff.

Suddenly, the comatose patient's hand jerked, hitting the doctor's leg, as if stimulated by an electrical shock. The doctor's attention coalesced onto Artemio. "You are right, nurse, he is fighting for consciousness!" In his new-found excitement, he leaned in towards Artemio's face. "Hello, Captain, can you hear me?" he said, loud and slow.

"Ye—yes," Artemio struggled to say.

"Oh my God, it's a miracle!" exclaimed the nurse in astonishment. Her duties in this hospital all too frequently consisted of wheeling young men's bodies to the morgue.

"Where am I?"

The leaning doctor again replied as if speaking to a foreigner who does not understand the language. "You are in Tobruk Hospital. You were wounded in a gun battle with SAS troopers. You are lucky to be alive; most men don't survive that."

The nurse proudly added, "You have won some metals, sir." The obese doctor showed his annoyance with the nurse by furrowing his brow and glaring at her. Artemio did not respond. He'd had so many bizarre dreams, he was not sure if this was just another one; or worse, reality.

The doctor introduced himself, then said, "Come, Captain, wake-up. Drink some water." Artemio pressed his dry lips to the glass the doctor held for him and swallowed, then coughed, spitting up most of the water. He pushed the glass away and looked around. It was a private room, and the bed had clean white linens. There was a wooden and brass crucifix on the wall across from him. He tried to remember the last time he had been in a bed with clean sheets.

"How long was I out?"

"Over six weeks now." The doctor had a heavy German accent, but his Italian was understandable. Artemio gazed dubiously at this overweight, scowling fellow. He had a completely bald head and beads of sweat were forming on it. His appearance did not inspire confidence.

"What?! What happened to me?"

The nurse interjected quickly, still wanting to be part of the conversation, "A grenade went off very close to you, sir."

The doctor answered authoritatively, "You sustained head trauma from the explosion. Your left hip is shattered, and your left ankle is broken from a bullet wound. It is by God's hand that you are even alive today."

"Can I walk?" Artemio asked. "I'm in a lot of pain."

"No. I'm afraid not. You need more intensive care than we can provide for you here," the doctor said, lamenting his hospital's inadequacy, "but we could not move you until you came out of your coma." Bauer scrutinized his patient to assess his level of consciousness. "General Montgomery has won the battle of El Alamein, and his armored forces are approaching Tobruk very quickly. There is a good chance that we will be overrun again. Now that you are awake, we can try to transport you to a rehabilitation hospital in Sicily."

"I don't remember anything of what happened."

The doctor pulled up a chair and sat alongside him. The busy nurse left the room to attend to other patients. Dr. Bauer started to explain the missing time to Artemio. "This base was attacked by a large-scale invasion, from air, land, and sea, but we fought them off. The British Special Forces are calling their failure a 'commando-style' raid. Commando, my ass. They threw everything they had at us." He began getting excited as he recounted the story. "It started with American B-17 bombers dropping their payload on the harbor complex and Tobruk city."

"I remember B-17s. I wanted a Macchi fighter, and tried to get airborne."

"The part of the operation that you thwarted was the airfield raid by the Long Range Desert Group, who traveled many days by truck from El Alamein. A German officer saw you on the tarmac, fighting as a lone gunman, like a cowboy. The Colonel's report said you were running and shooting a light machine gun, taking on truck after truck of SAS troopers, only stopping to put in fresh magazines. This officer was coordinating two armored vehicles with 20 mm cannon fire, a German car stationed at the airfield and an Italian recon vehicle that just happened to be in the area. Probably passing off Intel at the field command office."

"*Il Mulo*! And Lorenzo!" Artemio said. "That had to be Lorenzo!"

The Doctor looked puzzled by his patient's outburst, not knowing anything about a mule or a soldier named Lorenzo. He touched the patient's head to check for fever.

Artemio babbled, "The English met their match when Lorenzo appeared. That man should get a medal, not me."

The doctor continued, discounting his nonsensical outburst. "This German Colonel was the one who saw you get blown up by a grenade. The security forces at the airfield were sure you were dead. The Colonel put in papers for you to be awarded the German Iron Cross second class, posthumously." Bauer stopped to brush some dandruff off his lapel. "Your Italian flight commander has awarded you the *Medaglia d'Oro al Valor Militare* for the fighter tactics you developed. The Italian Fighter squadrons here in North Africa have used them to shoot down over 50 British Hurricane aircraft."

Artemio shook his head in disbelief that he could wake up in a bed and find out that he'd won two medals from two different countries. The pain on his left side was now starting to intensify, but he wanted to hear more about the attack.

"You said there was also a seaborne part to this invasion?"

"Oh yes, a British cruiser, six destroyers and dozens of PT boats and small motor launches sailed from Alexandria, Egypt. The cruiser and destroyers launched several regiments of Royal Marines, who began an amphibious assault on the seashore. It was quite a spectacle at 3 o'clock in the morning, with only moonlight. Our coastal batteries exchanged salvos with the warships in the Mediterranean Sea. Simultaneously, in the Port of Tobruk, their PT boats and motor launches came in under the cover of darkness to discharge two regiments of Scottish Highlander infantry with engineers to blow up port facilities and fuel storage depots. I've been told the noise was God-awful."

Artemio now sat up in bed; he was like a little boy wanting his father to finish reading an exciting book before bedtime. "How could we have possibly withstood such an onslaught?"

Dr. Kurt Bauer wiped the sweat from his forehead with a well-used handkerchief and explained, "The flotilla was hours behind schedule. As the sun came up the last of the Royal Marines were still loading into their landing crafts; the first wave had just started to approach the shore. Your Italian aviator friends in their Macchi *Folgore* fighters took off at first light and attacked the cruiser and destroyers with bombs. They then turned their heavy machine guns onto the wooden landing craft, and the strafing sank the little boats. The Royal Marines went down like lead weights to the bottom of the sea. Their kits must have dragged them down. The planes went back to the airfield, rearmed, and repeated this all over again."

The doctor checked the pockets of his long, white coat and fished out a partially-eaten German chocolate bar. He gestured to the Captain as if to share. Artemio refused.

"The Italian destroyer *Castore* had her boilers fired up and was waiting to put to sea. After passing the mouth of the harbor, she fired all her torpedoes in a fan pattern. Three of those deadly fish sank the British cruiser. In the early morning hours, German Stuka dive-bombers arrived from our airbase on Pantelleria Island and dropped 1000-pound bombs down the smoke stacks of the remaining destroyers. They have very good aim, those bombers."

Bauer lit a cigarette and blew the smoke to the ceiling. "It was a rout, really. The *Castore* spent the rest of the day picking British sailors up out of the Med." The doctor paused, as if observing a moment of silence for the departed. "The small English ships in the harbor fared little better. Some Highlanders and Royal Engineers landed, but Italian Marines were waiting for them—in prepared defensive positions. The Highlanders, who are a very tough bunch, realized they'd walked into an ambush of superior firepower and surrendered."

Artemio shifted and squirmed on the bed. Finally he broke down and told the doctor his leg pain was becoming unbearable.

"Oh, yes, of course." The doctor again searched his pockets, and this time found two pain pills. He handed them to the patient with a glass of water.

Artemio thought, *Pills in his pockets?*

The doctor went on. "And that wasn't all! When the PT boats and launches tried to get out of the harbor, they were shot to pieces by German flak guns mounted on Siebel ferries."

Artemio scratched his head; it strained credulity that a battle could have gone so well for the Axis forces. The history of the Italian and English conflict in North Africa had overwhelmingly favored the British.

Staring at the doctor, Artemio wondered how Bauer had ended up in such a godforsaken place as this. This German doctor must have pissed someone off. His white lab coat was wrinkled and had food mixed with bloodstains on the lower hem. It was unbecoming to see such an unkempt, corpulent man as a medical doctor.

"Tell me, Doctor, how could such a drubbing have taken place?"

Bauer smiled and answered with a question. "Well, do you want the truth, or the party line?"

Artemio was intrigued by this response and said, "Both."

Bauer enjoyed listening to and telling gossip. He leaned back in his chair, took another drag on the cigarette, and crossed his legs. "The scuttlebutt, which is never wrong, says that a Cairo prostitute working with a German agent got the plans of the raid. You see, every Friday night a British Naval attaché would frequent this woman. The Englishman was a regular of hers because he enjoyed a particularly unusual skill that she was noted for. While the attaché was tied up in the bedroom, no pun intended," Bauer coyly smiled, "the German spy would photograph the entire contents of his briefcase with a small Leica camera. That is how we knew where and when, and could prepare an adequate defense."

The pain was starting to subside as the narcotics took effect. Artemio thought for a moment on how insane the world we live in actually is. *We are all connected by a web of human actions, most of which we don't even know about. So many soldiers could be killed or captured through the behavior of a single man a thousand miles away. This one idiot, who could not control himself, compromised an entire mission.*

But for Artemio, the great victory felt hollow. He had a mental image of Mussolini waving his hand over a military map of Greece, giving a pompous speech on the glory of Rome to a group of compliant generals. The Italian men who would die in that invasion would see no glory. *Are our lives as soldiers so valueless? Was my generation sold a lie? There is no justice or fraternity here. As children we wore black shirts, marched in parades, waved flags, and sang songs about the greatness of Mussolini and Italy. Fifteen years later, is the payoff to die an ignominious death in the sands of the Sahara? What was it all for?*

"Hey, Captain. Do you want to know what the Allies' party line is for this failure?" Bauer said in a louder voice, as he saw Artemio's mind drifting off to the land of nod. The change in volume brought his patient back to the present.

"Yes. Please, Doctor, go on."

"Whitehall put out a press release that a German listening post on the island of Crete picked up heavy radio traffic when the Naval Squadron left the Port of Alexandria, so the Germans informed an anti-shipping unit of the Italian Air Force based on the island of Rhodes, and they sent up a four-engine heavy bomber to monitor the convoy and continuously relay back their position to Tobruk. Ha!"

Artemio was now lying on his back and staring at the ceiling. He shifted to get into a position that would ease his leg pain. The drug was starting to numb his brain. He said plaintively, "Winston Churchill would never have authorized the release of that statement. It is pure fiction. When Churchill lies, it is so good you want to believe it."

"What do you mean?" Bauer asked, as he checked his patient's chest with a stethoscope to see if fluid was building in his lungs.

Artemio answered with no passion in his voice, just cold calculation. "First of all, an operation of that scale would have warranted a separate predawn raid to take out that listening post on Crete. If the British knew it was there, they should have blinded the Germans before setting sail. Secondly, all Royal Navy fleet activity with cruisers and destroyers would have had fighter cover all the way in. With air coverage, any four engine heavy would have been seen and shot down. But most of all, the British know better than to allow heavy radio traffic! That story makes no sense."

The doctor slapped his leg and gave out a yell. "I knew it! I knew it was the hooker story!" His attention returned to Artemio, "You have a gift for tactics and strategy. Now I understand that you do deserve those metals."

Artemio looked down at his white sheets, his cheeks flushed. *What is this dreadful "gift"? I don't want it,* he said to himself. Seeing things that other people miss to improve the planning of operations that involve the killing of men—there is no honor in being an expert in the art of destruction and murder.

"Doctor, I'm feeling tired. Can we talk again later?"

"Absolutely! You get your rest. You have done much for Fascism. Herr Hitler and Il Duce need more men like you."

That evening, a large, ominous figure entered the room. Artemio, gripped by fear and pain, imagined it to be the Angel of Death walking the halls. A cold hand reached out and clutched his shoulder.

Artemio yelled out, "No! Get away from me! I'm not

ready!"

The startled voice of Dr. Bauer, calmed him. "Captain Battaglia, are you all right?"

"Yes. I'm sorry, I must have been dreaming."

"Captain, we have transport for you. This night a single plane will take some wounded back to Sicily, and I got you on it. We must get our wounded war heroes home."

"An airplane?" he said nostalgically. "I thought I would never fly again."

Dr. Bauer knew Artemio was heavily medicated. He explained anyway. "In the past we used hospital ships to get our wounded back to Europe. This ended when an English spy found out we had wounded soldiers only on the top deck; our Red Cross ships were full of ammunition and fuel for the Africa Corps. After that, the white-painted ships became high priority targets for RAF bombs and Royal Navy torpedoes."

"Leave me alone... I just want to sleep," said the groggy Artemio.

"Ha, ha! That's the methadone talking. I hate using the stuff, but it is all we have. The war has left us cut off from markets. We have no access to opium, from which morphine is made. So our scientists and chemical companies synthesized a new narcotic that is not opium based." Bauer looked into Artemio's eyes with a flashlight to see if his pupils were constricted. "There are other examples of German ingenuity, you know. We make our own diesel fuel, of which we have very little, from our abundant supplies of coal. My father went to school with Hans Tropsch, the chemist who invented the process. Even more ingenuous, this fuel gets here by submarines that never surface. Away from the prying eyes of British reconnaissance planes, these submarines pull up underneath what looks like an ordinary fishing boat a thousand feet from shore. Your Italian divers attach a flexible hose to the sub. The fishing boats conceal large engines that both recharge the submarine's batteries and pump its cargo to buried storage tanks in the rocky bluffs behind the harbor."

Artemio could feel the room spin, the effects of the last pain injection the nurse had given him. He didn't speak, but listened intently.

"We Germans have the best scientists, planners, and doctors, and no shortage of any of them. Our problem is medical supplies: antibiotics, gauze, rubber tubing, morphine and the like. These items are like gold to the German army. The British are lavishly supplied by the Americans with these, but they have few doctors. We have a gentleman's agreement with the English: our doctors cross over to the British lines at night and treat their wounded. In return, we are given medical supplies as payment. Even at war we can compromise with each other. We are all connected; humanity survives. I think you can understand me, Artemio, no?"

Artemio could see the doctor was in a melancholy mood and wanted to talk, so he nodded his head for 'yes'.

"I must stay away from the morphine we get from the British. The effects of that drug are not like methadone. It yields a beautiful, full-body warmth, a true internal glow. Then I love to play Wagner loud on the Victrola." His face drooped in sadness as he continued, "The nectar of the poppy is sweet and bitter. Ah, it cost me my marriage and a lucrative Berlin medical practice."

Artemio could see the perspiration on Bauer's bald head and the slight shake in his hand.

"Are you an addict then, Doctor?"

Bauer cleared his throat and straightened up. "I am a recovering addict. I was a very good orthopedic surgeon before my problem. You are probably wondering how such an accomplished doctor ends up in the Sahara desert. I was given a choice by a Nazi judge: to practice my skill on the battlefield or be interned in a reeducation camp. I do not know anyone who has come back from either choice." He said this as if talking with his own conscience.

"General Montgomery is moving fast from the east and General Patton is moving faster from the west; I think our time here is limited. Now there can only be disgrace and defeat in this war. I fear living; I fear the future. When the world finds out what we have done, the German people will not recover for a whole generation. I often think I should end my life with a syringe full of morphine and 'Ride of the Valkyries' at full volume. The furies will either take me to Valhalla or to some underworld to be tortured. I do not care which."

Artemio, startled by this admission, fought though to a conscious state. "No! Doctor, you cannot do such a thing. Your life is still valuable. You have saved my life. There are hundreds of German, Italian, and British soldiers alive today thanks to your healing hands. This counts for something in heaven. You must never think these thoughts again."

Dr. Bauer sat in a chair next to the bed and stared at the floor. Artemio had never seen a man this low in spirits. The actions of his government were so heinous, he could not stand to live with the knowledge. Artemio looked at him and saw a specter staring back through white skin and hollow eyes.

"Every man in this war has a burden. We will all wear the scars of our actions on our souls. They are invisible now, but will be prominent in the afterlife. We must use this time to repair what we destroyed. We will never make it perfect; that is not the point. God only demands that we try."

"What do you know of shame, you, a big war hero? You will always be able to hold your head high," the doctor retorted, heavily.

"I have my own shame that I must bear. Out of vanity, I requested that I be transferred from my position in the reconnaissance unit to active combat. My first mission involved escorting Italian bombers to what I thought was a conventional bombing of British military emplacements. With my reconnaissance knowledge of the terrain, I informed the squadron leader we were off course and flying away from the British line. I was told to shut up and maintain radio silence. We approached a Libyan village whose allegiance was with the Allies. I saw the bomb bay doors open and poison gas canisters fall from them. Villagers, even the women and children, ran from their tents, grasping their throats as their lungs burned. It was mustard gas. It causes blindness and death. I was sick to my stomach that I took take part in that mission, that the honorable and respected Regia Aeronautica was capable of doing such a thing. I told Command back in Tripoli that I would expose this crime against humanity to the international press. Their answer was to send me to the most active fighter squadron in North Africa. Here in Tobruk, I was to die in combat and be silenced forever. It almost happened!"

"The war is not over yet, my friend. Do you think your flight to Sicily will be easy? We send only one bomber a night, full of wounded, so that the Royal Air Force won't pick it up on their new radar sets. If they do find you and shoot you down, your death will be a watery one in the

Mediterranean Sea tonight."

"What about you, Herr Bauer?"

"Me? I will wait for the British army. They are only a few days away. I will have a better chance with them. One or two wounded soldiers might vouch for me. There's no sense in retreating, up into Tunis, then Sicily; it will all end in Berlin for our army. For me, if I go that path, a Russian firing squad will be my fate. I intend to cheat the Communists of that little victory."

CHAPTER 11
Sicily

Artemio lay in bed, staring up at the slowly spinning, leaf-shaped blades of the ceiling fan and listening to the monotonous click-click of the motor, so different from the rapid whine of the four-engine transport plane that had flown him here to Siracusa. That transport was the pride of the Italian aircraft manufacturing industry. The Americans and the British had them, but for all their industrial might, the Germans did not.

It felt good to be back on Italian soil, even if it was only Sicily. On his flight to Tripoli some 20 months ago, his squadron had landed in Sicily to refuel. He remembered flying above the snow-capped peak of Mount Etna, dipping his wing slightly for a better view, seeing the puffs of steam rising ominously from its core. *The Italian people are like that sleeping volcano,* Artemio ruminated. *They may show a cold, hard face to the world, acting like their war-loving German confederates. But deep inside the truth reveals a warm center, filled with a passion to create, to erupt and bring forth great art, music, and architecture. These are Italy's gifts to the world. The Germans should be left to their war machines and ruination.*

Nothing mattered to him now. He lay in bed with his

cauldron of emotions. A great sadness overwhelmed him when no one else was in the room, and he would sob for hours in his depression, like a cold, fall rain in his home town of Piacenza. The crying was not for the physical pain in his leg, but for the anguish of being discharged and his unknown future. He would never pilot a plane again. Sitting in a cockpit, high above the earth, would only be a cherished memory. He had become like the old veterans of the Great War, each man missing an eye or an arm, seen in cafes throughout Europe. A charitable passerby would buy a drink for one of these miserable men where they sat, waiting for their monthly government stipend.

This military hospital in Siracusa was one of the busiest rehabilitation hospitals in Italy. All the long-term wounded were brought here from the African Wars, to be healed of the unhealable and trained to live with their permanent disabilities. But recently the great numbers of incoming wounded had dropped radically. Once the Americans had landed in French Africa with General Patton and the British Commonwealth forces broke out from Egypt, the North African battles ended in hundreds of thousands of Italian and German prisoners being captured. *Where do the Allies put all these men, and feed them?* wondered Artemio. He knew from reports that the British and Americans treated Italian prisoners very well. The condition of Italian soldiers captured in Russia was much worse. In that theater of war, prisoners were beaten, starved, and eventually shot.

One day, a light caught the corner of his misty eye, and as he turned his head, his heart started to flutter. She moved like a dream out of his woozy head and into his room: a celluloid beauty, a vision all in white, her dress and jacket a mix of leather and fur. This was a little warm for the temperature of Sicily in early spring, but she made her own fashion trends. The Roman goddess of all his desires spoke.

"Oh, my poor baby, are you all right?" It was his beloved Donatella, at last! She ran across the room and kneeled at his bedside.

"What are you doing here?" he said, as he tried to sit up. He was in so much pain that he could only muster an attempt.

"No, don't get up; stay where you are," she said, her voice full of concern.

"I can't believe…. What are you doing here?" he asked, in disbelief and joy.

"I flew in, the minute I heard you were in Siracusa."

Artemio knew this was not true; it had probably taken a week before she'd left the filming of her new movie. "I am so happy to see you, but you should not have come. It is too dangerous for you here."

"Nonsense, Artie. Now that you are back in Italy, we will be together forever." She sounded splendidly dramatic.

"It is great to see you. I missed you so much." His heart ached for her.

"I know you have, baby, and I missed you too. Tell me, how badly are you hurt?" She scanned him up and down.

"I don't know, but I am getting better every day."

"It was your leg, they told me. Can you walk?" She felt the sheets to see if two legs were present.

"Yes, but I have a limp, and I am in pain when I do."

"What happened to you in Tobruk? I heard you won metals," she quizzed him, her full red lips smiling at him. It stirred passion within him.

"I was in a firefight with British soldiers. I am told a grenade went off near me."

"Why is your head shaved?" she asked, as she rubbed the back of his head. Her hand had long red finger nails. He craved her touch.

"It is not so bad now. You should have seen it a month ago." He reached for the back of his head, to hold her hand as he explained, "I needed stitches in my head to stop all the bleeding."

"Are you okay? Do you still remember me? Do you still remember us?" she asked persistently.

"Donna, please, how could I ever forget you? I would have to be dead." He smiled at her. "And even then, I would tell all the angels in heaven about you."

"Do not say that. That is terrible. You poor baby, what can I do for you?" As she said this, she pouted her lips and batted her long eyelashes. It was that exact look that made movie audiences swoon over her. "Artie, I am bringing you back to Rome! These doctors don't know what the hell they are doing. They are Army hacks. We will get you private, Roman physicians, the best money can buy."

He looked at her face in the early morning sunlight coming through the east window. She had lost her girlish complexion. There were wrinkles, small crannies around her mouth, smile lines. She was wearing more make-up than she used to. Donatella was all woman now; the playful little girl in her was gone. Why did everything perfect have to end? Even a goddess can be mortal. The year and a half separation had not been good for either one of them. The parties, the alcohol, and the men seemed to have taken a toll on her.

"Tell me about you. How have you been?" he said, to change the subject.

"Well, I am filming a movie." She tilted head proudly. "I play a mistress to a wealthy businessman who is stuck in a loveless marriage and cannot divorce his wife for religious reasons," she boasted, while looking into space as if telling a non-existent journalist who was doing a story on her.

"Is it a Massimo film?" he asked quickly.

"Why, yes it is. How did you know that?" she asked, surprised and self-absorbed.

"You and he are always photographed together in the gossip papers and the society columns," he replied coldly.

"You read those papers now! You used to make fun of me for reading them." It was Donatella's turn to change the subject.

"Well, now that I'm back in Italy, I have to get up to speed with your career."

He turned his head toward the doorway and asked, "Who is the guy with the white poodle?"

Donatella turned also and said, "That is my dog Luca, and you remember my bodyguard, Armando, from Capri."

A tall man in sunglasses was standing in the doorway, scanning the hall for possible threats. When he heard his name, he turned and looked into the room. His muscular build, like a weight-lifter's, threw off the fit of the expensive suit he wore. The pistol in its shoulder holster made an obvious bulge. It was a comical sight to see this tough guy holding a perfectly coiffured poodle with a red bow. At the same time, the sight angered him.

"Oh yes, I forgot you never leave Rome without a bodyguard." The tone of his voice was edged with anger now.

"You said yourself, it is not safe for me here!" She was trying to use his own words against him. "I don't like Sicily. It is full of criminals. *Il Duce* has yet to clean it up," she said contemptuously.

"That is not what I meant, Donna. Traveling around Sicily now is not wise because American airplanes can reach us here from their bases in Tunisia. Marauding fighter-bombers roam the skies over roads and railroad tracks looking for targets of opportunity. I am worried something could happen to you."

"Artemio, you are such a worry-wart. Daddy had Italian fighter planes escort my plane to the airfield here."

"You had a fighter escort?" he repeated in disbelief. Only cabinet ministers got fighter escorts. The power and influence of the Capoletti family kept surprising him.

"Baby, I have bad news for you," she said hesitantly. "I am not convinced now is the right time to tell you, but Daddy thinks you should know. Do you want to hear it?"

He was scared by the question, but said, "What is it?"

"Your friend, remember Gitano?"

"Of course I remember Gitano; he is one of my best friends. What about him?"

"His plane went down in Libya. No one ever found him. I'm so sorry." She barely held back her tears.

Seconds passed like minutes, in a void of silence. Then Artemio demanded, "Are you sure? Did he bail out? Maybe he landed; that is what happened to me, and I didn't get a scratch." He was grabbing at straws.

Donatella just shook her head sadly, biting her lower lip, then added, "No, baby, he couldn't get out. He went all the way down with the plane. Mario witnessed it and wrote the after-action report."

Artemio started to tear up slowly, then he wept uncontrollably. Donatella climbed on top of the sheets, over his broken body, and held him. Artemio knew this was not conduct befitting an officer, but he could not stop the tears. She felt so good against him, yet her powerful body could not drain away his pain. Through his tears he spoke, "Gitano's biggest fear was to be trapped in a burning wreak of a plane. He told me, in confidence, that he had nightmares of crashing in the desert while he was still alive." Artemio's crying was so intense now it could be heard in the hallway. A nurse came running to see why her patient was in distress. Armando put his arm out in front of the nurse to prevent her from entering the room. She took one look at the bodyguard's tree-trunk arms and turned to go back to her other duties.

"Baby, it's okay, it's okay," Donatella said softly, as she stroked his almost-bald head. Artemio thought fondly of the times he'd spent with Gitano. He was a soft, gentle boy who should never have gone to war. He was not cut out for the rigors of combat. But Gitano always followed his two best friends, whatever antics they got into. Artemio knew he was responsible for this young man's death. He'd trained Gitano, looked out for him; in his absence, how long could the lad have survived? He felt as much to blame for Gitano's death as the Englishman who lined him up in his sights and fired the wing guns.

Artemio wiped the tears from his face and forced a smile for Donatella. His voice cracked as he said, "Do you know that Gitano once punched a guy?"

They both laughed a little through their tears. Donatella said, "No way. The Gitano I knew would never do that." She remembered him as a bashful young man from the propaganda film shoot back in Rome.

"Yeah, he did! We were drinking a lot at the officers' bar in Tobruk one night." Artemio's mind travelled there as if it were happening in front of him now. "Captain Klaus Meyer, a German ace, said he trained his men to follow injured British planes all the way down to the deck to watch them crash. It was known that the English, to get you off their tail, would fake their own deaths. They would dive as if they were crashing, then at about five thousand feet they would pull back hard on the stick. You'd think they were out of the action, but then they would join right back in. Klaus also said that if his men saw a parachute open they would shoot at the hapless airman. This enraged Gitano so much! To execute a fellow pilot, of any flag, is beyond the pale. He hit Klaus with a perfect straight jab into his jaw. Klaus went lights out and hit the floor. Mario grabbed Gitano and pulled him out of the bar. I jumped on Klaus so he could not get up. I held him down until they got away."

"You guys were crazy," she said lovingly, as she gazed into his scarred face.

"That Kraut wrote Gitano and me up for that. I guess in the German Air Force that is a big deal, but we got into very little trouble with our commanding officers, who hated the pompous Germans anyway." He chuckled and added, "Gitano got free drinks from every Italian pilot for a month."

Donatella rested her head on his chest as they lay in bed and thought how wonderful life could have been.

"Is Mario okay?" he asked with trepidation.

"Yes. He and your whole squadron got out of North Africa before the defeat. They were sent to Milan to be refitted and trained on the new Macchi 205 fighters."

Artemio didn't say anything. He knew that, if he hadn't been injured, he would be a Bird Colonel by now and in command of that squadron. He would love to fly in one of those new fighters. Reality brought him back to earth and his hospital bed.

Donatella looked into his sad, red eyes. She smiled at his disfigured face. Artemio knew what she was thinking: that she loved him but knew they could never have a life together now. He could not keep up with her lifestyle. She needed her own space, to be with other friends, party all night, sleep over at a new, interesting man's apartment. She considered herself a free spirit that could never be tied down with a man like Artemio, whereas he needed what she could not give. He was from peasant stock. He would expect a monogamous relationship, with marriage and children. Why didn't Donatella want that too? What drove her to be so self-destructive? A cold chill ran up his spine at the thought of a nomadic wanderer, Haadi, and the story of his fall from grace because of a non-traditional woman.

As Artemio looked into her sapphire blue eyes, they reminded him of the refracted light of that grotto on Capri. He knew. They both knew. He was not right for her anymore. With these deformities he could no longer complement her beauty, no longer hold her as the gravitational pull of the earth holds the moon. He was ugly with scars and walked like a cripple. When he gazed on her perfection he felt hideous. Artemio knew he would have to leave her, even though it would kill him inside.

"I am still bringing you to Rome with me, for better doctors." Her voice cut into his thought.

"No, I am not going with you," he said as he stared out the window, unable to look at her.

"Why not?"

"The doctors here are not finished with my care yet. I feel I am getting stronger every day." He added, "And you cannot stay in Sicily; this is the next battlefield."

"Do you think the Americans would dare to invade Italian

soil?" the Roman woman demanded arrogantly.

"It is part of their plan. The Allies will invade Sicily, then cross the Straits of Messina. Eventually they'll fight their way up our beloved boot to Rome."

"You know the plans of the Allies, eh? Do you know the plans of Mussolini? I do! He has trained these men in Sicily to fight to the death. They will not give up one inch of beach to the Americans. Herr Hitler has pulled out his best troops from the eastern front, the 1st SS Division, with Tiger tanks, and brought them here to stop the Allies." She said this defiantly, propping herself up on her elbow.

"Donna, you listen to the propaganda on the radio. Fascist governments create their own truth. The problems start when the liars believe their own lies. You are caught up in your parties and your movies. You don't have any idea what is really happening because it has not affected your world yet. The reality is, we have lost all our colonies in Africa. The fighting in Russia is going badly for us. Just today the Allies captured our fortress of Pantelleria Island in the Mediterranean. Next they will come to destroy Italy."

Donatella quickly tried to climb off the bed; she almost fell in her high heel shoes. She stood over him, confused and angry. Stern-faced as he had never seen her before, she accused him, "You are a defeatist!"

"The war has destroyed my body, not my mind." His voice trembled a little as he spoke. "I have met the Sicilian troops here; they will surrender rather than die. They hate Mussolini. The Americans have already encountered Tiger tanks in Tunisia. They have tank-killing aircraft that will knock them aside like toys." He stopped to catch his breath, then forged on. "Worst of all, the SS Division from the eastern front that you thank Hitler for, they will kill more

Italians than Americans. Ask the people of Kharkov in the Ukraine. Actually, you can't ask them; the city was razed." He grabbed the handrail of the hospital bed to lift himself.

Donatella glared at him furiously, not knowing what to say, she was so mad. After a moment, Artemio confessed, "Donna, I dropped poison gas on innocent civilians in Libya. We all did. We killed women, *children*! What you see in this bed, this shell of a man, I brought this upon myself! It is justice. There is nothing left for me anymore. But you, you have a chance. There is a coming firestorm, everyone will be consumed by it. You must get out of Italy, go to Switzerland. With your father's money and connections you can do it. Convert all your lire to Swiss francs and diamonds."

"Artemio, you have gone mad! I will not hear another word of your ravings!" She started to leave the room. Her hysterical voice made Armando come in to check on her.

"Wait! You must know this, Donatella. My men and I were following orders to drop those poison gas canisters. Other men, Generals in Regia Aeronautica, conceived the plan and made the poison. Yes, Donatella, your father is a war criminal: he planned the mission. The blood of those Bedouins is more on his hands than mine. His retribution will be greater than mine!"

Donatella ran out of the room, crying. Artemio could hear the rapid tapping of her stiletto heels fade down the hallway. Armando looked at him with a face of disgust, then turned and strode after Donatella, still holding the poodle. Artemio lay in bed and wept. He would never again see the most precious thing he'd ever held in his hands. Life meant nothing to him now.

CHAPTER 12
Enrico

"Come on, Captain, two more reps; c'mon, you got this. It's only 20 pounds; give the leg full extension. That's it." The therapist, Enrico, voiced encouragement like Artemio's high school soccer coach.

"I am not a captain. Not anymore!" he replied angrily, as he stared at his withered lower leg. It was attached to a mechanical exerciser by leather straps.

"I know who you are. You're the hero aviator who won two medals—one German, one Italian." Enrico smiled, showing his front gold tooth. His young face was topped with thick, black, curly hair. He was a native Sicilian, one of the few whom Artemio could understand when he spoke Italian.

"Were you in military service?" asked Artemio.

"Me?" He shook his head. "No, I was arrested by the Carabinieri for stealing their car."

"Why would you steal a police car?"

"I needed it for a special job. Those Lancias are very fast, you know."

"Yes, I imagine they are," Artemio said with a grin. He extended his leg again, pushing hard against the weight.

"While I was hot-wiring it, the two cops returned." The therapist counted the repetitions silently. "A Beretta was pressed against my head and a *poliziotto* said, 'You're under arrest, punk.' I had to appear in front of a local magistrate." He looked at Artemio's face, to see if the story surprised him. "I was only 16 years old. The judge gave me community service. It is great; I can go home at night and Mom cooks dinner for me. And I am now unfit for the draft because of my criminal record."

"You should have had a lookout," Artemio said, always running strategies in his head.

"Yeah, I did, but he wasn't so good. He ran when he saw the police."

Artemio thought of his friend and wingman Gitano, and how Gitano had let the Hurricane get on his tail and shoot down *Contessa*.

Enrico grinned. "I should have had someone brave like you with me."

"Military tactics are a lot like criminal activity," Artemio explained, seeing parallel worlds. "They both involve precision timing, proper equipment, and well-trained men."

"I like you, Captain." Enrico gave Artemio his winning, gold-toothed smile again. "Tell me something else; there is a rumor going around the hospital that a *movie star* came to visit you a while back." Enrico leaned in close and asked, "Is that true?"

"I didn't know this hospital had a rumor mill. You can put your little fan club to rest. That never happened!" Artemio said angrily. He leaned away from Enrico.

"Wow, there was a lot of passion in that denial, Captain. Now I am suspicious. Do you know Donatella Capoletti, the film star?"

"Why do you care? Do you want her autograph?"

"No, but like your shoes, who visits you tells me a lot

about the man you are.”

“You mean the man I was. I am just the wreckage of a man now.” Artemio had a flashback of a transport plane burning on the airfield at Tobruk after the SAS men blew it up.He was like that plane. “I had to let her go.”

“That must have been tough; not many men would have done that.” Enrico shook his head sadly.

“Enrico, life is about loss. It is important to do the right thing, even if there is great pleasure in doing the wrong thing. She is better off without me”

“You broke up with a beautiful movie star, and you’re telling me you did it for *her*?”

“Yes, but something inside me makes me feel I did it for another reason. I just don’t know what that is.”

Enrico looked at him like he was insane. Artemio thought about personal loss. How horrible he’d felt when his father died in his arms. The loss of his friend Gitano—just the news of a plane crash, and then separation from him forever. How many children are dying as our cities get bombed? How can a parent handle that loss?

Enrico saw his distant stare and brought him back. “Captain, are your future plans to get out of Sicily, or stay and become an American POW?”

“I haven’t thought much about it.”

“Well, you’d better. Your rehabilitation potential has reached its peak. We will discharge you soon. If you want to get back home, you should leave quickly.”

“I suppose you know the American landing schedule,” Artemio said sarcastically.

“Hey, don’t laugh. I have relatives in America working with elements of their military. They will get pardons and get out of jail for the help we give them here in Sicily, information like where the sand can support a Sherman tank, currents and tides, where the German bunkers are, even helping General Patton figure out the crazy Sicilian road net. We will also cut German phone lines and mine roads when the time is right."

"Really, you and your friends are willing to do this?"

"We must do this! It is *cosa nostra*. Mussolini was no fan of ours, and we suffered. Now it is his time to get it in the neck. I am giving you the early warning; when the Allies land our soldiers will surrender fast. The Germans are setting up machine guns behind Italian positions to kill them if they surrender. So we will help the Americans with a few well-placed grenades while the Krauts are sleeping. This will make the American transitions smoother." He winked one eye, then continued. "If you stay here you will become a British or American POW. This is not so bad; you sit out the rest of the war in Liverpool or Alabama. Some even go to Bermuda!"

The young Sicilian put his hands on his hips. "Think of our poor brothers in Russia who will never make it back home. They are executed in the snow at the end of a battle, like dogs."

"Those Soviet bastards!" Artemio said in solidarity.

"If you want to get back home to the mainland, you must cross the straits of Messina. This is wild country now, very dangerous. An Italian soldier must have proper papers, or the Germans will shoot him as a deserter. The English bomb the straits all night with their Lancasters, and the Americans all day with their B-17s. The Germans are committed to keeping the straits open. They need supplies to come in and their wounded to get out." He unstrapped the captain from the therapy machine. "They have many flak guns on both sides of the strait, and Messerschmitts to shoot down the Allied heavies."

"I must get back to Piacenza to see my mother," Artemio said. He thought of her living alone on the mountain for so many years since he left to study at the University. She was always so proud of him and had pushed him toward greatness, but the price was her loneliness. He had to see her again. She would not be able to bear the thought of her son in a prisoner of war camp; that would kill her for sure.

Enrico must have seen something of these thoughts in Artemio's face, for he said, "I have a cousin who could drive you close to Messina, then get you on a fishing boat at night —for a fee."

"How much?"

"I'll give you a good price because I am a big fan of your girlfriend, and you are a war hero." He helped Artemio dismount from the machine. The patient's face revealed the pain of his movements, and Enrico said, "I noticed you take pills for pain. Do they make you sick?"

"No, but I get vivid dreams when I take them at night. The nightmares frighten me. In them I see men, some I know and some I don't know. They are fighting and dying. Explosions are going off everywhere. I hear cries for help, but I cannot help them. Some men are stuck on barbed wire in the desert. Some are locked in boxcars with their arms reaching out to me from an air vent. Some cannot breathe, their lungs burning, skin blistering; all of them expect me to help. Once I saw a dirty orphan child, sitting alone on the side of a road in a bombed-out city. As I walked past him, he said to me that he was my future." He rubbed his forehead as if to erase the dreams. "I don't know what any of it means. I stopped taking the pain pills at night because I don't want those dreams." He stared into the young man's face for an answer. "But if I stop the pills altogether, I can't sleep. The burning in my leg is too intense."

"I never heard of that side effect before; that's serious shit! It's probably from that synthetic German crap we give you here at the hospital. I can get you real morphine, the good stuff. It takes the pain away with no unpleasantness. I'll throw in a bottle, no extra charge."

With the headlights off, Enrico's cousin drove the battered old car from the hospital to a secluded inlet on the Straits of Messina. The hot June evening was uncomfortably humid. The silent driver finally spoke, "I had to work very hard to get you a boat this evening. This time of year is *La Mattanza,* which means 'the kill.' He laughed—his breath smelled like a dinner of onions—and rubbed his unshaven chin. "The kill. I bet you have done your share of killing, eh, Captain?" Artemio did not answer.

"You see, all the boats want to be out there getting tuna." Artemio looked out at the black night and saw nothing. Enrico's cousin decided to give him a history lesson while they waited.

"The tradition of *La Mattanza* dates back to Phoenician times. The men of this island go out in their boats with nets, and other men working in concert wade into the water with spears. We kill hundreds of fish a night, a real blood bath."

Artemio could see an unlit boat making its way to shore. The cousin introduced the boat owner as Pino and said, "This is an Air Force captain and fighter pilot. He wants to go home, rather than be pampered in an American prison camp." Pino shook hands but did not even look at Artemio;

he acted as though he didn't care who his passenger was. Pino was another Sicilian just trying to get to the other side of this war alive.

Half way across the straits, Artemio broke the silence and asked the boatman, "How's the fishing for tuna going?"

Pino answered, "It is not fishing, Captain. It is killing with spears." Artemio saw a bleakness in this man's face, as if he wished to have nothing to do with this world. "The tuna return from the Atlantic Ocean. They only desire to make love and have babies. If you ever get out of Sicily, it is a mistake to return, for fish and for men. For their effort of being strong swimmers and returning to their homeland, we net them. These magnificent creatures, they fight for their freedom. They only wish to get away from us. What do we do? We spear them alive, we kill hundreds. The sea turns red with their blood."

The hot breeze from the straits of Messina reminded Artemio of the North African Sirocco wind. He thought of Eduardo, the Sicilian mechanic who escaped to America and returned, only to be killed in battle. He knew he would never forget Eduardo's empty face, the blood-soaked clothes where the shrapnel entered his neck. Artemio looked north, to the city of Messina, and saw English bombs exploding at the seaport: sharp flashes of white light, then red balls of flame as munitions and fuel were set off as secondary explosions, followed by a muffled bass drum roll. The inferno of the city gave off an illumination, an eerie reflection on the water. Artemio could see that indeed the sea was red. *La Mattanza* was more than man killing nature, it was man destroying himself.

CHAPTER 13
Train Ride North

"Biglietto, prego, grazie. Biglietto, prego, grazie." Artemio heard this repeated, "Ticket please, thank you," from the front of the train car as the conductor slowly made his way back. A discharged Italian soldier, Artemio sat in his seat with his eyes closed, pretending to be asleep to deter the locals from attempting to engage him in conversation. The passengers riding with him were a mix of Italian culture. There were women and children together; perhaps the father was dead or in a POW camp. Some children rode alone; these were the saddest of the travelers. They may have been orphans, or just placed on the train by their parents to escape the bombings. The cities were now under regular Allied air attacks. The battle for Sicily was in the mopping up stage, and the Allies were transitioning to the invasion of Southern Italy; the "softening up" of the Italian mainland had begun.

The largest group of travelers in the train car consisted of German soldiers. These men were all from the same unit. Their uniforms were dirty and torn, and their faces showed exhaustion, with a bloody bandage here and there, and sunken eyes haunted by the violence of the battlefield. Artemio knew by their collar tabs and shoulder board insignias that these men were regular German Army. He kept his eyes closed to avoid the contemptuous stares of these frontline soldiers. These men did not respect the Italian armed forces. How could they? Most Italian soldiers had little desire to fight after Sicily capitulated. Mussolini could not even defend his own country without German assistance. These veterans of the Russian offensive hated being ordered into Italy to prop up the tinhorn dictator of a failed state. The Wehrmacht was losing all along the Eastern Front. The average German soldier wanted to be facing the Red Tide, defending the Fatherland. They knew what the Russians had in store for their families back home. Artemio remembered how the Messerschmitt pilots had been reluctant to fly with Italian pilots. Their former distrust had turned now to outright hatred.

The Conductor made his way to the rear of the car, continuing his droning, *"Biglietto, prego, grazie."* He was wearing a clean, pressed uniform. His hat was round, with a well-polished visor in the front, gold-colored rope on the top, and red piping around the side which matched the red piping along his pants seam. He was a short man in his late forties, with a little mustache. Everyone on the train could tell this job was very important to him and that he took it seriously. Mothers with children handed him their *biglietti* and he would deface it with his hand-held punch tool, but most of the passengers did not have tickets. Children traveling alone had nothing to offer, except an anxious expression. He would walk past them as if they were not present on his train. The German soldiers, holding their submachine guns, rebuffed him with more sinister stares. The Conductor's response was to look down and moved to the next person. *"Biglietto, prego, grazie."*

Artemio had his ticket and valid papers of Air Force discharge. The hospital in Siracusa had drawn up travel documents for him to return home.

The chubby conductor with his Errol Flynn mustache stopped in front of Artemio. *"Biglietto, prego,"* he said loudly to the Italian soldier with the closed eyes. Artemio faked a surprised look as if just awakening and handed him the little paper stub of a ticket. Their eyes met for a second. The Conductor punched the ticket and handed it back, saying, *"Grazie."* Both men felt humiliated to have armed German soldiers in their country. There was an internal solidarity of shame. This was unspoken. Outwardly they behaved as if it were just another day in Italy. It was important to maintain order, to wear uniforms, to buy tickets, to pretend trains could keep schedules in a sea of anarchy; it preserved sanity.

Belching thick, pungent smoke, the black steam engine slowed, then came to a complete stop. Another delay, this time to wait for track repairs after Allied bombings. Artemio thought that stopping on these train tracks in broad daylight was not wise. He remembered the crew of *Il Mulo;* they would never be caught out in the open. He started to sweat, then his right leg, the uninjured one, began to twitch uncontrollably. The woman passenger in the seat next to him gave him a bothered glance. He said to her, "I'm not feeling well. I am going to step outside for some air." He stood and she adjusted her legs to let him pass into the aisle. With his pain and injuries, he passed her with difficulty. The nervousness was starting to overwhelm him; he had to get out of the train car immediately. He pushed forward to the exit as quickly as his limp allowed. The German soldiers observed his movements suspiciously.

Once outside the passenger car, the open expanse of southern Italy calmed him. The land with its gently rolling hills, dotted with tall cypress trees, let him breathe easier. The sky was clear and blue, but storm clouds were on the horizon. His dread of losing control was passing. He had never felt like that before. Was that a panic attack? A lot of things had changed since the grenade explosion. The physical scars were obvious, but he also had new feelings and thoughts he wished he didn't have.

A middle-aged woman who had also disembarked from the train approached him along the railroad tracks and demanded, "What are you doing in that uniform!" Artemio was surprised by this stranger's intrusion. "Haven't you heard? The British have crossed the straits of Messina and are in Calabria!" she yelled over the clanking train noise. "Mussolini has been deposed from power!" Artemio too stunned to ask any questions. "The King has asked General Badoglio to assume command of the military." She stared at his face to see if he understood. "General Badoglio's first to act was to surrender to General Eisenhower. The war is over!"

"Oh my God!" he whispered softly, though his chapped lips. "Is it really over?"

"We must get you out of this uniform. If the Germans see you, they will arrest you." The woman had long, black, curly hair with streaks of gray. Her eyelids were low in her sad but gentle face. She went on talking as they walked, telling him she had been working for the International Red Cross Aid Agency for several years.

"Mostly telling wives and mothers that their husbands and sons were never coming home, and delivering what personal effects get sent back from our dead soldiers in foreign countries. Now I fear I will be representing the dead and missing right here in Italy!"

"You should be proud of your of work. It may be gruesome, but families want to know what happened to their loved ones. It is good to helps others in this time of misery."

"And what about you? Is there a wife waiting for you to come home?"

"No, I have no wife." He thought of Donatella and their last fight, of her running down the hall to get away from him. How he wished he had just died in her arms the last time they made love on the isle of Capri. The perfect life would have no war and Donatella by his side as long as he lived, but cruel fate had laid other plans for him.

White steam shot out of the side of the long, sooty, iron machine, enveloping those standing beside it. Then the whistle blew three times, signaling the track was repaired and the train would soon be on its way.

"My name is Artemio. What's yours?" he asked the kind woman.

She answered that her name was Adriana. "Come into my train car. There are no German soldiers there. I have civilian clothes you can wear so you don't stick out like a sore thumb. I hope you don't mind that the last owners are deceased."

Artemio did not hesitate. He was glad to be able to avoid Germans soldiers.

The rail car Adriana was riding in was a private sleeper. She picked out a set of pants and a shirt for him, then left the room to allow him to change. Artemio could not believe his good luck. Italy had surrendered and the war was over. Meeting this Red Cross worker who had civilian clothes was also fortunate. As he changed, he noticed a poster along the wall. A cold chill ran though him. In bold, black lettering across the top the poster read: "JEWS RATS VERMIN." A colored drawing depicted rats running on a city street at night, moonlight reflecting on the wet pavement. More words were printed on the bottom in bold black: "The Jews are the enemy of Italy. Exterminate the rats and the Jews."

Artemio's heart sank. He knew what this meant. A Jewish professor at the University of Milan had told him he was afraid Italy was moving too close to Germany. He'd said, "In the country where they burn books, soon they will burn people." He was right; this was the beginning of atrocities. *Italy is losing the war. Allies are bombing the cities, Germans have occupied the country, and the Fascists need a scapegoat. The Jews will be blamed for all the failures of Mussolini*, Artemio thought with a shudder.

Adriana knocked on the door and entered suddenly. Artemio was only partially dressed.

"Not bad for rummaging through donation boxes, eh?" she said, pleased she'd been able to fit him. She was not embarrassed by his state of half dress, until her eyes picked out the numerous wounds. The tone of her voice changed after she saw the long scars on his leg and back. She slowly walked over to him. Humiliated, he would not turn around to face her.

"Are they painful?" Adriana asked compassionately, as she touched his shoulder.

"It's getting better each day."

He spoke to the wall, ashamed of his disfigurement. In his nervousness he continued talking. "I feel bad. These clothes should have gone to a more deserving person."

"Artemio, you don't know the danger you're in. You think you are less deserving of these clothes then someone else?

Think again! The Germans are executing Italian deserters!" She desperately wanted to help. He was not fully comprehending the new normal in Italy.

"I have been overseas, fighting for my country, for two years. I have seen men under my command die. I am not a deserter!" Almost in tears he continued, "I have sacrificed everything for my country. My body, my future, my love. So much here has changed. I feel like a stranger in my own land." He pointed to the poster on the wall and asked, "Is this anti-Semitic hatred just a show put on for the Germans?"

Adriana looked at the poster, then closed her eyes for a second and took a deep breath. She answered with a voice of resignation as she sat on the bed, "It was just bluster when Mussolini passed the dreadful Racial Laws. All the people ignored them. Lists were made of Jews and anti-Fascist journalists. Nothing ever came of it, except maybe losing a job or not being able to travel abroad. Now with the German soldiers here, things are different. They are using those lists. I have heard rumors that in Rome, and further north, they are rounding up Jews and labor leaders. Some say they shoot them in the woods, some say they put them on trains going to death camps in the Reich."

This news of his country's behavior was hard for Artemio to accept. To go from being a frontline soldier, fighting and willing to die for his beloved country, only to hear of atrocities when he came home, made him feel betrayed by Mussolini, betrayed by his government. *There is no coming back from this.*

"Sit on the bed here with me." Adriana's hand gently patted the blanket. He sat near her silently. "In this compartment we are safe. I am traveling as far as Rome. As a

Red Cross official I can vouch for you until then." They continued to sit next to each other as the magenta hues of the setting sun filtered through the dirty windows of the train car. Adriana put her arm around him as a mother would her little boy. Their two bodies moving together, they slowly stretched out on the Pullman bed. Artemio closed his eyes and laid his head on her chest. He was comforted by this lonely stranger. She softly spoke to him as her fingers slowly combed his hair, and her words spoke directly to his soul. "Many good men fall in these times; this is a daily occurrence. Do not be ashamed of your appearance. A man's true mettle is his ability to rise from the ashes like a phoenix and refashion the rubble of his spirit and body to become an even greater man then he was before."

He thought of the error of Fascism. Life cannot improve only for some at the expense of others. *Life was supposed to improve for my country, but now everything is destroyed. What will happen now? I don't know. I need rest; I have not slept in days. These pills are making me sicker.* In Adriana's arms he felt replenished, as if she had known him from birth. For a few hours he slept soundly, without pain and without nightmares. Even the rumbling of the engine and its loud discharge of steam as it probed northward in the night did not disrupt the tranquility of that rest.

CHAPTER 14
Piacenza Rail Station

A cold fog covered the train station. The silvery brume swirled around the wooden floor, conjuring memories of the Libyan ghibli wind and its eddying currents of sand. Steel rails buckled and heaved from the weight of the locomotive engine rolling over them. The steam whistle signaled the conductors to open the passenger car doors and discharge their occupants. Artemio stepped out onto the slippery platform and pulled up his shirt collar. Adriana had given him only a worn shirt and pants. He shivered, wishing there had been a coat in that box of clothes. His old leather Air Force issue shoes had holes in them, and his feet felt the moisture on the northbound terminal.

He did not recognize the Piacenza train station. Six years ago his mother and father had hugged and kissed him here, then placed him on the train to Milan for the start of his university education. The train station then had been a two-story brown stone building, with four main tracks and multiple sidings. There had been trees and a well-manicured green area. Today the station was an unpainted wooden one-story structure built over the original foundation. It had only two usable tracks, one northbound and one southbound. There was a lone siding track for stray freight cars awaiting a destination. Turned-up dirt and mud pools were all that was left of the former lawn; the trees were gone. Artemio thought, *This is what the American B-17s do. They change landscapes, lives, and the course of history.*

All along the rail line from Rome he had seen Italian men forced into work gangs, Nazi guards and vicious dogs overseeing them. Their job was to repair bomb-damaged track. It made him furious that his countrymen were now slaves in their own land. To the left and right of the station house, he saw the long barrels of German 88 mm anti-aircraft guns pointing to the sky. On the wooden platform itself there were machine gun emplacements, surrounded by sandbags to protect the gunners from the shrapnel of exploding bombs. The train station was a nexus for activity, with German soldiers of every branch of service scurrying around. Officers pulled up in staff cars and barked orders to Aryan infantrymen, who were eager to please. Not surprisingly, there were very few Italian travelers. Movement in Italy had become extremely hazardous, what with Nazi road blocks, American fighter-bombers seeking targets of opportunity, and now a new group of combatants: partisans. These Italians had varying allegiances. In the chaos that followed Mussolini's imprisonment, bands of armed men and women roamed the countryside. In all this confusion, the German war machine had one primary directive: supplies from the Reich must get through to the front. Military transports were the lifeblood of the German Army. Tanks and large formations of men could only move by rail. Geographically, neutral Switzerland sat on top of Italy, preventing direct supply movement. Nazi rail traffic went from Austria into Northern Italy via the Brenner Pass. Piacenza was one of the main arteries for getting badly needed supplies to the frontline soldiers. The Allies knew this and bombed the railway extensively.

Artemio cringed when the shriek of a train whistle blasted behind him. An express rumbled past the station. He could see flatcar after flatcar carrying a succession of factory-fresh Tiger and Panther tanks, interspersed with rail cars conveying anti-aircraft guns, which gave the impression of a porcupine bristling with quills, all headed south to carry on the fight against Allied forces.

As the clacking of the express train diminished into the distance, there was a new sound, a voice calling him. "Artemio! Artemio! Artemio Battaglia, is that you?"

He looked around in disbelief that anyone here, in this beehive of activity, would know him. He saw a man wearing a filthy but originally white POW uniform. He did not recognize this man, but the friendly POW said, "Oh my God, it *is* Artemio Battaglia."

To silence this man from yelling across the station platform, Artemio walked up to him and asked, "Do I know you?"

"Do you know me? I am Rocco Beati—your friend from high school! You may have been the greatest center forward our school has ever seen, but I was your second striker who fed you the ball and made you look good."

Artemio became weak in the knees as he recognized this haggard old man as his high school friend and soccer teammate. *What has this war done to us?* he thought. "Rocco, what has happened to you?" he asked.

The man in the POW uniform pulled him into an alcove on a train station platform.

"It is not safe to talk. With the surrender of our forces, the Germans are arresting all Italian soldiers." He looked around to make sure no one overheard them before continuing. "I was a pilot also, but I was sent to hell on earth. For two years I flew a Savoia Marchetti transport plane in Russia. Supplying our forces while we were winning was easy work. When the defeats came, so came all the Russian fighter planes. They had built squadron on top of squadron and unleashed them all at once at us. The worst was flying the relief effort to get our boys out of the Stalingrad pocket." He scratched his head as if he had lice. "The Russians butchered our forces on the ground. Those not killed in battle shot themselves rather than be tortured or frozen to death. I would land the Marchetti in the last remaining air field we controlled, held by a small group of desperate men, the last resistance. We unloaded meager rations and took out the wounded. I still have nightmares, seeing the faces of ghosts begging me to take them home. I had to kick them off the plane so I could shut the cargo door." He wiped his eyes and continued in a lower voice, "I know hell has a torment devised just for me." He stared into Artemio's face as if he were still on the Russian steppe, seeing another ghost.

"Rocco!" Artemio shook him. "We have all suffered in this war. Pull yourself together."

"Oh, I know you are the great war hero," Rocco said, now back in the present.

"I am no war hero. I did my duty, as all Italian soldiers did." Artemio said the last part as if he were reading from a script.

"Really? A five-kill fighter ace, recipient of the *Medaglia d'Oro*, our nation's highest honor, and the German Iron Cross. Did all Italian soldiers get those?"

"How do you know so much about me?" He was astonished that Rocco was so well informed.

"Everyone in the Air Force knows of your exploits,

Artemio. You cannot expect to have any secrets when you date a general's daughter." Rocco had a sly smile as he lightly punched Artemio's shoulder.

"Those days are over for me," he replied in serious tone.

"No, Artemio, that is not true. Our war is not over yet, not until we drive these German invaders from our land."

Artemio looked at this frail man in a POW uniform, and thought of his own disabilities.

"How are we supposed to do that?"

"I am not really a POW. Right now I am spying for the American Office of Strategic Service, the OSS. I record in my head all the rail traffic moving north and south and the time. Then I radio the information to my American contact person."

Artemio recoiled. "I am sorry, I must go; I cannot participate in this. My war is over! They took my health, they took my future, and I have nothing more to give!"

Rocco reached out his arm and tightly grabbed Artemio's shirt and pulled him back in. "Yes, you do, Captain Battaglia. You have your life to give for your country," Rocco said fiercely.

"Look at me; I could not even fight a boy in my condition."

"In Russia, boys destroy German tanks with magnetic mines. They run up behind the tank and attach the mine to its metal surface. The mines usually blow up prematurely, killing the boys, but they do it anyway. It is only with this fortitude that the Germans can be beaten."

Artemio understood him. He had seen small bands of men who were highly motivated defeat much larger forces. He thought of the 300 Greeks at Thermopylae taking on the entire Persian Empire.

"What do you want me to do?" asked Artemio.

"Do you still live in that stone house on the top of San Giorgio Mountain?"

"Yes, my mother lives there, and I'm moving back."

"The Luftwaffe has constructed a fighter base on the western side of that mountain. Messerschmitts and Focke-Wulfs intercept the American heavy bombers as they approach Piacenza. This tactic is very effective in shooting down the bombers. I'll arrange for a radio transponder beacon to be delivered to you. Hide it in your house. That's all; the American Air Force will do the rest."

A high-pitched woman's voice yelled across the railroad platform. "Artemio, is that Rocco Beati? *Madonna mia*, I haven't seen you two boys in years!" Both men froze in place. Terrified, they slowly turned to see who was calling them. A small, frail woman with a thick head of gray hair walked quickly up to them.

"Hello, Signora Battaglia," Rocco said respectfully, as if he were a 15-year-old boy again.

"Mamma?" Artemio could not believe how much his mother had changed. She looked much older than he remembered, her face drawn and wrinkled. He hugged her for a long time, and they both started to cry. Rocco smiled, happy to witness a pleasant sight, so rare in this war. The three were starting to get stares from the Germans at the train station.

Artemio noticed the German attention. He wiped the tears off his cheeks, then took his mother's arm as he turned, and they walked away.

"Artemio, I think you are being rude. I have not seen Rocco in many years, and I did not ask about his mother."

"Mamma, just keep walking. We have a long way to go to

get home and I'm freezing cold."

"My baby!" She lovingly touched his face, as she noticed the scars. "What happened? Are you alright?"

"Yes, Mamma, we'll talk later. Let's just get out of here." The two of them made their way silently to the end of the platform.

A voice that could not be distinguished above the din of the train station called something out. Artemio and his mother kept walking, oblivious to the activity behind them. A second, louder shout of "Halt!" registered in Artemio's mind. He felt a strong push on his back; he lost his balance and fell. Looking up, he saw a giant dog growling in his face.

"Back off, Mouse," a German sentry commanded the dog. Mouse was a 65-pound Belgian shepherd with a mean temperament and bad breath.

"What is the meaning of this?" Artemio yelled angrily from the wet ground.

A German officer stepped forward from behind the dog handler and said, "It is always best to stop when commanded by the authorities." This man had strong features, a square jaw and a prominent chin.

"Allow me to introduce myself. I am Colonel Gunther Mueller of the SS Division Leibstandarte. I am in charge of security in this sector." Artemio got up from the ground slowly and in pain, brushing himself off. Mouse lunged at Artemio with his mouth open, about to bite. The young sentry held the dog back with all his strength while the dog barked ferociously.

"Soldier, shut that animal up," ordered the Colonel.

"*Jawohl, Herr Oberst,*" the sentry responded, and he kneeled next to the dog. The soldier petted the Belgian shepherd on his head while giving him a dried pigskin treat.

Artemio could see this young man loved and cared for his dog, but suspected he would kill another human being without a second of hesitation.

"I am Artemio Battaglia, and this is my mother, Rosa. Please tell us why we are being detained?" the wounded Italian officer demanded indignantly. He looked directly at the Colonel as he spoke. There were two additional soldiers behind the Colonel who were pointing submachine guns at him and his mother. An inconspicuous figure of a man stood off to the right in the shadows. He wore a white trench coat and a black hat. Artemio assumed he was German Gestapo.

"Signore Battaglia, you are walking right through a checkpoint. We merely want to see your papers, unless you have a reason we should detain you?" replied Colonel Mueller, as he intently scrutinized him with piercing blue eyes. Artemio handed over his discharge papers and travel documents. The Colonel took his time and read all the papers thoroughly. Artemio was poorly dressed for the cold, wet weather; the fall had hurt his leg and he needed a morphine pill.

"Well, well, it seems Signore Battaglia is an Italian pilot," Mueller said loudly, as if he had unearthed a secret. He glanced toward the Gestapo man, as if waiting for orders.

"I was a fighter pilot stationed in North Africa, but now I am discharged from service because of my injuries," said Artemio, shivering. The German Colonel in his woolen coat now turned fully around to look at the figure standing off in the shadows. The Gestapo agent nodded his head.

The Colonel continued, "My cousin in Hamburg is a fighter pilot, *ja*. The whole family is very proud of him. They thought he was so smart, because he got into aviation school. Now the Americans train monkeys to fly fighter planes.

That's right, we shoot down P-51 Mustangs with black men in the pilot seats. Did you ever think a monkey could do your job, Signore Battaglia?"

Colonel Mueller was trying to provoke Artemio into saying something he would regret. Artemio remembered the black soldiers in the Italian Army who'd fought bravely in Africa. The Germans' brand of racism was misguided and hurt their own cause.

"My son is a war hero who received both the Italian *Medaglia d'Oro* and your German Iron Cross!" Rosa said, irritated by this officer.

"The Iron Cross!" Mueller repeated in disbelief.

"The Iron Cross second class for extreme bravery on the battlefield of Tobruk," Artemio said proudly. Upon hearing this, the two German soldiers pointing their submachine guns at Artemio and Rosa lowered their weapons.

Rosa inquired tartly, "Have any of your cousins received an Iron Cross, Colonel?"

Mueller regained his composure and proclaimed, "Italian soldiers who have deserted their posts can be shot or put to forced labor. You have an honorable discharge, and with the severity of your wounds, Signore Battaglia, you may take your mother and go home."

He handed back the travel documents. Mother and son slowly made their way to the icy steps. The two weary souls descend carefully from the platform, holding each other for support.

Once on the ground, Rosa said loudly, "What a pompous ass that Colonel was."

"Shhh, Mamma, you know you almost got us killed."

"Artemio, my dear boy, the Colonel just needed things explained properly to him."

Heaven Cries

He looked at his mother, shook his head, and smiled. Ahead of them was the long walk home, and he had holes in his shoes. All his fingers were becoming numb in the cold, damp air. He knew the forecasts would have no word of warm, sunny days. Winter had arrived.

CHAPTER 15
Eureka

The Battaglia house that Artemio had grown up in had not changed in three generations. Two bedrooms came off a central room. The front door, made of heavy oak, opened into the main living area. A large, concrete hearth was built against the side wall, and a wood fire in it burned and crackled all day long. Above the embers was a cast iron pot, hung by a chain. Rosa always had something good simmering, either soup or polenta. The place had a warm, restful feel that he had never found anywhere else in the world. The walls were stone and mortar, covered by a wooden roof. As a young man, Artemio's grandfather had built this house for his bride. He had been a bull of a man, a stone mason by trade, who wanted many children to fill the house, but the pertussis epidemic had left them with only two children who survived: Rafaello, Artemio's father, and Bruno, his uncle.

All the Battaglias felt a strong affinity for this house—except Artemio. He had watched his father die in his bed here. He thought it was probably the same bed he had been conceived in. He had hoped to escape this mountain life. He had wanted something better for himself. Now, with his physical limitations, he doubted there was any other future for him.

Outside the house was an expansive mountain view of the Po River valley. On a clear day you could see for miles, but unfortunately in this part of Emilia-Romagna there were very few clear days. Cold, dry mountain air coming down from the Alps clashed with the warm, moist air resting above the river, creating turbulent weather patterns. The winters were mostly fog and snow; fall and spring were overcast with cold rain. The ancient god of winter blinds men's eyes here.

The thick, low-ceiling cloud cover hampered Allied bombing efforts. The American bombardiers, even with their advanced Norden bombsights, still needed to see their targets before dropping their explosive cargo. Artemio watched from his elevated perch as bombers flew low over the Po River; they were an easy target for the German flak guns waiting for them. In the river were barges loaded with anti-aircraft guns, and along the tracks were dug-in gun emplacements. This elaborate tactical plan to protect one asset reminded him painfully of Tobruk's defenses. However, the most effective element of the German *Wehrmacht's* strategy was right next to his mountain home. According to his mother Rosa, it was Mussolini and Regia Aeronautica who first built and operated the fighter base. Now, with Mussolini under arrest in the Gran Sasso prison, the Luftwaffe and elements of Regia Aeronautica still loyal to the Fascist cause flew interceptor missions from the base.

Artemio would sit for hours watching the activity of the airfield below him. It felt like when he was young and the biplanes would fly over on the way to Malpensa airport. He had been a boy who fantasized about flight. He had become a man who saw the awesome lethality of air combat. Now he was a disabled war veteran who would never fly again. This was the full circle of his life. When the leg pain became intense he would take his morphine pills and sit under a tree. From this vantage he could see the little, single-engine planes at the base of San Giorgio Mountain taxying and taking off. He was close enough to tell the difference between a Messerschmitt, a Focke-Wulf 190, and a Macchi fighter. One of the approaches to the landing strip was right over his house. Artemio could see the pilots' faces when they had the cockpit canopy open and wheels down for landing. His heart sank at being so close to the planes, knowing he would never sit in one again. He didn't miss the combat; the killing revolted him. It was the freedom of being airborne he missed.

Two carefully placed beacons around the city of Piacenza would make the bombing runs safer for the Americans because they would not have to always fly the same route over the river. Artemio knew from his Air Force days that radio beacons could be used to guide planes at night and in bad weather so that the Fifteenth Air Force out of Foggia could fly above the clouds the whole distance to the target. Radio transmissions helped navigators bring the bombers in without the need for ground landmarks. Once over the city, the pilots would pass control of the plane to their bombardiers. Previously, they would fly their planes low over the train station, where amassed German anti-aircraft artillery would greet them. With this new blind bombing technique, the B-17 pilot could fly above thick clouds, riding in on a beam from a signal generator. When the bombardier heard a signal from a receiver placed near his seat, he would release the bomb load.

Artemio realized why he had been asked for the use of the house on San Giorgio Mountain. His would be the second beacon; its transmission would allow the Allies to triangulate their position for the drop zone. Another reason for using the mountain as a signal generator was its proximity to the fighter base. Separate missions could be planned to destroy the enemy airfield, with the goal of reducing the numbers of German fighters mauling the lumbering bombers.

The smell of pine brought back childhood memories as Artemio gathered firewood. He was starting to enjoy his solitude—quite a contrast from military life. Even his mother was gone today. Rosa had left early to go into town, shopping for supplies. Gathering fallen branches on the high mountain meadow, he was considering the dangers inherent in helping the partisans when he saw movement at the tree line below him. A man was standing by a horse, holding its reins. Artemio instinctively dropped the wood and lay down behind a fallen tree. He could see that the rider was trying to be evasive. The stranger stopped at the end of the woods and scanned the open field before him, then looked up to the sky, wary of aerial reconnaissance. The horse was a strong stallion, the kind the Fascist police rode; the man wore a drab brown shirt and pants like the peasants, but with a bright red bandana around his neck. Artemio knew the stranger was trouble; they didn't get guests up here on the mountain. As the intruder mounted his horse, he saw that a rifle was slung across his back. *A Communist partisan!* Artemio had identified the trespasser at last. The man rode on when he thought the coast was clear. Artemio waited several minutes to make sure no one was following the rider. Once he was convinced that the intruder was a solitary horseman, Artemio, who had, after all, grown up on this mountain, took a short cut back to the house.

Moving as fast as he could with his weak left leg, he entered the home and loaded his father's shotgun. He left the house, making sure the front door was unlocked. Facing the entrance fifty yards away was a vantage point he had often used as a child when hiding from his father: a pile of rocks that gave a good view of the area while concealing the observer. Artemio stretched out on the grass and peered over the rocks. The partisan rode up the slope, approached the house cautiously, then dismounted and walked around the house, examining it. Artemio kept the stranger's upper body in his sights the whole time. The stranger carried a short Carcano rifle across his back, like the cavalry troops, and a canvas bag tied to his belt. When he appeared confident the house was not an ambush, he banged on the front door loudly. When no one answered, he cautiously opened the door, peeked his head in, and entered. Artemio slowly got up from his position and approached the house stealthily. He followed though the front door. It was disturbing to be in the house with a stranger. The double barrel shotgun gave him courage. He raised the long gun to his shoulder, pointing it at the stranger's back, and said, "Looking for something?" The startled horseman spun around and drew his pistol, all in one motion. There was an awkward moment as the two of them pointed guns at each other.

"I am looking for a man named Artemio," the intruder said in a strong but unmistakably female voice.

Artemio stuttered at the shock of seeing a woman dressed as a man. "I, uh, I, I am Artemio."

"I was told to give you something." She holstered her pistol and untied the canvas bag from her belt. He could see now her very feminine facial features. She had long black hair under her cap. She was tall, but with a slighter build than a man. The pants needed a rope belt to stay on her narrow waist. He was staring at her when she added, "Can you stop pointing that gun at me? Those old shotguns have a hair trigger."

Artemio lowered the shotgun but demanded, "Who sent you?"

"We do not use names." Her initial look of disapproval changed to one of dawning realization: he was new to this cloak and dagger business.

"Your mount outside has the 'M' brand on its rump for Mussolini."

She looked at him with fresh contempt. "Where we get our horses from is no concern of yours."

He plainly saw the red bandana of the Communist forces around her neck. *I never thought Rocco Beati would associate himself with the Red Brigades,* he thought.

She continued, "I inspected your house, and the most effective location for this is in your attic." The partisan removed an electronic device from the pouch.

"Is that the transponder? I was hoping it would be smaller."

"It's not. This is only part of it. I have the battery unit in my saddle bag."

Artemio was starting to regret the decision he'd made at the train station to help his high school soccer friend.

"The English agent said this half is called 'Eureka'. It will emit a wave that will be received by a unit in the bombers call 'Rebecca'."

Artemio could see the partisan was fascinated by all this espionage. *English agents, Eureka, Rebecca. I am in way over my head,* he thought. Nevertheless, he showed her the access to the overhead storage in the roof. As Artemio propped up the ladder to the open attic doorway, they both awkwardly started to climb it. Their faces came close together for a moment, then they recoiled—two like poles of a magnet repelling each other. She gave him a frown, then ran up and installed the signal broadcaster. Artemio got a good look at her mud-speckled face. This fighter was a pretty girl, but she was tough, as if she had grown up in a house of all brothers.

After the transponder was safely hidden in the attic, she was about to leave when he asked shyly, "Can I make you an espresso?"

She was very curt with her reply. "No. I must leave now."

She was almost out the door when he blurted out, "I know you."

Her body stiffened. "How do you know me?" she demanded with her back to him.

"The day of Mario Piaggio's graduation party."

The partisan woman drew a knife from her waistband and, fast as a snake, turned on him. "Are you friends with Mario Piaggio, that Fascist bastard?" she yelled, pressing the sharp edge against his throat. He backed up to the rear wall of the house. Her face was nose to nose with his; he could smell her breath.

"Yes," he struggled to say as the blade cut him slightly. "And you, you know him too. You were at, at the party,"

Artemio stuttered. He'd not expected such a violent reaction from this once-gentle girl.

"Who are you? Tell me who you are or I will cut your throat and bury you on this mountain!"

"Gabriella, go ahead and kill me! You would be doing me a favor." He grabbed her hand and pushed the knife harder against his neck. "Look at me. You don't even recognize me. I was good-looking once; now I am grotesque." She struggled to get the knife off his throat. He slowly slid to his knees and started to cry.

She was unprepared for this. Tough partisan though she was, she felt sorry for this pitiful man. She kneeled in front of him and wiped his tears. Her big dark eyes looked closely at his scarred face and finally she said, "Artemio! What happened to you?"

"This damn war, it has destroyed everything. It has destroyed me," he said through his sobbing.

"Ah, I know this as well," she lamented. "This war has changed me also. I feel dead inside. The emptiness is filled with hate. Artemio, I enjoy killing. What does that say about me?"

He studied her face, as if the image would stay with him forever. He touched her hair. "You were the sweetest girl I had ever met," he said, mourning the loss of her innocence.

"That girl is long gone. So far gone, I don't even remember her," Gabriella said, and even though her voice shook, he heard the hardness in it.

The two of them helped each other get up. Over a cup of coffee he told her about his life in the Air Force and North Africa, how he flew with Mario, and the loss of his close friend, Gitano. Gabriella told him she had heard that Mario was still flying, but for the new Republic of Salo, the name for the German puppet state of northern Italy.

"They shoot down the American heavy bombers and strafe us partisans if we ride out in the open," she said with contempt. Artemio understood her feelings. When the Italian armed forces surrendered, that had been Mario's chance to get out of the service. *He is misguided*, Artemio thought. *He does not see the end of Fascism, where it leads.* Now there was no hope for his college roommate. *He will die for sure, either in combat or by firing squad with all the other hardcore Fascists. If the Germans do not kill him, the Allies will.*

He held Gabriella's hand and said, "Mario and I believed, as most Fascists did, that to better the lives of Italians we had to invade weaker countries and subjugate the population, to steal their wealth and enslave their people." After a deep breath he continued, "I now understand this was wrong. We must work to improve the conditions of the least among us. We must be humble and labor selflessly."

The front door swung open abruptly, revealing Rosa with packages in her arms from shopping. Both Gabriella and Artemio jumped up from the table. They had been so engrossed in each other that they were caught completely by surprise. Gabriella was angry with herself for having forgotten to be vigilant, Artemio was embarrassed, and Rosa had a shocked expression on her face at seeing a woman in her home. Then she smiled at her son.

She said, "Oh, *Buon giorno*. I hope I didn't startle you."

Artemio saw Gabriella had her right hand on her holstered pistol. Quickly he said, "*Ciao, Mamma*, this is—"

The young woman stopped his introduction with a gesture, saying, "It is getting late, and I must go." She leaned in to kiss Artemio on the cheek and whispered, "No names, remember." She whisked to the door, only bending to pick up her rifle. Rosa gave Artemio a big smile, and he frowned back at her.

He watched from the window as Gabriella rode away into the woods. The horse galloped off, and clumps of sod kicked out from the hooves. The figure on the stallion with a rifle across its back again looked like a man. Artemio could not stop thinking about her; he was glad that she had remembered him eventually. He thought of what a fool he had been to brush her off, so many years ago, because of his youth and arrogance. He should have written to her, but Donatella had been too bright a star. Like the sun, her light blotted out all others in the sky. Would he ever see Gabriella again? She rode off so fast, and he knew nothing about her. She must want it that way, he realized. However, this war had so many strange twists and turns, anything was possible.

CHAPTER 16
Mortality

Artemio had observed bombing missions against Piacenza's rail lines. In his mountain home, he felt like a hawk atop a tall tree. He could see the American B-17s come in under the low cloud cover. The flak guns would start their black, shrapnel-laced puffs of smoke. The bombardiers tenaciously stayed on course, straight at the target. Unfortunately, a formation flying in a straight line made an easy target. Artemio figured that from their long flight up the boot from Foggia, along the Adriatic Sea, the flight crews were fatigued. Artemio saw the melees that ensued. Some bombers exploded in midair, their wing tanks full of aviation fuel. Others fought back, every fifty-caliber machine gun blazing. Fighter planes of many nations swirled for position. It was elevated carnage. Damaged Flying Fortresses slowly fell to earth with thick plumes of smoke coming from the engine cowlings. The controlled decent towards the ground was not how these gawky birds naturally died; it was the result of the consummate skill and willpower of the two pilots trying to give their crew members enough time to bail out, transforming the plummet to a glide. The sky was peppered with little white mushrooms descending to the ground. All the men who flew into combat were brave. Death rode along as a copilot, always ready to harvest souls. Artemio looked on as heroes fell from the sky.

On touching down to earth, each airman was either retrieved by Italian civilians who would transport them to the partisans, or captured by the German forces. If apprehended by regular German army units, the airman would be afforded full Geneva conventions. The American and English bomber crews were sent north to internment camps. The German Luftwaffe treated the Allied forces with respect because Axis POWs were humanely treated, and courtesy evoked the same response from men of honor. Being rescued by a partisan band was a much more chancy affair. Worst of all were the German search teams that went house to house, looking for allied airmen and partisans. The anti-partisan SS were specially trained; only the most ruthless and devout Nazis made the grade for entrance into their ranks. These men were utterly devoid of compassion. They were very good at extracting information through torture, then finally murdering their victims.

With the transponders up and working, bombing missions changed. The bombers could now fly above the clouds, out of sight of the anti-aircraft artillery along the railway lines, and drop their payload from a safer altitude. Spies on the ground would radio back bomb damage assessment. This informed Allied Air Command when targets were successfully hit. Axis interceptor tactics had to change to meet this new threat. The Italian Fascist Air Force of the Republic of Salo would send Macchi fighter planes up from their base at the foot of Mount San Giorgio, their mission to soar above the clouds as sentries. These pilots would reconnoiter over the Po River and its delta to the sea. If bombers were seen, they would radio back to base, reporting enemy heading and speed. It was left to the Luftwaffe fighter squadron to scramble at a moment's notice and fly up to attack them. This new role for the Italian airmen forced them to continuously take off and land in any weather, searching for their nemeses.

Artemio woke early to stoke the previous night's embers in the hearth. Every morning was the same routine: Rosa slept late and he would tend to the fire. After an adequate flame started to heat the house, he would go down to a mountain stream that ran through the meadow. It was a long walk back up the hill, carrying two buckets of cold water. This morning, a fog lay heavy and visibility was poor. He had to walk the path back to the house from memory. Suddenly, from out of nowhere, the loud whine of a single engine propeller plane passed overhead, followed by a bang, then sounds of metal scraping and bending. There was an awful sound of aluminum crumpling, which Artemio had heard more than once in his Air Force career, then a return to complete silence.

The old pilot in him took over. He put down the buckets and ran through the mist toward the sound of catastrophe. In the clearing above the tree line was a wrecked plane. Artemio made his way past fragments of propeller blades and landing gear to get to the larger, central mass. As he got closer, he could smell leaking hydraulic fluid. He stopped, and only slowly approached the cockpit. The canopy was open; he saw the pilot slumped forward over the instrument panel. He reached in to check the limp body for a pulse. A strange feeling overtook Artemio in the depth of the fog. In this surreal atmosphere he began to feel as if he were in heaven. The dead pilot in the plane was a young Artemio Battaglia. The face bore no scars. He was a good looking lad, as Artemio had been. The dead man's head had thick black wavy hair, just like his. It was like seeing himself, dead. Artemio stepped back in horror. *"Am I dead? Is this what really happened?"* He felt his chest with his hands, to see if he was solid or a specter. He started to tremble at the thought of his own mortality.

"God, don't take me yet. Please give me more time," he whispered. He felt his legs weakening, and he went to the ground. *How could a life with so much potential end with a whimper?*

In time the feeling of panic passed. He looked up and wiped tears from his face, then slowly uncurled from the fetal position he found himself in. With renewed curiosity, he approached the fighter plane again. He pushed the airman's shoulder, placing him upright in the seat. The young pilot had a cherubic face. There was no blood marring his features; he had died by breaking his neck. As Artemio struggled to pull the body from the tight compartment of the cockpit, his thoughts went to Giovanni in *Il Mulo*, saying how much he hated disassembling weapons in the desert with dead men lying on them. Artemio checked the body for identification papers, to discover that this boy was only 21 years old. Like himself, this pilot must have been very bright to get through flight academy that fast. Artemio wondered if they'd attended the same flight school, had the same instructors. Out loud he cried, "Who trained this boy?"

To himself he thought, *"If I had not been wounded in North Africa, I would be commanding a fighter wing by now, and this boy would have been under my command. I would have trained him better; he was not watching his altimeter.*" He looked squarely into the boy's face and said, "Son, I would have taught you to lower your landing gear after you passed over the mountain. It is my fault that you are dead. I should have been there training you young airmen, passing on my skills." He hugged the lifeless body and began to cry anew, not just for this boy, but for all the dead the war generated.

As he leaned over the body, a voice caught his ear in the fog.

"Why are you here, living this solitary existence?"

Artemio froze, feeling as if his sanity were being challenged.

"Artemio, you have so much to give, yet you bury your talents on this mountain." The voice in the air echoed from all directions in the fog.

"I have to be here. I was wounded and I take care of my elderly mother," he said feebly, not knowing whom he was talking to.

"Artemio, my sweet child, just now you were begging for more time. I am a messenger sent to many like you. All want more time, but most will not use it properly. You do not get more time unless you use it in His service. You will be called soon. Listen to the messenger, and obey." Artemio stood up and backed away from the dead airmen. He turned and stumbled in the fog, then ran back to the house.

CHAPTER 17
Colonel Mueller's Visit

The gray sky obliterated the sun, and the trees had lost their leaves. Days like this made joints ache. Artemio and Rosa both felt the chill through their heavy winter coats as they looked down the tortuous mountain road. A German armored column was approaching the house amid a cloud of dust and the clacking of caterpillar-track fighting vehicles. The two lead motorcycles turned off the road and approached the house. A four-wheel drive armored car advanced past Artemio and his mother. Finally it stopped, its turret scanning the upper slopes of the mountain with its 20 mm gun to protect the convoy. The next vehicle was an open-top staff car that followed the motorcycles off the road. The car, with its officer in the back seat, stopped in front of the two Italians. It was Colonel Gunther Mueller, who looked at them with disdain. Rosa and Artemio tried as hard as they could not to return the expression. The remainder of the vehicles parked on the road: a collection of Opel trucks interspersed with Hanomag fighting vehicles.

When all the transports came to a stop, about a hundred men dismounted with their rifles and submachine guns and searched the property. Colonel Mueller stood in his convertible Mercedes and barked commands and curses in

German to his soldiers, making sure each man was as destructive as possible. "You there, Private, turn over that barrel." "Sergeant, you idiot, inspect all of the wood pile. A man could hide in that." Artemio, also an officer, never approved of treating enlisted men as animals to be whipped.

Mueller turned his gaze to the two homeowners and spoke civilly. "It is terrible that I have to travel with this heavily armed group just to visit you."

"Will all your visits consist of ransacking my home?" asked Rosa. Gunther Mueller smiled at her, not in a way to show friendship, but to instill fear. His expression was unnatural, like the face of a mad man who'd just gotten a sinister idea.

"Italian partisans control all these hills above Piacenza." The German Colonel pointed to the far peaks across the valley floor. "Without all this show of force I would not be able to get through to you." He looked down and asked, "Captain Battaglia, why must Germany, an ally of Italy, be treated in this way? Don't you people know, we fight together against a common enemy, Bolshevism?"

Artemio knew these questions were rhetorical and did not want to offend the Colonel with a rebuttal. He only said, "Are you looking for your missing plane and pilot, *Herr Oberst*?"

"Yes, tell me what you know." The Colonel looked down on him greedily.

"The wreckage and the pilot's body are higher up the mountain behind a ridge line." Artemio pointed in the direction. "The morning of the crash, visibility was poor. A fog as thick as soup blanketed this mountain. The pilot misjudged the crest and his altitude. He was young and inexperienced. He lowered the landing gear too soon, before he cleared the mountain."

Mueller lost interest in the story of the plane crash. He was a man with no sympathies. This would only keep him from his true goal: crushing dissent among the local population.

"Tell me, Artemio, how many partisans operate on San Giorgio Mountain?" The Colonel scrutinized the war hero with his piercing blue eyes. The use of the familiar, the first name, was a deliberate insult.

"I have not seen any, Herr Mueller," he lied. A German sergeant came out of the front door of the house and called to the Colonel, indicating it was clear.

"Artemio, let's go inside and you can pour me a glass of wine."

Colonel Mueller followed Artemio inside the house. He sat at the large engraved oak table, the fire crackling in the hearth behind him, so that his own features were in shadow. Artemio sat uncomfortably across from him. Mueller's head swiveled around the room, inspecting. Two SS storm troopers posted themselves inside the front door, pointing their MP44 submachine guns at the Italian captain. Rosa brought two glasses of red wine to the table, then retired to her bedroom. The Colonel unbuttoned his top collar and lit a cigarette. He offered one to Artemio, who declined. Then he removed his P-38 pistol from its holster and placed it on the table. Most SS officers had the older model P-08 Luger pistols, because all new production of P-38s from the Walther factory were earmarked for regular Army officers. This created an inequality, a rival between the two services. Nazis, not to be out done by their Wehrmacht brethren, used a slave labor camp in Poland to manufacture a low-grade copy of the gun. Artemio thought of the terrible irony of a soon-to-be-murdered Jew or Gypsy working to make the guns that would be used to kill them.

"Artemio, my friend, I checked on your war record. The Iron Cross incident at Tobruk is quite impressive. One man against a swarm of English special forces, and you survived." He shook his index finger at Artemio, and with a creepy smile said, "I always knew you were a killer." Mueller took a slow drag on his cigarette and continued. "I have to tell you I feel uneasy with a man of your capabilities out of the Fascist uniform."

The two men glared at each other. Finally Artemio spoke. "I am only out of uniform because of my injuries."

Mueller, not believing anything he said, continued. "My job is to catch partisans and kill them." He ran his fingernails along the grapevine pattern carved into the thick wooden table with his left hand, while the right rested on the pistol's grip. Artemio could see the Colonel marveled at the beautiful artwork a skilled craftsman can make with a natural product like wood. The cold steel weapon in his other hand was fabricated solely to take life. Without looking up from the table, in a low detached voice he said, "I don't like it, but I am good at it." He then turned his head to Artemio. Looking directly into his eyes, he said, "Aerial reconnaissance has spotted horseback riders on this mountain. Partisan riders!" With a loud, firm voice he continued, "I will ask you again, Captain, have you ever seen any anti-government activity on this mountain?"

"*Nein, Herr Oberst!*" he answered back loudly, as if he was one of Mueller's soldiers. Then in a calmer voice he added, "I have done such work in North Africa. Flying at low altitudes in the Sahara Desert, a truck can be mistaken for a tank, or a Bedouin on a camel for an English messenger on horseback."

The Colonel sat back in his chair and relaxed. He started to talk about all the things he loved about Italy. He believed the Uffizi was the greatest art museum in the world. He dwelled on the magnificence of Michelangelo's David at the *Accademia* in Florence, Luca Signorelli's mastery of the brush stroke in the Orvieto Cathedral, Verdi's operas as the only rivals to Wagner's, and Italian cuisine's superiority to French. Artemio could see the dichotomy in this man. He was cultured and well educated; nevertheless, he lacked some basic human essence. Something was missing. He was drawn to a dark force. Mueller could not understand why Italians hated the German occupation of their country. He saw the shooting of ten Italians for every dead German soldier as a proper intellectual way of dealing with partisan activity. He could not recognize that the German policy of indiscriminate murder as retribution was turning the entire country of Italy into a partisan base camp.

The front door opened, and a young lieutenant burst in with a Heil Hitler salute, then informed his Colonel the Italian pilot's body was loaded into the armored personnel carrier.

"Very good, Lieutenant." Mueller said, as he stood up and quickly downed the remainder of the wine. He was holstering his pistol when the lieutenant spoke again.

"There is something else, *Herr Oberst*," he announced from his at attention stance.

"Well, what is it?" the Colonel snapped, irritated by the slow delivery of information.

"We have detected a radio transmitter signal."

"Excellent work, Lieutenant! Where is the location of the beam?" Mueller asked as he prepared to follow.

The Lieutenant answered with no emotion, "It is coming from this house, *Herr Oberst*." The expression on Mueller's face changed in an instant, from surprise to rage. He pointed his pistol at Artemio, still sitting in his chair. Mueller barked orders to the guards at the door. "Arrest this man! And get the old woman. Lieutenant, get your men in here and find that God damn transmitter!"

Once outside the house, Artemio could see the radio direction locator truck. The enclosed back of the vehicle was loaded with electronic sensing gear. Atop the truck was a circular antenna: a slowly spinning radio detection loop. His heart sank. His hands were tied together with rope, and the barrel of a gun was pressed against his back. His mother was by his side, saying nothing. She did not know about the transmitter, although she must have guessed the girl in her house a few weeks ago was a partisan. She did not want to incriminate her son, so she remained silent, but Artemio knew his mother was a strong, defiant woman.

Mueller paced in front of the two Italian prisoners. "I know the bombers have changed the altitude of their runs because the partisans are aiding and abetting them. We always travel with RDF equipment, looking for radio beams on these hills. But I never thought *you*, Captain, would be a traitor to your country." He stared at Artemio for a long minute. The captain held his head low, like a snake about to strike. "So you want to switch sides and help the Americans. All right, I will show you the price it is going to cost you." Looking back to the sergeant he said, "Run a steel cable around the house and attach it to that Hanomag. Pull the house down while the traitors watch."

One of the goliath Hanomag personnel carriers backed up to the house.

"No!" shrieked Rosa, and she ran toward Mueller.

"Mamma, no!" Artemio called after her. The Colonel was still holding his pistol and fired one bullet point blank into her chest. She fell to the ground with a choking cry. Artemio lunged forward, but a German soldier grabbed and got him in a chokehold from behind. He struggled violently to get to his mother, but he could not breathe. The last thing Artemio saw before blacking out was his mother, face down on the land she loved so much, in the garden she faithfully tended, German invaders smirking above her body.

The Nazis pulled down the stone house with the powerful half-track personnel carrier. That house had been the bridge that connected Artemio to his ancestors, to this mountain. With the house destroyed, his mother dead, that connection was abruptly severed. His childhood, his whole past life, ceased to exist. Now he was a man without his reputation, a German prisoner. What would become of him? In the hands of his enemies, would that splinter grow, the one the nomad Haadi had seen in his eye?

CHAPTER 18
Train Car to Auschwitz

The side-to-side motion of the rumbling half-track revived Artemio. Rural wagon ruts were ill-suited for modern mechanized conveyances. He could smell the heavy exhaust fumes of the open-top behemoth as it lumbered along the narrow dirt path. His stomach queasy from the pain in his leg; the stench only made him sicker. He partly levered himself up from the debris-covered floor of the vehicle, and his brain finally registered what was below him: a human body, the dead Italian pilot, half-decayed and terrible-smelling. Revulsion propelled Artemio to his knees. German soldiers sitting along the benches laughed at his scrambling confusion. When the Hanomag came to a stop, the two steel doors at the rear opened up and the German SS men dismounted. As the first soldier passed him, he spat in Artemio's face; the next man hit him with a wooden ax handle, which knocked him out of the vehicle. When all the troops had exited, they took turns punching and kicking him. The beating only ended when Colonel Mueller approached the group. Artemio, held up by two SS troopers, faced Mueller and another figure he remembered earlier from the train station platform—the Gestapo agent. The secret policeman's freshly polished shoes were like black mirrors.

He was quite dashing, at a time when few Italians had money for food. This man clearly had a penchant for nicely tailored clothes. Even Mueller's uniform, which was standard SS issue, designed by Hugo Boss and sewn by slave labor, paled in comparison. It was evident that the SS Colonel was subordinate to the Reich legal authority.

"Is this our brave Italian fighter ace?" the Gestapo man asked cynically, as he watched the blood stream down Artemio's face.

"Yes. Unfortunately for our little bird, he got disoriented and flew over to the other side," snickered the Colonel.

"Your medals won't help you now, Battaglia," pronounced the secret policeman, who was both judge and jury. Artemio said nothing in his own defense; he was in too much pain to argue the inevitable.

"What should we do with him, sir?" asked Mueller.

From under the brim of his hat the Gestapo agent said, "The orders from Herr Hitler are clear. All partisans are to be shot when apprehended, or sent to death camps in the Reich." Executing the Italian captain in front of his countrymen on the train platform would create quite a scene. Secret, non-incriminating murder was more his style. "Put him in the train car leaving for Auschwitz tonight."

"*Jawohl, Herr Gruppenfuhrer*!" the Colonel yelled, then clicked his heels and gave a Nazi salute. The *Gruppenfuhrer* did not return the salute; Artemio realized that the Gestapo agent was uncomfortable with drawing attention to himself in the Piacenza railway station. He wore civilian clothes because he wanted to distance himself from the military arm. He was fooling himself into believing he was not part of this wretched affair, that he was somehow above it all; or at least, he was wishing he was.

Sweat and blood stinging his eyes, Artemio looked directly into the face of the plain-clothed policeman and, in a raspy voice, said, "The war is lost for Germany. You better hope I die, or I will hunt you down and kill you myself. It may be years from now; you will never know when it is coming. You may be walking with your wife, or eating in a restaurant with friends; you will see me, then there will be blackness, and you will be no more. I will be the nightmare that haunts you"

"Trust me, Captain. After your internment in Auschwitz-Birkenau, you will not be heard from again."

"My disappearance will not be forgotten, *Herr Gruppenfuhrer*, nor will your face. You think you are inconspicuous, but everyone in Piacenza knows who you are. You wear suits no peasant could afford. Your Horch sedan is so ostentatious, one like it has never been seen here before." Even while being held up by soldiers Artemio struggled to get closer to the Gestapo agent. "Trust me, *Herr Gruppenfuhrer*. Justice will find you in whatever hole you crawl up, in whatever country you think will protect you."

Mueller nodded his head curtly to another soldier on the platform. The SS trooper hit Artemio with the butt of his Mauser rifle and the soldiers holding him let him fell to the ground. Artemio knew this was the end for him. Auschwitz was a place no one returned from—a death sentence. He thought of his poor mother, her body lying on the freshly turned garden soil, unburied. It was his fault she was dead. He had made the decision to hide the radio beacon in her home, to save American airmen's lives. *Was it worth it?*

There were half a dozen POWs on the train station platform watching these events unfold. They had stopped working to watch the Italian hero beaten and dragged away. Artemio noticed one face that shone out among the rest: it was Rocco Beati. His expression was filled with pity for Artemio, for his suffering; it was because of him that his old friend was in this predicament. It crossed Artemio's mind to tell his tormentors that Rocco was his accomplice so that the punishment would cease. He did not. He imagined what he must look like to the people in the station. Perhaps it was all the blows to the head, but he felt as if he were sharing the fate of Jesus Christ. He was being scourged by Pontius Pilot's Roman guards. They mocked him as they beat and spit on him, then led him through the streets of Jerusalem, while onlookers stared at the man about to be crucified. No hope, no rescue, only final judgment.

The German soldiers dragged him to a single boxcar parked on the rail siding. The train car was painted red and had a small compartment built onto the front of it. An SS guard came out of this separate space and asked, "Who is this?" The guard was an older man in his fifties, probably a veteran of the Great War, too portly for frontline duty. The two younger SS troopers holding him up announced him as "Artemio Battaglia, partisan."

This response chilled Artemio. He, a graduate of the prestigious University of Milan, first in his class in flight school, an officer in the Regia Aeronautica, a fighter ace, awarded two metals of honor for courage on the battlefield, reduced to 'partisan,' an epithet that proclaimed him a criminal under a death sentence. He hung his head low. The SS train guard grabbed him by his collar and pulled him to the red sliding door of the boxcar, like Charon the ferryman of Hades who carries souls of the newly deceased across the river Styx. Artemio perceived he was traveling into the Underworld.

Inside, the boxcar was a macabre view of hell, a foretelling of the future. Gaunt bodies were packed inside this dark waiting room of evil, eyes staring out of their emaciated heads, specters, not even hoping for freedom; that dream had long ago died. The huddled people squinted at the daylight, ghouls inspecting a fellow traveler. Artemio started to shake, and his legs could not follow commands from his brain. Tears streamed down his face.

"No, no, not me! Not like this!" he sobbed.

He would have fallen on the train tracks, but all three soldiers were holding him up. They heaved his shivering body onto the wooden floor of the boxcar. To get the door to shut, they shoved his body with the barrel end of their rifles, as if he were a sack of potatoes. There was a sound of rolling thunder as the iron wheels turned, then the great door slammed shut. The next sound was the lock engaging, and all prospects for escape vanished.

Artemio's burning eyes tried to focus in the low light. He looked at his arms, they were only bone covered by skin. Like his fellow travelers, he had changed. His view from the floor was of old, tattered shoes, or cut and bleeding bare feet. No one touched him or spoke to him. In this crowded train car where everyone could expect the same demise, the suffering was very solitary. The odor of human feces and urine filled the confined space. As he lay on the floor and people stepped on him, he thought, *Why me? All the partisans in Italy, and they catch me.* His mind raced. *Maybe Rocco turned me in to the Nazis. I saw him at the station. I should never have trusted him.* Artemio tried to stand, but the pain in his leg and back was too great. He did manage to get to his knees. Looking around, he felt the fear and shame of every one there, lost in the knowledge of their future deaths. He hated them. He thought, *How did we all end up here? Wasn't there something we could have done differently? A better place to hide? A more convincing lie?* He knew only death awaited him in Auschwitz-Birkenau, his final destination a crematorium. The words of the Good Friday service echoed in his mind, and he cried them aloud through his sobs, "My God, My God, why hast thou forsaken me?"

A young girl, about 6 or 7 years old, came through the crowd and approached him. She put both her hands on his face. Her gentle caress rubbed his cheeks, chin and eyes. She wore a burlap blouse with the Star of David sewn onto it. Her face was soft and cherubic. Her hands wiped his tears, her touch soothed him. All of his pain left his body and his bleeding stopped.

He whispered, "Who are you?" His ears barely heard his own voice.

Her smile was sad and gentle. Her lips did not move, yet she said, "I am your daughter." Artemio did not understand this; he had no children, but he loved this ethereal being as if she were his own.

"How can you be my daughter?" he asked.

She answered only by looking into his eyes. "The children today and children not yet born need a safe home. Artemio, you are a great warrior, but the world does not need any more warriors. Humanity is collapsing; the end is near! I cry in heaven for all my children." He suddenly knew who he was communing with.

"I am too sinful and unworthy to be in your presence."

"You all are."

"I do not know why you call on me. I am condemned to die here. Why can't you wave your hand and fix all of this? Destroy the Nazis with a swat of your hand, like a bug."

"It is not for me to undo what man has done. This is your trial by fire. In this furnace, you will be forged as hardened steel, or as the hardest ice you will melt."

"I will do whatever you command. As a soldier I will obey." He was emotionally willing, but... "But how could I do anything? Look at me, at where I am! Look at us!" The angel moved back into the crowd. Artemio got up on his feet in an attempt to follow her. "No! Don't go without me! I am ready to come home!" he said through his tears.

"Not yet; there is still much to do," was the response that came back to him. He looked around the dim car, but she was gone. When he stood, all his pain was gone. His body was not just numb, as if on narcotics, this was a rejuvenation. He was not sure if he had ever felt this good physically; joy and exhilaration ran through his veins.

Artemio saw a woman next to him with a handkerchief held up to her mouth in a futile attempt to ward off the stench. She was staring at the wall in shock after losing her whole family. He touched her shoulder and said, "It is terrible, I know; but you are going to be all right." The woman turned and looked into his sympathetic eyes. She smiled tentatively. He turned to a man on his other side, desperately worried about how his family would carry on without him. Artemio held his hand and told him they would be fine. "I can only hope so," the stranger said.

Sitting on the floor was the Rabbi of the Piacenza synagogue. He had been hidden by a Christian couple in their attic. An informer had turned them all in to the authorities, for money and food, the rabbi's wife explained to Artemio. The Rabbi sat huddled and despondent on the floor.

Artemio bent down to the hopeless religious leader and whispered in his ear, "Be at peace; all will be well, Rabbi." The Rabbi answered without looking at him. "Why bother? We are all going to die. Sooner or later, we all die."

"No, Rabbi!" Artemio responded firmly. "We all have work to do. Ezekiel tells us, 'Get ready; be prepared, you and all the hordes gathered about you. Take command of them. After many days you will be called to arms.'"

The Rabbi now looked up at him. "You, a gentile, quote Ezekiel? Where are you from?" Artemio smiled back, knowing a faithful man would understand. The Rabbi pointed his finger at Artemio's face and said, "I see a holy spirit in your eyes."

"Yes, Rabbi, I feel it. A splinter has been plucked from my eye. I can see again." Artemio turned to everyone in the train car, bound for the concentration camp, and yelled, "Renounce death and prepare for life!" People closest to him were filled with hope and believed, their faces illuminated from within. However, the effect was like a stone cast into the water: the farther back in the darkness, the weaker the ripple of faith.

Sometime after midnight, air raid sirens started to blare. The entire troupe of the condemned panicked. Being residents of a city with a railroad, they knew that Lancaster bombers flew over at night to destroy the tracks. Women started to cry and men prayed. The idea of being imprisoned in a train car as a formation of heavies dropped their payload was too much to bear. The next sound they heard was the powerful German anti-aircraft guns along the tracks, firing into the night sky, like a boxer taking blows but punching back. The prisoners clung to each other. Strangers hugged strangers. Some looked up as if they could see through the roof, imagining the planes above them. The floor of the dilapidated wooden car started to vibrate from the impact of English bombs striking the ground far in the distance. What terrified everyone was how the vibrations got stronger as the bombing swept closer. Artemio's trained ear picked up a new sound—small arms fire. "Why rifle and submachine fire here at the station?" he murmured under his breath.

A metal-hitting-metal sound could be heard on the boxcar door. Jubilation engulfed the passengers as they realized that partisans were attempting to open the door. Some laughed and some cried with relief and joy. The lock broke from the mighty blows of a sledge hammer. Slowly, the heavy door rolled back along its iron groove, pulled by determined hands. This created a large gap, a portal back to the living. Sweet night air entered the dank space. Artemio's lungs breathed in the cool freshness, filled with the scent of life. Prisoners no more, the freed men, women, and children poured out the great opening. They jumped from the red prison car onto the dirt siding and ran. Artemio saw Rocco Beati standing in the vast doorway. Rocco's head moved side to side, scanning every face. He was looking for him. When they saw each other, Rocco yelled, "Artemio! Over here!"

Rocco grabbed his arm to stabilize him as he jumped from the opening. Artemio almost stumbled as he landed on a soft, irregular surface. When he looked down he saw he was standing on the dead German guard, who earlier had asked, "Who is this?" Artemio spoke to the body of the slain SS man, announcing loudly, "Artemio Battaglia, partisan— escaping!" Rocco gave him a puzzled look. It lasted only for a second; both men knew the pandemonium of the assault would not last long. The Germans would regroup and mount a counter-attack.

Rocco directed Artemio away from the railroad siding. As they ran, they passed dead German soldiers on the platform and Luftwaffe anti-aircraft gunners slumped over their weapons. Partisans with submachine guns scanned side to side, looking for German reinforcements. The two men reached the street in front of the train station to see a lone car, a Topolino, waiting for them. Rocco opened the passenger side door, then skillfully inserted Artemio onto the seat of the gray subcompact. This all happened so fast, the former prisoner barely had time to thank Rocco for the daring attack and liberation. He managed to gasp, "For a time back there I doubted you, my old friend."

The partisan smiled and answered back, "I got you into this. You are my brother, and I will look after you." Artemio's whole family was now dead; this man calling him brother made him feel part of a family again.

"We need you," Rocco continued. "There are still many Germans left in Italy to kill. God willing, I will see you again, and we will fight together." He slammed the car door closed and began barking orders to other men with guns to clear the way. The diminutive two-door coupé sped off.

Holding on to the armrest of the door, Artemio looked out the windshield as they took a high-speed turn around a traffic circle. The Fiat was traveling so fast it went up on two wheels and almost veered into a flower cart. With a thump that shook all his bones, the car righted itself and sped on, taking turns at ferocious speeds. As nerve-wracking as the ride was, this automobile was a welcome refuge from the extermination-camp-bound boxcar.

CHAPTER 19
Quaraglio

They left the city and the driver slowed the car so as not to draw attention. The country roads were even more dangerous than the urban ones. During wartime one had to drive with the lights out or risk being seen and attacked by roving fighter planes. Artemio asked the silent chauffeur, "Hey buddy, where are you taking me?" The driver removed the cap and long, raven locks fell to her shoulders.

"Don't you recognize me?" the driver asked.

Artemio was stunned, first that the driver was a woman, second that her voice was familiar. He leaned closer to the chauffeur to get a better view. He knew her scent. It was Gabriella, the horseback partisan who'd delivered the transmitter beacon. For a second time he had assumed a masculine assignment could only be performed by a man.

"Gabriella, I am astonished to see you here!" he managed to say. He was glad to see her, but at a loss for intelligent conversation.

"They asked me to drive today. I prefer being in combat, killing Germans." Her eyes never left the road and she showed no emotions. Artemio was starting to realize this woman was a serious fighter, and that he'd better treat her as such. "Did they beat you? Do you need a doctor?" It was obvious from her tone that she asked only for practical reasons.

He answered, "No, I don't need a doctor. I was treated with good old fashion German hospitality." He saw her smile ever so slightly for the first time. He continued, "You said 'they' asked you to drive; who are 'they'?"

"Your friend Rocco, and our leader, Fermo."

"Who is this Fermo?" He asked, thinking how fortunate he was to be with her again.

"Both Rocco and Fermo are partisan group leaders. Rocco's area of action is inside Piacenza. Fermo's area is the surrounding countryside. Rocco is a brigade leader under the command of the freedom fighters *Giustizia e Libertà*. They work closely with the Americans. Fermo, on the other hand, is a rogue operator. He meets regularly with the Communist Garibaldi Brigade, but he's not a Communist. Fermo was the first partisan in Italy. He was killing Mussolini's men back in the 1930s, before it was fashionable." Gabriella pulled the car over to the side of the road. "Enough talk, take your clothes off," she demanded.

Artemio, a little put off by the curtness of her request, said, "I usually like a little more romance, but okay."

"You must get out of those bloody, stinking clothes. We have a change for you, and bandages. We expected a few bullet holes in you." *Bullet holes!* he thought, and suddenly realized how dangerous a mission this was. The shoot-out at the train station could have gone badly for the partisans.

She continued, "The area behind the seats has a hidden compartment with a change of clothes and a gun. At the Fascist road blocks they check our papers and only look in the trunk." She constantly looked up and down the road. "Now you must drive the rest of the way. It will be too suspicious if a woman drives a man." Gabriella unashamedly took off her masculine partisan clothes in front of Artemio. He pretended not to notice her as he changed also. From the corner of his eye he observed her muscular body. She was tall for a Romagna woman, strong and athletic; yet in the moonlight her skin looked soft and her figure had all the feminine curves. Gabriella caught him stealing a glimpse of her. While looking down the road and adjusting her bra she said, "Well, I guess we cannot use you in our spy service, because your eyeballs pop out of your head." Artemio turned around, embarrassed at his indiscretion.

"When we are stopped, this is our cover story: you are my husband, I am your pregnant wife." He turned toward her to see her place a rag filled canvas sack under her dress. A hidden slit on the side seam allowed access. She inserted a gun into her artificial baby bulge. He gave an astonished nod of agreement.

Artemio drove the car in darkness, watching the side of the road and keeping the leading edge in view. They were coming to the end of a wooded area. Suddenly, two German Regular Army soldiers stepped onto the road and held up their arms to stop them. A young man leaned into the car and looked around with a flashlight, then demanded their papers. Having recently been beaten by German soldiers, Artemio was very uneasy. He shifted around in his seat as his pulse quickened. Gabriella could see the amateurish movements of this nervous driver; he could not control his fear. He began to sweat profusely. She hoped the guards didn't notice.

Gabriella reached into the glove box and handed the papers to Artemio. The other German soldier stood in front of the car, training his submachine gun on the two Italians.

After inspecting the documents, the young man, so young he could not even grow any facial hair, signaled his friend to let them pass.

Artemio slowly accelerated the car and followed the road to the end of the forest. He turned out of the wooded area to an open stretch of road. By the light of multiple fires, he could see the reason for the checkpoint. During the bombing of Piacenza that night, RAF fighter planes had found a column of German armor. The tankers had thought there would be safety under cover of darkness; they were wrong. An hour earlier, this must have been a scene of bedlam. Even now the Germans were attending to their wounded and lining up the dead. Panzer tanks with steel cables were pulling disabled trucks out of the mud. The drivers had scrambled desperately to get off the road when the British Spitfires strafed them. Artemio knew that RAF pilots were ruthless when they discovered a soft point in their enemies' defenses, like English bulldogs that, having bitten, would not let go.

The most unnerving aspect was the expressions on the faces of the shell-shocked German troops as Artemio and Gabriella drove past them. They could see in their grimy faces the loathing they had for the Italians witnessing their ignominy. Even this moment of terror and confusion could not erase the contempt they had for the rest of the world. Unlike Colonel Mueller, who had a sadistic smile he used to disarm his prey, these men could not disguise their hatred, which was accentuated by the firelight. With the high level of tension in the air, Artemio feared an enraged soldier might empty his magazine of 9 mm bullets into their car.

Gabriella broke the silence. "Dirty krauts! I wish the English had killed all of them." Artemio noticed she was shivering and had her hand on the gun's grip still hidden under her dress. He did not reply to her comment. They slowly drove past the carnage.

Artemio was surprised at how well the little Fiat drove off the paved road up a winding dirt trail that would imperil larger vehicles. Gabriella directed, "See that rock face? It has a hidden door; drive up to it."

There was a high, exposed granite cliff with grass growing in front and to either side of it. Long, thick ivy grew down over the flat rock. Closer inspection revealed a recessed wooden door. Gabriella exited the car to push the vines out of the way and opened the hidden doors. This brought the last rays of afternoon light into the cavernous storage space. "Before the war, shepherds dug out these caves," she explained. "They would provision them with dry beans and bottles of wine for an overnight encampment. The next day, they'd move on with the herd."

The car ensconced, Gabriella changed back into her partisan garb. Her brown cap had a red piece of cloth that was originally a five-pointed star sewn onto the front. Her pistol now holstered, the matron's dress and fake abdominal roundness were placed in the secret compartment of the Topolino. They shut the weathered doors to conceal the car, making sure the vines lay naturally again. Then the two partisans set out on foot up a steep incline of gravel. No vehicle could travel any further.

Artemio asked as they approached the tree line, "Is Fermo's camp close by?"

Gabriella answered, "No, but the horses are."

He thought of the day she'd ridden up to his house to deliver the transmitter beacon. He remembered his surprise when she'd taken off her hat and he'd seen a feminine nose and narrow neckline.

"Where? I don't see them?"

"They, like everything else we have, must be concealed. Over there is a box canyon with a dense tree canopy. Planes flying above them would see only the green leaves."

Artemio saw a young man suddenly appear from behind a boulder.

"*Ciao*, Pepe," Gabriella called to the sentry.

"*Ciao*, Gabriella. Who is your friend?"

"This is Artemio. He is the one Rocco told us about."

Pepe had a handlebar mustache that he used to try to hide crooked teeth. Around his neck he loosely wore the red Communist bandana. He was a city boy who had learned how to move in the woods quickly and quietly. Like most of Fermo's gang, he was a crack shot with his sniper rifle. They were just young men who wanted the German invaders out of Italy. Not many youths wanted to serve in the existing National Army. The military forces in northern Italy were an affront to many; the Republic of Salo was only a veneer for the German occupation, like the Vichy government in France. Artemio had heard stories of these boys becoming good fighters under partisan leadership. Even early in the war, the Italian military command had been corrupt. Artemio remembered how this had led to a feeling in the lower ranks that no one cared about them. They endured winters with no warm clothes, equipment with no spare parts, even being rationed bullets on an active battlefield.

In the horse corral, Pepe saddled up two horses and addressed Artemio with a grin, "I knew you were Gabriella's friend."

"How did you know that?"

"I was tracking you for ten minutes. In that time, I counted two occasions when Gabriella would have cut your throat if you were not who you were supposed to be." He smiled, exposing his brown, chipped teeth. Artemio rubbed his neck as he looked at Gabriella. She adjusted the saddle on her horse and grinned, knowing Artemio was feeling vulnerable.

Pepe continued, "The horses are kept hidden under these trees until night fall, when I let them graze in the meadow. Before dawn I must gather them up and bring them back into the canyon, or observation planes will see them." Artemio thought of the conversation he'd had with Colonel Mueller about partisan activity on Mt. San Giorgio. Aerial photographs of horseback riders was evidence the Germans used for planning missions.

Gabriella asked him, "Do you know how to ride?"

"Of course I know how to ride! I grew up in these mountains," Artemio replied, annoyed that his competence would be questioned.

"Then enough chit chat. We have a hard ride ahead of us, and not much sunlight left," she yelled behind her as she mounted and rode off. He had to ride spiritedly to catch up.

When the horses got closer, he asked, "Gabriella, why do you treat me as if I'm a stranger? You keep a distance between us. We have a past, you and I."

She did not look at him when she spoke. "You don't know me, Artemio. You only think you do. I am one of the leaders of this attack group." When she did turn, her face was emotionless. "We met once at Mario's graduation party. If I told anyone here of your Fascist connections, you would be arrested and shot."

"That is not fair, Gabriella. I was young and idealistic before the war. Yes, I did believe Mussolini was the best thing for Italy. He did much good in the early years; not until the friendship with Hitler and the Nazis did things turn to shit."

"You were a nice boy. I did like you, but your friend Mario and the Piaggio family are rich, arrogant bastards. They support Mussolini and that whole rat's nest in Rome." Artemio knew *Il Duce* was playing the puppet-master with the old-money aristocrats and the new-money industrialists. "Well, these bourgeoisie who prop up Mussolini, they will all meet the end of a rope!"

Artemio thought of Scarafaggio and his rabid Fascist way of thinking. *How will these two Italies come together at the end of the war?*

"Gabriella, you know our side will win this war. Is there not any room for forgiveness? We will have to make Italy a country for all Italians again. That will require healing the hate." Artemio looked into her face and her heart. He saw anger at this talk of reconciliation; perhaps it was too soon. He continued, "Is Fermo as anti-Fascist as you?"

"Fermo is my spiritual father. We despise the Fascists. When you meet him, you will see. He has a vision of the future, a vision of freedom. He believes all governments, by their very nature, grow bigger and more powerful, eventually enslaving the people who live under their influence." This idea struck a chord with Artemio. He had been a valuable asset to the Italian government, a decorated fighter pilot in the Regia Aeronautica, yet he had been discharged from service after being wounded. Totalitarian governments see their people as machine parts, and when they are broken they are taken out with the garbage.

Gabriella's horse nuzzled Artemio's horse as they trotted alongside each other. She continued.

"Fermo grew up dirt poor on Quaraglio Mountain. The only food his family ate was what he hunted. The government gave them nothing, but wanted taxes from them. One day a *carabiniere* rode up Quaraglio Mountain and came upon Fermo hunting. The policeman on his horse asked Fermo if he had a license for his old shotgun. Fermo replied he never heard of needing a license for a tool. He said the gun had belonged to his dead father, who had given it to him years ago. The *carabiniere* demanded the gun from him: 'No license, no gun.' Fermo explained that the only way his family could eat was if he shot rabbits and birds. The policeman dismounted from his government-issued horse and grabbed the barrel of the shotgun. A tug of war with the gun ensued. The way Fermo tells the story, when he pulled the trigger and shot the Fascist pig, he looked into his face and saw surprise there. The hubris of this man sent from Rome, to not even consider that a peasant would fight back! It was at that moment Fermo knew that the common man could beat the arrogance of tyranny."

"It's one thing to bury a man on a mountain, but I am sure his fellow policemen wanted to know what happened to him."

She nodded and went on. "Fermo was not discreet. He rode the Fascist's horse into town. Everyone saw the Mussolini 'M' brand on the horse and the leather mark on the saddle, the ax wrapped with sticks. Fermo had never owned a horse in his life, and the town's people knew it. He is a charismatic man and attracts people to his cause. In the beginning, he had like-minded followers, poor men who were tired of a life of poverty. Some were veterans who felt screwed by the politicians in Rome. They all felt abandoned and disaffected. The *Carabinieri* did not want to make a martyr of him and his growing band of supporters. They left him alone on his mountain, until a new police chief was installed in Piacenza. He was young, stupid, and a coward. This inexperienced chief told everyone he would bring in the renegade tax cheat named Fermo. He never left the station house, but sent twenty of his best men. Their commander was a lieutenant from Puglia, where they eat horse meat. There are no roads up Quaraglio, so armored cars and trucks are useless. The policemen rode their stallions up the mountain, while the lieutenant waited in his staff car on the perimeter road. The twenty horsemen, like the first *carabiniere*, never returned; they are buried on this mountain. The legend goes, when the chief of police asked the lieutenant what happened to the men, he replied that they were all killed in action. Then he was asked, 'What happened to their horses?' The lieutenant thought for a moment and said, '*Braciole!*' In the south of Italy they cook tough horse meat for hours in a tomato and wine sauce; this is called '*braciole.*' As this story circulated among the other *carabiniere* units, the name '*Braciole*' became the moniker for the Piacenza police station. They are jokingly called the *Braciole* Troop. Fermo is greatly feared and respected by these Fascist police units. He is hated by the Germans, who cannot catch him in the open. Their nickname for him is 'Inferno'.

The horses were walking in a culvert, in a slow, single file. The terrain became steeper, with a loose gravel base. At a dry stream bed Artemio got off his mount and walked beside it. Gabriella looked back to see what the holdup was.

He answered her question before she asked it. "With the incline and the moving gravel, the animal is not stable. I'm afraid she might slip and hurt her ankle. She can handle this better without a rider."

Gabriella shook her head. "You do have a good heart, Artemio. The stories we have heard about your fighting skills from Rocco don't fit your caring nature."

"Whatever you have been told by him may be true, but I have changed. Now I am tired of the politics and the killing."

Gabriella gave him a long look, as if she were evaluating a dress on a display rack that she was thinking of buying. Then she said, "This war is not over yet. The fighting here in the north is going to intensify as the Allies move closer. The faint of heart will hesitate in battle—and get killed. You must reach down inside yourself and find that warrior spirit again. You will need it."

"I want to say the opposite to you, Gabriella. On a few occasions you should reach down inside yourself and find the tender girl I knew in Milan."

Her eyes narrowed with rage, and she scowled at him. She kicked her steed and galloped off.

Artemio knew what he had seen, what he had done, and how that had changed him since his college days. But what had happened to sweet Gabriella to have brought about such a profound change? She had more than just anger; she was self-destructive.

The upper camp was also guarded by sentries, who signaled them to pass. Evidently Gabriella was well known and easily recognized. Artemio noticed that the guards appeared, then vanished.

"The ground here is good for defense!" Artemio shouted up to her.

Gabriella turned her head and shouted back, "We have just passed through a minefield and a bunker complex, and you didn't even notice!"

He contemplated Fermo's thorough preparations and thought, *He is a natural tactician.* The sun was now setting behind the mountain. In the amber light two men in thick wool uniforms, a mix of German and Italian Army issue, walked out of the tree line and took the reins of the horses. They both wore the red armbands of the Garibaldi brigade. Gabriella jumped off her animal as if she were an equestrian athlete. Artemio dismounted only as fast as his disability allowed. She proclaimed loudly, "We are here!" He looked around and saw only a gentle, rolling meadow and woods, towards which the horses were led. There was absolutely no sign of human activity anywhere.

CHAPTER 20
Meeting Fermo

Artemio searched for a command post, but only saw the natural beauty of trees, sloping mountainside, and a stream. If he had not known the mountain's reputation, he would have deemed it tranquil.

"The Germans know we are here," explained Gabriella. "They have attacked us in the past, but they paid for it with heavy casualties. Even with air power they cannot beat us on this mountain; it is our fortress." She looked up in the sky. He could see the pride in her face. "When they have a few extra bombs that are not needed in the south, they drop them here on Quaraglio. The bombs explode but are ineffective, because the pilots cannot find any targets. Our stables and barracks are higher up the mountain, in that forest." She pointed up the jagged rock face. Her expression hardened as she talked of aerial bombardment.

"The Axis pilots are cowards. Many a good partisan has been killed by a fighter coming out of the sun. They strafe us if they catch us in the open. We have no defense for this. I believe you should see a man's eyes before you kill him. An Axis pilot who bailed out of his plane would not live long after touching down on Quaraglio."

She adjusted her long hair up into a bun. Her movements betrayed her anger. Artemio thought, *This is no life for a young woman. We were all cheated. Our generation is tarnished forever. None of us will have a normal future, not even after the war.* He was afraid to show his feelings for her. There was that pain, that rage: whatever she had endured, he must understand first.

She went on. "The camp operations are underground. That old, burned-out barn is the entrance."

Artemio saw rubble in the center of the meadow. "One lucky bomb dropped from a Messerschmitt last year did that. So now we use the damaged building as our front door." She gave a sly smile. "Why would the enemy waste another bomb on an already blown up barn?"

They walked over to the destroyed building with its collapsed roof. Artemio saw a machine gun emplacement across the field, hidden by foliage and built into a naturally occurring crevasse. The gun crew protected the entrance from unauthorized access. It was only because of his grasp of tactics that he noticed the camouflaged automatic weapon. He pointed at it to show Gabriella that he saw it. She answered, "You only get in if they let you in."

Once in the tunnel complex, Artemio had to stop to let his vision adjust to the darkness. Fermo's band of outcasts had been digging these shafts for years. As the partisan group expanded, so did the tunnels. The rock walls were close and damp, the tool marks evident, as if freshly hewed, and the ground underfoot was uneven. At first, he was expecting to have a problem in this dark, confined space, but since his time in the Auschwitz-bound train car and his encounter with the healing spirit, he had not needed any pain medication, and the claustrophobia with panic attacks had ended. Nevertheless, his eyes started to tear. Smoke from cooking fires filled the close air of the tunnels. Gabriella told him that the fumes got bad at dinner time. "We have a ventilation system that works to bring fresh air in and hides the exhaust smoke, but it is not perfect."

She stopped at a doorway along the narrow tunnel. Artemio could hear the low voices of men coming from the room. Inside were a table and chairs, and two officers were leaning over the table reading a map. In the center of the table was a small pot-bellied carbide lamp such as miners use. It gave off an unnatural bluish light while it hissed. Everything about this place was aberrant, Artemio thought; humans were not meant to live like this. In the corner of the room was another man operating a large radio set. The antenna travelled up through a bored hole and probably continued along a tree trunk above ground. He sat at a separate table, listening through head phones while staring into the black box of electronic tubes. There was a partisan team out on mission, and these men were waiting for the patrol to radio in at a checkpoint.

"Fermo, I bring you Captain Artemio Battaglia," announced Gabriella from the doorway. One of the two men at the map table stood and walked over to them, smiling. Fermo was a burly man in his late forties, short, but with broad shoulders. The gray razor stubble on his face was as thick as the palisade defenses of Quaraglio. Even in this low light, his eyes had a vibrancy to them.

He stood directly in front of Artemio and said, "No one will call you "Captain," because you have no rank here, and last names are not used, to protect our families back home." His forthrightness surprised Artemio. This protocol was a complete contrast to a Fascist army, in which your last name gave you prestige and your rank was determined by how wealthy and important your family was.

Fermo continued, "Your friend Rocco has told us how you risked your life for the cause and did not break under interrogation." Fermo put his hand on Artemio's shoulder and with a heavy voice said, "I am sorry for the murder of your mother. I promise, you will avenge her death."

Artemio nodded and replied, "Thank you. I have heard much about you as well, Fermo."

The second man now stepped forward quickly and introduced himself. "I am Maurizio. We hear you like to kill Germans, eh?" the young man said, with a smile.

"I have fought side by side with Germans, and against them. They have strengths and weaknesses that we can use to our advantage." Artemio thought of flying with Klaus Meyer, an accomplished fighter pilot and ace. Now he would be fighting with these partisans of unknown abilities. In fact, his life would be in their hands. Artemio felt very uncomfortable about that.

Fermo seemed pleased by Artemio's answer. He turned to his junior officer and said, "Did you hear that, Maurizio? I told you this man could help us with our dilemma."

The smile had disappeared from Maurizio's face. He studied the newcomer, then asked suspiciously, "In what capacity did you work with the Germans?"

"I flew combat missions with a German fighter squadron in the Africa Corps. I found them to be very tough, capable men. There is no turning them from their objective. An Aryan soldier must carry out his orders; for them, there is only victory or death. No way back is allowed the Germans."

Gabriella added, "He won the Iron Cross for bravery at the battle of Tobruk." Artemio nervously cleared his throat. He felt strange to have her singing his praises.

Maurizio said with a frown, "We know—for killing *Allied* soldiers."

Fermo interrupted to change the direction of the conversation. "Yes, yes, this is a confusing war. One day you are killing Englishmen, the next day you are asking them for supplies."

Gabriella remembered her message for Fermo. "Rocco told me, before the attack on the train station, that the English agent assigned to Rocco's brigade said there will be no aid or equipment for our group as long as we fight under the Communist Garibaldi Brigades. Winston Churchill has refused the transfer of any help to Red Brigades."

Fermo said bitterly, "I know this already. *Il Volpe* told me the news this morning. The Communists have spies in Churchill's personal office and at 10 Downing Street. We know these things before that British MI6 agent in Piacenza does." Fermo's face showed his disappointment as he spoke to Artemio. "Churchill knows that in the war after this one, his enemy will be Stalin and the Soviet Union. So he will not aid any Communist fighters in Western Europe, no matter how many Germans we are killing."

Artemio maintained a calm composure outwardly when he heard the name *Il Volpe*, the Fox. *Could this be the same man I met in Milan? The man from whose face I wiped the blood after the Fascists beat him to within inches of his life?*

Maurizio trumpeted, "Ah, dinner is here!"

Women in partisan olive drab uniforms with the red scarfs of the Garibaldini brought in plates of food. The men refolded the map and took it off the table. As the four sat down to eat, Fermo poured red wine from a glass bottle with a straw wrapping. In the unnatural light given off by the lamp, the wine looked like the dark, blood-stained waters of *La Mattanza*.

Fermo said, "Artemio, in the old days my family and I would say a prayer before a meal. If you grew up around here you did also. But now things have changed. In the Communist structure this is forbidden. I miss it. Now there is no good way to start a meal except to say, *Buon appetito*."

All four raised their glasses and said, "*Salute*," but Artemio wondered how, if Communists were not allowed to pray, this new order was supposed to bring freedom to Italy. Already, the chains were tightening. Who was pulling them?

Artemio took a long sip of the Lambrusco. He had missed his hometown wine with its carbonation. Carefully, he addressed the three partisans. "Communism will not be well received in the south. They are still religious people and say grace before a meal."

The officers froze for a moment, then their eyes darted around the table. They did not know the politically correct response for their new guest, whether to be good Communists and educate him, or let it pass.

Gabriella, poking at her food with her fork, broke the uncomfortable silence.

"Fermo, no meat again?"

Fermo looked at Artemio across the table and said, "We are getting to be a large group. The rabbit and pheasant population have long been hunted to extinction here."

Maurizio raised his wine glass and added, "This war is total war. It kills all life."

Fermo looked at the young Communist officer and frowned at him, then continued, "We occasionally get lamb or chicken if the local farmers sell them to us. The Germans go through the villages and take all the livestock, hoping to starve out the local population. If the farmers can't feed their families, how can they feed us?" He paused and then added, "We have a local man, Don Orscini, who lives on the next mountain over; he makes the best dried duck sausage in all of Italy."

"We won't be getting any more of that sausage," said Maurizio.

"Why not?"

"German aerial reconnaissance discovered the pens where he was hiding the birds. The SS foot soldiers had checked before, but never found them. When they returned, they accused him of food hoarding. They shot him outside his home in front of his wife and children."

"Don Orscini's grandfather fought alongside Giuseppe Garibaldi in the Italian war for unification!" said Fermo, aghast at the news.

"I don't think the Nazis cared about that," Maurizio said, then inflated his chest and proudly stated, "It doesn't matter. Our proletarian army will beat the Germans, even if all we have to eat is polenta."

Artemio added, "Rocco told me that, at Stalingrad, the Russian soldiers had only eaten potatoes and black bread for nine months. If a Russian soldier complained of no meat, his commanding officer would say, 'Do you hear Soviet rockets traveling over our heads and landing on the German positions? We can stop the supply of these *katyusha* rockets and bring in meat instead. Is that what you really want?'"

Fermo, thinking of the poor Italian soldiers on the Eastern Front with frost bite and dying of exposure, said, "Marshal Zhukov, supreme general of all Soviet forces, is a genius. He manipulates the Germans to do what he wants on the battlefield. He made Hitler commit his best units to attack straight though the middle of the front, and this exhausted the Wehrmacht. Zhukov held back his own vanguard until the time was right. He then encircled the Germans with his fresh winter tank forces from Siberia and won a major victory!"

"Yes, I heard the winter tank army paint their tanks white for camouflage and use a secret, Soviet-invented oil that will not harden at even 30 degrees below zero," said Maurizio.

Gabriella, bored by the conversation, added, "Rocco also told me the Americans air drop tins of chipped beef to all the non-Communist Action Party Brigades."

Maurizio's eyes narrowed with anger as his right hand clenched into a fist. "We fight the hardest and take most of the causalities, yet the Allies still play favorites! I am tired of being the black sheep of the family!"

"Come now, Maurizio, I taught you to be proud of your accomplishments and not to be envious of others," said Fermo paternally. With this, all the diners fell silent and ate their polenta with wild mushrooms harvested from the local woods. The only sound was the radioman trying to communicate with the lost patrol. Static mixed with the sound of his growing concern as he said, over and over again, "Straw man, this is Tin man; come in, Straw man...."

After dinner, the camp women picked up the empty plates, then served espresso coffee with Sambuca, an anise-flavored liqueur. Both Gabriella and Maurizio finished their drink as a shot, head back and elbow up. They quickly excused themselves from the table.

Fermo struck up a conversation with Artemio, his new friend and fellow tactician. The talk centered mostly on how the Germans were killing civilians to drive a wedge between partisans and the local population. Fermo explained the importance of the people and their continued support in this war. Italians had so many mixed emotions and allegiances: Should they be loyal to Mussolini or the king? Which partisans should they support, Communists or non-Communists? Who to befriend, the Germans or the Allies? Fermo was sensitive to the difficult balance between killing Germans and having the civilians suffer the wrath of Nazi retribution. "The locals *must* support the activities of the Resistance; if they side with the Germans, they could finish us. They know where to find us, they know where we go. Comrade Stalin says, 'The partisans are like the fish and the local people are the sea. The fish must live in the water because the water gives them sustenance; they are inseparable.' He is right."

Artemio let him ramble. He also paid attention to the radio operator, who appeared to be having difficulty. Then, interrupting Fermo abruptly, he asked, "I heard you are not a Communist in your thinking, Fermo, and we both see how the Allies are reluctant to help Communists. I do question why you fight under the banner of the red flag. If you hated the tyranny of Fascism, why would you accept the tyranny of Communism?"

Fermo looked into Artemio's face as a chess player would. "You were a Captain in the Regia Aeronautica, the Air Force of the Fascist state, yet you profess not to be a Fascist. Why did you fly their airplanes?"

"I was a supporter of Mussolini in the early years. His ideas were revolutionary at the time, and they seemed to be good ones. The government building projects, agricultural land reform, and universal health care. We were so progressive, we were the envy of Europe. But then things turned dark, and now I reject his policies." He paused as he thought about his life. "It is wrong to put men in ships and sail to foreign lands to conquer and subjugate the native people. I have seen atrocities I will not repeat here. I know there will be a reckoning in the future for my actions." He looked directly at Fermo. "Now I must be as correct as possible."

"Correct as possible?" Fermo's voice changed, becoming angry. "Is that like the difference between Germans who commit genocide and those who only fight Americans? Artemio, you would be the only man on the Titanic throwing buckets of water overboard as the ship is sinking."

"No, Fermo, I would be one of the many men who gave up his seat on a lifeboat for someone else," he answered back solemnly.

Fermo respected his answer but did not agree with it. He continued to argue. "In the early days of the resistance, I was the only one who stood up to the Fascists. I had no political inclination. They called me a bandit. I was not; I was an anarchist. I wanted *no* government on my mountain. The Communists approached me after their defeat in Spain. *Il Volpe* is a political animal, not much of a military man. He is my friend, not my commanding officer. We work together to disrupt German supply lines. I need him for information, like which trains have valuable supplies, or the troop movements of the anti-partisan SS and Blackshirts. I collaborate with him for intel only."

Fermo turned to the radio operator to see if he had raised the lost patrol. When the radio operator shook his head, he frowned and turned back to Artemio. "The Communists have a brilliant spy network. All the governments around the world have Communist sympathizers hidden in them. These agents pass on information. It gets to *Il Volpe,* whose area of influence is the triangle of Milan, Genoa, and Bologna; here he can coordinate all the Garibaldi Brigades' activities.

Artemio asked, "What must you do for his valuable information?"

"Nothing! I am an independent operator. However, I cannot convince the English of this, so I get no supplies from the Allies. All our weapons are German and Italian Army issue that we pick up on the battlefield after victorious combat." He leaned in and lowered his voice, as if he were confiding a big secret. "I love the American M-1 carbine. It is lightweight and more accurate than a submachine gun, a great partisan weapon, but we cannot get any. We go on ten times as many missions as any other partisan band. All my men are here to kill Fascists. Many men in the other units are only there to escape government conscription. They are young playwrights and musicians, useless in a fight." Fermo shook his head in disgust and added, "Some brigades are riddled with Fascist informers."

Artemio remembered the anger in Colonel Mueller's voice, when he'd complained of how difficult travel was on the roads because of Fermo's partisan activity. "I know the Germans would love to destroy this outpost. Do you ever worry about traitors in your midst?"

"We have a process for dealing with informers." Fermo looked at the radio operator again and demanded what the problem was. The radio operator, who was obviously afraid of him, answered with a shoulder shrug. Fermo turned back to Artemio and said, "Maurizio sets up a panel of judges that reviews the evidence. If there is a conviction, Gabriella is sent out. She is only told the name of the informant. I have seen her gallop off on a horse with her rifle across her back. In a day the problem is solved. I never ask her any details. Gabriella is our enforcer and is autonomous." He gave the Captain a serious look and repeated, "The problems are solved permanently."

Artemio remembered her riding fast up to his farm house, a natural athlete in the saddle. She had looked like she had just won the *Palio di Siena* horserace.

He said to Fermo, "When Gabriella dropped the transmitter off at my San Giorgio Mountain home, there was a misunderstanding between us, and I did feel her blade to my throat."

Fermo laughed loudly and said, "You are the only man to survive that. She must have a soft spot in her heart for you." Artemio weakly smiled back, even though he did not think it funny. He swallowed hard, glad to feel his throat working properly, then said, "She has a deep hatred for the Germans, I have noticed that."

Fermo's jovial face saddened suddenly. "Her whole family was killed by an SS murder detail, right in front of her eyes," he explained. "A group of partisans had blown up a railway bridge with a German troop train on it. Hundreds of soldiers and their tanks fell into the gorge. Colonel Mueller personally received a phone call from Adolph Hitler. He was ordered to kill every Italian living in the nearby town. Gabriella's father was the butcher and the town's part-time mayor. He confronted Mueller and begged him not to harm the town's people. Gabriella was coming home from soccer practice when she saw her father, mother and little sister machine-gunned while they were on their knees. Gabriella ran away. She is the only survivor of that massacre. The whole town was executed; all were innocent. They had nothing to do with that train attack. She is ashamed of running away that day. She told me she wished she had died with her family." He rubbed his stubble on his chin.

"Gabriella joined our band to avenge her family's death by killing as many Germans as possible. As a young girl she trained with us to ride horses, set booby traps, and shoot rifles and machine guns. If Maurizio is my right hand, then Gabriella is my left hand. I have lost my only son Ramon to this war. He was a hero. He gave his life helping others escape a Nazi ambush. With only his pistol and a sack of hand grenades, he held back the SS assault long enough for everyone else to get away. Then, to avoid torture, he saved the last bullet for himself." Fermo's voice had begun to shake. He stopped talking to compose himself.

"I miss him so much! The Communists won't let us pray, but, secretly, I ask God every night to give him back, and take me instead." Fermo looked away as his eyes welled with tears. He blew his nose in a handkerchief, then continued. "I have no more family; they are all dead. I call Maurizio and Gabriella my family now."

Artemio felt compassion for this seasoned fighter. He said, "I have met the SS colonel in charge of anti-partisan activity in this sector. He's an insane bastard. He killed my mother, and I know he wants me dead."

"Yes, I am familiar with Mueller and his Gestapo boss. I respect the Colonel; he goes out with his men and fights alongside them, as I do, unlike most of these Fascist leaders, who are afraid of death. They come from rich families and will have a good life after the war, no matter which side wins. They won't take risks." Fermo took a straight shot of Sambuca, then filled both glasses again. "Rocco told me you are a good strategist and expert in military tactics. Is that true?"

"I am very good at aerial combat, but I don't know if I can help you. On the way here I saw your bunker complex and covered trench lines. You are very good," he replied, complimenting him, one strategist to another.

"My problem is with our roadside convoy ambushes. We plant mines in the road that detonate on pressure. The damaged vehicle blocks the road and stops the column. Unfortunately, this is not reliable. The spot that the vehicles must be stopped at has to be precise, so that the later incendiaries will be as effective as possible." Artemio thought of the name the Germans had given this man, 'Inferno'.

Fermo went on, "The lead vehicles are often motorcycles. When they detonate the mine, the column is not hindered. Another problem: if many vehicles miss the mine, then the first explosion is late and many enemy soldiers escape the kill zone."

Of necessity, Fermo made his own incendiary bombs, using a mixture of gasoline, benzene and soap flakes, carefully heating them together to form a gel. The Allies would not supply him with dynamite or napalm, so the resourceful terrorist had adapted. His signature on a battlefield was like a lurid artist's rendition of hell. The German relief column would arrive long after the partisans had fled, leaving only blackened, burned out vehicles and cadavers with scorched flesh.

"I will consider your problem. Could I see the terrain you plan to work in and what weapons you have?"

"Of course! I will have Pepe show you the target area in the morning. As for weapons, we have what a German Army Platoon would have. It is a mix of captured German and Italian rifles, MP 44 submachine guns and MG 42 medium machine guns. The Americans give their front line weapons to the non-Communist Justice and Liberation Brigades. Yet these ex-Fascist units fight very little. I don't care, because there was a time when I fought Mussolini by myself. I am proud of the fact that I have killed more Germans than any other Italian. But I would like a little respect from the American and British forces. When we return a downed airman back to them, they give us money. They make us feel like we are just mercenaries. Money for a pilot! I would give them whole bomber crews for free, if only they would air drop us tins of meat and medical supplies."

Artemio could see he was upset by this.

Suddenly the radio operator started talking loud and fast. Both men turned to stare at him. By the stricken look on his face, Artemio knew it was not good. The man looked down at the table, afraid to tell his leader the bad news.

Finally, Fermo bellowed, "What the hell is going on?"

Filippo answered in a distressed voice, "The night patrol we sent out was ambushed by anti-partisan forces, and none made it to the checkpoint. They are all dead!"

The partisan strategist rubbed his forehead and thought for a moment. He told the radio operator to have Maurizio put together a raiding party to intercept the SS and counter-attack. He got up from the table and checked that his side arm had a full magazine. He said to Artemio, "My friend, someone will show you to your quarters. I must leave now to try and find the scum who did this, before they reach their base camp." He slammed the full magazine into the pistol and racked the slide. "If I can destroy them quickly, it will steal their victory."

Fermo was a guerrilla at heart, a master of the game.

CHAPTER 21
Mission to Genoa

Artemio was woken up by a silent hand on his shoulder; it was Gabriella. He was startled at first, but then a serenity overcame him at seeing her face.

"Come along, we have a mission today," she said with a serious expression, then left the room. Artemio looked at his watch—it was four a.m. *What was the mission at this hour of the morning?* he wondered. One of the camp women brought him a cup of hot coffee and a piece of last night's stale bread for his breakfast.

"Grazie, signora," he said to her politely. He also asked for her to bring him a big kitchen knife. When she did, Artemio slipped it into his belt. She gave him a dumbfounded look, but left without asking questions.

He and Gabriella rode their horses along the serpentine trail down the mountain, with only the dim light of the waning moon to see by. Artemio was picking thorns from a briar patch off his pant legs, when he asked, "What is the mission, Gabriella?"

"You will know the mission when you need to know it," she, the senior partisan fighter, informed him.

"Why the secrecy? Who could I tell?" he asked. They made their way back to the dirt road where Artemio had left the car during the ascent up Quaraglio. The car was now parked on the road, and some of the partisans were standing by it. Two of Fermo's men held the horses while the riders dismounted. Artemio was handed the ignition key by a man he had not seen before. Lanzo was a young partisan who had a belly that hung over his belt. He was the first guerrilla fighter Artemio had seen who could stand to lose a few pounds. Lanzo smiled at him and said the car had a full tank of gas. Another partisan, Tino, spoke only to Gabriella, in a low voice. "There are three checkpoints along your route, all of them manned by Blackshirts." He then turned to Lanzo and commanded, "Give him your knife."

"But Tino, this is my war trophy," the fat one whined.

"I will get you another one; give him this one now." Reluctantly, Lanzo took from his belt a Hitler Youth knife. The blade was etched with the inscription, '*Blut und Ehre,*' 'Blood and Honor.' This was a fighting knife for hand-to-hand combat that was only given to the best in the class. Artemio thought of the honor of the German boy soldier who had died rather than surrender. He shuddered, thinking of the mother waiting for her young son to come home; he would never arrive.

He hid the fighting knife up the left sleeve of his coat, then removed the big kitchen knife from his waistband and placed it under the front seat of the car. On seeing the two knives, Tino yelled to his friend, "*Madonna*! This guy is ready for a serious street fight!" Artemio grinned at him, knowing these men were inexperienced partisans who did not understand behind-the-lines, asymmetrical warfare, with its deceit and subterfuge. As he looked over at Gabriella, he saw her loading a fully automatic Broomhandle Mauser Pistol.

Lanzo said, "He is perfectly safe; she has her trumpet." Both partisan boys laughed for a bit until they saw her glare at them, and they abruptly stopped. Gabriella concealed the large handgun in her fake pregnancy bulge.

The sun started to clear the horizon as a new day began. Artemio drove the Topolino onto the Quaraglio service road. "You really should tell me the mission so I know what to expect, Gabriella."

She was looking out the side window, immersed in thought. "I keep things from you for a reason," she said, then decided it was time to explain. "The fat one, the one who gave you the key to the car, he is being investigated by Maurizio's tribunal. Until we can trust him, you might have let something of the mission slip out."

"The young boy with the pimples? Lanzo? I do not think he could be a double agent," Artemio said in disbelief.

"I don't know all the facts. It is his father. The new recruits were talking in socialism class about the need for land reform after the war. Lanzo said he was against it because his father is a pig farmer and needs his land."

"That's it?" Artemio said exasperatedly. "His father is a pig farmer so he is under investigation?"

"Everybody gets investigated eventually. A good Communist has nothing to fear." She said this as if investigation were a minor event, even though some people were sentenced to death by investigators. "They don't tell me all the details, because I would be the one to carry out the sentence."

"You mean, you would be the one to kill him," he said solemnly. "Doesn't that bother you? They make you kill and you do not know why."

Gabriella looked at the permanently injured pilot driving the car and asked him, "When you fired your machine guns into a British fighter plane, did you know the man you killed?"

"No, but that was different. We were at war with England. It was every Italian soldier's duty to fight and kill them."

"So does that make the killing justified in God's eyes?" Her words stung him. The gnawing pain in his stomach returned; he knew he was wrong. There was much he still had to atone for. How upside down this world had become, when a murderer can lecture on morality. All he knew was he had to save Gabriella from being the tool of politicians.

"I do not profess to live a good and spiritual life. I am not a monk. But I know we are on the wrong path. As a young student in Milan, I believed only a strong nation could better the lives of its citizens. But the politics of Fascism threw the whole world into war; it was a mistake. I will live the rest of my life trying to repair the damage I have done."

"What is the point of it all? What you say and think is meaningless. If you save a little girl standing in the road during a firefight, you risk your own life running across the street under gunfire to pick her up and bring her to safety. Later, you find out she was rounded up by a German SS patrol and shot for partisan retribution. What was it all for?"

He was encouraged by her wanting to have a discussion. "Saving the little girl in your example is the point. Nothing else matters after that. Risking your life for hers is what makes you human. It is what connects us all together. We all die. It is what we do with our lives that matters. Who we are as people is determined by how we treat our brothers and sisters." He stopped to let her think about it. "Another example is, each government believes that if they win the war, no matter how heinous their troops were on the battlefield, it will be justified. Machiavelli was wrong when he said 'the ends justify the means.'"

He turned from looking at the road and looked into her deep brown eyes. "Every action we take now will be marked on us for eternity. We will pay for our hate with our souls. I know this." He remembered how, in the fog of his mountain home, an angel had told him he did not have much time left. "My only hope is to repair some of the damage I have done before I am taken."

"You could start by not judging me. I see the way you look at me, like I am a crazy murdering bitch." Gabriella's voice went an octave higher as if she was about to cry.

Artemio saw the tears in her eyes. "No, no, you misunderstand. My look is one of regret. I hate myself for rejecting the life I could have had with you. I turned away from you to worship false idols. You were the right girl for me. I know now what a fool I was. Gabriella, I love you."

She could not believe he had just said that.

"How could you love me? You never wrote to me, you never telephoned. I dreamed you would come home on leave in your Air Force uniform and meet with my father and ask him if you could call on me. We would go on dates and fall in love. You never did any of that." She put her hands up to her face and wept.

"Gabriella, I never got leave! I have been in continuous combat for two years. I am only here now because of my wounds. Otherwise I would be dead or in a POW camp. I knew the day I saw you at my mother's house you were the one for me. I am sorry I hurt you by not writing, but my life was chaotic. I know now I made mistakes on the path I travelled; even so, look, it led me back to you. I have been given a second chance. That is why I am sure about us. But these times are so dangerous, I had to tell you how I feel! If something happens to me... well, now you know."

He wanted to kiss her and dry her tears, but a Blackshirt roadblock appeared up ahead.

Artemio shifted into neutral and applied the brake. Two Italian soldiers from the Republic of Salo approached either side of the car. The one closest to Artemio said, "Exit the vehicle and show me your travel documents." Gabriella got out slowly and heavily as a pregnant woman would. The soldier on her side of the car yelled to his friend, "Hey, get a load of this one." Then he put his hand on Gabriella's swollen abdomen. Artemio shouted at the man to get away from her or he would kill him. The sentry next to Artemio put his rifle barrel up against his back and said, "Hey, calm down, cowboy. No one will harm your woman."

Artemio, without taking his eyes off the Blackshirt next to Gabriella, said, "Before I kill your friend, I will shove that rifle up your ass!" Gabriella for the first time had a look of fear on her face, not knowing what would happen next.

Their commanding officer swiftly walked over to the car, clearly in a bad mood. "Let's move, search the car; we don't have all day." The two sentries slowly walked back to the Topolino with their guns pointed at Artemio. A cursory inspection discovered the kitchen knife under the front seat.

"Look what we have here! A weapon!" the soldier held it up in his hand as if it were a trophy.

Artemio said, "I use that to protect my wife from the criminals who prey on this road." The Italian officer looked at the two traveling misfits; a cripple and a pregnant woman. He turned to his subordinates and cursed at them. "Idiots, do you think I have nothing better to do than baby sit you two?" He turned away and walked back to the sentry post.

The embarrassed private asked, "What do I do with the knife?"

"Give it back to him, *stupido!*" the commander answered without turning around.

As the relieved partisans drove away from the checkpoint, Gabriella looked at him in wide-eyed amazement. Finally she asked, "What did you think you were doing back there?"

"If I had acted calmly, I would not seem like a typical Italian husband whose wife is being groped by another man. I felt passion when that man came at you. You don't need my protection, Gabriella, but something rose up inside of me, a blinding rage, when that man touched you. I would have killed everyone at that checkpoint."

Gabriella felt a warmth coming over her whole body. She had never seen a man become angered and violent in order to protect her. She liked it. With her hand she fanned her face, then lowered the window for fresh air. "And what about the kitchen knife?"

"Oh, that ridiculous thing! It is a prop. When a guard sees something that silly, they automatically underestimate you as a fool. While they were fixated on that kitchen knife, I could have stabbed all three of them. Up my sleeve I still have the combat knife that they never looked for."

"Well played, Captain Artemio Battaglia, well played." She had a newfound respect for his abilities as a partisan, not just as a good fighter but a man who could think under pressure. This was the hero who earned those bravery medals. She saw him in a new light.

CHAPTER 22
American Navy

Gabriella gently placed her hand on his while he shifted gears from the center console. Neither one said anything. He looked out the window as the tall cypress tress passed by like a picket fence. Finally she broke the melancholy silence. "Do you want to know the mission?"

"What, now you're going to tell me? Are you sure it's safe?"

She smiled at his dry humor.

"We're smuggling an American pilot to Genoa."

Artemio was surprised, even though he had heard of such missions before. He kept silent and let her speak.

"He's in the back right now, in the secret compartment I showed you. This evening we will rendezvous with an American PT Boat and make the exchange."

"Do you mean the cash payment Fermo says he hates?"

"Oh, I don't know why he goes on about that."

"Money cannot buy the supplies or the weapons he needs."

Artemio felt strange, knowing there was someone else in the car with them. He pressed hard on the brake as a deer ran in front of the car.

"Oh my God! That scared me!" Gabriella exclaimed, with her hand on her heart.

Artemio smiled to himself at her being startled. She so rarely showed any spontaneous emotion. He shifted into second gear and said, "Fermo loves you. He told me he thinks of you as his daughter." He glanced at her, and they both smiled.

"Fermo trusts you, too. I have never seen him warm to anyone so quickly. He has told you a lot about how we operate." She thought of how Fermo usually refused to allow strangers on the mountain. "Does he want you to help him with the planning of a roadside ambush?" she asked.

"Yes, he explained to me that the problem in the past has been that the troop convoys travel too far past the kill zone. This leaves a lot of the German soldiers and their armor safe from the pre-positioned incendiaries."

"Incendiaries; what a nice word for it. Don't you mean hellfire?"

He looked at her, puzzled.

She added, "You know, an all-consuming flame which will return Satan's minions to their hellhole." Gabriella was entering that dark place in the back of her mind, her eyes focused on a nonexistent form in the distance.

"I have been in combat, too, and have suffered loss," Artemio said somberly. He thought of Gitano, his friend and wing man. "I used to think aerial combat was spectacular, like a graceful ballet. The color of machine gun tracer fire is vibrant against a backdrop of puffy white clouds. I would bank my plane on the tail of an Englishman who was trying to evade death. He would bank or dive; I would anticipate and follow. Try as he might, I would not let him escape. The red lines that arced into the enemy's plane were so symmetrically elegant. The fifty caliber bullets would hit the cockpit, and pieces of glass canopy and aluminum fuselage would fly off into the atmosphere, glittering in the sunlight. It was beautiful." He was silent as his mind raced. "There is no morality to a body being blown apart. The physical world has laws: the restraint of gravity, movements of the planets, even time itself. The strange and macabre, the improbable, become commonplace on the battlefield. I have seen horrible things. A man shot in the head, medically dead, still able to throw a grenade and kill the men in the trench that shot at him. An Englishman with his lower jaw shot away, begging for water. The Germans gave him a full canteen just to laugh at him, while they watched him try to drink out of it. After an action, as a soldier reflects on what he saw, it can seem surreal to him. Some soldiers choose to be outsiders, looking on as if it were all just a movie, hoping these things they have witnessed will be of no consequence to them, the mere viewer." He rubbed his brow as if he could erase memories. "However, that is not the case. These images are permanent."

He debated whether to tell another incident. As a confession for his soul he said, "I once saw a British pilot in my gun sights try to escape his burning plane. He opened the glass canopy to bail out, twisting and turning futilely. His legs were pinned by the wreckage. His Hurricane was a casket falling to earth. I gave him an additional burst of machine gun fire just to end his torment." He was contemplative for a moment. "That is what I thought, but on reflection, I was ending my own torment of watching that man suffer."

She looked at him as he continued his introspection. She knew his eyes had seen more than any man should endure. Both her hands rested on her artificial maternal belly bulge.

He explained, "I wanted no part of the killing at first. Reconnaissance missions were all I did. Then later, to get promoted to a higher rank, I requested front line duty." He thought of the advice his rival, the German ace Kurt Meyer, had given him: *Advancement can only be gained through combat and kill counts.* "On the same mission when I became an ace, I was shot down in the desert. I should not have survived that ordeal. Those were my last moments on earth when he came to me."

"Who came to you?" she asked, afraid of the answer.

"The Evil One." Her mouth opened but she could not speak. She turned her imaginary fetus slightly away from him.

"He asked me to join his flock of winged furies. I refused him. I chose an inglorious death, abandoned by my squadron and its powerful machines. To have sand blow over my face as my body decayed close to Saint Anthony in the desert. I found that preferable to living only to serve in hell."

Gabriella, unsure, asked, "You are here now. How is this possible?"

"At the last moment before my death, a reconnaissance team found me and poured water down my throat. As my last thread of contact with this world severed, I heard Sergeant Major Niccolo giving orders to his men, and the sweet sound of the Italian tongue brought me back from the abyss."

Gabriella turned away and started to tremble in fear.

"Did he," Artemio asked pensively, "visit you too?"

She said nothing for quite a while, then broke the silence.

"There is no beauty in killing."

Artemio lowered his head; he was glad she had started to open up.

"At first, I got satisfaction from killing Germans. Fermo and Maurizio think I get pleasure out of it. I do not. I have a, a... *need* for it." Her dress had white lace and fashionable buttons running along the sides. A partisan seamstress had made a hidden slit on the right side of the dress under the lace. Gabriella's hand reached in through this access to feel the comfort of the Mauser pistol. "After combat I have a mental clarity, a sense of purpose. Without warfare I am dead inside. During the fight I am numb. I feel indifference for the men I kill. German, Italian, it does not matter, only the killing is important. After every action I feel alive. Every rabbit and bird is bright and full of energy; colors of roses and tulips are vibrant and alive. One time, after a battle, I lay down in a meadow and I became part of the earth; it enveloped me. Vines, and plants, even a red cardinal making a nest, I was part of it. I never wanted to come back." She turned her head and looked out the side window and somberly said, "The light eventually leaves me. A day or two later, when the excitement fades, the blackness returns. A shawl of sadness lies on my head and shoulders. Thoughts about my parents' death, and the annihilation of my town by the SS, return. I question why I am even alive."

Artemio felt her grief. He loved her, and being a romantic, he wanted to see her happy. The conditions in which they lived made this almost impossible. Could God have wanted man to live like this? Surely God had something better planned for humanity. He spoke softly to her, saying, "Gabriella, our time here is not our own. We want to think it is ours, so we fill it with simple pleasures. As partisans fighting in northern Italy against the Germans, our lives will be short. Very few of us will see the end of this war. Heaven will take us soon unless we improve the lives of people."

"What are we to do? Everyone here is just concerned with daily survival: finding food and staying away from Germans." Even as she said this, her face had a look of yearning, a desire to understand the confusion of their lives.

"I do not know. I try every day to solve the puzzle. Look at me, my body is scarred and I walk with a limp. I am considered a deserter. How can I effect change in a world at war?" Artemio said, loathing himself.

"I am not a religious woman, but I would like to think of God as a great general, one who knows what is in our hearts." She looked at him as she said, "One who will always pick the best person for the job. Like the Moses story from the Old Testament: God picked an unlikely man in the desert, a man who had rejected the Pharaoh, a man with an impediment, a stutterer, to perform an insurmountable task. There were miracles along the way to accomplish the job of leading the Chosen people out of Egypt. I know the Italian people today need a miracle."

He looked at her and saw beyond her beauty. She also was searching for a higher knowledge. They both were travelers along the road of good and evil.

After a long drive, they knew they were close to their destination by the smell of the sea. He pulled the coupé over onto a desolate seaside road; there was nothing as far as the eye could see but scrub brush and sand. Artemio pushed his seat forward to find the hidden compartment. He hit the wooden door with his open palm and said in English, "I am a friend out here. We are getting you to freedom. Please remain calm." After unhooking the secret latch, he lifted the door. In the compartment was a man compressed like a baby in a womb in order to fit in the small space. He was black. Artemio was surprised at first, then offered his hand to help the American pilot unfold. Slowly, the pilot limped stiffly to the side of the road and sat down, stretching his limbs and rubbing his neck. Artemio sat near him; Gabriella stood lookout.

"My name is Artemio and this is Gabriella. We are partisans who are going to reunite you with the American Navy tonight. Are you hurt from your parachute jump?"

With an agonized look on his face the man said, "Yes, my leg hurts, but I don't think it is broken. I am Captain Joseph Bates of the 332nd fighter group."

"Oh, the Red Tails," Artemio said matter-of-factly.

Joe had an astonished look on his face as he asked, "How did you know that?"

"I was a fighter pilot also. I make it my business to know who is flying above me."

"Your English is good. Where did you learn it?"

"The University of Milan. Please excuse me, but I have not used it in a long time."

"No, it is very good; I understand you quite well."

"I am sorry, I do not understand you well; it is your accent. It is south of America, yes?"

"It is southern. I am from Mississippi."

"I do not understand Italians from the south either," grinned Artemio. Joe looked a little puzzled. As both men sat in the high grass of the sand dunes, swatting away mosquitoes, Joe Bates asked the Italian pilot, "What kind of plane did you fly?"

"I flew a Macchi 203 fighter in North Africa."

"I have shot down a few 205s, the new ones. They are no match for the P-51 Mustang."

Gabriella approached and asked him, "Are you thirsty?" She offered a wine bottle that had been refilled with water.

"Yes, thank you." He took it and drank from the bottle.

Gabriella and Artemio decided they all might as well eat; together they got the supplies that Lanzo had packed in the trunk. Gabriella offered the American a thick slice of *sopressata*, a dry Italian sausage, saying, "We will wait here until dark, then walk onto the beach. A PT boat should arrive at 2:00 a.m. to pick you up."

Joe nodded his head to indicate that he understood, then added, "Thank you for risking your lives for me."

Gabriella smiled at him and said, "We are Italian partisans. We live in danger every day. This is just another mission. You are a fighter pilot. You understand risk too, yes? We both fight the Germans. It is natural that we help each other."

"I did not know what to expect when I bailed out. We bomb you people day and night. I was afraid I would land in a field and get a pitchfork in my belly from an angry farmer. Instead I was helped by a farmer and his wife. They hid me from a German patrol at great risk to themselves."

Artemio wagged his finger in the air. "So that is a lesson for you not to pre-judge. The Italians are a very hospitable people. We see the Allied bombing as necessary to kill Germans. In Italy, the Americans are seen as liberators."

"I wasn't sure how I would be treated because I am black."

Artemio's thoughts went back to his experience with black soldiers in the Italian Army in North Africa. He was proud to have served with them. They had been very brave and aggressive fighters on the battlefield. He also remembered Colonel Mueller's rantings at the Piacenza

Train Station, and repeated them to Joe. "I met one SS officer who said, 'How hard could it be to fly a plane? The Americans have trained monkeys to fly their P-51 Mustangs.'"

"You see, that's what I mean. That is exactly the type of racism we black pilots are afraid of if we get shot down."

Artemio did understand. "Yes, the Germans practice this racism. In fact, it is an important part of Nazism; the superiority of the Aryan race is a tenet of their Fascism. Mussolini was never able to use anything like that with Italians." He did not say it out loud, but he knew that if Captain Bates had fallen into the hands of the SS, they would have tortured him to death. Perhaps they would think of it as revenge for Jesse Owens winning four gold medals in the 1936 Berlin Olympic Games, embarrassing Hitler and the Master Race theory.

Joe said, "Did you know there are white people in the U.S. who are racist? Black men have been killed in America just because they were black."

"Not in America! This cannot be possible!"

"Absolutely in America. You think there is no racism in America?"

Artemio defended the U.S. as if it were his adopted home. "America is the land of opportunity! There is no king or ruling class; there is justice, there are courts. How is this possible? Your slavery ended eighty years ago."

"Trust me, a black man does not get a fair shake in America."

"They trained you to be an officer and a pilot; is that not a 'fair shake'?"

"This was an experimental project, just in case they ran out of white pilots. It worked out so well they gave us front line duty, but only after years of keeping us waiting, and using us as a way to fast-track promotions for white officers." Joe waited a minute, watching how his new Italian friend absorbed these facts. Then he said, "My uncle Jasper was hung from a tree five years ago in Mississippi. There was no investigation, no judge, no jury, and no justice."

"I am sorry. I did not know that things like that occurred in America."

"I understand. How could you know? We black folks have to go to different schools and use separate bathrooms, because of the Jim Crow laws."

Artemio had never read anything like this in his Uncle Bruno's letters from New York. Joe had never been to New York. He had gone to college in Jackson, then Tuskegee, Alabama, for flight school.

The two pilots talked until the sun went down. Gabriella looked at her watch, then broke into their conversation. "It is time to go to the beach. Come on, I have the flashlight." Artemio helped Joe to his feet. With Joe's arm around his neck, the two disabled men struggled onto the beach. Artemio had feared he would not be able to help, but for some reason Joe seemed light, and he enjoyed helping this man in need.

There was no moon; in the complete darkness Gabriella flashed the light across the Ligurian Sea. Two lights flashed back out of the darkness. This was a dangerous time; Axis forces patrolled the beach looking for partisan activity. Soon the distinctly American sound of the rumbling Packard engines could be heard long before the patrol boat could be seen. Suddenly a bright search light from the PT boat turned on and scanned the beach for enemy soldiers, for a possible trap. Then the big light was aimed at the partisan and the airman. The two struggled in the cold water up to their hips.

A voice from behind the light yelled, "God damn, can you believe this? We risked our necks through waters full of Kraut E-boats, only to pick up a nigger!"

Artemio could not believe his ears. He had heard that word before and understood its meaning. He put his hand above his brow and squinted into the harsh light saying, "This man is a captain in your Air Force. He is very brave to fight in the skies above Piacenza."

Another voice, the skipper of the boat, yelled out to his men from the helm. "Johnson, Swede, Abrams, keep an eye on the dagos. Do they have weapons?"

"No, sir; they're friendlies," a voice on the blacked-out ship stated.

The sailor manning the searchlight shut it off and leaned over the boat. He grumbled something about a wasteful mission, then gave an outstretched arm to bring Joe onboard. As the two men struggled alongside the shallow draft boat, a wave of frigid, murky water hit them chest high. Artemio, angry now, stabilized himself and Joe so as not to go under water. He saw the foul-mouthed sailor's arm and purposely pulled hard on it to unbalance him. The man gave out a yelp as he tumbled out of the boat. With all three men in the water, Artemio punched the sailor in his face several times. Two other sailors jumped in the water to pull Artemio off the dazed, bloodied man. The dry sailors on the deck were laughing at their beaten shipmate as he got back in the boat.

"O'Neal, you ass, get below deck to sick bay and have your nose patched up," commanded the skipper. He yelled his next orders over the din of the three 12-cylinder engines.

"Hey, Johnson, get Rocky Marciano on board. Watch out for his right hook; it's fast."

On the bridge of the PT boat, Artemio sat in a fold-down chair, with a blanket for warmth, while the skipper stood over him. He was tall with a red beard. His voice boomed when he spoke, "*Parla inglese*?" He said with a New England accent.

"Yes."

"Listen, the way we handle the exchange for our air men is to give you commie Red Brigades only cash."

"I am not a Communist, nor mercenary. I am a freedom fighter, a partisan warrior trying to get German soldiers out of my homeland."

The skipper and first mate were surprised by this. "We were told the exchange would be with the Red Brigade."

"I am an ex Air Force captain; my name is Artemio Battaglia. I fight with this partisan band but I am not politically aligned with them. The men of this group are the toughest in all of Italy. We kill many Germans here, and that saves many American lives in the south."

"We thank you for your service on our behalf, Captain, but our orders are to give you the money and send you on your way," said the Celtic-looking commander of the PT boat.

"Service! Is that what you call it?" Artemio became indignant. "My mother was murdered, and our home knocked down by the Nazis, all because we had an American radio transponder in our attic!"

The first mate gave an insider's glance at the skipper. Artemio knew they were using poker faces to communicate.

Finally the skipper demanded, "What? What are you thinking?"

"C'mon, Lieutenant, we have to help this guy out," the first mate said sympathetically.

Artemio looked at the sailors on the boat and said, "I see the American Navy issues M-1 carbines for on-shore missions."

"Yeah, so what?" said the first mate, whose hat was on crooked. His demeanor was of a man who had experienced combat and was disgusted with regulations.

Artemio sized up the American naval officers. "We could use a weapon like that. It's short-barreled, and the caliber is more powerful than our nine millimeters. Good for close-in combat; you know, ambush work. Those M-1 carbines would be perfect for us."

"Really?!" said the commanding officer. "You like the carbines, eh?"

"Skipper, give them the guns," said the first mate.

"Ensign, stand down and let me think a minute."

He rubbed his beard and asked the first mate, "Back at base, won't they ask where the guns are?"

"Jonesy at the gun locker owes me a big favor. He's been losing at poker all month. I'll take care of it with him."

"Alright, do it. These poor bastards are fighting and dying to take pressure off our boys south of Rome."

"Thank you," said Artemio.

Another officer entered the bridge and the skipper ordered, "Scotty, go below and check on the men. Make sure they maintain battle stations until we put to sea."

"Aye, aye, Lieutenant." The man left the bridge without saluting.

Artemio took the blanket off. "I travelled for a short time with a crew on a recon vehicle in the Sahara desert. It is much like a ship at sea. Your men like you. However, you must maintain respect and discipline on this ship at all times."

The naval commander could feel an easiness with Artemio. "I'm sorry for the way we initially treated you. We are not racists on this PT boat, Captain Battaglia. You saw O'Neil cracking under the pressure. On this patrol to get the airman, our sister PT was sunk by a German E-boat, all hands lost. The men are pretty shaken up about that."

"I have never travelled to America, Lieutenant, but I can tell you I love it. America is a refuge for humanity. In your history you have taken in the poor and the hungry. You have no walls." The first mate handed him a cup of hot coffee. "As Europe destroys itself, hope can live on, there. The rest of the world has limits imposed by kings and oppressive governments. Americans love freedom. You love it so much you are willing to fight to make other men free. This is unique in human history." He sipped the hot coffee; it tasted good. "I will tell you, governments hate personal freedoms. They get power by crushing liberty. The Italian people put all their faith in Mussolini. When he started to fail, he believed he needed more power to be successful. Fascism slowly stole... no, we *gave* our rights and liberties away."

"I hope we meet again under better circumstances," said the skipper as they shook hands.

True to the lessons of Artemio's Reconnaissance days, he did not take the same route back to Quaraglio. Even in the dark, the starlight gave a luminescence to the sea foam as the waves broke on the rocks. At this point the coastal highway was cut onto a mountain face, elevated above the sea.

He said to Gabriella, "They say Christopher Columbus learned his seamanship skills here." She had a grin on her face as she told him, "I am more interested in your negotiating skills."

"What do you mean?"

"The American sailors. If they knew we were Red Brigade, how were you able to get those carbines?"

"You have to understand what motivates men. Sometimes it is money, but oftentimes it is not. If you are honest with people, they can tell."

"You knew those were Fermo's favorite rifles, didn't you?"

"Yes. They will be like a birthday present for him."

They both smiled, thinking of Fermo as a kid with a toy.

Gabriella gave him an inviting look and said, "You should pull over somewhere along the beach." She kicked off her shoes and played with the curls in her hair. "I am not in a hurry to get back."

Artemio felt an emotional bridge connecting the two of them before they even touched. He knew she wanted him. He wanted her. For a short time, the darkness and the surf blotted out the rest of the world.

CHAPTER 23
Bobbio

It was the first spring day of strong sun. It burned with brightness and hope, as if Persephone had returned to the arms of her mother, Demeter. The fields were blooming with their first flowers. Eaten by cows in the field, their scent could be detected in the milk. Three Quaraglio partisans were sitting outside at a small café operated by party faithful in the town of Bobbio, which on the map was a small dot south of Piacenza. Its importance came from the fact that the Germans had decided not to occupy it. The mayor and town council, as well as its residents, were apolitical, unlike Bologna to the east, where the heavy hand of Nazism clashed with the red fist of the Italian Communist Party. Bologna regularly had outright urban warfare in its streets. Sleepy little Bobbio was a place apart from the war.

Artemio and Gabriella sat at an outdoor table with Fermo, enjoying the weather. Fermo took a sip of hot espresso before saying, "The Germans are starting a new initiative in the Milan-Piacenza area. The roads are almost impossible to travel now. A German SS sergeant is stationed at every Italian checkpoint to oversee more thorough searches." He looked up and down the street. There was no traffic except for a three-wheel farmer's truck delivering produce. "*Il Volpe* hopes to be here today if he can get through. He tells me often how much he wants to meet you, Artemio." After another fortifying swallow he added, "*Il Volpe* is very impressed with you two. All your missions together are successful, without a single shot being fired." Fermo beamed; he was proud of his fighting group.

"We have not fired a shot because of Artemio. He is a skillful negotiator. I have seen him get whatever he wants." Gabriella smiled at Artemio and he returned her smile, the way lovers do. Then she looked at Fermo and said, "He has taught me that not all conflict must end with an empty magazine in your gun."

Fermo smiled, put his hand on hers, and said, "As your adopted father, I approve of your romance with Artemio."

"Thank you, Papa, that means much to me." Her eyes welled up with held back tears.

Fermo turned to Artemio and told him of a raid when the M-1 carbines had been used to good effect. Afterwards, Tino had been able to barter with the Justice and Liberation partisans for more thirty-caliber carbine ammunition. Fermo always had a cheerful face when he told of a successful operation. Then he asked, "Have you given any thought to our dilemma with stopping convoys?"

"Yes, I have." Using his hands, Artemio demonstrated: "We will place two .50 caliber machine guns in the road. At your signal they will fire into the lead vehicles. Even armored cars and Hanomag half-tracks will be penetrated by that caliber. This havoc will create a pileup that will stop the entire convoy."

Fermo frowned with disappointment. "This is a good plan, but I told you, we have only medium machine guns.

They do not have the penetration we need to knock out those armored vehicles."

"I have the answer to that as well. There is a crashed Macchi fighter plane on the top of San Giorgio Mountain. Only the landing gear and propeller are damaged. Send some men up there to disassemble the two heavy machine guns out of its nose. In the skies above Piacenza, the Italian pilots are only used for reconnaissance, so it should have a full complement of armor-piercing ammunition." He remembered Eduardo from the recon team and how he could field strip all the useable parts from damaged equipment. Surely Fermo had a few men like that.

Fermo was still not convinced of the operation's chance for success. "You cannot just place two machine guns in the middle of the road and expect Germans with motorcycle scouts to drive right into them!"

Artemio, who had never done this sort of work before, was nevertheless confident. "Of course, the stretch of road where you want to place the ambush will need some engineering. I will prepare the ambush to your specifications to give us the biggest advantage. Here is how we will set about it...."

Morning began to fade into afternoon. A black sedan pulled up in front of the café. The driver exited first; his eyes first scanned the street for threats, then the patrons at their outdoor tables for unusual characters. Only then did he open the rear door. His eyes still roved the area, scrutinizing the church across the street as an afternoon funeral procession passed by. A thin man with a graying beard exited the car. It was *Il Volpe,* the leader of all the Red Brigades for Milan and Emilia-Romagna.

Was this the same man I helped escape the beating from the Blackshirts? Artemio wondered. This man appeared much older than he remembered. His time in Spain, serving the cause, had aged him. Suddenly Artemio was sure it was him. *Il Volpe,* however, gave no sign of recognition. As was the Communist way, few pleasantries were exchanged, no salutes or handshakes. *Il Volpe* either did not remember him or pretended not to know him.

Fermo made the introductions. "This is the new man I was telling you about, the one working with Gabriella."

Il Volpe looked directly at Artemio and tried a little humor. "Ah yes, Gabriella's jealous husband." They all smiled and chuckled out of respect for his position. "It is a pleasure to meet you, Artemio. I have heard the pregnant wife ruse is quite successful." He looked around to see if he was being watched. The Fascists had spies too.

"You are a good partisan fighter, even under pressure." *Il Volpe* looked Artemio up and down. "Despite your obvious handicap, all the men want to fight alongside you."

Fermo addressed *Il Volpe* with reverence; Communist officials had to be respected because of the power of life and death that they wielded. "We were just discussing a roadside ambush. Artemio is planning a new method to stop the lead vehicles."

The Communist leader turned from Artemio. He intently stared at Fermo and scowled. "I need action from you, and soon!" *Il Volpe's* disposition had changed from cordial to serious.

"Of course! Tell me what you want and I will perform it," said Fermo, concern in his voice.

Il Volpe leaned forward and spoke in a low voice. "I am getting intelligence reports that Colonel Mueller is well liked in Berlin. They think he is doing an excellent job here. There is talk of promoting him and expanding his command to a new SS anti-partisan division, probably to be based in Piacenza. Do you know how bad this makes me look to the Russian Bear?"

Artemio knew the Russian Bear was a KGB officer assigned to northern Italy, a ruthless taskmaster. The difficulty they were in registered with everyone at the table. Without a direct order being issued, they knew their next mission was to kill Mueller.

"I understand. Just tell me times and locations of where he is operating. We will take him out," Fermo said huskily.

"Fermo, you are a good soldier. I have relied heavily on you in the past. Now this war is changing; it is going to get very hot. As the Americans push up from the south, the Germans will fight harder. They feel they are being compressed in a box. Hitler is going to send his vaunted Waffen SS units into this tight space. These men are trained in both Nazi ferocity and solid infantry tactics. You will know them by their camouflage uniforms. Their mission will be to kill everyone—everyone! The Nazis here know they are dead-enders. They have no future; after the war, any who have survived will be put on trial and hung for war crimes. So for now they are on loan from hell. To all the Red Brigades, I need a doubling of your efforts. That means more patrols, more strikes, and more assassinations."

"Yes, *Volpe*! We will all work harder and push through to victory." Fermo said this enthusiastically, even though he knew he would be doing the work while the Communist leader sat in his command post.

Il Volpe leaned back in his chair as if exhausted. He signaled to the waiter for an espresso. His gaze turned to

Artemio. There was silence for a long, uncomfortable minute. "I know of your rejection of Mussolini and Fascism. Tell me, how are you embracing our socialist experiment here in northern Italy?"

Gabriella kicked him under the table. Artemio was not sure if that meant *"Be careful of your answer"* or *"Conceal your true feelings."* He cleared his throat, giving himself a second to think. "These are difficult times, and it is hard to make an evaluation of how socialism could work here. After the war we will have a better economic environment."

Il Volpe, not really concerned with his answer, asked a second question. "I am told you go to the required socialist education classes but never participate in the question and answer period." Clearly he had spies everywhere. "Why is that?"

This political inquisition had to be negotiated carefully, or Artemio could be arrested for impure thought.

Fermo jumped in with a stutter, "*Volpe,* he, he, he is new to this information. He is my best fighter, he likes to kill Germans—that's all!"

"Really! He is a graduate of the Italian university system; I don't expect to be talking to an idiot."

Artemio took offense to this browbeating of Fermo, and to being called an idiot. He started in again. "I believe that for communism to take root in Italy it must be another flavor than Russian communism. Italians have their own way of doing things. Mussolini's brand of fascism was very different from Hitler's. The Italian way is subtle, like the spices in our food. The flavor of borscht is too bitter for the Italian palate."

Il Volpe was confounded by this because it was not the usual dogmatic regurgitation. Artemio forged on.

"There are elements of communism that appeal to most Italians. The social aspects, such as the government providing healthcare and housing for all its people. Worker's rights, fair wages, free childcare, and the idea that all people are equal, these are noble goals. However, there are some tenets of communism that would never work here, such as political imprisonment and loss of free speech. Internment camps of people who have dissenting opinions will never be tolerated again. We are fighting the Germans because we reject the holocaust of humanity. The Italian people will never accept a totalitarian and oppressive government again."

Gabriella was shocked that he'd opened up like that to *Il Volpe*. She injected quickly, "*Volpe*, he needs time to fully appreciate all the benefits communism yields to its people. I know this man well, and he is a good socialist in his heart."

Il Volpe raised his hand as if to stop her. "No, it is okay, Gabriella. I will make allowances because he is a war hero. Tell me, Artemio, what of the Italian Blackshirts who tortured our people; are we to just let them go free?"

"I know this is an unpopular opinion right now, while we are fighting and killing each other, but yes. When the hostilities are over, we must forgive all atrocities from both sides. It is the only way Italy and all of Europe can heal and move on as a society. We will not forget; but we must forgive. Vladimir Lenin executed all of the people associated with the czar. A repeat of that here would be a mistake."

Both Fermo and Gabriella were horrified that Artemio spoke so frankly to the regional Communist party boss.

Il Volpe stood up from his chair without drinking his coffee and said, "Artemio's views are not correct and should be adjusted if he wishes to continue in the Brigades."

Artemio saw the frightened look on Gabriella's face.

Without changing his monotone voice, Il Volpe gave new orders to Fermo. "We have shot down and captured a Republic of Salo pilot. He is to be tried for strafing partisans in an open field. Then he is to be convicted for crimes against humanity and executed. The trial and execution will take place, Fermo, at your mountain fortress of Quaraglio. There must be no chance of Mussolini's men rescuing him. This order comes directly from the Russian Bear."

Artemio knew the Bear was in direct radio contact with Moscow. All orders for assassinations of government officials came from the Bear. Now it seemed the purging of the military had begun. *Il Volpe* was making it clear that Artemio's ideas of reconciliation with Fascists after the war was out of the question. With terrible clarity, Artemio realized, *If the Communists come to power in Italy, the firing squads will operate night and day. All of this will happen under the auspices of their Soviet puppeteers.*

CHAPTER 24
Bella Ciao

After dinner in the underground bunker complex of Mount Quaraglio, Artemio sat silently by himself and reflected on the coming morning's ambush. Fighting as a partisan in northern Italy was unlike aerial combat over the Libyan desert. The air war in North Africa had more variables and uncertainties; attacks were quick, violent, and often came from a blind side. In some encounters you saw the enemy first and were able to position your squadron for maximum effect of a first strike; other times your adversary got the jump on you and you had to resort to defensive tactics. Asymmetrical guerrilla warfare had the advantage of always striking first, choosing the time and place of battle. Fermo prepared his battlefield so the enemy would not see the first punch coming. Then all successive hits diminished the enemy, like a prizefighter getting his opponent on the ropes and delivering blow after blow so there was no hope of recovery.

Maurizio came up behind him as he sat in his chair finishing the evening's spartan meal, and said in a low, official voice, "*Il Volpe* wants a word with you."

Maurizio's background was not much different from Artemio's. As boys, they both grew up poor, distrusting and fearing the rich ruling class. Artemio, who was older, had believed Mussolini's promises of a better life for all Italians. Less than a generation later, younger men were growing up disillusioned with the regime and they found bolshevism attractive.

Artemio was escorted to a deeper level of the wood and earth fortification. Timbers sagged and cracked under their heavy burden. Dirt would trickle down and land on his head or shoulders. *This is what a rickety coal mine must be like*, he thought, *never really safe, always on the verge of collapse.* How many men died in places like this, mining for coal or metal that made other men rich? How many families lost fathers and sons because no one cared enough to make the mines safe?

Il Volpe was at a table with two other Communist party officials. The single carbide lamp in the room gave off a glaring light. The men were smoking and drinking; a pistol lay on the table. They were planning, not war, but politics. The high-ranking socialists were always fabricating back room deals, even now on the eve of battle. When *Il Volpe* saw Artemio in the doorway, he quickly flicked his head to the side, a signal for the two men to stop talking, get up and leave the room.

"Artemio, please sit down." He motioned for him to take a just-vacated chair. The regional party leader poured a clear liquid from a bottle with no label and pushed the glass towards Artemio.

"Vodka! From the Russian Bear. It must be good, right?" He smiled, revealing teeth broken by a Fascist policeman's night stick.

Artemio warily smiled back.

"You think I forgot you and our meeting in Milan?"

Artemio took a shot of the vodka and answered, "Yes, I thought you did not recognize me because of the scars on my face."

Il Volpe paused to take a good look at his face. "I find it better not to tell anyone of our first meeting. People like to believe I left for Spain to go into battle. I prefer that version to one of me running away from a fight with the Blackshirts."

"Sir, I am sure you fought valiantly in Spain," he said, not really knowing the truth.

"Artemio, Spain was a disaster. The Fascists kicked our asses. It is not something I am proud of." *Il Volpe* looked away for a moment, then resumed.

"This is not the reason I sent for you. I know you are not a Communist and do not believe in a socialist world order. Those can be very serious charges, leading to your arrest. However, I do owe you a debt of gratitude for saving my life in Milan." The Communist commander refilled the shot glasses.

"You are a good partisan fighter. Your mother was killed by Colonel Mueller because you put that transmitter in your house. These acts of bravery and sacrifice must be rewarded."

They both quickly swallowed another shot of vodka. *Il Volpe* made a pained face as the alcohol burned his throat.

"The problem I have with you is your mouth. In the Red Brigades we must all toe the party line. I know you cannot; you will always follow your conscience. This behavior is unacceptable for a Communist guerilla." He was being firm with Artemio, and he was obviously disappointed. "You follow some misguided religious concepts, the old ways."

Artemio could not hold his tongue any longer. "Is it misguided to put your fellow man's best interest ahead of your own? Is it misguided to love your country more than a political ideology?" He could see *Il Volpe* did not agree, and ire was stirring in him. He went on, his voice rising.

"I believe in a heaven after my death. It is because Communists have no faith in God that they must create ideals to control man's actions and economics. These constructs are artificial and must be propped up, because they cannot stand on their own naturally."

Il Volpe yelled, "It has been two thousand years of nature and the cold hearts of men chasing profits that has led to poverty, inequality, and war!" He would not be lectured to, not in his own command post.

Artemio looked at him and saw a man at the end of his rope. His hands had a slight tremor when he poured the vodka; his eyes were glassy. The man he remembered in Milan had been sharp-witted and clear-eyed. The pressure from the Germans, who wanted to kill him, and from Moscow pushing him to do more, was taking a toll on his mind and body.

Artemio answered the dangerous Brigade leader. "In Spain, what did you tell the townspeople when you executed their priests, mayors and school teachers? 'The priest was the cause of your poverty!'? Maybe you did not do so well in Spain because the common man does not approve of Stalin's purges."

Il Volpe continued to drink. It seemed to Artemio that he drank to anesthetize his soul. "I do not have the time to explain the entire Communist Manifesto to you. In the unlikely event that you do not get killed tomorrow facing down 200 elite German Waffen SS troopers and their armor, only then will I think of you as my problem," he said dismally.

"I think of you as my brother. I will cross the battlefield to save your life again tomorrow if I have to."

The drunk Communist laughed out loud. "You will save my life?" He shook his head. "Artemio, I have seen your plan; surely you know you will be the first to die." He stopped laughing, and in a serious tone he said, "Twin .50 caliber machine guns still attached to the nose of a Macchi fighter plane pulled on a wooden cart. In front of the entire German convoy! It is total madness!"

"It is not exactly as I had envisioned it," Artemio admitted. He had found out that Fermo's men were not as good as Eduardo when it came to taking apart derelict equipment, so the machine guns had stayed in the aircraft's nose, meaning Artemio would have to sit in the pilot's seat to fire them. The engine, shattered propellers, wings, and most of the fuselage had been removed to get what they needed off the mountain.

"The heavy automatic weapons will be on a stable platform once the wagon comes to rest. My team will be in concealment until Fermo gives the signal. Then they will wheel me and the cart across the road. There is some armor plating the men welded to the cart in front of me. It is not much protection, but enough if the motorcycle scouts open fire first. Hopefully it will buy enough time for a heavier piece of armor to present itself in my sights."

"Why were you against the mules pulling the wagon across the road?"

"The mules would have to be tied to the front of the wagon. If one were shot, it would fall in our path and then everything would stop. If a man is shot, we can pull him out and another man can immediately take his place."

"Your part of the ambush is a suicide mission. Yet there is no shortage of volunteers to fight with you. Even Gabriella wants to die by your side. I wish I knew how to motivate soldiers like that."

"Look at me, *Volpe*, I am ugly and disabled. It is not a skill that you can learn, a style to mimic. It is basic. Start by being honest with men. Tell a man the danger of the mission and why this goal is worth the expense of his life. They must be assured you do not waste men's lives needlessly. Most importantly, you must fight side by side in the trenches with them. Make their hardship your own. If you freeze with them in the winter, if you bleed with them in battle, they will follow you and fight with you."

Il Volpe looked into the lamp as water dripped onto the calcium carbide and hissed as it formed acetylene gas, then burned bright. "Artemio, have one last drink with me, then get a few hours rest. You must be at the battlefield before the sun." The brigade commander raised his glass; he was quite inebriated. "I will miss you, my ugly, disabled friend. These conversations are like a look back in time to a bygone age. A toast. A toast to the last of the dinosaurs, and the new age of enlightened men, God help us."

Artemio did not feel like sleeping, he was too nervous. What was he doing, planning a ground offensive? He was a pilot! His mind played *Il Volpe's* voice over and over again: 'You will be the first to die!' The thought of getting fresh air appealed to him. In the meadow the night was cool. Although past midnight, there was enough light to see the other partisans had the same apprehension. Some men walked together, talking quietly. A few men and women sat on a blanket under a tree, while Tino strummed a guitar. They sang a sad song Artemio had never heard before, a plaintive melody:

Heaven Cries

One morning I woke up
O bella, ciao, bella, ciao, bella, ciao ciao ciao
One morning I woke up
And found the invader.

Oh partisan, carry me away,
O bella, ciao, bella, ciao, bella, ciao ciao ciao,
Oh partisan, carry me away,
For I feel I'm dying.

And if I die as a partisan
O bella, ciao, bella, ciao, bella, ciao ciao ciao,
And if I die as a partisan
You have to bury me.

But bury me on Quaraglio Mountain
O bella, ciao, bella, ciao, bella, ciao ciao ciao,
But bury me on Quaraglio Mountain
Under the shadow of a beautiful flower.

And the people who will pass by
O bella, ciao, bella, ciao, bella, ciao ciao ciao,
And the people who will pass by
Will say to me 'what a beautiful flower'.

This is the flower of the partisan
O bella, ciao, bella, ciao, bella, ciao ciao ciao,
This is the flower of the partisan
Who died too young, for freedom!

CHAPTER 25
Roadside Ambush

The moon peeked over the trees, yielding its pale light, as if observing the activity on the road. Artemio, while haunted by *Il Volpe's* prediction, nevertheless worked tirelessly with his men to assemble the war wagon: a strange device, as if born from the inventiveness of Leonardo da Vinci. On the road Fermo and Maurizio were moving quickly, making sure all the preparations were accomplished precisely as planned.

Maurizio started yelling at Pepe, who had dug a pit for Fermo and the igniters along the east side of the road. The deep hole was too close to the jellied fuel; when it was set off, Fermo might get injured. The Quaraglio Commander broke up the fight, saying to Maurizio, "The risk is acceptable and there is no time to dig a new shelter." Maurizio accepted Fermo's decision, but he did not like being countermanded in front of the men.

The sun began to brighten the sky, although it was not yet in view, and Artemio knew the German column was approaching. He looked up and thought the moon and the sun were also going to fight today. The moon, however, was a good guerrilla warrior and knew to retreat back into the night.

The road was a main thoroughfare for traffic moving south from Piacenza. When the railroad tracks were bombed out, the Fascists would unload the train cars and truck the men and equipment south. The frontline German combat troops desperately needed the supplies, like an addict needs his drugs. Colonel Mueller and his SS men were responsible for keeping the road open, at all costs.

Artemio checked his position over again. A farmer's stone wall ran perpendicular to the road. It was over 4 feet high and was a good defensive position. It was thick enough to protect them from small arms fire and shrapnel. The tall overgrowth of trees and hedges hid the wooden cart. Mounted at a right angle on the cart was the propellerless nose of the Macchi fighter plane. Armor plate was affixed to the side of the cart that would be facing the German convoy. At the appropriate time, his men would move the hidden four-wheeled wagon onto the road, stopping in the middle to block the German progress. At this time, Artemio would fire the two heavy machine guns into the SS armor column.

He looked to the west side of the road: a sloping hill overlooked the valley. It was on this hill that Maurizio had dug in the entire partisan force. Unseen from the road, these partisans were prepared to fire their rifle and automatic weapons at the Germans in an enfilade pattern.

He was pleased to see *Il Volpe* on the hill shouting words of encouragement to the men before battle. It was not like him to be present at the fighting. He must have taken their talk last night to heart. *He is a new man today, a better leader of men*, Artemio thought. Fermo, standing in the middle of the road, made eye contact with Artemio and raised his right arm, and in it was the M-1 carbine gift Artemio had gotten him. Artemio returned the salute with the raising of his own M-1. Fermo smiled at him; he was in his element: love of combat ran through his veins. He then jumped into the hole Pepe had dug for him, completely disappearing with his igniters. Next to Artemio was Gabriella; they crouched behind the safety of the stone wall together, waiting. He looked at her as if to memorize the sight. Her hair was pinned up in a bun; there was no fear in her face. Not saying a word, he touched her cheek to feel its softness, maybe for the last time. At that moment he had no greater love for anyone. Her look back said, "I love you too." Neither spoke; they didn't have to, their souls were intertwined as lovers. He felt secure that this mighty stone wall would protect her during the battle. No matter what happened to him, she would live.

A huge dust cloud appeared down the road. It snaked closer to them, and gradually the loud clanging and squeaking of a mechanized army could be heard. Artemio, with the help of his men, got onto the wagon and into his pilot's seat. Everything felt natural and correct; his pulse was slow as a calmness overtook him. He was in the moment, experiencing serenity before the tempest. He placed his feet on the now useless pedals, and his hand naturally went for the control stick. He remembered crying in the hospital that he would never fly again, yet here he was, in a Macchi fighter plane, about to unleash a torrent of lead at his enemy in a life and death struggle. He did not care if he died in the pilot's seat today; it was how he wanted to go out. Not as a cripple, but as a fighter pilot. He could now see the lead elements of the German column approaching, and he felt exhilaration.

The coming battle made his heart beat loudly in his ears, time started to dilate as everything moved more slowly.

Fermo fired a red flair—the signal to attack. Artemio's group of men strained to push the heavy armored wagon. It did not move. He yelled from the pilot's seat, "Come on, men, let's go!" The men groaned as their muscles strained to roll the heavy cart. Timing was critical to this operation; all movements were synchronized with each other. It was not budging, as if its wheels were stuck in the fine dirt. Gabriella lunged forward from her position behind the wall. Wild-eyed, she shrieked at the men leaning into the wagon, her voice full of urgency. "Push! Push, you dogs! Push this wagon into hell! We have devils to kill today!" Other men from the wall came to help. They all feared Gabriella more than the Germans. Even so, the heavily loaded armored cart was slow to start; then, with gathering momentum, the wheels turned freely. Seconds felt like minutes to Artemio. At last, the wagon was in its proper position on the road, and he charged both machine guns from the cockpit bolt handles. In his gun sight were two motorcycles, followed by a four-wheeled armored car. The car had a 20 mm auto cannon in an open-top turret pointed directly at him. The two German soldiers operating the cannon had seen the wagon come onto the road. This caliber gun could easily pierce the thin iron plate protecting Artemio, and the Germans were furiously trying to load the cannon, their helmeted heads exposed above the turret. Artemio took a deep breath, then depressed the trigger on the control stick. The heavy machine guns gave out a roar.

Airplanes with spinning propellers and guns that must shoot through them have a rate-limiting device called a synchronization gear. This prevents the pilot from shooting off his own propeller. Artemio's machine guns, with no propeller, fired all their bullets within seconds. In the blink of an eye the view of the road changed. Smoke was coming off the red-hot barrels of the emptied machine guns. The motorcyclists had dissolved into a pink mist. The .50 caliber bullets had passed though the armored car, killing everyone inside. The carcass of the vehicle blocked the road and stopped the convoy at the planned location.

The next phase of the operation began when the partisans on the western hillside overlooking the road opened fire with all their rifles and medium machine guns. This produced a hail of bullets the entire length of the stalled convoy. The natural instinct for the Waffen SS men in the trucks was to jump out and find cover. The deep drainage ditch on the east side of the road was the obvious choice: an embankment to hide behind and return fire. Many of the Nazis were wearing the green and brown camouflage pattern of the SS Death's Head detachment. These men were transfers from the Russian front, where they had honed their combat skills in daily hand to hand fighting. Shovels, knives and handguns had been the weapons of desperation which had held back the red tide. These men were good soldiers, well trained in classic infantry maneuvers and willing to fight to their deaths.

But Fermo had used this tactic of deception before and had anticipated this reaction. Along the floor of the trench he had placed jerry cans filled with napalm, white phosphorous mortar rounds, and an electrical igniter, then pigtailed the wires together and run them to his foxhole. All the cans and wires were covered with a thin layer of dirt, so the poor devils in the trap wouldn't see it coming.

Fermo waited until the maximum number of casualties was possible, then he electrically ignited the incendiaries. Multiple red balls of fire streaked skyward, black smoke and the foul smell of burning napalm and burning human flesh flowed across the road and filled the air. Thin white lines of hot phosphorous flew upward, then fell to earth, scorching men's skin and scattering as they bounced on the road. One white line fell down into Fermo's foxhole. Germans were running about, screaming, with white phosphorous burning their bodies. They ripped their clothes to get it off.

The partisans should have charged down the hill and finished off the remaining Nazi soldiers while they were disoriented. In the ancient world, to stop a hemorrhaging wound a hot iron was used to cauterize it. When the iron was red hot, that was the proper time to apply it. If the physician waited and it cooled, the opportunity was lost. The partisans waited. They did not charge down the hill, because a single armored half-track was still in the fight. Its driver was dead, so the behemoth could not move, but two machine guns continued to fire at the partisans on the hill, pinning them down. Artemio and his men on the road could not get a clean shot at the Hanomag, owing to all the burning vehicles in between. There is a critical time in combat, when a loss of initiative may push a victory into defeat as the momentum of battle shifts. The remaining Waffen SS were starting to rally and counterattack. The partisans on the hill were not a disciplined army. In the past, these irregular units had been known to break and run off the battlefield.

Artemio looked onto the road from his vantage point and saw something that made his spine tingle. Gabriella had left the security of the stone wall and was walking on the road. She held a German MP 44 submachine gun on her hip and was firing at running SS troopers. She was in some kind of trance-like state, a killing machine. Painfully he struggled to get down off the wagon. As he got to the road, he noticed the partisans on the hill had stopped firing so as not to hit Gabriella. She walked up to Fermo's position and looked in to see if he was alive. She turned and continued firing her submachine gun at the Nazi troops along the road, only stopping to reload fresh magazines. The fearless female partisan worked her way between the burning trench and the open-top armored personnel carrier. Having exhausted all the 9 mm ammo, she threw down the submachine gun. With her back against the last functioning fighting vehicle, she pulled the pin on three grenades. Each grenade was thrown one at a time, up into the fire-breathing dragon's mouth. One grenade was thrown back out at her and detonated in the burning trench. She heard multiple taps of shrapnel hitting the personnel carrier behind her. The other two grenades exploded in the Hanomag, and the machine guns fell silent. Artemio had almost reached her when she drew her Broomhandle Mauser pistol from its holster. He yelled for her to stop, but between the adrenaline rush and the grenades going off near her, she neither saw nor heard him. She walked to the back of the vehicle, opened the two big steel doors, and entered. He was running towards her as fast as his limp allowed when he saw movement in the open-top personnel carrier—it was Gabriella. She stood in the personnel carrier, her face looking down as she aimed her pistol. Coldly, methodically, she executed each wounded German soldier in that vehicle.

The Italian partisans on the hillside let out a blood-curdling scream as they charged the remains of the convoy. The few remaining Germans fired a shot or two, then dropped their weapons and surrendered. Artemio ran over to

Gabriella, who had climbed out of the vehicle, and hugged her tight. Her body was stiff, like a mannequin, her eyes cold and lifeless. He tried to lay her down in the grass on the side of the road. She resisted and finally spoke, saying, "We must get to Fermo. He is burned."

When they got to the foxhole, Maurizio was already there, helping Fermo out. He was badly scalded on his face and neck by the phosphorous that had fallen back to earth.

"Where is Dr. Fugazza? Get him to Dr. Fugazza, now! You, Tino, go find the Germans' medical supplies! They will have morphine and bandages. Move!" Artemio shouted.

He saw across the road that the Italians were laying out their dead and wounded. The pudgy young boy, Lanzo, was on his back, struggling to breathe. Artemio went over and knelt down beside him. The partisan had a chest wound. Pink frothing blood was coming out his mouth, and a sucking sound could be heard from his chest. Lanzo looked up. His face was full of fear, and his body quivered. Artemio got even closer, leaned over, and spoke to the young man.

"You are a brave soldier, Lanzo, but your fight is over now. I promise you, I will visit your father and tell him you were a hero today. All of Italy owes you their gratitude." Artemio saw the boy's face become calmer and colder. "Relax now, soon you will be with your other Father in heaven. There will be no sorrow or suffering when you are in His bosom."

Lanzo closed his eyes and departed.

Artemio was standing in the road with Gabriella when *Il Volpe* approached. He was smiling from ear to ear, and he kissed Artemio on both checks. "It is good to see you alive, my brother." He then hugged Gabriella's rigid body. "You are our greatest asset," he said to her, "better than a tank! We have Archangel Gabriel, and she blows her trumpet of destruction." Artemio could see the post-action exhilaration in him. He continued talking rapidly. "And you, Comrade, did not have to save my life today! But I got you a present anyway. Come with me."

As they walked along the road, unexploded ordnance detonated around them. Wounded German soldiers were crying out in pain, but no one tended to them. On his knees, in front of an armored personnel carrier, was a stunned Colonel Mueller.

Il Volpe was like a little boy, exclaiming, "We got him, we got him!" A partisan soldier, standing behind Mueller, pressed the barrel of his Beretta submachine gun against the officer's neck, while his left hand clutched a tuft of blond hair to keep Mueller's face up. The brigade commander taunted, "Come on, Artemio, this is for the murder of your mother. Go ahead, put a bullet in him. We all know he deserves it."

Artemio was caught up in all the chaos. The shouts and cries, the sights and smells of battle, had roused his blood lust. "This bat deserves to be sent back to hell!" he cried. He reached for the M-1 carbine slung across his back.

Il Volpe grabbed his arm to stop him. "Oh no, you must use his own gun," he explained. "A man's pistol is who he is. Be he a military officer or a policeman, he trains with his gun and cleans it. He cares for it like a baby. This gun gives him authority. He may have even taken others' lives with his gun." *Il Volpe* looked at Mueller with contempt, then looked at Artemio and smiled. "Now is the ultimate betrayal: his own handgun is turned on him. His own gun will take his life!" The bearded Communist put the P-38 Nazi-issue pistol in Artemio's hand.

Artemio looked in the eyes of the bewildered German and put the 9 mm to Mueller's temple. In his mind he saw hundreds of Jews toiling away in prison garb at Auschwitz-Birkenau, some of them making this gun. They all stopped to look up, to see this Nazi officer shot in the head with the gun they'd made. This would be pure justice. Then a bodiless voice from the Sahara desert spoke into his left ear. "So you think your God will take you into heaven after you've murdered five men, *Ace*?" Another voice in his mind seemed to say, "The combat is over. This is murder!"

Artemio relaxed his index finger off the trigger. He gave the gun back to *Il Volpe* and walked away from the execution.

"Do it for your mother! What? Do you think you are above all of this? You're not! You are just like us!" *Il Volpe* yelled at his back. Artemio knew he was right. He was not feeling clean, just less dirty.

Then he heard a familiar voice proclaim, "This is for my family and my village!" A loud pistol shot rang out directly behind him. He turned quickly to see. It was Gabriella who had grabbed the P-38 from *Il Volpe's* hand and shot Mueller in the head. His body jerked up, then slumped over lifelessly to the side as it landed on the cobblestone road. Evil drained from the head wound.

The few German prisoners were standing next to a knocked out half-track. Partisan guards fired submachine guns into the disarmed men. This was standard procedure for the Red Brigades: no prisoners taken. The Nazis would have done the same to them if they had been victorious. Artemio wondered, *When will it ever end?*

A cold rain started to drizzle down onto the road. The fires still flickered. Steam came off the hot metal touched by the cleansing water. He knew Heaven was crying. Looking upon this scene of carnage, he started to get a pain in his stomach and his knees buckled. The nausea was not from the smell of burning flesh or the sight of dead bodies strewn everywhere. The road was littered with disabled trucks and armored half-tracks burning a black, oily smoke. He realized at this moment, above the moans of the wounded and the smells of fire and brimstone, that there was no need to book a passage to hell; man had created it right here on earth. This is the road to perdition. Satan has triumphed over good. The Evil One is a deceiver, he tricks man into believing there is a good side and a bad side. The truth is, only a single man's action can be moral or immoral.

He was convinced, now more than ever, that all of mankind was doomed unless individuals changed. He himself did not have much longer to live. Why should he? He was part of the problem. The angel in the holocaust-bound train car had told him. The world does not need warriors, now it needs peacemakers.

CHAPTER 26
Interpretation of Dreams

After a battle is a rousing time. Survivors are so elated to be alive that there is no desire for relaxation or sleep. The mind has clarity of thought and purpose after an engagement; ideas whiz around like bullets. The change in brain chemistry brings forth an ability to understand and produce complicated schemes, even planning for a future after the war.

Artemio decided to go for a jaunt uphill to the horse stables, thinking it would burn off some of his nervous energy. The terrain surprised him with how steep the incline became. His breaths came short and quick—the hallmark of exercise at this altitude. He came to rest on a plateau and looked up at the strong mountain sun, its rays energizing him. For a moment, he dreamed of bringing all Italians onto Quaraglio Mountain to keep them safe from the war. He heard a familiar sound behind him: a rifle bolt open, a cartridge chambered, then a bolt close. He raised his arms above his head and turned around slowly. Both men were surprised to recognize each other.

"Artemio, what are you doing up here?" demanded Pepe.

"It is such a beautiful day, I was in the mood for a walk."

Pepe thought the notion of an afternoon stroll when the Luftwaffe was searching for partisans was ludicrous. "Okay, but stay under the trees. I have already seen two German Storch reconnaissance planes fly over. I think they are mad as hornets after our raid on that convoy."

"Pepe, that was no raid! We killed over two hundred of their best troops, and Colonel Mueller. That is victory!"

"Yes, we did well. The war is not over, though." He played with his handlebar mustache, making the ends pointy. "Last night they delivered the Fascist pilot. He was guarded by ten men! That is a big detachment, easily noticed by informers looking to sell information. I don't like this idea of keeping high-value prisoners on our mountain. It needlessly increases clashes with Blackshirts."

Pepe had a sudden muscular eyelid twitch. Artemio had never noticed this tic before. Pepe seemed different; maybe it was from digging the foxhole too close to the incendiaries and causing Fermo's injury. The mountain sentry continued, "He is a captain, like you. I think the Fascists are looking for him. What if they find out he is here?" There was a note of fear in his voice.

"The Blackshirts will not attack Quaraglio. That is the reason the Russian Bear wants him held here. They are afraid of us."

"*They* are afraid of *us*? How is that possible? They have tanks and planes!" he exclaimed, his anxiety starting to build.

"Pepe, the two of us were not here during that massive assault on Quaraglio last fall, but I am told the Fascists took heavy casualties. Not only that, but the guns and equipment they lost in the attack became ours, to use against them! I don't think they will risk that again."

Pepe looked up into the sky for more planes, not comforted by the disabled man's words of encouragement. But Artemio had an ulterior motive for being at the stables, and it was not for fresh air. "I will show you how broken in spirit these men of Mussolini are," Artemio said. "Where is the pilot being held? I would like to meet him."

"You cannot! He is here in the horse barn, but I have strict orders, from Maurizio: no one is to have contact with him."

"Pepe, come on. I can question him as only a fellow pilot could. I will extract information out of him. You can come along and watch." Pepe pondered this, then slowly nodded. "Bring your rifle to protect me," Artemio said sarcastically. Pepe snickered, knowing Artemio would protect him.

His eyes widened as they beheld the prisoner. The partisans had given their captive tattered peasant clothes to wear. The threadbare shirt and pants were filthy and malodorous. The hair on his head was disheveled, and he had a beard longer than a few days growth. Artemio showed no emotion, so the prison guard would not know they had a history. The man sitting in the hay, handcuffed to the wall, was Mario Piaggio, his wingman and college roommate.

"Oh, my God," Mario said in a low voice as he saw his best friend walk into the horse stall. Artemio made a facial grimace and shook his head, warning Mario not to reveal their friendship. Mario went silent.

Artemio behaved like a grand inquisitor. "So this is the brave *Repubblica de Salo* pilot who strafes our men in an open field?" Mario stared at the unpainted wall in complete silence. He would not look at nor speak to his captors.

"What type of plane did you fly, Captain?" Again, no response from Mario.

"How many planes in your squadron? Where is your airfield, Captain?" Artemio looked at his friend, once the dashing aviator, the one all the girls wanted to meet. Now he was pathetic, with one hand manacled above his head. He had bruises on his face, probably from beatings, although nothing that would leave a permanent scar. He sat on hay with horse manure all around him.

"Are there German planes at your airbase?"

Still no answer. The prisoner glared furiously.

"Pepe! Go find Maurizio. If he is to be the judge in this matter, I want him to see the guilt of this Fascist pig refusing to answer questions."

"Yes, sir." Pepe turned to run out of the barn.

Artemio yelled, "Wait! Let me have your weapon so I can keep guard on him."

The gullible partisan handed him the rifle saying, "Be careful! He is devious."

After Pepe was clear of the barn, Artemio moved closer and crouched in front of his old friend, "Are you hurt?" he asked quietly.

"Your friends roughed me up a bit, but I'm fine." Artemio thought of the pounding Herr Mueller's men had given him, and grinned sardonically. "They are not the experts the Germans are at roughing up prisoners."

"I am thirsty. Do you have any water?"

Artemio walked to the horse trough and dipped a ladle into it, then brought it to the beaten man. Mario reached out with his free hand to bring it to his lips. He drank the stale, equine water greedily, the excess streaming down both sides of his mouth.

"What are you doing here with these commie bastards?" he asked between gulps.

Artemio was shocked by that language. These men had rescued him from the death camps of the Reich. They were his new family, and he was in love with a partisan commander. How far had he traveled from Mario? How could Mario be so callus to his fate, or did he just not care? Could they ever be friends again?

He cleared his throat and answered, "Mario, I am a respected partisan fighter now, killing German invaders and driving them from our homeland."

Mario's face turned stone cold. "You? In league with this rabble? Then you are a traitor to Italy and should be shot."

"*I* should be shot? Like your friend Galeazzo Ciano, Mussolini's son-in-law?" Mario's face changed at hearing that name. "That's right, the man who got you into Regia Aeronautica. Your hero. The Blackshirts lined up the whole Fascist Grand Council, under orders from *Il Duce* himself, and shot them in the back. Galeazzo was his own son-in-law, yet that could not save him from a Blackshirt bullet!" Artemio knelt on one knee and in a solemn voice said, "I have news for you, airman. The plan is to put you on trial and shoot you tomorrow. With a Communist bullet." Mario paled as his situation became clear. Unless Artemio could help him, this was his last day on earth.

Now that he had Mario's full attention, he asked again. "Did you strafe any partisans?"

Mario was sick and tired of this war. His hands had blood on them, but he would not be convicted of something he had not done.

"No! My men and I have only one mission. We maintain a 24-hour air surveillance over Piacenza, watching for Allied heavy bombers. If a pilot detects them, he radios back to base the coordinates and heading. Then the Germans scramble up their Messerschmitts and Focke-Wulf fighters."

"The charges will say that you were strafing partisans, and it was their return fire that brought your plane down."

"That is a lie!" protested Mario. "I was jumped by three high-altitude RAF Spitfires coming down from the sun. I never saw them. The engine started to smoke and hydraulic fuel sprayed all over the cabin. I lost control of my plane. No flaps or rudder response. I parachuted into a field and was picked up by a band of *Giustizia e Libertà* partisans." He looked away, humiliated, and added, "Later they traded me to the Red Brigade for a German machine gun. That's what my life was worth to them—a lousy machine gun."

Artemio was now able to piece it together. The *Giustizia e Libertà* partisans did not fight the Germans much, so an MG-42 was quite a prize to them. Also they would never execute a fellow Italian, Fascist or not. The men of the Red Brigades, however, relished killing any Fascist they could get their hands on.

"Artemio, unshackle me. Give me a rifle and let me make a run for it. C'mon, old friend, it is the only chance I've got."

"Do you know where you are?" Artemio demanded, almost mad at that stupid idea. "This is Quaraglio! You would not get five hundred yards before a sniper took off your head. These men train with their rifles daily. They are all marksmen." Artemio thought for a moment. "The only chance we have for you to survive is for you to denounce Mussolini and this new Italian Social Republic."

Mario was not enthusiastic about that plan. "I know Mussolini is a sad character in this tragedy we call Italy, but what are we to do? He is still our leader, and like a drunken father, we must stand by him." He added, "The King's unconditional surrender to General Eisenhower was an insult. We are a proud people and should fight to a negotiated peace accord that would give us guarantees."

"Mario, your way only prolongs the killing. The Americans bomb our cities because of Mussolini, the Germans shoot our civilians because the *Repubblica di Salo* lets them."

"No! The Germans kill our civilians because partisans blow up their convoys! Artemio, *you* are the traitor who gets our civilians killed."

"How can I be a traitor?" Artemio turned his head away, feeling shame. "My country has surrendered. The Italian Army has walked off the battlefield. It is now the duty of every Italian to force the Germans off our land. You must understand this and become a freedom fighter also. It is the only way you can persevere through a trial."

Mario became quiet and thought for a minute about his life. Finally he asked in a low tone, "You once told me back in Milan that the mural of The Last Supper spoke to you and revealed a betrayer in our midst. Was it me? Do you think I am the Judas?"

"No." Artemio looked at his forlorn college roommate. He remembered the wilderness, being tempted by the devil. The voice in his head resounded simultaneously in the past and present. "I know now, it is not just I who was deceived. All Italians were seduced by *Il Duce*, then double-crossed. Mussolini is the Judas Iscariot who sold us out for thirty pieces of silver. Like the wayward apostle, Benito fell under the influence of that devil Hitler."

Mario was uncomfortable with this kind of talk, but knew it was true. "I know of the atrocities in Yugoslavia," he admitted slowly. "I have flown over the Rab concentration camp, low enough to see thousands of people behind the barbed wire fences."

"Mario, this is your time. You must recant Fascism publicly at the trial and save yourself. I don't want to see any more of my friends die."

"Friends die? Save yourself? You mean like I should have saved Gitano! You think I wasn't looking out for him, don't you? You blame me for his death!" His guilt was burning inside him and he could not wait for Artemio to accuse him first.

"I heard about Gitano when I was in the hospital in Sicily, from Donatella. What exactly happened to him?"

"He tried to be you, as always. He tried to fly like you and become an ace." Mario turned away to hide the tears that were forming. "You. You should have been there to protect him. You were always better at that than I was."

"I was in a coma and almost died in that hospital. Why weren't you looking after him? I told you, you are your brother's keeper!"

Mario stared at his filthy peasant shoes. Artemio wondered how three boys with so much promise in life had ended up so wrong.

Finally Mario spoke, "I came to look in on you once, at the Tobruk hospital. I could not stand to see you like that, so I never went back. Gitano went almost every day to see if you would regain consciousness, until we were ordered to pull back, then we had to leave you."

Artemio became melancholy and started to miss the old days in Milan, thinking about their friendship. Then he remembered their present reality and jumped to his feet to look out the window to see if Pepe was on his way back, but the hillside was bare.

"Tell me exactly how Gitano got shot down," he said quietly, squatting down in front of his old roommate.

Mario's voice got choked up as he recounted the tale. "After our defeat at the battle of El Alamein, we were always falling back as the British advanced. Our squadron was ordered to make a stand at Tripoli. Gitano was my wingman. We flew sorties against the RAF; by now they had squadrons of their new Spitfire planes. On this one mission they hit us by surprise and our formation split up. Gitano climbed to a high altitude, then dove down onto the English in their four-lines-abreast battle formation, exactly the way you taught us to do. His machine guns were firing as he closed with them. Then he banked perfectly, but the Spitfires have a tighter turning radius. An Englishman followed him into the turn and fired his eight machine guns into Gitano's plane. His Macchi fighter dropped like a stone. It was found later, on a farm, burned to ashes.

Tears welled up in Artemio's eyes. It seemed it was the tactics he'd taught them that killed Gitano.

Then he asked Mario, "Were his parents told of his death?"

"I personally drove out to their farm commune. It was close to Tripoli. When his parents answered the front door their expression was like they were afraid of me. I expected sadness and crying. There was none. I was thanked for coming out to tell them, but not asked in. This is the weird part: they shut the front door in my face."

"Artemio! Get away from that man."

A group of partisans stood in the doorway of the stable. "I gave strict orders the prisoner is not to be spoken to!"

Maurizio commanded. Pepe ran up to Artemio and snatched his rifle back.

"Maurizio," Artemio replied calmly, "I am glad you are here. This man wishes to defect to our side and he disavows all the tenets of Fascism." Seeing resolute contempt in the senior partisan's face, he added, "He denies ever shooting at partisans." Seeing no softening, he added, "This man could prove very useful to us in the future."

"It is only because Fermo has great respect for you that I don't knock you down and lock you up in the next stall!" Maurizio yelled. He turned and stormed out.

A group of Red guardsmen, an internal security force, escorted Artemio to the dormitory cabin in the woods. He was told he was under house arrest and would not be allowed to leave.

Much later that evening, Gabriella arrived, exhausted from leading a night patrol. While she ate cold, leftover spaghetti, Artemio sat across from her in the community kitchen. He informed her that the captured pilot was Mario Piaggio, and the plan was to execute him on trumped up charges. Gabriella did not seem interested. Her troops had run into a patrol of Blackshirts and there had been a fierce gun battle. Her mind was on the recent combat she'd barely survived.

In bed that evening Artemio could not stop talking about the pilot's innocence of the charges. "Mario's life must be spared," he repeated to her. Somehow they had to derail the trial.

The tired officer was getting annoyed. "I know he is your friend, but he did continue to fight after Italy surrendered. He will get what he deserves!" she said loudly. Then Gabriella held him close and whispered in his ear, "The

Communists want—and will get—a conviction. There is nothing we can do about it tonight. Let's get a good night's sleep and work on it in the morning."

"I can't," he said, mad at himself. "I will get the nightmare of my father and the donkey again."

"Are you still getting those?" She sat up in bed, leaning on one elbow. "I thought about it, and I believe the dream is a message of some kind."

"A message! What kind of a message?"

"Orders for you to do something."

"Orders?" He was puzzled and dumbfounded.

"Well, as I see it, your father, in the dream, is really the voice of God. He is telling you to get the donkey off the road, right?"

"Yes," he said apprehensively, waiting for the next part of her explanation.

"What if the donkey represents all of us? You know, people going in the wrong direction. You are to change our direction. Direct humanity out of danger's way, back into the light, back to Him. If we don't change, we will bring disaster upon ourselves." She looked at him and saw he was taking it in. "The policeman in your dream shooting Contessa seems to me to be the Evil One."

"Wow, Gabriella that is really profound. I think Sigmund Freud would have a field day with that." Even though he was trying to make a joke of it, the sense of her words shook him profoundly. What she said felt... right. True.

"There is more." He looked into her eyes, fearful of what else she would say.

"You said your father untied the load of wood from the donkey and put it on your back."

"Yes, that is what happened."

"Don't you see? The wood on your back! The wood is the cross, like Jesus carries. This mission in front of you is your cross to bear to lessen the suffering of many."

Artemio stared at the ceiling, contemplating Gabriella's interpretation of the dream. Where would this mission lead him? What would happen to him?

CHAPTER 27
Piacentina

The diminutive Topolino was easy to maneuver through the narrow streets of Piacenza. Artemio had to navigate a maze of bicycles and pedestrians that shared the cobblestone roadway. Piacenza had been a garrison town for the Roman Empire; Julius Caesar's army had used it as a place to water their horses, where a centurion could get a hot meal before continuing the march north into the provinces. The Germans had found a similar use for the city. They refueled their war machines there and rested the men before the ride south to fight the Allied forces.

On this warm spring day, the sunlight came down between the buildings. It warmed wet clothes pinned on a line, strung overhead. What light fell to earth produced a dappled pattern on the streets. Last night's rain had left a shine that glistened on all the stone. Gabriella, with her belly bulge, looked over at Artemio driving and gave him a smile, the kind that made her whole face brighten. It was the look that would make any man melt inside. She only gave that smile to him, and he never tired of it. Artemio secretly wished Gabriella were carrying his baby.

"Oh look, Artemio, a man selling gelato on the side of the street! Please, please pull over and buy me a cone."

"Okay. Sometimes you are such a little girl." He loved when that side of her emerged.

Behind the pushcart was an unassuming man with long, thick sideburns and a thick mustache. The ice cream vendor's uniform consisted of a red-striped shirt and a white straight-brim hat. He had three different flavors that he had made only hours before. Gabriella decided on two scoops of mint chocolate. Elated, she walked away, licking her cone, her gait one that could almost be classified as a skip, if not for the additional weight in the front of her dress.

There was a soccer game going on in the street, the way city kids play the game: buildings as boundaries and movable goals in the road, to be shifted as traffic appeared. Her love of the sport got the better of her and Gabriella stopped to watch. Artemio paid the vendor at the pushcart. As he handed over the *lire,* he also made a clandestine signal all partisans would know. Artemio's left hand scratched the side of his neck then gave a slight tug of the ear lobe. On seeing Artemio's hand signal, the man said, "A fine day to be traveling." This response meant, *Yes, me too.*

Artemio grinned as he thought that everyone in the city was probably a partisan. On Quaraglio, men carried their weapons outright and wore red armbands. Here in the city, the cause was hidden. The passion was just as strong, but it had to be subversive. The Germans could look at a map with shaded areas and think they knew what territory they controlled. Piacenza was considered German territory. The irony was that *Il Volpe's* headquarters was also here. The partisans operated a shadow army that mirrored the German army. Knowing nothing of this secret war, children kicked and passed the soccer ball: boys and girls enjoying the good weather after a long winter.

All of a sudden, a solitary German supply truck careened around the corner. A young girl playing the goalie position caught the ball with her two hands to prevent a score. Her back was to the goal—and to the rumbling truck. The driver saw the children playing in the road and slammed on the brakes. The worn out pads produced a squeal like metal on metal, but the heavily laden Daimler-Benz truck could not stop soon enough. The girl had a look of terror on her face as she first heard the truck brakes, then saw Gabriella running toward her. The soccer player flew through the air into a doorway as the sprinting, five-foot-10-inch woman pushed the girl out of the way. Daimler's three-pointed star on the hood was all Gabriella saw as the truck hit her.

Artemio, standing beside the pushcart, watched in horror as Gabriella's body was tossed like a rag doll. She was thrown onto the sidewalk, landing on her back, her body writhing uncontrollably. When the transport did stop, a feeble, elderly man climbed out of the driver's seat. Frightened by the havoc he had created, he approached her cautiously. The German soldier was astonished to see a Broomhandle Mauser lying on the street. On impact, it had fallen out of Gabriella's hidden compartment.

"Ah! Partisans!" he yelled. The driver nervously fumbled with the clasp on the leather holster as he tried to draw his own pistol.

Artemio raced down the street. His heart was pounding and he gasped for breath. All he knew was that his precious Gabriella was in danger. In the terror of the moment, the injury to his left leg was forgotten. There was no reality except the imperative to protect her. With his right hand, he drew the Hitler Youth knife that Lanzo had given him from his left forearm sleeve. The German soldier had his right arm extended as he pointed his pistol at Gabriella, about to shoot. Her face was frozen as she stared down the barrel of the 9 mm Luger. Artemio ran in front of the German driver, taking him by surprise. He grabbed the driver's gun hand with his left and pushed it skyward. The pistol discharged a single round into the air. The two men were now face to face; Artemio could smell the stench of alcohol on the driver's breath. He slowly and deeply ran the edged weapon in his right hand across the driver's throat. The German's face went from wide-eyed surprise to dazed lifelessness as arterial blood from both carotids spreyed in the air and splattered onto Artemio's shirt. As the heart continued its beat, more bright red blood spewed onto the street, the truck hood, even onto the door above Gabriella's head, before gravity pulled the standing corpse down.

Artemio quickly came to Gabriella's side. He thought he had seen her die. She was still shaken, first by her desperate effort to save the girl's life, then by the sight of an enemy soldier with a gun pointed at her, about to fire. She could not move. The little girl whose life she'd saved got to her feet and ran away. Gabriella started crying hysterically. "No more, no more killing!" Her head was not bleeding outwardly, but it was starting to swell under the skin. She quieted down but still mumbled, "No more killing. Please, no more killing!" Artemio hugged her and held her head.

The gelato man picked up both pistols and helped carry her back to the car. He gave them ice for her head. The experienced partisan said to Artemio, "Here is a towel to clean the blood off of your face. Take this extra shirt of mine to change out of that bloody one." After a quick wipe down, he spoke again. "Get out of here, now! The Fascist police will have heard that gun shot. I will take care of this mess. Don't worry, neither that German's body nor the truck will ever be seen again." He handed Artemio back Gabriella's Mauser.

Artemio nodded to the urban guerrilla. "Thank you, Comrade, for everything you have done here today." Then the two Quaraglio partisans sped away towards *Il Volpe's* lair.

The warehouse at the end of the street had an old faded sign indicating they sold olive oil. Past the loading dock were the offices of the highest ranking Communist party member. In a small side room, Dr. Fugazza examined Gabriella: looking at the way her pupils reacted to light, determining if she knew where she was, posing a simple math question, conducting a full neurological exam. Further down the hall, behind a closed door, Artemio visited with *Il Volpe*.

"What are you doing in that asinine red stripped shirt? Are you trying to stand out for the Nazis to find you?" *Il Volpe* demanded.

"It is a long story. We risked our lives to get here to see you, *Volpe*." Artemio explained who the pilot in captivity on Quaraglio Mountain was. The Guerrilla leader had many other things on his mind and had almost forgotten about the trial. Artemio pressed his case to spare Mario's life, but *Il Volpe* refused to listen.

"I would never prevent the execution of a Fascist. I could not! Artemio, look at my position in the Communist party. I would become suspected of subversive activity."

"You told me once that you owed me your life. I stopped the Blackshirts from beating you to death that night in Milan. Well, I am calling in that favor, for my friend Mario's life."

"I respect how you honor friendship, but you are misguided about this man. He is a *Repubblica di Salo* fighter pilot. He rejected the chance to disarm; instead, he took up arms with the German invaders. Now he shoots at partisans and American bombers. These are the actions that condemn him."

"*Volpe,* he never shot at any Italians. Mario only radioed in positions of Allied planes for the Germans. He told me that he rejects all Fascist teachings and ideals."

"And you believe him, do you? Ahh!" He threw his right hand up in the air to accentuate the absurdity. "He would say anything to save his skin."

"He is my friend. No, more like a brother to me. I would lay down my life for him, as I did for you."

Il Volpe frowned. "You might have, too." He thought for a moment.

"The best I can do is to not answer future requests for orders. With Fermo in the hospital, Maurizio can't shit without a confirmation from a superior. When they call me for what to do about your Fascist pilot friend, I will not respond. This will buy you hours, perhaps a day."

Hiding his disappointment, Artemio said, "Thank you, sir, for your help." He wished *Il Volpe* could have done more, but this gave him time to plan a strategy.

"Sit and have a drink with me, while the good doctor finishes up with Gabriella."

Il Volpe poured two shots of grappa—a distilled spirit made from the pomace of the leftover skins and seeds of grapes.

"Where did you get grappa? I have not seen a bottle of that in two years."

"Artemio, my friend, even in Nazi-occupied Europe, there is not a vineyard that is harvested without the approval of the Communist Workers Union."

"I did not know that they were still so pervasive." Both men swallowed the contents of their glasses. *Il Volpe* refilled them.

From under his black beret he added, "The sign out front says olive oil wholesaler, but grappa is our real money maker."

"Be careful, you are starting to sound like a capitalist."

Both men let out a big laugh. Artemio had almost forgotten how good humor could make you feel. *In these times, laughter is found in few places*, he mused. He said to *Il Volpe*, "I never understood why Italian Communists fight so hard on the battlefield when they know Churchill and Roosevelt will never stand for a Communist government in Italy."

The man across from him looked like a fox as his eyes lit up. "Now you are on a subject I love to discuss," he said, as he swallowed the next mouthful. "We will become political after the war, no more throwing Molotov cocktails. When we put the bombs away, then the real work begins, at the election box. Churchill and Roosevelt will have nothing to say if Italy *votes* in a Communist government. Hey, that's how democracy works, right?"

Artemio knew that after this favor, if he succeeded in freeing Mario, he would never again see the man he'd rescued in Milan. So he said, "I will miss you, *Volpe*; I know you have a big heart. You keep up a façade before your comrades, who would mistake kindness for weakness."

"I wish you could stay longer. Maybe with enough time I could figure you out. You are an influential man with no agenda."

"My agenda is mankind. Gabriella says my dream is to save humanity."

The older man thought about that for a moment. "Yes, I can see that. As a diplomat or ambassador maybe." Artemio's face turned white.

"What is the matter? You look like you just saw a ghost."

Artemio spoke faintly, "I met a Bedouin living in a tent in the Sahara desert. He was a mystic. A tall, spiritual Muslim man who wandered the sands, like Mohamed himself. He told me the exact same thing. I never understood him, but all his prophesies are coming to fruition."

Il Volpe stood up. "I would not put any stock in the ravings of this Mohamed character. Your most important job now is to live long enough to realize your dream."

At that moment Doctor Fugazza passed through the door, Gabriella standing behind him. He announced, "Artemio, it is my medical opinion that your girlfriend has sustained a mild concussion. Get her back to base as soon as possible and let her rest a few days."

"I don't need any rest. I'm fine," the tough partisan protested.

"Gabriella, please listen to the doctor," insisted Artemio. Then he looked at Doctor Fugazza and asked, "How is Fermo doing in the Bobbio Hospital?"

"Oh, he is an even worse patient then she is. He has second-degree burns on his face and neck. His right shoulder has third-degree burns from the phosphorous. He almost lost an eye. All he talks about is getting back to his mountain home."

Artemio was relieved to hear he was recovering, and Gabriella managed a wan smile.

Back at the car, Gabriella lowered the seat of the Topolino as far back as it would incline. She closed her eyes but could not sleep, not with the day's events running like a loop in her mind. Artemio knew all the streets of Piacenza; he'd run them as a boy. Now they seemed out of place to him. He saw them as a foreigner would, because he was already becoming a stranger. After tonight, he would never be able to return home again.

CHAPTER 28
Manhunt

Artemio steered the nimble Italian car into the hidden cavern at the base of Quaraglio, then locked the olive wood doors of the ancient garage to secure the Topolino. Dusk was settling in.

Gabriella, although not usually vain, combed her hair to cover the head bruise. Standing behind him, she said stoically, "Don't say anything, and just follow my lead."

"Gabriella," Artemio protested, "you took a hit on the head; please let me handle this." He stared at the black and blue welt; it had improved with the ice, but he was sure it was still painful.

She frowned, knowing he could not perform her duties without raising suspicion. "You can't. When it comes to prisoners and the carrying out of sentences, these men know it's my job. They will only follow my orders. If you speak for me, they will know something is not right."

The two collaborators walked up Quaraglio Mountain, signaling at every checkpoint and bunker. She told key men along the route that there would be riders coming down later with the Fascist pilot to execute him. Sentries should not get involved; let them pass unmolested. The men she spoke to nodded; some grinned. They had seen many men take their last ride accompanied by this angel of death.

It was dark when they got to the top of the mountain. Artemio parted from her and ate dinner alone. He followed the plan and saddled three horses. Nervously, he waited below the corral in the darkness of the early morning.

Gabriella made her way to the stables on the upper hill. She knew the stall that housed the prisoner was at the end of the building. Pepe was on guard duty. He put up his rifle and commanded, "Halt!" She did not stop. She walked right up to him as he held out his Carcano rifle in a blocking manner.

She sneered as she looked into his eyes. "Stand down, soldier. I have orders to take this prisoner."

"Wait a minute, Gabriella! No one has told me that," Pepe said, confused.

"I am telling you now. I am taking the prisoner with me. He has been found guilty of all charges and I will carry out the sentence, as is customary."

He scratched his mustache; he didn't think the trial had even started. Puzzled and stalling for time, he said, "Maurizio himself has put me in charge of guard duty."

Her face scowled in anger. "Are you saying Maurizio has a higher rank than I do?" She seemed to swell with menace and looked ready to fight.

"No, Gabriella. It is just that I expected Maurizio to relieve me of this duty." He looked away as he became more timid.

"You fool, he has more important things to do now that he has to run this camp, with Fermo in the hospital."

"Please understand, *Comandante,* these are my orders and I must carry them out until properly relieved," Pepe said anxiously. Gabriella was now furious with him. She grabbed his shirt lapel in her fist and pulled him toward her face. She was much taller than he was.

"Listen to me, Pepe." she snarled, "*You* dug that foxhole too close to the explosives. Fermo has third-degree burns because of *you*. When he gets back, there will be a reckoning for what you did." She studied the fear in his face. "I will be the one that will extract payment from you. Do you really want to piss me off now?"

Pepe realized that his life was in her hands. Quickly he turned and entered the stall that contained the captured pilot. His fingers trembled as he unlocked the wall chain from the wrist ligatures. Mario got to his feet and cautiously moved to Gabriella.

"I'm sorry, Gabriella. Please forgive my insubordination," Pepe pleaded.

Without a word, she grabbed the prisoner by his wrist shackles and pulled him roughly out of the stall. She stalked forward, not looking at the scared partisan as she passed.

The three confederates walked down the hill, each leading a horse by its reins. Mario was the first to whisper, "Artemio, I am guessing that because we are sneaking down the mountain at night, you were not able to get *Il Volpe* to pardon me."

Artemio took a minute to formulate an explanation. "He is a good man, but he has to work in a suspicious, authoritarian system. He is very limited in this matter. You know how this is, because our Fascist government is just as paranoid."

Mario, dejected, stared out into the bleak night. "Is this truly an escape? Or when I least expect it, will she put a bullet in the back of my head?" He pointed the thumb of his closed fist at Gabriella behind them.

"If I wanted you dead, Artemio would be digging your grave by now," the executioner retorted.

He looked back at her, then continued sadly, "I know this mountain has hundreds of Fascists like me buried on it."

Artemio smiled at him. "Yes, but you are no longer a Fascist. So we must leave this place with you alive."

The first rays of morning sun began to creep over the mountain top. "I know we cannot simply leave this mountain. Tell me the plan, my brother."

Artemio did not really have one. Saving Mario's life was only the first stage. This was not yet accomplished, so everything was a work in progress. He had discussed it with Gabriella, and she had agreed that Artemio would not survive much longer in the Communist brigade either. Their future was uncertain, so he only told Mario the immediate plan.

"Gabriella, as a partisan scout, knows all the mountain passes around Lakes Como and Lugano. We are going to make a run for the border, to get into Switzerland."

The newly released prisoner, with his hands still bound, contemplated the plan and after a deep breath said, "You will have to bribe the border guards. They won't take *lire*; it must be gold or diamonds."

"I know."

"Do you have any?"

"No."

Even with this answer, Mario felt confident in Artemio's abilities to achieve his objective. He always did. Ever since they had become friends at the University, Artemio had succeeded at everything he set out to do. *More importantly,* Mario thought, *he never leaves his friends behind.*

The sun was high over the mountains now. They had ridden for hours on a gently sloping incline out of the Po valley heading north, away from Quaraglio, rolling green hills on either side of them. Gabriella rode back from her lead position to inform the two stragglers, "There is a lone man on horseback in front of us. Do not try to cover me or point weapons at him."

Artemio nodded, knowing that she was familiar with all the partisan bands in the area, communist and non-communist alike. She turned her horse and galloped off to meet the man. Despite her assurance, Artemio felt worried and said under his breath, "Mario, this could be a problem."

"Get me out of these handcuffs and give me a submachine gun. I will cut him down if he tries to harm her."

"You have been a fighter pilot too long, my old friend. In the world of guerrilla warfare, this rider is merely a diversion for your attention. There are men with rifles trained on us right now."

"Where?"

"Don't look, but they are on the high ground to your left, in the evergreen copse. You won't see them, but you are in their crosshairs." Mario uncomfortably tried to look in another direction. "Deception must be met with an even deeper deception. They must think you are our prisoner."

Gabriella rode back and in a serious tone said, "I told them that he is a Fascist pig who is to be taken into the woods and shot." She looked at Mario unsympathetically, and said, "They agreed and will let us pass."

"I know they are going to radio this in to Maurizio, and he will be on us like flies on a horse. We must double our pace now," said Artemio. With Gabriella out in front, they maintained a brisk trot. In a short time the horses began to tire, as the terrain was all uphill.

Mario announced from his steed, "I don't know how this will end for us, but I wish to thank you now, my friends, for doing this for me. I know you both have put yourselves in great personal danger for me. And for what? Everyone wants me dead."

Artemio could see Mario was at an emotional low point. He had been there himself. When you realize that your world is crumbling and all your efforts in it were in vain, that the country you loved has forsaken you—that is when you have hit bottom. Artemio knew that now was the time to show Mario a new direction forward, one with a promise of a better future.

Mario was saying, "When those Spitfires came out of the sun and opened fire on me, I felt relief. I thanked God the nightmare was over, and I was ready to die. To have it end in my Macchi fighter was preferable to an Italian firing squad. But no bullets reached me, the canopy opened, and the parachute deployed; death was not there for me." Mario's bound hands gripped the saddle horn as he looked into the past and saw himself jump out of his burning plane. The fall to earth had been both physical and spiritual for this man without a country. "I am filth, fighting for the Germans against my own people. I deserve any punishment handed out to me." He was about to cry, but no tears fell. "I don't know why you want to save me. I thank God for having friends like you and Gabriella. I see now you were right, I, too, should have quit the day Italy surrendered."

Artemio smiled warmly at him. "Mario, you are my oldest friend. I have no regrets taking on this risk for you. I am just glad we can be together again." He had an image of the three roommates, in the rathskeller drinking and laughing. "I just wish our little friend Gitano could be with us."

"I know. I miss him too." Artemio could see the tears now, as Mario went on. "There's not a day goes by that I don't think of him. I should have watched out for him. He, too, was my brother."

Their mounts were exhausted by the long ride and fast pace, so Gabriella ordered, "We will rest the horses at this stream for ten minutes." The horses drank thirstily of the cold water; it was winter snow melt. The crystal clear water moved rapidly around the rocks, making a gentle, babbling sound. The flat, green meadow was surrounded by a thick tree line. Mario asked Artemio, "This place is like heaven, so secluded; how did Gabriella ever find it?"

"As a scout for the Red Brigade she has been all over this land," he explained, and looked around to enjoy the natural beauty. "It may feel like heaven, Mario, but this is not our time to die. We have a lot of work to do before that happens. I will need you sharp." He cut the ligature that bound his friend's wrists. "Can you stay focused on our future?"

Mario had seen men who had seemed invincible die terrible deaths. All his family's wealth and influence had not been enough to save him from capture and imprisonment in a stable, under a death sentence from his own countrymen, and he had despaired of ever seeing those he loved most ever again. Now the friend he had once envied and even despised was risking death to rescue him.

"I will do whatever you ask of me, Artemio," he said.

Gabriella acted as a sentry with her submachine gun, circumnavigating their perimeter. Mario said reminiscently to Artemio, as they sat together in the green mountain grass, "Do you remember Scarafaggio?"

Artemio's face puckered as if biting into an unexpectedly bitter apple. "Sure! How could I forget that madman?"

"Did you know he became a highly decorated Blackshirt major? That's right! He was wounded while fighting in Greece and received a medal for bravery. The same one you did Artemio, the *Medaglia d'Oro al Valor Militare*." Mario looked in his saddle bag for food, then continued. "The story I heard was this: an Italian army platoon was cut off by a Greek counterattack. When volunteers were sought to help them, all the army officers refused to fight the aggressive Greeks. Scarafaggio stepped forward to embarrass the army men and said his Blackshirts would charge the Greek line to rescue the lost platoon. He was misguided, but loved by his men. After the fight, surgeons were unable to remove a Greek bullet lodged in his lung. Even so, Scarafaggio refused to retire. He stayed in active service."

Artemio thought about that for a minute and said, "Maybe we are not all that different, eh?"

"Yes, we all seem to be connected at some level; only our circumstances keep us apart." Mario took a bite of the bread and cheese Artemio had packed.

"He was promoted in the '*Covo*' den, in Milan, the highest honor bestowed on a Blackshirt."

"I always knew he was dedicated to the cause. Too bad the cause was insane," mumbled Artemio.

Mario took a minute and swallowed hard against the lump in his throat before saying, "He is dead. I saw him die. It truly affected me. I knew I would be next."

Artemio could see the remorse on Mario's face and asked, "What happened to him?"

It was a difficult story to recount, but Mario needed to get it off his chest. And here, on this quiet mountainside, beside the clear, sweet water that had refreshed them, it was easier to tell the truth.

"It was the last assault on Quaraglio in the fall. I flew air support that day, looking out for enemy planes, but there was nothing for me to do. 'Inferno' would never get any help from Allied air command. American fighter-bombers would not come to their aid, because they think those partisans are Communists. Colonel Mueller ran the entire operation, planning and coordination. Hell, I even heard his voice in my headsets. He had a tent and a map table, and I could see him from my plane, waving his arms and yelling at his troops to get into position."

Mario looked right at his best friend as he continued. "Scarafaggio was in charge of all the Italian forces, the Carabinieri, Blackshirts, and local police units that took part in the attack that morning. He sat tall in the saddle, a proud man. He believed completely in Mussolini and was willing to die for him."

Artemio, with his interest in strategy and tactics, asked, "Why do you think Mueller's plan failed?"

"Hubris," Mario said simply, then continued. "The Colonel was given some obsolete German Mark 3 tanks from division headquarters. These tanks were unfit for frontline duty against the newer Allied armor. They were of no use at Quaraglio, either. No vehicles of any kind could travel up that mountainside. The Colonel placed them in a hull-down position along the perimeter road. Each tank fully elevated its main gun, a 50 mm barrel. Mueller used them as fixed artillery along with some 80 mm heavy mortars. They fired barrage after barrage onto that mountain, until they ran out of ammunition. In his arrogance, Mueller believed just having tanks would win the battle for him. Maybe he thought the partisans would run when they saw them. The Germans believe in a mental condition they call tank fear. When they invaded France, the French army ran off the battlefield screaming, 'Tank! Tank!' That rapid defeat in the west is something they try to reproduce everywhere."

He ripped another piece of bread from the loaf. "Mueller fired a red flair to signal the start of the ground offensive. The Germans stayed on the road while the Italians advanced up the hill. Scarafaggio moved his infantry first, up the slight elevation. Cavalry was placed on both flanks and in the rear of the foot soldiers, just as a Roman Emperor would have arranged a Legion in battle. About eight hundred men total, from different sectors of the *Repubblica di Salo*.

"At first, a few of the infantrymen stepped on land mines; this was expected. Medics took them down the hill. The formation continued its march forward at the same slow pace. Then the sniper fire started. This was very accurate, and the snipers targeted the officers. I saw men shot out of their saddles. Others died on their horses. Next came the light 45 mm mortar fire. Soldiers would get blown up into the air and fall down to earth, dead or crippled. Even so, Scarafaggio and his troops continued their advance towards the tree line. Where the hill became steeper, all the concealed partisans opened fire with their rifles. Even this did not deter the Blackshirts, who fired back and continued their progress."

Artemio watched Mario dip his hand into the stream and drink. They were next to the three horses, all sipping the cold mountain water. Mario washed his face, then checked Gabriella's position. Seeing she was out of earshot, he went on.

"At 300 meters things got bad. The Communists' forces had pre-positioned heavy mortar bombs to land there. The Fascists' casualties started to become significant, and the remaining officers had to dismount from their horses and physically pull on the enlisted men to get them up off the ground and force them to move forward. I saw this! When the army reached the tree line, the partisans' gunfire became even more intense. From my plane, I could see the infantry dug into the earth with their entrenching tools, as if a few inches of scraped dirt could save their lives."

Artemio thought of that SAS trooper with the beard and flowing white Arab headdress firing his machine gun at him, and how he'd clung to safety behind a sand bag wall. He refilled the canteens while Mario spoke.

"All the cavalry dismounted to fight as foot soldiers. Most of the surviving officers sent their mounts down the mountain, riderless. Not Scarafaggio, he sat upright in the saddle, directing his men. Bullets were whizzing all around him, but none hit him. As a pilot above all this carnage, I saw the dead mixed with the living, all lying in the red-brown Quaraglio dirt. Horses walked aimlessly around the battlefield; mortar shells exploded. The German soldiers did not advance from their position on the road; some friends, eh?" Mario poked at the cheese with the knife.

"The partisans simply withdrew deeper into the woodlands. They disappeared like ghosts, except for the snipers, who were still firing to maintain a level of confusion. Scarafaggio could have given orders to withdraw. He was too proud for that." Mario wiped his forehead and said contemplatively, "I think he was proving a point to Mueller, that Italian soldiers could be as dedicated as German soldiers. He regrouped his last remaining men, about 200 souls, and they fixed bayonets onto their rifles. Then they charged into the woods. I saw them disappear into the forest. The last I saw of Scarafaggio, he was walking behind his men, not even shouting orders anymore. Perfectly dressed, no dirt or blood on him, holding his pistol, his cap still on his head and his trouser legs tucked in those shiny black riding boots. He walked forward to what he had to know would be his death. He chose to die on that battlefield, rather than face a mob's tribunal, which would be only a parody of a court, and the certainty of a noose around his neck. For me, Fascism died that day with Scarafaggio."

Artemio empathized with the heartache his friend was feeling. Mario glanced at him sideways and said, "Fermo lived up to his nickname that day. The men still loyal to Mussolini entered a trap. As they entered the enemy fortification, they must have felt safe, to be out of the hail of gunfire. But the Communists had set incendiaries in their earthworks. The remaining infantrymen and Scarafaggio were incinerated. I saw a huge mushroom cloud of flame and black smoke rise up through the canopy of the forest.

"Only five or six of Scarafaggio's men made it down the mountain. Herr Mueller was disappointed by the Blackshirt performance that day. He ordered his German soldiers back into their tanks and trucks and returned to Piacenza. The

Colonel did not care about the loss of Italian life. Fascist or Communist, the men who died on Quaraglio meant nothing to him. He knew enough to cut his losses and not risk his own men. That mountain was a killing ground prepared by Fermo for his enemies. Mueller, who was not a fool, would never underestimate him again."

The retelling of the story had disgusted Mario. He wished its memory could be erased.

"I heard later that partisans captured and executed Colonel Mueller."

Artemio's thoughts flashed back to the moment he held Mueller's P-38 pistol to his head, *Il Volpe* egging him on to avenge his mother's murder and pull the trigger. He had killed many men on the battlefield and in air combat, always in a fair fight with some modicum of honor or dignity. But never, as he had told the voice in the Sahara desert, in cold-blooded murder.

"Mueller's death?" Artemio said in a low voice as if he were talking to himself. "Yes, I saw it done. It was battlefield partisan justice. No clean, fancy courthouse. No lawyers in white-powdered wigs and black robes. No book of law or statutes to quote. It was carried out by a woman whose whole family had been machine-gunned by Mueller's SS troops in front of her eyes." Now it was Artemio's turn to look for where Gabriella was on her mini patrol. "She took his own handgun and executed him in the dirt, like a rabid dog."

"Good!" yelled Mario. "I wish I had been there, I would have done it myself."

"Mario, you are a proud, respected Italian Air Force officer; do not sully yourself with such things," counseled Artemio. "We must plan ahead. The three of us must prepare for Italy's future. This war will end, and we know the

Americans will be the victors, but for the next few months northern Italy will be awash in turmoil and confusion. It is our duty to help others. I don't know exactly how we can accomplish this; I am waiting for a sign. The most important thing for us now is to stay alive over the next 24 hours."

Gabriella came running at full stride across the meadow. Both men stood and saw the panic in her face. As she neared them she yelled, "Get the hell out of here!" In a single bound she jumped on her horse and galloped away as if chased by a pack of wolves. The two men quickly mounted their horses, leaving all their gear behind except their Berettas. Calvary horses are bred for speed. They rode them hard across the open grass. A single crack of rifle fire was heard from the tree line, then a whizzing through the air as the bullet passed. Another and another followed. Maurizio's men had found them.

CHAPTER 29
Como

Artemio, holding the reins of his horse, walked up to Gabriella. She was crouched over the wet forest floor, examining foliage. Ferns were starting to overgrow the seldom-used path. An earthy smell of mushrooms and humus arose from the ground. The partisan scout was inspecting a freshly broken branch; she read it as if it were the latest edition of a newspaper.

Artemio broke her concentration. "It's been four hours since they shot at us. As slow as we've been going, Maurizio's men should have overtaken us by now!" She didn't answer, just continued her exploration of the ground for tracks. He persisted, "Why have they not made contact?"

"I don't know," she said, annoyed by the interruption. "I'm looking for signs of an ambush. They may have passed us and be lying in wait. That is what I would do."

"We must change direction again." Now Artemio was looking around for an ambush.

"It won't matter. Maurizio knows where we are headed."

He was surprised by that answer. "Where is that, exactly?"

"My partisan contact in the town of Como. He is a scout with a *Giustizia e Libertà* Brigade."

"Will this scout help us?" He checked the magazine on his submachine gun again.

"I have trusted him with my life for the last six months, and he has never let me down. At the very least we can water the horses and bed down for the night."

The stillness was broken by a loud *"Buon giorno!"*

Both partisans turned quickly in the direction of the greeting, weapons at the ready. The man who stepped out of the brush to startle them was a tall, well-built man in his late twenties. He wore a green alpine hat with a feather on the brim, brown corduroy pants and a blue sweater. Across his waist was an ammunition belt full of 6.5 mm Carcano cartridges for the rifle hanging over his shoulder.

Gabriella yelled up the hill to him, "Salvatore, you fool! We almost filled you full of bullets."

"No, Gabriella, I do not think so. I am the only hope you have to get out of this mess." He walked through the thick underbrush of pine needles and fallen branches to greet them. Gabriella introduced her traveling companions to Salvatore. He had a strong grip to his handshake and a sincere smile. Artemio was surprised by his easy manner, as if he knew them. His blue eyes were not uncommon among Italians in the northern parts, a product of the mixing of Celtic, Germanic and Italian bloodlines at this latitude.

"Is the path in front of us safe?" Artemio asked the affable woodsman.

"Yes."

"Are you sure?"

"Nothing happens in Como without the birds telling me about it." The three travelers gave anxious smiles. They could tell Salvatore was holding back information. He did not seem surprised to see Gabriella with two strangers. All he said was,

"My friends, we must go. A fast-approaching rain storm is moving across the mountain."

The four horsemen made their way to Salvatore's home, a hidden wooden shack, built under a canopy of walnut trees. When not spying on Fascist troop movements, he spent most of his time here.

Mario tended to the horses while Artemio started a fire in the hearth. Being a good host, Salvatore made a fresh pot of espresso for his guests.

"I am sorry I have no grappa, or sugar for the coffee."

"Tell me, what did you mean when you said back there, the mess we were in?" Gabriella asked timidly, trying to find out what he knew about their circumstances.

"I know the whole story, except for the why. Why would you risk your life for these two Fascist pilots?" he asked, as a grimace appeared on his face. His disappointment with her showed. Artemio did not like being called a Fascist pilot, or the tone of the man's voice, or the questioning of his girlfriend. The mood in the cabin was not as light as before.

There was a long pause as she thought of how to phrase her answer for Salvatore.

"The Communists were going to kill Mario, after convicting him on false war crime charges. His friend Artemio could not let that happen."

"So what! We have seen the Communists kill people for political reasons before." He spoke to Gabriella as if they were the only two people in the room. "What's so special with these two?" Salvatore tilted his head at them.

There was another pause before her response. Artemio had never seen her have so much trouble with a conversation —or was this turning into an interrogation? His eyes scanned the room for the location of the guns.

"Sal, all the killing.... It's just wrong!" she pleaded.

"You jeopardized it all for them! Why, Gabriella?" he demanded with anger in his voice.

She blurted out, "I am sorry, Salvatore. I love him. I am so sorry." She put her hands over her face and started to sob.

None of the three men in the room had expected that. Artemio went to her and held her, but that only made the sobbing louder. As he tried to comfort her, his eyes caught Salvatore's. Both men glared at each other, and realization struck Artemio—they were both after her heart.

The woodsman fell back into a worn chair and watched the roaring fire in the hearth crackle. His facial expression said it all: *When did I lose her?*

Gabriella, still weeping, went behind Salvatore's chair and hugged his head, then kissed the top of it. He gently patted her arm and said, "It's okay, it's okay, *bella*. This war makes people do crazy things."

They ate dinner in silence. Artemio's eyes would meet Gabriella's, then she would look down quickly, as if she were in a Catholic school afraid to be caught out by a nun. Salvatore waited in frustration, then finally asked, "Isn't anyone interested in why Maurizio didn't hunt you down and kill all of you?"

The guests looked up from their wild mushroom and barley soup, but were silent. He explained, "Gabriella, that little girl you saved from being hit by the truck in Piacenza. Did you know who she was?"

Gabriella, who remembered pushing the skinny girl out of the way of the military transport, then only darkness, replied, "She was just a little Piacentina, no?"

"That little girl's father is on the council of the National Liberation Committee. He is in London as a liaison with the British Special Operations Executive." Salvatore took a long drink of water, and added, "Before the war, her father married Rocco Beati's sister."

"She is Rocco's niece?" asked Artemio, amazed.

"That's right, and the ice cream vendor is her bodyguard."

Artemio had given the hand sign to the man in the candy-striped shirt and gotten the correct partisan response. He had known the vendor was connected, but hadn't figured out it was protection duty. Now he was thinking, *If the random little girl playing soccer in the street was Rocco's niece, we are all interconnected in some way. There is a web that binds all of us. Some strands are thick and strong, you can see them. Others are thin, too faint to be seen. Right now I have to figure out the web between Gabriella and this scout.*

Salvatore was saying, "When Rocco heard of the truck incident, he was about to go to Quaraglio to thank you for saving her life. Then he got word of your prison break with Mario here."

Artemio looked at Mario and said, "I told you that lone man on the horse would send out word of our position."

Salvatore confirmed this, saying, "Yes, we have informers in each other's camps."

"You mean little gossipers," said Gabriella.

Salvatore smiled at her lovingly, the way he was used to doing, then caught himself, and the serious expression returned. "I was in camp when we got the information. Rocco changed his plans from three men bearing a gift of American tinned beef to a heavily armed assault group of two dozen men. We rode hard for 12 hours to overtake Maurizio's force."

"Some of Maurizio's men did make contact with us. A few shots were fired, but we rode like the wind to get away from them," said Artemio.

"Was there any fighting between your men and my Brigade?" asked Gabriella, concerned.

The man with the broken heart scornfully said, "Gabriella, you do not have a Brigade anymore." Her stricken expression showed her feelings. "No. Rocco and I insisted that the Quaraglio men stand down. They were not committed to a mission that involved killing you, Artemio. You have earned great respect among the Garibaldi brigade."

"When they were shooting at us, I did not feel any respect," grinned Mario.

"Without any direction from Fermo or *Il Volpe* they could not continue. Maurizio is good at yelling, or spouting verse of Communist manifesto, but he is a poor leader of men. They argued amongst themselves, then turned around and went home."

Gabriella leaned back, obviously relieved. Then she looked directly into the eyes of their host. "Thank you for all your help up to now, Salvatore. I have one more favor to ask of you."

The Como scout quickly replied, "Let me guess, you want safe passage into Switzerland."

Artemio leaned back in his chair, astonished. How could he have known of their plans? Salvatore laughed at his guest's quizzical expression.

"This is my plan. I know that when the Americans punch through the German Gothic line, all hell will break loose here. We have intercepted orders from Berlin. When the line collapses, the Nazis are to withdraw to Austria, but not before killing as many Italians as possible. The Germans call it their scorched earth policy." He looked at Gabriella as her eyes darted away from his; her face had gone white. "I had already planned to take her to safety in Ticino," Salvatore said, looking now directly at Artemio, "but the Germans have sealed the borders tight. They now control, with the Blackshirts, all access points between the two countries."

Gabriella interjected, "Not at Chiasso on Lake Lugano."

He looked down at the table and nodded his head. "Yes, I agree that would be possible. I have been told by Rocco to give you everything you need. I will make two passports for the pilots." He looked at Gabriella with pain in his eyes and said, "I already had yours ready with mine."

The Chiasso border crossing was a stone building made from the local mountain granite. It was a good fortification that blended into the mountainside. A retractable wooden gate painted with red and white stripes could be raised and lowered for cars and trucks. Italian guards were outside, smoking and talking to each other. No Germans were present at this out of the way, rarely used crossing. Artemio assessed the situation, leaning back against the rocks, out of sight from the border guards. He looked into Gabriella's face. Under her kerchief, she forced a nervous smile back.

"Are you okay?" he asked tenderly.

"I will be when we get across."

"Back there with Salvatore, I did not know...."

"Of course not, how could you? Thank you for being understanding."

"I don't know our future, but I love you very much."

"Oh, Artemio, it feels so good to hear you say that! Before I met you I was hoping to die. I could not kill myself, but I wanted to die in battle. I could not see any future promise in my life, only the blackness, with death the only end for me. Since knowing you, I desperately want to live. Your love gives me hope."

He gently kissed her forehead. "For my plan to succeed, we must all get into Switzerland. Today we have no weapons; we must be good actors and have some luck."

Inside the border station they waited in line till it was their turn. The guard looked at the passports, then up at their faces. The uninterested young man stamped the freshly minted documents with an "Exit from Italy" ink mark. The three concealed their nervous excitement and walked normally toward the exit that had a sign over the door marked "To Switzerland."

A senior officer, leaving his office, shut the door behind him. He looked at the three almost out of the building and said, "Excuse me, please. May I see your passports?" He allowed Gabriella and Mario to leave. Over Artemio's documents he lingered. Then he called out to a soldier who was standing at attention. "Sergeant, arrest this man!"

Artemio froze in bewilderment.

Mario yelled, "He is with me, I will vouch for this man." The lieutenant looked Mario up and down and said, "Arrest both of these men." Artemio, as he was being taken away, called out, "What is the problem here? I demand to know the problem!"

"The problem here is that I knew Artemio Battaglia, and you are not him."

Artemio stared deeply into the man's face and did not recognize him either. "I assure you sir, I am Artemio Battaglia!"

"You cannot be him." The officer looked up from the forged documents. "I saw him die on the battlefield of Tobruk." Artemio was sure this border guard knew him, but who was he? He looked at the officer's face a second time, intently. He noticed the man's nose was surgically reconstructed and his left eye was made of glass. Typical, low-quality Italian Army surgeon work. Then he saw the deep crow's feet on the outer angles of both eyes. These are the skin changes of a man who has looked into the sun, waiting to see the airplane that will swoop down and kill him and his crew.

"Niccolo? Are you Sergeant Major Niccolo Sansone?" he whispered.

There was no answer from the stolid Italian officer.

"Yes, yes, it *is* you, you old Baresi pirate!" Artemio's face brightened.

Slowly the man smiled from ear to ear. "Artemio, how is this possible? I saw the explosion. They told me you received the Iron cross—posthumously."

"I was in a coma for six weeks; everyone thought I would die. But God had other plans for me, so he sent me back," Artemio said with a sad smile.

The two war-wounded men hugged. The border guards, viewing this, wondered what to do.

"*Mi scusi, tenente,* Excuse me, Lieutenant, should I continue to process the arrest?"

"No, you idiot! Get away from us!" Niccolo said curtly, and he took Artemio and Mario into his private office, sending for the anxious Gabriella when Artemio quickly explained the three of them traveled together. He looked at the three of them and asked, "What are you doing, crossing the border with these obviously forged documents?" Behind

Niccolo was a large plate glass window showing the Swiss side of the border and their objective.

Mario said, "Your corporal thought they were valid."

Niccolo gave a condescending smile through his scars. "He is the grandson of a general. That's the sort who get these off-the-frontline, cream puff jobs: fellows high on connections, low on intelligence."

"But tell me, now *Lieutenant* Sansone, how did you get here, and what happened to the crew of *Il Mulo*?" Artemio demanded eagerly.

Niccolo's face winced with pain when *Il Mulo* was named. "It was a sad day, Artemio." He turned his head to take in all three of them, then fixed his gaze back on his old friend. "We had fallen back into Tunisia. Unlike Libya, Tunisia is green and fertile. Our scouting duties involved probing the American front lines." He shook his head in disgust. "You can fool the Americans once, but don't try it again. The Germans sent all reconnaissance units across the battlefield late at night. We had successes mapping the American step-off points, and the Germans brought up their 88 anti-tank guns. They cut up their Sherman tanks at dawn when they tried to advance. On the next American offensive, the Germans ordered us to repeat the same tactic. This time the Americans were waiting for us. They had partially buried gun emplacements in advance of their front line. *We* never saw them. Too late, I saw a flash, and then I was lying on the ground, looking at all my men dead, their bodies scattered, and *Il Mulo* ablaze. Somehow another recon unit got me to a hospital. I was discharged from the Army with my wounds. The border service offered me this job and a promotion to lieutenant."

Artemio took the news hard. "Paolo, the Muslim, and his friend, Giovanni, are dead?"

"Yes, and our gunner Lorenzo, also dead. I was the only survivor of the blast."

Artemio remembering what a capable soldier he had been, knew the war was lost for Italy without men like Lorenzo. He thought back to his time in the desert and asked, "What happened to that cunning Bedouin, Haadi?"

"My friend Haadi was a man of mystery and intrigue; there were many things about his life he kept secret. We assumed he sold all the English guns and bullets we gave him. I later found out he was arrested by British Intelligence for plotting to bomb the King David Hotel in Jerusalem. It turns out he was a top man in the Muslim Brotherhood. That hotel is where the English diplomats and senior military staff live while in Palestine. The Arabs think the British are about to create a Jewish state, so they are fighting a guerrilla war of their own." Artemio knew Haadi had had multiple agendas. Like a chameleon, he was comfortable in many different settings.

Niccolo moved his arm in its shoulder socket and grimaced; it hurt because it was freezing up. After a minute, he continued, "I took this position here because after my discharge from the army there was nothing for me. I send most of my pay home to my parents. I hate this job! Turning poor, starving Italians back to their villages where there is no food and German death squads waiting for them."

"So, why do you turn them away?" Artemio asked, already knowing the answer.

"These border guards look stupid, but they will inform on me in a minute if I do not follow government protocol. I don't want to do it, but my alternative is a Fascist jail cell."

"The world does not have to be this way." Artemio patted his long-lost friend on the back. "I will call on you soon, Niccolo, to work for me. First I must establish a base of operations in Switzerland. We will work together to let even the weakest among us get the security they need."

"Artemio, I trust you. The crew and I all knew you were special. I will give my life if I have to. It is not worth much, though. Our generation is lost forever. We grew up as children believing in Mussolini and the Fascist cause." He became depressed, thinking about his wasted youth. "There is nothing for us now. Older men have wives and families to go back to. Younger men have not seen as much violence and destruction as we have. They can rebuild their lives with a fresh start. We believed and were led astray; there is neither past nor future for us."

"Take heart, my Baresi friend. The work I have in mind will give meaning back to your life." They hugged as brothers.

CHAPTER 30
Swiss Bankers

Stepping out of the border crossing station into a different land felt liberating. Across the border the air was fresher. An invigorating wind blew, carrying the fragrance of edelweiss blossoms. All three smiled at each other and said nothing. The unseen freedom flowed around and through them.

The land from Bellinzona to downtown Chiasso was filled with small farms, A-frame chalets with green grass lawns, and dairy cows grazing. As they walked, they heard an occasional bovine guttural sound mixed with a neck bell clank. Artemio had tasted the semi-soft cheese from this region, along with its three-grape varietal white wine. He was remembering these flavors when Mario whispered to him in a low voice so that Gabriella could not hear, "It is a good thing your friend Niccolo let us pass through the border crossing."

"Yes, if anyone else had been manning that post it could have gone badly for us."

"That is not how I meant it. If the border guards had been foolish enough to arrest you and me, Gabriella would have come back with a machine gun and leveled the place to get you out."

"I see your point. They were indeed lucky." He grinned.

A few more minutes passed, then Mario broke the silence again. "My father-in-law is hiding out in Switzerland."

His two traveling companions looked at him in disbelief.

Artemio asked, annoyed, "When were you going to tell us that?"

"I could not say anything while we were still in Italy. If we were captured, it is information that could be extracted from us. The Communists have put a death sentence on his head, because he was close to the Fascist regime."

Artemio remembered Luigi Mercati. He was the banker who made easy interest loans to his friends, like Mario's father. He thought back to the graduation party, the line that formed of people paying respects to Signore Mercati, and the drive the four of them had taken in Mario's car. What a different time that was, just a few short years ago! He could have had a relationship with Gabriella back then, but he had been self-centered, thinking he could do better. What a fool he'd been! Now that time was running out, he could make no more mistakes.

Gabriella asked about her old friend. "How is Olympia? I heard she is working in Zurich."

"Yes," said Mario, with a big smile that lit up his whole face. "We were secretly married at the courthouse in Piacenza. I then immediately sent her to Switzerland. Her father has many banking friends here who were able to give her a job." Mario's expression turned to puzzlement. "Wait a minute, who told you she was in Zurich? That was kept confidential."

"Oh, I don't know. It was just something I heard in passing and didn't think much about."

Artemio, still thinking about Luigi, asked, "Where in Switzerland does your father-in-law live? Because after a hot bath and a good night's sleep in Chiasso, that is our new destination."

"He lives very discreetly in Lugano and rents a house under an assumed name. I am told it is a nice place right on the lake. I don't think he will be any help to us, however, as he is here illegally. That quiet old banker will not want to rock the boat, for fear of being deported back to Italy and a Communist noose."

"Don't worry about him; leave that to me," Artemio said under his breath. The planning for the new operation, not a military one, but just as dangerous, had begun.

Switzerland had different politics from the rest of Europe. The Swiss people were proud and fiercely independent. Neutrality is a difficult card to play when the poker table is encircled by sharks. Still, they managed good relations with Hitler and Germany, even though the Nazis had drawn up plans, Operation Tannenbaum, for the invasion of Switzerland. Amicable diplomatic and banking ties were also maintained with England and America. Warring countries need access to capital; they can print it, but must also borrow it. All potentates, from Napoleon and the King of England to Roosevelt and Hitler, had to finance their wars. America sent gold to Swiss banks and they repatriated greenbacks. No other country in the world would accept Reich marks, so Germany sent gold to Zurich in return for other currencies that they could spend internationally.

The composition of the Swiss people consists of French, Germanic, and Italian descendants. Artemio liked the idea of different people being able to live in harmony with each other. He saw this small country as a life raft for the ship of Europe, which was sinking fast.

Gabriella, with her knowledge of the Ticino Canton, instructed the men that Lugano was just around the mountain. Artemio persuaded Gabriella and Mario, still exhausted by their recent ordeals, to rest by the side of the road while he scaled the crest and looked for a possible short cut. As he reached the top, he became fatigued and short of breath. These mountains were a higher elevation than San Giorgio, where he'd grown up. The view was like standing on the top of the earth. In the foreground were mountains with green pastures and sharply descending rocky patches. Beyond lay the snowcapped Alps with their glaciers sliding into valleys. Directly below was the tranquil, blue Lake Lugano. It stretched for miles, with little houses along its shore, as well as hotels and quaint bed and breakfasts, attended by owners who only knew of war by reading the newspapers. A combination of the thin air and the exertion of reaching the top gave him a sense of euphoria. He sat and rested next to an ancient oak tree, and became introspective.

This is my time. I feel it deep in my aching bones. I did not choose this, but I was born in the middle of this madness. My path is clear. As my father told me on a mountain similar to this one, I must make a change in the world, to right this listing ship. There has been a coalescence of forces on the earth into massively destructive ideologies. They are like speeding freight trains heading toward each other. The immoral and treacherous nature of man has always been present, but something now is different. A malevolent hand has intervened to upset the balance that previously existed in nature. The influence of this dark force must be reversed. Not by military might. That was my original error. The counter measure to evil is not more evil. The proper tactic in this war is to unleash goodness. The opposite of wickedness is hope, trust, and compassion. Only these will neutralize the atrocities and brutality of our time. I must reach out to make a sanctuary, a place to heal wounds and repair lives. To offer safety and security in this little harbor until the tempest has passed.

They were experienced guerrilla fighters who knew not to knock on a front door. From the road, the three Italians gazed at the house. Mario had indicated this was where the banker lived. The large roof and second floor were at street level. A sharp hill with steps down and a stone and mortar pathway led around the back to the entrance. Artemio and Mario took an observant position across the road, concealing themselves behind shrubbery about 100 meters up the mountainside so they would not be seen by neighbors, while Gabriella circled the house. Watching her reminded Artemio of the time she'd reconnoitered his mother's house for the radio transmitter. Who would have guessed a love would grow between the two of them? She signaled that no one was in the house and returned to a hidden position in the backyard. Now the waiting began.

Mario said, while looking at the ground and picking through pebbles, "When we were training at Airbase Foggia, I desperately wanted to make captain Sin over you."

"I know you did. We were rivals for that position."

"You made a better captain than I ever did. After you were shot down and I was promoted, I could not hold a candle to your memory."

"Oh, come on, Mario, I'm sure you were a fine captain." He elbowed his friend and continued his surveillance of the house.

"No, I mean it. Our leadership styles were different. I pushed the men of our squadron too hard. Klaus Meyer commanded us to be aggressive and always 'attack, attack, attack.' I wanted more and more kills. What I got was more Italian pilots being shot down because of the risks we were taking."

Yes, Artemio thought, *the Piaggio family pride was all-consuming.* Mario looked at Artemio sincerely and said, "When you were our captain, we trained always with an eye to safety. You drilled us in efficiency and cohesiveness. All the men looked after each other."

Artemio completely understood. "Klaus Meyer had a black knight with a lance painted on the nose of his Messerschmitt for a reason. He believed he was the lone man on the battlefield who would bring victory to his Führer. Many Axis pilots died to keep his kill count growing. I could not subscribe to that ethos. Being captain was a terrible weight on my shoulders. Every mission, I counted our Macchi fighters as they landed. If there were one or two birds missing from the flock, it ripped at my heart."

Mario said sadly, "I was a stupid young man who did not know England had so many airplanes they would never run out. But Italy had only one Gitano." Artemio put his arm on his friend's shoulders and pulled him in, as if to hug him. Mario heaved a sigh. "These last two days with you have made me understand. I want to be a part of something good, something redeeming. I don't want the world to know the Piaggio family for the war machines we make, but for our kindness and generosity."

"You were my wingman in combat above North Africa. You will be my wingman for the rest of my life."

An hour later a portly man with a bald head under his chapeau walked along the road. He carried a canvas bag full of groceries. As he entered the home, Mario said, "That's him, let's go."

"No, wait, give him some time to settle in. We don't want to spook him."

The two men left the seclusion of the hedge and crossed the street. Knowing that only Luigi Mercati was in the house, they used the brass door knocker. Gabriella remained out of sight. The man looked cautiously through the peephole. They heard a jubilant, "Oh my God!" from within the house, and then a hurried fumbling to unlock the door. It was flung open and Luigi embraced his son-in-law.

Mario eventually broke away and said, *"Mio padre*, do you remember my friend Artemio?"

The older man did not remember, nevertheless he gave a polite nod. As Gabriella walked up the stone pathway, Mario was about to introduce her, but before he could say anything Luigi yelled out, "Gabriella! Thank God you are all right!" He pushed past the two men and hugged her and kissed both her cheeks, as if she were his long lost daughter. He put his arm around her waist and walked her into his house, brushing by the two astonished men. Mario and Artemio gave each other dumbfounded looks. Once in the house, Mr. Mercati offered her something to drink: "Water, beer, wine, anything?" She shook her head no. Then he turned to the two men. "My housekeeper will be here in an hour and she will prepare a special meal for all of us." He was so elated, he looked like he would dance. "I just purchased sausages, cheese and veal chops. We will celebrate."

Gabriella understood the overly affectionate banker's reaction to her, but said nothing. Finally Luigi himself noticed the puzzled expressions on the faces of his two male guests and said, "I think you do not know this, but she saved my life." Her two traveling companions looked directly at Gabriella. She remained silent, so he explained. "Remember, Mario, when I told you the Communists put a price on my head?"

"Yes," Mario replied, quite interested in this revelation.

"Well, Gabriella here"—he turned and smiled at her— "was supposed to be my executioner. She was tasked with the job of killing me." He swallowed hard to clear the lump in his throat. "I was traveling from Milan to Piacenza, when someone abducted me. I was brought to the woods, forced to my knees. Praying to God, I asked the Lord to take care of my family after my death. I could feel the cold rain beating on my clothes, the steel of a gun barrel against the back of my head. I knew my time had come. Suddenly the hood was pulled from my head, and I saw my guardian angel." He kissed Gabriella's hand, then continued. "She brought me here to Ticino, and then told the Garibaldi Brigade Tribunal I was dead."

Artemio looked at her and loved her even more. He had reprimanded her once for doing the Tribunal's dirty work without knowing the facts of the case. She had never let out the secret that she ferried men, not over the river to Hades, but to freedom in Switzerland.

Gabriella broke her silence and said, "When I was twelve years old, Mr. Mercati would come over for Sunday dinners. My mother would make a feast of beef and pork for him. My father's butcher shop had run into some economic difficulties. Luigi gave him a loan when no one else would; it saved the family business. I came to think of him as a favorite uncle. When I got the orders to execute him, I did not hesitate for a second to bring him here to Ticino."

Mario nodded his head at the revelation. "That's how you knew Olympia was living in Zurich." He turned and pointed to the banker. "He told you." Luigi smiled sheepishly as Mario continued. "Tell me, father-in-law, do you like living here in this comfortable life you have made for yourself in Ticino?"

"Yes, I have many friends and business acquaintances here. There are Italian lawyers, politicians, and artists, all expats. A lot of wealthy people had to get out of Italy, for many different reasons, to escape torture and death at the hands of the Nazis, Blackshirts, or Communists. Life there was unstable and becoming too dangerous."

Artemio asked, "What of the poor, who cannot afford a bribe payment, or are not influential enough to get out?"

"Ah, yes." He hesitated a second and continued in a lower voice, "I feel so sorry for the ones that can't make it out. The future for them is dismal."

"What if we were able to get many people out of northern Italy? To safety here, at least until the war is over."

Luigi looked at him strangely and said, "That is a nice dream, but that could never happen. The federal government in Bern would not allow it. They are very sensitive to the feelings of the Nazis in Berlin." He sat down in an expensive Louis the XVI chair and continued his explanation.

"Switzerland as a nation is concerned about this Operation Tannenbaum. They have reservists on a permanent state of readiness for the invasion. They know they cannot beat the German army, but they will go into the hills as a guerrilla force and harass them."

Artemio sighed in exasperation. "This is not going to happen. The Germans are losing to the Allies in both Italy and France. The Russians are retaking huge chunks of Europe, the Eastern Front moves closer to us each day. This Operation Tannenbaum is an old plan. There is no way Germany could open up another front to fight on."

Luigi admitted the Italian-Swiss in Ticino Canton would not mind helping their brethren, but the Germanic-Swiss in the northern part of Switzerland would not allow it.

Mario stood next to his father-in-law and told him, "We know the banking community in Zurich and the government in Bern are aiding and abetting Hitler and his henchmen. Olympia has seen documents wherein Swiss banks gave gold to the German Reich Bank, never expecting to be repaid. The Nazis give signed-over life insurance policies and bank accounts of dead Jews who were tortured. This payment in gold is not just a war crime, it is blood money!"

Luigi did not want to talk about this, but guilt was boiling inside him. "I don't need to see documents. Every banker knows this is going on, and worse."

Mario repeated, "Worse?! What could be worse?"

"An art dealer in Lucerne has been buying paintings looted by Borman, Goebbels, and von Ribbentrop from Jewish collections. They are transported into Switzerland by diplomatic pouch. These men are getting rich from the extermination of the Jews. Then there is the German national policy of refilling its coffers by looting all of Europe.

The Nazis hate modern art, the Impressionists, Picasso and the like. They strip museums of these works and sell them to Swiss art dealers for a fraction of what they are worth. The Swiss are guilty of financing these maniacs. At first it was for security, to deter the German Wehrmacht from turning its attention to Switzerland."

Artemio injected quickly, "And for profit!" He could feel his blood pressure banging in his head. "This is an outrage; these men must see the injustice they have created. This cauldron of war has been financed and prolonged by these bankers and art dealers. The Nazis will get what they deserve for their sins at the end of a rope. The Swiss have an opportunity to help heal mankind through penitence."

"Are we to take care of everyone? This is not practical, Artemio," admonished Luigi.

"Our brothers' and sisters' blood is being spilled. Can you not hear it?"

Luigi became afraid of Artemio's rage. He pushed himself further back into the soft chair.

"No! No, you can't hear it! But it cries out to me from the ground; I hear it, and I will make you hear it."

Luigi believed in what Artemio was saying, but he had less faith in his fellow man. "The Swiss people are not Nazis. They are a clannish people. They don't like the Nazis and they don't like Italians, but the national government in Bern has learned to peacefully coexist with both. I think they are too comfortable with Germany."

"Like a tick living under the sleeping dog of Germany," said Mario.

Artemio was committed. "Luigi, you do not deserve to live here, nor do your rich friends. You know I'm right; without your money and influence, you would be swinging by your neck on a lamp post in a Milan piazza." He looked at Gabriella, and she nodded in confirmation. He went on. "You must give back. You are your brother's keeper. Now it is your turn to sacrifice. Sacrifice this comfortable lifestyle and work for the downtrodden. Europeans are suffering under this yoke of war. Your anonymity ends tonight. You and your powerful friends will get the Swiss government to let in the suffering people from all over Europe. We will cajole, beg, and bribe the national government to open its borders and allow refugee camps in Ticino."

"And if we meet resistance to your ideas? Then what?"

"Everyone has an eye on the future, after the war. We will remind the Swiss of their Nazi-sympathizing ways." Artemio looked at Mario and smiled. "I can convince them it is time to repent."

"There are soldiers on both sides of the border enforcing this policy," Luigi pointed out.

"I have fought behind walls my whole life. The barbed wire of Tobruk, or a farmer's stone wall at a roadside ambush. That part of my life is over. It was unproductive. My future is to tear down walls. There are barriers across countries and in men's hearts that must and will be overcome." He was leaning over the sitting banker, Artemio's hands on both chair arms, nose to nose with Luigi. "Tomorrow, your job is to work the phones, call in all your favors and bank loans. We must get this job done; our souls depend on it."

CHAPTER 31
The Wedding

The groomsmen smiled at him and patted his back when they saw the bride start her procession down the aisle. Artemio thought she looked radiant as she approached. Gabriella kept her eyes straight ahead and walked slowly in her white silk dress. Escorting her was her spiritual father, Fermo. The height difference between them seemed comical unless you knew their history.

The war was over and Fermo was lauded as a hero; had circumstances been different, he would have been tried as a war criminal. The men by Artemio's side were honored to be there. Only three men stood on the solea that was one step elevated from the floor that the pews were on, but hundreds of men loved him and were glad for him. Mario, as best man, fumbled for the ring. Olympia, standing with the bridesmaids, rolled her eyes. Even a fighter ace can be nervous around women who expect perfection on such a special day.

The band at the reception played exuberantly, and everyone danced. They were elated by the nuptials. At a deeper level, they danced to celebrate life. Not just their survival, but a reinvigoration of humanity, a continuation of the spirit. Like the survivors of a shipwreck in the South Pacific, stranded on an island that will never be found, they are happy to be alive, but would rather have their old lives back, their lives before the war. Mario and Olympia were dancing, holding their one-year-old daughter, Gabby, named after her godmother. Fermo, with a few too many drinks in him, held Gabriella's abdomen and announced to the room, "It was my idea to have her play the pregnant wife of Captain Battaglia! Now I want my premonition to come true. I want grandchildren!" Gabriella slapped his hand away and pretended to be annoyed, but he was only saying what the whole room wished for them.

Later the bride and groom circulated around the tables, thanking everyone for attending. Artemio turned to his new wife and said, "Honey, do you remember Gitano from the graduation party in Milan?" Gitano rose from his chair and hugged and kissed both of them.

"Gitano, tell Gabriella the story of how you survived."

The bride had a look of surprise on her face. "Yes! All these years we thought you were dead."

The airman still had a boyish body and a nose too big for his face. "With a lot of luck, and good people to shelter me." He explained how, in his last sortie with British Spitfires, his plane could not outmaneuver theirs. His Macchi fighter had been raked with gunfire. "From the engine compartment black smoke billowed out. I could tell oil was spilling onto the exhaust pipes and burning. It looked bad, like an engine fire, but I still had full control of the instruments."

Almost in tears, he hugged Artemio. "My brother here, our great Captain, had always taught the pilots in the squadron to prepare for all contingencies. I am alive today because of this man."

Artemio felt warm inside, hearing one of his junior officers praise him. He thought of the young man that crashed his plane on San Giorgio Mountain. If only he could have trained him, another life would have been saved.

Gitano continued, "I purposely went into a tailspin, as if I were out of control. At four thousand feet I let out the flaps and pulled hard on the stick. The plane leveled off, but not soon enough to let me clear the ground. I rode the sand like a skier in the snow.When I finally stopped, black smoke rose all around me. From the altitude of the dog fight, they were sure I was dead." He stopped, as if mourning the loss of his own life, certainly a previous life.

"I opened the cockpit canopy to exit and smelled aviation fuel everywhere. The wing tanks had ruptured. I ran to a farmer's shed, and as I got to the big double doors, the plane detonated like a bomb. If anyone thought I might have survived that landing, the explosion would have convinced them otherwise. The farm was owned by Fakhim here, and his family. It was my chance to get out of that stupid war." He placed his hand on Fakhim's shoulder. "His family hid me in their house. No one in the village knew I was there. One time Fakhim and I did make a short trip into Benghazi to see my parents. I was disguised as an Arab woman in traditional dress. I wanted them to know I was okay, but not to tell anyone."

"That explains why Mario got the door shut in his face, when he went out there to tell them you were dead!" The whole table laughed. Artemio turned to Gabriella and explained, "They live together in Libya, even now."

Heaven Cries

"Yes," said Gitano. "I am a citizen of the new free country of Libya. I never even had an Italian passport." Gabriella hugged and kissed both of them. She thanked them for making the long journey from their homeland.

The table across the room also had a distinguished guest. Sitting with a girlfriend was a famous New York City restaurateur. The successful man was very proud of Artemio and the humanitarian work he was doing at the U.N. It was Artemio's *zio*, Uncle Bruno. They had never met before, but the younger man had idolized Bruno his whole life for having the fortitude to leave Europe for the promise of the New World. Bruno greatly admired his nephew for weathering the storm of war and coming out the other side a hero and a diplomat.

"I am sorry I never visited before the war, but I was building my business. There never seemed to be a good time." Both men's thoughts converged. Bruno said it first: "I miss your father so much. I have fond boyhood memories of him. Because of the war I could not come to his funeral."

"I know, *Zio*. He loved you very much, and missed you from the day you left Piacenza. He told me that often." Bruno held back tears. One lifetime is not long enough. He had cancer, and had been told at the new Sloan-Kettering Institute that he only had a year to live. He regretted the time away from his Italian family.

"I know the post-war economy in Italy is terrible," said Bruno. "When you finish up your work at the United Nations in Geneva, please come to New York and help me. I have a chain of Italian restaurants that are in need of a good manager." He gazed at his nephew, disfigured from combat, and saw past the scars. "I am a rich man with no family; I want you to share it with me. The job includes making you an American citizen."

"Thank you for that generous offer, *Zio*. I would love to do it. It has always been a dream of mine to become an American. However, the work I am now doing is taking up all my time."

Gabriella leaned in and said, "I barely get to see him. He is working on two massive problems with the English government. India wants independence; and a new nation, Israel, wants to be birthed. The English have screwed things up so badly, they need Artemio to fix it."

Artemio explained, "King George VI wants me to handle the negotiations. He believes only an independent third party can be trusted." Artemio snickered inside as he thought back to a time when Winston Churchill would not send his men food. *If only the English had known all our lives are interconnected.*

Gabriella looked at him in disbelief. "He is so modest! It is both Mahatma Gandhi and David Ben-Gurion that want him in the room during negotiations. They don't trust the English for a minute."

"When these two little issues are taken care of, I will come to America," he joked.

Bruno laughed. "Little issues! If you can fix the British Empire, I know you can manage my business empire."

But their good-byes at the port of Genoa would be the last they ever saw of each other.

CHAPTER 32
Sleep

The man in a wet trench coat unlocks the front door. With his weak left leg he manages the threshold step. He flips the wall light switch up, and a piercing white light fills the darkened room. Gabriella is sitting at the edge of the couch, holding a half asleep one-month-old infant. Her long, dark hair is flowing in every direction, defying gravity. She is wearing a stained nightgown covered by a robe: the image of a mother with an unsleeping baby. He quickly flips the light switch off.

"Sorry," he says softly. "I had hoped you would all be asleep."

"Arty, you are home late!"

"Yes, my love. It was awful, 72 hours of straight meetings and negotiations. This diplomacy stuff wears you down. Sometimes I think I prefer the days of open warfare; at least then you knew who your enemies were." Even in the darkness she can see he has a smile on his tired face. "Then the plane ride home was miserable. The heavens opened up and we hit thunderstorms the whole way. My head and neck are killing me." As he rubs his brow, he asks, "Is our son asleep?"

"*Si*, Fermo went to bed after supper. He was exhausted from playing soccer with his friends all day. He practically fell asleep at the table. Little Rafaella has been up every four hours for her feeding."

He kisses the head of the drowsy baby gently, so as not to wake her. He then kisses Gabriella on the same spot and whispers, "You are my baby, too." He feels warm inside now, being home with his family. He works hard for them. When the war ended and the peace treaties were signed, Artemio had thought he would find a quiet life; it was not to be.

"Did you get my telegram when you were in Geneva?"

"Yes, the one about Frau Meyer contacting you."

"When Helen invited me to lunch, she told me they have proof that Klaus Meyer is alive and a Russian prisoner of war." She adjusts the baby in her arms as she looks at him for a sign that he understands the problem.

"How could they know? All that information is kept in Moscow as a state secret."

"Apparently, there is a man they are bribing, but he wants his identity kept unknown. Klaus's family is old Prussian aristocracy. They were hated by Hitler, and now they are hated by Stalin. Helen told me they are willing to pay anything to get him out. He is the heir to the family fortune, which includes a vineyard on the Rhine and a machine factory in Stuttgart."

Artemio scratches his head as he asks, "Did she happen to say how Klaus got captured?"

"Helen said that after North Africa he fought as a fighter pilot in the Battle of Sicily, then was transferred to the Russian front. His Me 109 was shot down while holding back the Red Army so that the Wehrmacht could escape out the

Kuban Bridgehead to Crimea. No official record of his capture exists."

"I called in some favors at the Red Cross. My friend Adriana found a file on him, but they don't know where he is, or if he is alive. He is a twenty-kill ace, including three Sturmoviks in one day."

"Helen told me they are positive he is alive. Her contact had a letter that was smuggled out, with information only Klaus would have known."

"Where do they think he is?" His mind races with possibilities and hope.

"On a gulag island north of Murmansk, almost in the Arctic Circle."

Artemio's buoyancy sinks with the news. He hugs Gabriella as he tells her somberly, "Those islands are a chain of death camps that no one ever escapes."

"Oh my God. Artemio, is there anything you can do?"

"Yes, I have already gotten the ball rolling. The trick is to let the Russians know that you have information about the prisoner in their custody, and demand they give him proper human rights, like food and access to health care."

"So this is good? We put them on notice, they better take care of him?"

"It is a start. My friend at the UN Department of Relocation and Repatriation told me their big push with the USSR is just to get Stalin to stop killing his own people. Russian soldiers, captured in the early part of the war and put to work in German factories as slave labor, are being killed upon repatriation. The Soviets consider surrender to the Germans a capital crime." He shakes his head. "Getting Klaus out of a Soviet gulag alive would be a difficult task."

Gabriella, who has not slept in 24 hours, is saddened by the news of continued atrocities.

To change the subject, he says, "I'm sorry the kids are wearing you out."

"Oh no, I'm fine, but I'm worried about you. You really have been pushing yourself too hard. Honey, you have to slow down, you don't look good." Gabriella rocks the sleeping infant in her arms. "What happened to your plan that you would resign and we would move to America?"

"I know, and I still want to. But the problems in the world just seem to be getting worse, and I'm essential to these talks, as no one trusts each other."

"They do get worse, Artemio, and you cannot solve them all. You need a vacation. The cemeteries are full of people who thought they were essential."

"Yes, I promise we will take a vacation." He knows she is right.

She knows he will not slow down. With her head against his and little Rafaella between them, she whispers, "Arty, you are out of the wilderness now. Hundreds of people are alive today because of your tireless efforts. The wounds inside have healed."

"Yes, many have scarred over, but many remain. How will I know when the girl in the Auschwitz-bound train car is done with me?"

"Auschwitz is closed now. You must take care of yourself. Take two aspirins and get into bed. You need to sleep." She kisses him on his cheek. "You really don't look good; you're so pale."

The summer sun feels strong on his face. There are no clouds over the mountain today. The raspberries are bursting red on the vine, the fig trees blossoming. The colors and smells of the earth are intense. The young man is in the prime of his life, strong and brave, his muscles rippling under his shirt. He is the pride of his family. His father calls out to him, "Artemio, be mindful of that donkey!"

"Yes, Father, I am watching her!" he calls back.

"Keep her off the road. Make her stay on the grass. When she is full, bring her back to me."

"I know, Father, this world has many pitfalls and unseen dangers. I will protect her and guide her."

A loud, mechanical clatter sounds, and an unnatural vibration disturbs the peaceful earth. Two motorcycles and a limousine speed by the shepherd and his charge at a safe distance.

"You are a good son, Artemio. I am well pleased."

The father adds lovingly, "You have faithfully taken care of my inheritance. I know you are tired; your body is broken and in pain. You have sacrificed everything for your mission. We have beaten them back, a small respite from the darkness. Now it is time for you to come home and rest your weary head."

"Yes, Father. I would like that."

The End

About The Author

Stephan A. Silva

Stephan A. Silva is a practicing physician in Boca Raton, Florida. He lives with his wife of thirty years and their three children. They travel often to Italy to visit relatives in Piacenza and Switzerland.

Heaven Cries is a fictionalized account of Stephan's Great Uncle Artemio Silva and his exploits in the Royal Italian Airforce during World War II and subsequent internment under Nazi occupation. Air combat above the desert of North Africa and his imprisonment in an Auschwitz bound train car are factual, as was the barbaric nature of partisan resistance to Nazi atrocities.

Many of the primary witnesses to this history have passed on. Most renditions were told by the children of Artemio and Fermo with varying degrees of accuracy. To this day, few people who know of the shocking events of the Italian Holocaust, in which 40,000 civilians were transported to and exterminated in the Reich, wish to discuss it.

If You Enjoyed This Book
Please write a review.
This is important to the author and helps to get the
word out to others
Visit

PENMORE PRESS
www.penmorepress.com

All Penmore Press books are available directly
through our website, amazon.com, Barnes and Noble and
Nook, Sony Reader, Apple iTunes, Kobo books and via
leading bookshops across the United States, Canada, the
UK, Australia and Europe.

When the Jungle
Is Silent

by

James Boschert

Set in Borneo during a little known war known as "the Confrontation," this story tells of the British soldiers who fought in one of the densest jungles in the world.

Jason, a young soldier of the Light Infantry who is good with guns, is stationed in Penang, an idyllic island off the coast of Malaysia. He is living aimlessly in paradise until he meets Megan, a bright and intelligent young American from the Peace Corps. Megan challenges his complacent existence and a romance develops, but then the regiment is sent off to Borneo.

After a dismal shipping upriver, the regiment arrives in Kuching, the capital of Sarawak. Jason is moved up to Padawan, close to local populations of Ibans and Dyak headhunters, and right in the path of the Indonesian offensive. Fighting erupts along the border of Sarawak and a small fort is turned into a muddy hell from which Jason is an unlikely survivor.

An SAS Sergeant and his trackers have been drawn to the vicinity by the battle, but who will find Jason first: rescuers or hostiles? Jason is forced to wake up to the cruel harshness of real soldiering while he endeavors stay one step ahead of the Indonesians who are combing the Jungle. And the jungle itself, although neutral, is deadly enough.

PENMORE PRESS
www.penmorepress.com

THE LAUNDRY ROOM

BY

LYNDA LIPPMAN-LOCKHART

The Laundry Room dramatizes a fascinating moment in the history of the founding of Israel as a self-ruling nation. Based on actual events, Lynda Lippmann-Lockhart follows the lives of several young Israelis as they found a kibbutz and run a clandestine ammunition factory, which supplied Israeli troops fighting against Arab forces following the end of British occupation in the late 1940s. Under British rule, it was illegal for Israelis to possess firearms, so it was necessary not only to create and stockpile bullets for the coming war, but to do so in secret.

The ingenuity, courage, and sheer audacity displayed by the members of the code-named "Ayalon Institute" as they operated their factory right under the noses of the British military make for an intriguing tale. Lippmann-Lockhart shows readers what it might have been like to be one of the young pioneers whose work shaped the outcome of Israel's fight for independence. The Ayalon Institute remains standing to this day, but the secret hidden under the kibbutz's laundry room was not revealed until the 1970s. It was made a National Historic Site in 1987 and is open to the public every day of the year except Yom Kippur.

PENMORE PRESS
www.penmorepress.com

WILDFIRE IN THE DESERT

BY

BRUNO JAMBOR

Action Adventure, Crime, Mystery,
Southwest History

Highly entertaining, well researched
and original:

A Navy veteran returns home to his ancestral land to escape the pace of modern life. His nephew begs him to hide the drugs he is transporting to escape his pursuers.

An astronomer trying to find a replacement for his estranged wife finds solace in his work with the stars.

Police and the drug cartel try to recover the missing shipment, regardless of consequences, ready to sacrifice any opponent.

The antagonists crisscross the desert of Southern Arizona in a chess game where the loser will be eliminated.

Unexpected help comes from a famous missionary who blazed new paths through the same desert three centuries ago.

The climactic resolution will captivate readers of this thriller with deep spiritual undertones.

PENMORE PRESS
www.penmorepress.com

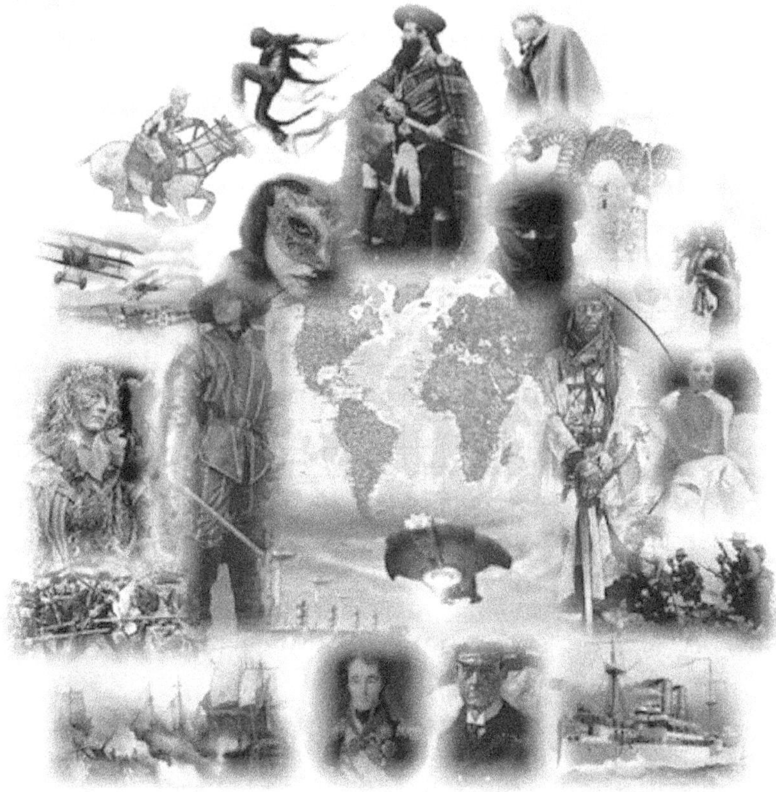

Penmore Press

Challenging, Intriguing, Adventurous, Historical and Imaginative

www.penmorepress.com